NEW YORK REVIEW BOOKS
CLASSICS

AGATHE

ROBERT MUSIL (1880–1942) was born in southern Austria, an only child whose older sister died before he was born. Sent to military boarding school when he was twelve, he enrolled at an officer's academy in Vienna at seventeen, before dropping out to study engineering at a university in Brno. He received his doctorate in 1901, and then another, in philosophy, in 1909. Musil's first novel, *Die Verwirrungen des Zöglings Törleß* (*The Confusions of Young Törless*, 1906), met with some acclaim, and he worked as an editor at a Berlin literary magazine while writing a short-story collection, *Vereinigungen* (Unions, 1911). That same year he married Martha Marcovaldi. During World War I, he fought on the Italian front, and in 1917 he and his father were ennobled and given titles that they would hold until the collapse of the Austro-Hungarian Empire the following year. After the war, Robert and Martha moved to Berlin, where his play *Die Schwärmer* (The Enthusiasts, 1921) was awarded the Kleist Prize. Several novellas and many essays followed, and in 1930 and 1933, he published the first two volumes of his unfinished magnum opus, *The Man Without Qualities*. His work was banned by the Nazis and, following the Anschluss, he and Martha, who was of Jewish descent, fled Berlin for Switzerland, where they would live in poverty while he worked on the next volume of *Qualities* until he died of a stroke.

JOEL AGEE is a writer and translator. He has been awarded a Guggenheim Fellowship and has received several prizes, including the ALTA National Translation Award and the Helen and Kurt Wolff Prize for his translation of Heinrich von Kleist's verse play *Penthesilea*. He is the author of two memoirs—*Twelve Years: An American Boyhood in East Germany* and *In the House of My Fear*. His translation of Aeschylus's *Prometheus Bound* was published by NYRB Classics in 2015. He lives in Brooklyn, New York.

AGATHE

or, The Forgotten Sister

ROBERT MUSIL

Translated from the German by
JOEL AGEE

NEW YORK REVIEW BOOKS

New York

THIS IS A NEW YORK REVIEW BOOK
PUBLISHED BY THE NEW YORK REVIEW OF BOOKS
435 Hudson Street, New York, NY 10014
www.nyrb.com

Library of Congress Cataloging-in-Publication Data
Names: Musil, Robert, 1880–1942, author. | Agee, Joel, translator.
Title: Agathe, or the forgotten sister / by Robert Musil, translated from the
    German by Joel Agee.
Other titles: Mann ohne Eigenschaften. English | Forgotten sister
Description: New York : New York Review Books, [2019] | Series: New york
    review books classics | Translated from the German.
Identifiers: LCCN 2019025132 (print) | LCCN 2019025133 (ebook) | ISBN
    9781681373836 (trade paperback) | ISBN 9781681373843 (ebook)
Classification: LCC PT2625.U8 M313 2019 (print) | LCC PT2625.U8 (ebook) |
    DDC 833/.912—dc23
LC record available at https://lccn.loc.gov/2019025132
LC ebook record available at https://lccn.loc.gov/2019025133

ISBN 978-1-68137-383-6
Available as an electronic book; ISBN 978-1-68137-384-3

Printed in the United States of America on acid-free paper.
10 9 8 7 6 5 4 3 2 1

CONTENTS

INTRODUCTION

We don't have too much intellect and too little soul, but too
little intellect in matters of the soul.

—*Robert Musil*

I

I AM LOOKING at a photograph of a late-middle-aged man in a
gray suit with broad lapels. He is wearing a bow tie. There are dark
leaves behind him and the lines of a sunlit house. His right hand
dangles across the armrest of a wicker chair in which he is sitting
with one leg draped over the other. The left hand, wearing a signet
ring, rests on a round table and is loosely holding a cigarette. The face
could belong to a European diplomat or businessman of a now extinct
type: refined, austere, intellectual. The dark, dense eyebrows add an
expression of calm virility. The only incongruous detail is the eyes:
they are closed. One assumes at first that the snapshot was taken
at the moment of blinking. But it is difficult to imagine this face with
the eyes open, because all its features and in fact the whole gesture
of the body, which at first glance appeared so urbanely relaxed in its
well-tailored suit, are drained of motility, as if drugged. At any minute, the cigarette may drop from between those slackly curved fingers.
Is this a picture of mortal exhaustion or of extremely attenuated
contemplation? Probably it is both. The man depicted is Robert
Musil, who died at the age of sixty-one, less than two years after this

photograph was taken. At his funeral, which was attended by eight people, the eulogist applied to Musil a statement Musil had made about Rilke: "He was not a summit of this age—he was one of those elevations upon which the destiny of the human spirit strides across ages."

Today no one would dream of describing a human being in such grandiose terms—a political program, perhaps, or a space mission, but not a person, and certainly not a writer. It may have something to do with the expectations writers have of themselves, and with a rather diminished sense, generally, of the human spirit having any sort of destiny. Perhaps it's better that way. A more modest perspective may open up a vision of what is staring us in the face: that unless we supply the essential necessities to the collective body of man, the spirit may have to find another planet for the fulfillment of its destiny. Musil himself was coming to a similar conclusion near the end of his life (chastened, perhaps, by the enormity of the Second World War and by his own experience of severe poverty): "The most important thing is not to produce spiritual values, but food, clothing, security, order.... And it is just as important to produce the principles necessary for the supply of food, clothing, etc. Let us call it—the spirit of privation." Elsewhere he described himself as "building a house of cards as the earth begins to crack."

The house of cards was a huge, phenomenally ambitious construction, more than twenty years in the making and never finished, titled *The Man Without Qualities*—a satire on the collapse of the Austro-Hungarian Empire, a utopian novel about untried possibilities of being, a meditation on the nature of history, a critique of the major ideologies of the twentieth century, an attempt to combine the different exactitudes of reason and mysticism. The book, a critical success after its first volume was published in 1930, was virtually unknown at the time of the author's death in 1942. Today it is frequently mentioned along with *Ulysses* and *In Search of Lost Time* as one of the great modern novels.

*

The term "novel" bears a great deal of stretching. Randall Jarrell's witty definition—"a prose narrative of some length that has something wrong with it"—seems designed to fit most if not all cases. But *The Man Without Qualities* does not match that description because it appears to be intent, from the beginning, on subverting narration itself. As soon as a lively scene or dramatic incident threatens to turn into a story, a train of reflection comes along to interrupt it. Some of these digressions exfoliate in the protagonist's brain or issue from his mouth in lengthy soliloquies, others accompany his reflections as a kind of meta-commentary, still others play themselves out in his absence, describing the mental and emotional states of other characters, or detach themselves entirely from the novel's plot to disport themselves freely in a chapter or two of their own.

But perhaps the idea of narration bears some stretching as well. Essay, in this quintessentially essayistic novel, is the mode for depicting a mind so active that it nearly constitutes a character independent of the man whose mind it is. That man is a thirty-two-year-old Austrian mathematician known to the reader only by his first name, Ulrich, who, disillusioned in his quest for intellectual glory after reading in a newspaper about a racehorse of genius, decides to take a year-long "vacation from life," which he conceives of as an experiment in pure philosophic contemplation—"living essayistically," he calls it—in the hope of perhaps, by that pathless route, discovering an occupation better suited to his abilities. If he does not find it within a year, he will put an end to his life, because, to his fanatically logical and consequent mind, an unjustified life is not worth living.

One of Ulrich's favorite maxims is that reality is just a possibility: everything that happens could have turned out differently. So it is no surprise to him when, almost immediately after he begins his retreat from active engagement with the world, his father, a prominent legal scholar, introduces him to a circle of socialites, aristocrats, financiers, and intellectuals who are nothing less than obsessed with action. They are planning a "great patriotic campaign" to celebrate the seventieth jubilee of Emperor Franz Josef in December 1918. They call it the Parallel Campaign because a similar festival is being prepared in Germany for the thirtieth anniversary of Kaiser Wilhelm II's reign in the same year. Upstaging the Germans is no small matter, especially as the Parallel Campaign's director, the benign and elderly Count Leinsdorf, seems constitutionally unable to make a decision without crippling it with dilatory maneuvers. But the ultimate goal is both noble and grand: to demonstrate, with a resounding festival, Austria's preeminence among nations as a fountainhead of culture, intellect, beneficence, peace, and, why not, military might as well.

Ulrich is appointed the honorary secretary of this cabal, and it is mainly through his eyes that we witness the high-minded pedantry, boondoggle, and oratorical pomp, with a dash of chicanery in the mix, by which its members contrive to get nothing done in their endeavor.

Ulrich's year of "vacation from life" begins in August 1913. Sarajevo is just ten months away. Of course he cannot know this. The Parallel Campaign's designs for a pan-Austrian peace festival will eventuate almost on schedule in the collapse of the empire following Germany's defeat in a pan-European war. None of the characters in *The Man Without Qualities* are prepared for the impending disaster.

Does that lead their endeavors and hopes ad absurdum? Not at all. Nothing was further from Musil's intentions than a grim demonstration of historical necessity, for the simple reason that he did not believe in such a thing. Every one of his characters, even the most foolish and most deranged, is an avatar of possibility. The war itself, even though it actually happened, was no more and no less than that.

One of the many received notions Ulrich takes pleasure in discarding is that a man—not just any man and not, generally speaking, a woman, but a man of account in the world—must be endowed with qualities for which he is known and by which he knows himself. Ulrich has many admirable and a few unattractive qualities, but they don't adhere to him, they are not, to his own perception, even tangentially his. Because he commits himself to this paradox and lives authentically within it, he exerts, especially on women, a mysterious appeal that one jealous friend characterizes as the empty glamour of "a man without qualities." That is a designation Ulrich is happy to accept, and in fact he is that in much the same way that a tightrope walker can be said to be a man or woman without gravity. Ulrich performs, on an often brilliantly funny level of abstraction, the dizzying, high-stakes adventure of divesting himself of all the cultural axioms that support what his contemporaries agree to call "reality," in order finally to arrive at the great Platonic question, and to ask it in earnest and without flinching: What is the good life—or the holy life, if you will—and how can one live it without self-deception, and without retreating into prerational modes of feeling and thinking, in a world that has lost its passion for the good?

This question does not crystallize in Ulrich's thoughts until he meets his sister Agathe more than seven hundred pages into the novel. Her name—which, significantly, is derived from the Greek word for "good"—has not been mentioned before: she appears, as it were, out of nowhere. As their relationship unfolds (how apt the floral image in that metaphor seems here: a continual, unhurried opening and disclosure), one has the impression that she has been present to him all along precisely by her absence. In all his dealings with both men and women before meeting Agathe, Ulrich has displayed charm, diplomacy, lust, aloofness, private scorn, occasional stirrings of compassion, but on the whole a notable absence of tenderness, let alone love. Something was missing. Now she is here.

Their encounter marks the beginning of a radical departure for Ulrich and for the novel itself. The narrator describes it in a rare address to the reader several chapters further on:

> But whoever has not already picked up the clues to what was developing between this brother and sister, let him put aside this account, for it describes an adventure he will never be able

to approve of: a voyage to the edge of the possible, leading past, and perhaps not always steering clear of, the dangers of the impossible and the unnatural, indeed of the repulsive; a "limit case," as Ulrich later called it, of restricted and special validity, reminiscent of the freedom with which mathematics occasionally employs the absurd in order to arrive at truth. He and Agathe came upon a path that had much in common with the business of the God-possessed, but they walked it without piety, without believing in God or the soul, or even in a Beyond or a Once Again; they had come upon it as human beings belonging to this world and walked it as such: and just that was the remarkable thing about it.

Agathe and Ulrich withdraw from society, eventually retreating to Ulrich's little rococo château in the middle of Vienna as if to an island. For a while, in obedience to social pressure, they attend elegant soirees with the idea of finding a new husband for Agathe (she intends to divorce the man she is married to), and Ulrich pays visits to various friends and acquaintances, including the luminaries of the Parallel Campaign. But before long, these worldly forays recede from the novel's horizon, until the siblings' retreat becomes near absolute. Their private adventure, both spiritual and erotic, becomes the central theme of the novel. That is the principal reason why it was possible for the editor of this book, without violating the novel's integrity, to excerpt thirty-six chapters, all of them centered on Agathe and Ulrich, as a self-contained narrative, in effect a novel within the novel. A loss of complexity and illuminating contrast is unavoidably entailed in this experiment; but that loss, I believe, is offset by the gain of unbroken concentration on what Agathe calls "the last possible love story."

*

The main part of the first volume, after a brief introductory section called, ironically, "A Sort of Beginning," is titled "Seinesgleichen geschieht"—"The Like of It Happens." This little gem of compressed bitterness expresses, with epigrammatic precision, a state of affairs in which the same thoughtless habits of speech and emotion, the same petrified rules and dogmas, inadequate moral systems, and ingrained patterns of behavior repeat themselves ad nauseam under the guise of novelty and innovation. If one extends that observation beyond the span of personal existence to history itself and perceives its epochs and eras succeeding each other like the meaningless trends of fashion with little or no advance in moral intelligence, one can begin to appreciate, if not necessarily share, Ulrich's revolt against the self-replicating ways of "reality."

The second volume, where Agathe makes her entrance, bears a starkly contrasting title: "Into the Millennium," followed by the parenthetical subtitle "(The Criminals)."

The Millennium, in German, is *das tausendjährige Reich*, a term that, irrespective of Hitler's use of it as a slogan for his twelve-year reign, carries a good deal more emotional charge and mythic resonance than the Latinate English word, which in our century most of us have come to associate with the turn of a page in the calendar. It is the name for the thousand-year Kingdom of peace prophesied in the Bible and fervently awaited by millenarian sects through the centuries and still today. One does not expect Robert Musil to invoke such a reference without irony. He was as imbued with the ethos of the Enlightenment as any twentieth-century author, a merciless critic of all kinds of mystification, secular as well as religious. Nevertheless, it is the skeptical, scientifically trained Ulrich, in many ways Musil's alter ego, who declares to his sister, only half jokingly, that together they will embark on a voyage to that fabled, improbable realm.

The source of his faith is not a belief founded in Scripture but a memory referred to by the title of an early chapter as "The long forgotten and supremely important affair with the major's wife"—an unconsummated romance when he was a twenty-year-old recruit that ended with his fleeing the object of his love and withdrawing to a remote island. There he experienced "the very state described by those believers in God who have entered the state of mystic love, of whom the young cavalry lieutenant at that time knew nothing at all." This condition is so different from ordinary consciousness that it constitutes a "second reality," in which "love is not a desire for possession but a gentle self-unveiling of the world for which one would gladly forego possession of the beloved." Ever since then, at transient moments in the midst of his otherwise worldly and alienated existence, he has felt intimations of that same state of being, which he calls "the other condition." The descriptions of this state in the writings of the mystics speak to him "in tones of intimate kinship; with a soft, dark inwardness" that is "the opposite of the imperious tone of mathematical and scientific language."*

Ulrich has no intention of renouncing science and mathematics. Their austere beauty is the passion of his intellect. But he rejects the rationalist prejudice against mystical experience, which has its own, necessarily poetic and metaphoric language, just as he rejects, with a good deal of revulsion, the sentimental cult of "spiritual" feeling pitted against the hard-won attainments of reason.

Is Ulrich unhappy or despairing? Not in the usual sense we give to these words. He is extremely lonely but is too tough-minded to indulge in self-pity, and he enjoys human company, though always at an ironic remove. Vaguely, he notices that he does not love himself as he once did, but it is in the nature of such lack that it largely occludes what was lost. It's probably fairest to say that he has a genius for disillusionment. In any case, by the time he departs for the provincial city of —— to discharge himself of his filial obligations on the occasion of the death of his father, he has shed almost all of his attachments and

---

*The word translated above as "intimate kinship" is *Geschwisterlichkeit*. It is usually translated as "fraternity," but the root of the German word is *Schwester*, meaning "sister." In such subtle ways is Agathe prefigured—announced as it were—early on in the novel.

ambitions and is open to whatever unforeseen possibilities life may have to offer him.

2

Agathe and Ulrich meet under quasi-magical auspices—a ready loophole for skeptical irony. But the magic is compelling. By pure coincidence they are wearing nearly identical Pierrot costumes. Perhaps I should say Pierrot and Columbine. But it is characteristic of such a pairing (Papageno and Papagena are another example) that male and female, even self and other, are subsumed in the charm of an impossible identity. Are they one or two? They are two of a kind.

In commedia dell'arte, these creatures of fantasy are never taken to be real, and yet they are super-real in the claim they make on our longing for such bravery of innocence and love, and maybe our secret belief that such feelings might be possible even for people like ourselves. Why not? Of course there are a million reasons why not. But here, by a trick of chance, a man and a woman of cultured sophistication, siblings separated since childhood, find themselves transformed into a semblance of this moon-enchanted couple.

Naturally, they are charmed, by each other as much as by the amusing coincidence, but they think little of it (although Agathe's quip—"I didn't know we were twins"—is prescient). But the reader, meeting them as characters in a book, knows that something out of the ordinary can be expected in the light of such an event. And that light, when we speak of Pierrot, is moonlight.

Skeptical Ulrich as Pierrot in love with the moon seems an unlikely stretch, but late in the story, on a moonlit evening, Ulrich says to Agathe, "You are the moon," and Agathe understands him. And it is not only Ulrich but Musil himself who gives himself over to "the fantastically altered reality of moonlit nights" and writes transportingly about them, only to have Agathe, three pages on, say to Ulrich, "Do you know what you look like now? 'Pierrot Lunaire.' This calls for prudence."

Ulrich immediately agrees, which saddens Agathe, but they both know she is right. The necessary prudence of rational checks on mystical intuition is a constant refrain in the exchanges between the siblings, not as a defense against drifting into kitsch—that would be merely a lapse in taste—but against deceiving themselves, or worse, each other, about something that matters to them more than life itself.

Ulrich contemplates Agathe's face, hoping to find it similar to his own. He sees no clear resemblance. And then: "There was something about this face that unsettled him. After a while he realized what it was: he couldn't make out its expression. It lacked whatever it is that allows one to draw the usual conclusions about a person. It was not an empty face by any means, but nothing in it was emphasized or summed up as a readable character trait."

A little later, as they smoke their last cigarettes before retiring for the night, he muses again about her appearance:

> He didn't know what to make of his sister. There was nothing either emancipated or bohemian about her, even though she was sitting there in the wide trousers in which she had received her unknown brother. It was more something hermaphroditic, it seemed to him now; as she gestured and moved in conversation, the light, masculine garment, which was semitransparent, like water, suggested the delicate form underneath, and in contrast to the independent freedom of her legs, her lovely hair was gathered up in decidedly feminine style. But the center of this amphibious impression was still her face, which possessed the charm of a woman to a high degree and yet had something missing or held in reserve whose nature he could not make out.

Ulrich never comments on the fundamental trait they have in common, but the reader is prompted to recognize it: Agathe is a woman without qualities and is thus Ulrich's counterpart in female form.

*

Not having known each other since they were children and now meeting as adults at a moment in their lives when they are at parallel points of isolation and estrangement from the worlds they have each inhabited, they are delighted to find in each other not just a sibling but a kindred soul. What is this kinship, what is its nature? The question is charged with ambiguous appeal. They are a man and a woman, after all. Moreover, they are young, attractive, highly intelligent, and not bound by any ties, aside from Agathe's marriage to an unloved husband, that might stand in the way of an intimate relationship. But they are brother and sister.

Agathe seems no more constrained by the incest taboo than she is by any other prohibition. In her education in a convent school, she has known moral authority only as rules laid down for the suppression of pleasure. And if she has lived a life of submission to her wifely duties, it was not out of conviction but in self-humbling penitence for her failure to keep her first husband, and with him her first and only true love, alive when he was dying of typhus. Ulrich, on the other hand, Nietzschean iconoclast though he is, and obsessed with discovering, together with his sister, the sunken continent of an ecstatic, primordial morality, is surprisingly wary of trespassing the moral and legal codes of his day.

It is Agathe who does that in his stead. Or rather, she does it for him: "Essentially she was making Ulrich the gift of a crime, by placing herself in his hands, fully trusting that he would understand her rashness." And Ulrich, watching her as she forges her father's will, "experienced a pleasure he had never known, for there was an enchanting absurdity in succumbing, for once entirely and without caution, to what another being was doing."

And yet, though her crime—and his by complicity—may well have grave consequences for them both, it is only a foil to a spiritual event that is made visible by the narrator briefly parting the curtains to a view behind the physical action:

An aura of justice with flames instead of logic surrounded her. Goodness, decency, and law-abidance, as she had experienced these virtues in the people she knew, Hagauer in particular,* had always seemed to her as if a stain had been removed from a dress; but the wrong that hovered around her at this moment was like the drowning of the world in the light of a rising sun. It seemed to her as if right and wrong were no longer general terms and a compromise arranged for millions of people, but the magical encounter of Me and You, the madness of a first creation, not yet comparable with any thing, not measurable by any standard.

There is no hint of irony in this description. It is meant to evoke a dimension of consciousness that knows nothing of the statutes by which the world of *seinesgleichen geschieht* conducts its business, and that knows instead something of incomparable value, power, beauty, and even utility, if people would only avail themselves of it. That, of course, is not a reasonable proposition. It is the view from within the precincts of the other reality.

Strolling together in their dead father's garden on paths that "turned back upon themselves," talking about the nature of morality, the siblings find themselves "in a state of mind that drifted in circular eddies like those of a current rising behind a dam." The entire image—of the current impeded by a barrier and the mental state that drifts in circles that rise as they turn—is a virtual diagram of Ulrich and Agathe's relationship and of the direction and even the form their conversations will take in the course of the book.

A circle that rises as it turns is describing a spiral. That is the peculiar form of the siblings' quest and of the novel within the novel that, in

*Hagauer is the name of her husband.

this edition, bears Agathe's name as a title. Unlike narratives that progress on the horizontal plane of a timeline, their story proceeds in a slowly cycling ascent to higher and higher stations. This asks of the reader a special kind of attention and imaginative participation. When, for example, the narrator says of Agathe, who is puzzling over the fantastical prospect of the Millennium, that "even now she was not sure yet if it was truly possible . . . . But for as long as she had been with him she had always had the feeling that a country was taking shape from his words, and that this land was not forming in her head, but truly beneath her feet," the reader is invited, or perhaps I should say more strongly "enjoined," to imagine—which is to say, attempt to intuit—the other condition as an at least conceivable reality, separate from the socially conditioned world we all inhabit.*

Reading in this way becomes a contemplative activity—one of inward listening to a resonance that responds to descriptions of subtle and profound, sometimes nearly intangible states of feeling and perception. Ulrich, in an earlier part of the novel, proposed half jokingly to Count Leinsdorf, the leader of the Parallel Campaign, that they institute a "world secretariat for precision and soul." That is Musil's motto as a writer as well, and nowhere more than in these late chapters where Agathe joins Ulrich in his investigations. Intellect and feeling, intuition and reason cooperate without abandoning their different criteria for truth in expression. According to Ulrich, this is the sine qua non of authentic ecstatic experience in our time. It is also the alchemy that infuses a sentence by Robert Musil with its characteristic balance of lightness and gravity, sensuousness and rigor, spiritual lucency and intellectual wit.

*

*The danger of falling prey to phantasmagorias is mentioned again and again, but at no point are we permitted to conclude from Ulrich and Agathe's exchanges that they are deluded.

Before they met, Agathe was the embodiment of lethargic, compliant indifference. Nothing mattered, because love had died. Virtually from the moment Ulrich arrives, as she talks to him about her husband, her capacity for decisive action is awakened—with a vengeance, one might say. Ulrich in turn begins, almost immediately, to experience the miracle of meeting himself in feminine form. He is entranced by Agathe's spontaneity, so different from his objective watchfulness and methodical habits of mind. And little by little, without any controlling intent on her part, simply by the convergence of his fascinated passivity and the energy and freedom she exhibits in his presence, he becomes an instrument of her will. At the same time he notices to his astonishment that her impulsive actions, from the charmingly outré to the criminal, are nothing less than enactments of his own ideas, which he has expounded to her in his role of "older brother and somewhat obtuse dispenser of edifying counsel," and to which she has attended with the eagerness of a disciple. And yet, at one point Agathe realizes that "much of what he said she had already thought: just not with words, for with only herself to rely on, as she had been until now, she would never have made such definite assertions!" Who is the leader, then, in this constellation, and who the follower?

Gradually it becomes clear to them and to the reader that their relationship is defined by a single astonishing fact: they are indeed related, not only as brother and sister but also in the painful and beautiful way in which the living halves of a severed whole are related and necessary to each other.

"You are my lost self-love," Ulrich says to Agathe at one point, and at another: "I would want to be a woman if only—women did not love men." It seems he can only love himself as a woman. Agathe has no great respect for women, no matter if they consider themselves emancipated or "raise a brood for which a male must supply the nest."

"Ridiculous parasites," she calls them. "They share a man's life together with his dog!" Clearly Ulrich and Agathe are renegades, not only to polite society but to their own sex.

Such a marginal position offers them a vantage from which to reflect with scorn and sorrow on the erotic theater in which men and women like themselves have been obliged to perform. There are two passages, a brief one from Ulrich's perspective (he is the less conscious of the two, at least at this juncture) and a longer one from Agathe's point of view, on 18 and 69–70, respectively, that are worth reading in tandem as mutually mirroring ethnographic descriptions of the stage directions by which the European bedroom dramas of their time were played out. It seems that men experienced sexual love as an opportunity to either enjoy "a hunter's delight" in amorous conquest or else grant themselves "an hour of weakness" in a variety of performance styles that strike Agathe "as cheaply melodramatic and overdone, since she had at no time ever felt herself to be other than weak in a world so superbly constructed by the strength of men." It is an exhausted and exhausting game for both of them.

"Sooner or later," Ulrich prophesies, "there will come an age of simple sexual companionship, where boy and girl will stand, like-minded and perplexed, before an old heap of broken springs that once drove the mechanisms called Man and Woman!"

Late in the book we are introduced to two men who are far from being players in the jousts of love. Both have a strong interest in Agathe, and both, it turns out, are experts in educational theory, one of them "progressive and forward-looking," the other a pietistic conservative fiercely opposed to his colleague's liberal views.

The first is Gottlieb Hagauer. The reader has been aware of him all along, mainly through Agathe's and Ulrich's uncharitable opinion of him. Now, in a single chapter, we get to know him from within, so to speak, as the understandably aggrieved husband of a wife who, with no forewarning and for no declared reason, is letting him know through a curt missive from her brother, whom Hagauer dislikes, that she wants a divorce. It is a devastating portrait, not least because Musil does not appear to be satirizing him. He is a prototype of conscientious mediocrity so justified in his self-conceit that he cannot imagine why Agathe might have cause for dissatisfaction and concludes, in a carefully reasoned chain of reflection that goes off to Agathe in a letter, that she is "socially feebleminded" and for that reason not fit to live without his protection.

The second exemplar of male authority is Professor August Lindner, whom Agathe meets by chance after fleeing Ulrich's house with the intention of killing herself, and in whom she believes to have found a paragon of empathy capable, perhaps, of helping her to close the gap between herself and the fullness of love that Ulrich's dialectics seem unable to deliver. Where Hagauer is merely pathetic and self-righteous, Lindner, goaded by sexual excitement that he cannot admit into his puritanical worldview, becomes a character both sympathetic and ridiculous. Both men are Kantian automatons, models of duty-bound rectitude and probity. They are epitomes of "men with qualities," completely entrapped in their social personas and professional identities.

Agathe slips in and out of the other condition with ease and without Ulrich's tutelage. Here she is, for example, in her father's house after Ulrich has left for Vienna to prepare for her arrival:

> During this time and from the moment when she had stayed behind alone, Agathe had been living completely at ease, released from the tension of all relationships, in a serenely melancholy suspension of the will, as if at a great height where there was nothing to be seen but the wide blue sky.... Nothing troubled the state she was in, no clinging to the past, no straining for the future; when her gaze fell on any of the objects in her vicinity, it was as if she were coaxing a young lamb to come near; it would either gently approach her, or else simply take no notice of her—but she never took mental possession of it with that

motion of inner grasping that imbues every act of cold recognition with something violent and yet futile, for it scares away the happiness that is in things.

Ulrich seems incapable of such humility before the unknowable, though he aspires to it with deep sincerity. In one scene, for example—they are lying in deck chairs on a sunlit lawn—he is talking about the terrifying immensity of pure sense experience unmediated by a conceptual framework. The apparently self-evident fact that grass is green, he laments only half humorously, is actually ungraspable, impossible to capture with words or even to nail down with a scientific measurement.

Agathe . . . found it very understandable that nothing could be understood, and replied: "I suggest you look into a mirror at night sometime: it's dark, it's black, you see almost nothing; and yet this nothing is very clearly something other than the nothing of the rest of the darkness. You sense the glass, the doubling of depth, some remnant of the ability to shimmer, and yet you see nothing!"

Ulrich's response to his sister's advice is to laugh at her "readiness to strip knowledge of all its honor; he himself was far from thinking that concepts have no value and was well aware of what they accomplish, even if he did not exactly act as if he did."

We are not told how Agathe felt about the laugh, but one can't help wondering if Ulrich isn't being obtuse in his thinking as well as his feeling. Of course concepts have value, and of course they accomplish a great deal, but they cannot open the gates to the liberated state in which self-centered existence comes to an end with the realization of the commandment to love one's neighbor as oneself. Agathe knows this with an instinctive clarity that tends to elude her theorizing brother, though she does not seem to know that she knows it.

*

Ulrich thinks of himself as "a believer who just didn't believe anything," but that is not entirely true. He believes in possibility. He
believes, in particular, in the possibility of translating the other
condition into a lasting state, not in heaven but in Vienna, or wherever
any given man or woman happens to be. That would be the Millennium. It is, ultimately, for all human beings—if not now, then in a
future that may never come—that Ulrich aspires to bring heaven
down to earth, because the eternal round of *seinesgleichen geschieht*
is not worthy of a species that is capable of such beatitude as he experiences with Agathe in their walks through the city.

Despite her natural aptitude for non-conceptual gnosis, Agathe
emulates her brother's gift for clear-eyed rational thought. She depends
on Ulrich to point the way to the Millennium, and he does, by engaging with her in loosely discursive philosophical inquiries that range
from questions of ethics and the nature of feelings to the baneful role
that chance plays in favoring the statistical average over individual
genius in determining the fate of humanity. All these themes are
contiguous to the other reality, and Agathe burns with impatience
for her brother to take a decisive step over that border. (Perhaps she
believes that then their union will become indissoluble.) Ulrich,
however, moves from one tentative proposition to another, even one
that may contradict the first, always stopping short of a definitive
conclusion. That is the experimental method he has learned from
science and is not willing to forfeit for the facile certainties of dogmatic
belief and emotional conviction. But for Agathe, doubt, necessary
though it is as a safeguard against illusion, threatens to undermine
faith itself. She carries with her a vial of poison with which she will
kill herself if hope dies again.

Her instinctive approach to their common quest is diametrically
opposite to his. She is *ardent*. The image of fire in its various manifestations shows up frequently when her inner state and even her
appearance is described. As one of the four classic symbolic elements,
fire is action itself. It does not hesitate. Its movements are unprepared

by any calculus of motive or conscious design. And of course, in its innocent heedlessness, fire can also destroy.

3

Ulrich: "It is an everlasting pity that there are no trained scientists who have visions!"

Agathe, tempting him: "Do you think they could?"

Ulrich: "I don't know. Maybe it could happen to me!" Then, hearing his words, "he smiled in order to limit their meaning."

It is hard to escape the impression that Agathe's and Ulrich's voices are expressing temptations and anxieties in Musil's own consciousness, and that by giving birth to Agathe from Ulrich's hyperintellectual head, Musil introduced a muse who helps not only Ulrich but his author to talk about aspects of mind that are not accessible to ordinary consciousness.

Every one of the gnomic sayings cited by Agathe as she peruses Ulrich's books comes from a single volume, Martin Buber's *Ecstatic Confessions*, an anthology of mystical writings from many traditions and historical periods.* I don't believe it is farfetched to regard the tale of Ulrich and Agathe's voyage to the Millennium as Musil's ecstatic confession. He could not pour it out in bursts of rhapsodic surrender. It had to be wrested from constraints set by his training in, and fealty to, science and mathematics, and by the no less exacting artistic deliberations that governed the composition of every metaphor and the shape and rhythm of every sentence. The "and" in his watchword, "precision and soul," is a sign of uncompromising, almost ascetic severity. But if there is any question that Musil belongs in the company of mystical poet-philosophers like Hildegard von Bingen or Meister

---

*It may not be insignificant, in view of Agathe's portrayal, that a great deal of space is given in Buber's book to the testimony of medieval Christian women.

Eckhart, I propose a reading of the last chapter, "Breaths of a Summer Day," in the light of such a comparison. Here time, which flowed like a slow-curving stream in earlier chapters, debouches into eternity. With a few concrete particulars—a garden, two deck chairs, sunlight and shade, a man, a woman, and a steady drift of blossoms in the air—an imponderable mystery is invoked. The presence of the miracle is never named, yet it displays itself with stunning simplicity—not as a deciphered riddle but as revelation through words.

Musil died of a stroke an hour after a morning's work on this chapter. His wife found him collapsed in a bathtub with a smile on his face that she described as *spöttisch*, which could be translated as "mocking" or "ironic." I find the second meaning more plausible.

The handwritten manuscript of "Breaths of a Summer Day," the latest of many versions he wrote over several years (not all of them under this title), is studded with deletions and inserts and stops on a note of inconclusion. Like the great novel of which it forms a part, it is a magnificent fragment.

—JOEL AGEE

A NOTE ON THE TRANSLATION

I FIRST read *The Man Without Qualities* sixty-one years ago, which happens to be the span of Robert Musil's life, when I was eighteen years old and living in the part of Berlin that at the time still called itself the capital of the German Democratic Republic. I found the thick, handsomely bound volume on my stepfather's desk, among other books published in the West that he had ordered for possible review in a literary magazine he edited. I asked his permission to read it. I couldn't have understood much of the book, but I read it with tremendous excitement. I think what bowled me over at first was its sheer stylistic brilliance and wit and the way even the more foolish characters spoke like philosophers and sometimes like poets. But the true entrancement set in with Agathe's arrival. I had never read anything that could compare for sheer erotic charm with the exquisite balance of forbiddenness and enticement that developed between this brother and sister. And there was something else for which I had no preparation. It was the news (I took it to be news, not an artifice of fiction) of a mystical state that had nothing to do with the worlds of politics and culture that surrounded me, and that bestowed on those lucky souls who discovered it a fulfillment of happiness and love that was unmatched by anything in ordinary experience. I believed in this "other condition" and was convinced that I already had intimations of it. It was of course Musil's prose that made me believe it.

Being invited to translate precisely those late chapters from *The Man Without Qualities* was a surprising and welcome gift. It was an opportunity to reacquaint myself with a work and an author that had shaped my own vocation as a writer like probably no other. The reacquaintance proved, in some important respects, to be a discovery. The enchantment I had experienced as a boy was no doubt due to my own receptive capacity, but on the other end, so to speak, was a versatility and subtlety of language I was not experienced enough as a reader to fully appreciate.

There exists a theory according to which, in fiction, particularities of language are not crucial, so that if one has read Dostoyevsky in translation, one can legitimately say that one has read Dostoyevsky; whereas the equivalent cannot be said if one has read Pushkin in translation, the reason being that the language of poetry entails rhythm and metaphor and other tropes of poetic diction that are not easy to carry across into another language. This theory may have merit in a general way, but it makes rather short shrift of prose fiction as a form of poetry, and it certainly does not apply to a novelist like Musil, who so clearly requires and rewards close attention not only to what he says but to how he says it. I can't think of another way to do justice to this immensely resourceful stylist than to attend to both the literal and the figural meanings of his words, and to strive to re-create in English the shape, the rhythm, the web of associations and implications, the nuances of irony, the lyricism, the architectural equilibrium, the pleasures to the ear as well as the mind in the composition of any sentence he wrote. There is also at times a strange newness of meaning—to borrow the philosopher Owen Barfield's prime criterion for poetic beauty—that startles not only the English but also the German reader in Musil's prose. With it, inevitably, comes some oddness in expression. Musil hardly ever employs a common turn of phrase, for instance, without varying it in a subtle and unexpected way. It is a temptation for a translator to mitigate strangeness in the original with something more familiar. In my view, this temptation must be resisted.

Such criteria unavoidably impose on the translator of Musil strictures and anxieties not dissimilar to those that tormented the notoriously self-exacting author. Again and again, as my work progressed, and despite a comfortable deadline, little zephyrs of unease beset me: Could this or that detail not have been rendered more accurately, or more aptly? At one point, to choose one of many examples, Ulrich says to his sister: "*Das Verstehen macht einem unstillbaren Staunen*

Platz." The adjective *unstillbar*, derived from the verb *stillen*, which denotes the settling of a baby's distress or hunger by suckling, here forms an alliterative unit with its noun, *Staunen*. That word presented me with a first puzzle: Was it "amazement" or "astonishment," or was it "wonder"? Feeling out the gradations of meaning in those three words, and comparing them with the vibration of *Staunen* in the passage in which the sentence appears, I chose "astonishment." For *unstillbar*, "unquenchable," "insatiable," and "unappeasable" offered themselves, but they all implied a voraciousness or greed that I didn't hear in the German word with its infantine connotation. I settled, uncomfortably, for "ceaseless astonishment." Months later, after a Google search for *unstillbar* in a variety of contexts, I saw that I had been mistaken: a hungry baby is indeed voracious, and *unstillbar* is very adequately translated as "unquenchable." I mentioned this to a friend, who suggested "unslakable" as an alternative: "After all," he said, "doesn't a mother slake her baby's thirst rather than quench it?" And so, in the end, "Understanding gives way to unslakable astonishment," odd as it sounds, seemed the best possible translation for the equally odd combination of words in Musil's sentence.

Several excellent translators have previously applied their skill and imagination to translating all but two of the chapters included in this volume: Eithne Wilkins and Ernst Kaiser in the first English-language edition of *The Man Without Qualities* in 1953 (which comprised only the chapters published during Musil's lifetime), and Sophie Wilkins and Burton Pike in the 1996 edition by Alfred A. Knopf. It would be disingenuous not to acknowledge the advantage to me, as their successor, of being able to consult their approaches to some difficult problems—not to crib them but to sharpen, by their relative success at or distance from ideal fidelity, my perception of the challenge posed by the German text. In a few instances, when there sprang out at me from their pages an ingenious and, it seemed, irreplaceable solution, rather than settle for something less felicitous, I adopted theirs and acknowledged it in an endnote.

—J.A.

EDITORIAL NOTE

ROBERT Musil's *The Man Without Qualities* is, notoriously, unfinished. Unlike that other seminal masterpiece of the first half of the twentieth century, Marcel Proust's *In Search of Lost Time*, there is no climactic passage that satisfies the reader by making sense of all that has come before. In fact, it is quite unclear what an ending might have looked like, and Musil had different thoughts at various stages of the book's genesis without clearly settling on an answer. Thousands of pages of manuscript exist from different periods of the book's composition, including chapters that Musil was working on when he died unexpectedly in 1942. The publishing history of these drafts is complex both in German and in English, and many English-speaking readers do not explore beyond the chapters that had been published in Musil's lifetime.

Some two-thirds into the published chapters of *The Man Without Qualities*, the focus of the book changes with the arrival of Agathe, the sister of Ulrich, the man without qualities. As George Steiner writes in his essay "The Unfinished" (from *The New Yorker*, April 17, 1995), "what was previously a kaleidoscope narrows to a laser." In both the published chapters and their continuation, which he was working on when he died, Musil changes his emphasis from the political and social satire that dominates the book until that point and turns the novel's philosophical inquiry into the search for a viable way to "be" in a modern world where the available modes of existence have lost their value. Musil explores what it is to lead an authentic life, even if that means contravening social norms. This exploration has an explicitly mystical character. It is shown through the burgeoning relationship between brother and sister, who withdraw from society and engage in a series of dialogues that they themselves conceive of as a spiritual experiment.

Agathe consists of a selection of these chapters, two of which have not previously appeared in English. Together they stand as a remarkable exploration of the human condition by one of the greatest of twentieth-century writers.

ON THE SELECTION

Two sections of *The Man Without Qualities* were published in Musil's lifetime, in 1930 and 1933, and he was still working on the novel when he died nearly a decade later. In 1938, he had withdrawn from publication a set of chapters that had been set up by the printers in galley proof as a continuation of the chapters published in 1933; these were the sections of the novel he was revising when he died. In addition over the years he left many thousands of pages of manuscript presenting alternative versions of the novel's key plots. In German, a number of different editorial approaches have been taken to these drafts, starting with Martha Musil's publication of 1943. It was not until the comprehensive Klagenfurter Ausgabe (Klagenfurt Edition, CD/online) of Musil's complete works that transcriptions of all of his manuscript workings were made readily available.*

In choosing the sequence of the chapters that make up *Agathe*, the editorial approach has been to favor narrative continuity over completeness. Episodes involving Ulrich and Agathe in chapters that include the cast of characters from earlier parts of the book have been left aside as their inclusion was not essential to creating a coherent

---

*Currently, the digital edition platform Musil Online is being prepared at the Austrian National Library in Vienna; a trial version will be available starting in December 2019. The plan is to make all 12,000 manuscript pages of Musil's posthumous legacy accessible on the Internet as facsimiles with transcriptions, reading texts, and text-genetic dossiers, along with the entirety of the works published during his lifetime and an additional interdiscursive commentary.

continuous sequence and would have involved substantial editorial interference. One exception has been made in chapter 22 where the dialogues between Ulrich and Agathe seemed too important to leave out. Other than in this chapter, a minimal amount of editing of what Musil actually wrote has been necessary in order to avoid references to story lines and characters that are not included in our selection. Chapters 1 to 22 of *Agathe* are drawn from part 3 of *The Man Without Qualities*, which was published in 1933, during Musil's lifetime. Chapters 23 to 30 are the first eight of the *Druckfahnen* (galley proof) chapters he withdrew from publication in 1938, in which he subsequently made stylistic and other revisions but which he did not alter drastically before he died. Chapters 31 to 36 are from the manuscript continuations of galley chapters that Musil reworked significantly in 1940–1942 during his exile in Switzerland; in fact he was working on *Agathe*'s chapter 36, "Breaths of a Summer Day," on the day he died. Chapters 31 and 32 have not been translated in any previous English edition. It is important to emphasize that we do not know which of the posthumous chapters Musil himself might have chosen to publish had he lived to continue work on the sequence and there is no claim that chapter 36 was designed by Musil as a conclusion to the story of the siblings' relationship, although it serves well as a resting point for the story.

The *Agathe* project was proposed to NYRB Classics by Nicholas Berwin, who would like to express his gratitude to George Steiner for a seminal conversation that suggested publishing the posthumous draft chapters as a way of introducing the English-speaking reader to Musil's most exceptional writing.

—EDWIN FRANK
Editor, NYRB Classics

AGATHE

I

THE FORGOTTEN SISTER

WHEN ULRICH arrived in —— toward evening of the same day and came out of the train station, a wide, shallow square lay before him that spilled out into streets at both ends and exerted an almost painful effect on his memory, as happens with a landscape one has seen many times and forgotten again.

"I assure you, incomes are down by twenty percent and life is twenty percent more expensive: that amounts to forty percent!" "And I can assure *you*, a six-day bicycle race creates bonds of friendship between nations!" These voices were coming out of his ear; coupé voices.* Then he heard someone say, very distinctly: "Nevertheless, opera means more to me than anything!" "I suppose it's a sport for you." "No, it's a passion!" He tilted his head as if to shake water out of his ear: the train had been crowded, the journey long. Drops of the general conversation that had seeped into him during the trip were now draining away. Ulrich had waited for the cheerfulness and bustle of arrival to pour out into the stillness of the square through the station gate, as if through the mouth of a duct, until its flow was reduced to small trickles; now he stood in the suction chamber of silence that follows upon noise. And along with the auditory disquiet induced by the sudden shift, he noticed an unfamiliar calm before his eyes. Everything visible was more pronounced than usual, and as he looked across the square, the cross-shaped frames of perfectly

*A train compartment in Austria and Germany was called a "coupé." The literal meaning of the French word—"cut"—adds a punning reference to the cutoff phrases still lingering in Ulrich's memory.

ordinary windows stood as black against the pale sheen of glass in the evening light as if they were the crosses of Golgotha. And all things in motion detached themselves from the stillness of the street in a way that does not happen in very large cities. Whether drifting or stagnant, everything here evidently had room to enlarge its importance. He detected this with some curiosity of reacquaintance as he regarded the large provincial town where he had spent some brief but not very pleasant parts of his life. It had, as he very well knew, a quality of rootless dislocation, like a colonial outpost. An ancient core of German burgher stock, transplanted centuries ago to Slavic soil, had worn away so thoroughly that, aside from a few churches and family names, hardly anything was left to remind one of them. Nor was there any evidence, except for a handsome palace that had survived, of the town's having become the old seat of the provincial diet later on. But in the era of absolute government, this past had been covered over by a sprawling vice-regency, with its district headquarters, schools and universities, barracks, courthouses, prisons, episcopal residence, assembly rooms, and theater, along with their attendant staffs and the merchants and craftsmen they attracted, until eventually an industry of immigrant entrepreneurs filled the suburbs with one factory after another, exerting a stronger influence on the fate of this piece of earth in recent generations than anything else had. This town had a history, and it also had a face, but the eyes did not go with the mouth or the chin with the hair, and over everything lay the traces of a life roiled by much change and motion, but inwardly empty. It could be that under special personal circumstances this might favor some great departures from the ordinary.

To sum it up in a phrase that is no less imperfect: Ulrich felt a "spiritual vacuity" in which one could lose oneself so completely as to awaken an inclination toward unbridled fancies. He had in his pocket his father's peculiar telegram, which was imprinted on his memory. "Take note herewith of my recent demise" was the message conveyed to him on the old man's behalf—or was it not, rather, a direct communication? For such it appeared to be, given the signature underneath: "Your father." His Excellency the High Privy Councilor was not given to levity at serious moments. The eccentric construction of the message, therefore, was devilishly logical, for it was he himself who was notifying his son when, in expectation of his end, he wrote or dictated those words, thereby declaring the resulting document valid as of the instant after he had drawn his last breath; indeed there was probably no way to state the facts more correctly, and yet this operation, in which the present sought to dominate a future it would no longer be able to experience, exuded an eerie sepulchral whiff of ragefully moldering willpower.

This mode of behavior, which Ulrich for some reason associated with the almost meticulously off-balance taste of small towns, made him think, not without some misgiving, of his sister, who had married in the provinces and whom he was supposed to meet in a few minutes. His thoughts had already turned to her during the trip, for he knew little about her. From time to time obligatory announcements of family events had reached him through his father's letters; for example, "Your sister, Agathe, has married," followed by additional information, as Ulrich had not been able to come home for the wedding. Then, about a year later, he had received notice of the young husband's death; and three years after that, if he was not mistaken, word came that "Your sister, Agathe, I am pleased to say, has decided to marry again." At this second wedding, five years ago, Ulrich had been present and had seen his sister for several days; but all he remembered was a ceaselessly whirling giant Ferris wheel of white lace, tulle, and linen. And he remembered the groom, whom he hadn't liked. Agathe must have been twenty-two years old then, and he twenty-seven, for he had just received his doctorate; therefore she must be twenty-seven now. But he had not seen her since that time, nor had he exchanged letters with her. He only remembered that later his father had often written: "Lamentably, all does not seem to be going as well in your sister's marriage as it might, though her husband is an upstanding man." Or, once, "Your sister's husband's latest successes have given me much pleasure." Such, more or less, were his father's remarks, to which, regrettably, Ulrich had never paid any attention; but once, as he now remembered quite clearly, there had been, in connection with a disapproving comment on his sister's childlessness, an expression of hope that she was nevertheless contented in her marriage, even though her character would not allow her to admit it. "I wonder what she looks like now," he thought. It had been one of the peculiarities of the old gentleman, who showed such solicitude in keeping them informed about each other, that he had sent them away from home at a tender age, right after their mother's death, to be educated in separate schools. Ulrich, who tended to misbehave, was often not allowed to go home on holidays, so that since their childhood, when they had loved each other very much, he had hardly seen his sister again, with the exception of one long visit when she was ten.

It seemed natural to Ulrich that under these circumstances they hadn't exchanged letters. What would they have had to say to each other? At the time of Agathe's first marriage, he was, as he now remembered, a lieutenant and confined to a hospital with a bullet wound he had received in a duel. God, what an ass he had been! In fact, strictly speaking, several asses at once! For he realized now that the memory of the dueling lieutenant didn't belong there; he had been on the verge of becoming an engineer and had something "important" to do that kept him from the family celebration. Later he learned that his sister had loved her husband very much: he no longer remembered who had told him that, but what does "loved him very much" really mean? It's a manner of speaking. She had married again, and Ulrich could not stand the second husband; that was the one thing he was sure of! He disliked him not only for the personal impression he had of him but for some books by him which he had read, and it was certainly possible that his subsequent forgetting of his sister may have been not entirely unintentional. It was not good of him to have done that; but he had to admit that even during the past year, when he had thought of so many things, he hadn't remembered her once, not even when he learned of his father's death. However, at the train station he had asked the old manservant who picked him up whether his brother-in-law had arrived yet, and was happy to hear that Professor Hagauer was not expected until the funeral. And though it would be no more than two or three days till then, it seemed to Ulrich a limitless retreat, which he would now spend with his sister as though they were the most intimate confidants in the world. It would have been useless to ask himself why he felt as he did. Probably the thought of the "unknown sister" was one of those roomy abstractions in which many feelings that are not quite at home anywhere find a place.

And while he was occupied with such questions, Ulrich had slowly walked into the town, which opened up before him, at once strange and familiar. He had arranged for a car to follow behind him with his luggage, to which he had added quite a number of books at the last minute, and with the old servant, who, already belonging to his childhood memories, had come to combine the functions of caretaker, butler, and beadle in a manner that over the years had brought imprecision to their inner boundaries. Probably it was this humble, taciturn man to whom Ulrich's father had dictated the telegram announcing his death, and Ulrich's feet led him homeward in a kind of pleasant wonderment, as his now alert senses took in with curiosity the fresh impressions with which every growing city surprises a visitor who has not seen it in a long time. At a certain point, which they remembered before he did, Ulrich's feet departed with him from the main street, and after a short time he found himself in a narrow lane formed by two garden walls. Diagonally across from him stood the house, barely three stories high, the central part of it taller than the wings, the old stable off to the side, and, still pressed against the garden wall, the little house where the butler lived with his wife; it looked as if, for all his dependence on them, the aged master had pushed them as far away from himself as he could while at the same time enclosing them within his walls. Absorbed in his thoughts, Ulrich had arrived at the closed entrance to the garden, raised the big ring-shaped knocker that hung there in place of a bell, and let it drop against the low, age-blackened door, before his attendant came running and corrected his error. They had to walk back around the wall to the front entrance, where the car had stopped, and only then, at the moment when he saw the shuttered facade of the house before him, did Ulrich take note of the fact that his sister had not come to meet him at the station. The butler informed him that Madam had complained of a migraine and retired after lunch, giving instructions to wake her when he, the Herr Doktor, arrived. Did his sister have migraines often, Ulrich went on to ask, and immediately regretted his awkwardness, which revealed his estrangement to the aged confidant of his father's household and touched on family relations it was better to pass over in silence. "Madam gave orders for tea to be served in half an hour," the old man replied with the politely blank face of a well-trained servant, giving discreet assurance that he understood nothing that went beyond his duty.

Inadvertently Ulrich glanced up at the windows, supposing that Agathe might be standing there observing his arrival. He wondered if he would find her agreeable, and realized with discomfort that his stay would be quite unpleasant if he did not like her. That she neither came to the train nor to the door of the house, however, seemed to him a confidence-inspiring sign, and it showed a certain kinship of feeling, for strictly speaking it would have been as unwarranted for her to rush to meet him as it would be for him to dash to his father's coffin immediately upon arrival. He sent word that he would be ready in half an hour, and went to get himself in order. The room that had been prepared for him was in the garret-like third floor of the main building and had been his room when he was a child; it was now curiously supplemented by several pieces of furniture brought together haphazardly to serve the convenience of an adult. "There's probably no way of arranging it differently as long as the body is still in the house," Ulrich thought, settling in among the ruins of his childhood, which was not easy, but there was also a vaguely pleasant feeling that rose like mist from this floor. He decided to change his clothes, and as he began to do so it occurred to him to put on a pajama-like leisure suit he had come across while unpacking. "She should have at least come down to say hello when I got here!" he thought, and there was a touch of rebuke in the carelessness with which he chose this garment, even though he continued to feel that his sister must have a reason for acting as she did and that he could like her for it, which in turn lent his change of clothes something of the courtesy that lies in the unforced expression of ease with another person.

It was a wide, soft, woolen pajama, almost a kind of Pierrot costume, checkered black and gray and gathered at the waist, wrists, and ankles; he liked it for its comfort, a quality that felt pleasant as he came down the stairs after the sleepless night and the long journey. But when he entered the room where his sister was waiting for him, he was more than a little surprised by his outfit, for by a secret directive of chance he found himself face-to-face with a tall, blond Pierrot swathed in delicate gray-and-rust stripes and diamonds, who at first glance looked quite like himself.

"I didn't know we were twins!" Agathe said, her face lighting up with amusement.

2

TRUST

THEY DID not greet each other with a kiss but merely stood facing each other amicably, then shifted positions, and Ulrich was able to look at his sister more closely. They were of matching height. Agathe's hair was lighter than his, but was of the same fragrant dryness as Ulrich's skin, the only feature he loved about his own body. Her chest did not lose itself in breasts, but was slim and sturdy, and her limbs seemed to have the long, slender spindle shape that combines natural fitness with beauty.

"I hope your migraine is gone," Ulrich said. "There's no sign of it that I can see."

"I had no migraine at all, it was just simpler to say that," Agathe explained. "I couldn't very well send you a more intricate message through the butler: I was just lazy. I took a nap. I've got into the habit here of sleeping whenever I have a free minute. I'm lazy in general: out of desperation, I think. And when I heard you were coming, I said to myself: Let's hope this will be the last time I'll be sleepy, and then I indulged myself in a kind of sleep cure by taking one more nap. After careful consideration, for the butler's purposes, I called the whole thing a migraine."

"You don't go in for sports?"

"Some tennis. But I detest sports."

As she spoke, Ulrich regarded her face again. He didn't find it very similar to his own; but maybe he was mistaken, there could be a resemblance like that between a pastel and a woodcut, where the difference of medium could distract the viewer from noticing an accordance of lines and planes. There was something about this face that unsettled him. After a while he realized what it was: he couldn't make out its expression. It lacked whatever it is that allows one to draw the usual conclusions about a person. It was not an empty face by any means, but nothing in it was emphasized or summed up as a readable character trait.

"How come you dressed the same way?" Ulrich asked.

"I didn't give it much thought," she said. "I thought it would be nice."

"It's very nice!" Ulrich said, laughing. "But it's quite a conjuring trick on the part of chance. And Father's death doesn't seem to have greatly upset you either."

Agathe rose slowly on her toes and then just as slowly sank to her heels.

"Is your husband here too?" her brother asked, just to say something.

"Professor Hagauer won't be coming until the funeral." She seemed to relish the opportunity to pronounce the name so formally and place it at a distance from herself as something alien.

Ulrich did not know how to respond. "Yes, so I've heard," he said. They looked at each other again, and then, as moral custom suggests one ought, they went into the little room where the body lay.

This room had been kept artificially dark for the whole day; it was drenched in black. Within it, flowers and lighted candles glowed and exuded odors. The two Pierrots stood tall and erect before the dead man and seemed to be watching him.

"I'm not going back to Hagauer!" Agathe said, just to have it said. One could almost think the dead man was supposed to hear it too.

There he lay on his pedestal, in accordance with his own instructions: in full evening dress, the shroud drawn halfway up to his chest, the stiff shirt showing above it, hands folded without a crucifix, decorations affixed. Small, hard orbital arches, sunken cheeks and lips. Sewn inside a corpse's ghastly, eyeless skin, which is still a part of the entity and yet already extraneous; life's traveling bag. Ulrich felt shaken at the root of existence, where there is neither feeling nor thought; but nowhere else. If he had had to put it into words, he would only have been able to say that a tiresome relationship without love had come to an end. Just as a bad marriage corrupts people who cannot get free of it, so does every onerous bond reckoned to last through eternity when the mortal substance shrivels away beneath it.

"I would have liked you to come sooner," Agathe continued, "but Papa would not allow it. He made all the arrangements for his death himself. I think he would have been embarrassed to die with you looking on. I've been living here for two weeks now. It was dreadful."

"Did he love *you* at least?" Ulrich asked.

"Everything he wanted done he told his old servant to take care of, and from then on he gave the impression of a person who has nothing to do and has lost his reason for living. But every fifteen minutes or so he would lift his head to see if I was in the room. That was during the first few days. Afterward it was only every half hour, then every hour, and on that horrible last day it only happened two or three times. And all those days he never said a word to me, even when I asked him a question."

As she was telling him this, Ulrich thought: "She's actually hard. Even as a child she could be tremendously stubborn, in a quiet way. And yet she looks soft." And suddenly he remembered the day he nearly lost his life in a forest that was being torn to shreds by an avalanche. A soft cloud of powdery snow, seized by an irresistible power, had become hard as a falling mountain.

"Was it you who sent me the telegram?" he asked.

"That was old Franz, of course! All that was already in place. He wouldn't let me care for him, either. I'm certain he never loved me, and I don't know why he had me come here. I felt bad and locked myself in my room as often as I could. And during one of those times he died."

"He probably did it to prove you had done something wrong," he said bitterly. "Come!" And he drew her toward the door. "But what if he wanted you to stroke his forehead, or kneel next to his bed—if only because he had always read that this is the proper way to take leave of one's father—and couldn't bring himself to ask you?"

"Maybe so," Agathe said.

They had stopped again and looked at him.

"It's just horrible, everything about it!" Agathe said.

"Yes!" Ulrich said. "And one knows so little."

As they were leaving the room, Agathe stopped again and said to Ulrich: "I'm imposing on you with something that of course is of no concern to you: but it was during Father's illness that I decided not to go back to my husband under any circumstances!"

Her brother could not help smiling at her obstinacy. Agathe had a vertical furrow between her eyebrows and was speaking vehemently; she seemed to fear that he would not take her side. She reminded him of a frightened cat who out of sheer terror launches a frontal attack.

"Does he consent?" Ulrich asked.

"He doesn't know yet," Agathe said. "But he won't consent."

The brother looked questioningly at his sister. But she vigorously shook her head. "Oh no, it's not what you think. There's no third person involved!"

With this, their conversation was finished for the time being. Agathe apologized for not having considered that Ulrich must be hungry and tired, and led him into a room where tea had been served; finding that something was missing from the tray, she went to fetch it herself. Ulrich used the opportunity to recall her husband as clearly as he could, in order to understand her better. He was a man of medium height with a rigidly straight back, pudgy legs in crudely tailored trousers, rather thick lips under a bristly moustache, and a fondness for large-patterned ties, evidently to show that he was no ordinary schoolmaster but a modern pedagogue willing to move with the times. Ulrich felt his old misgivings against Agathe's choice revive; but remembering the open candor that shone from Gottlieb Hagauer's eyes and forehead, it was inconceivable that this man would harbor some secret vice. "He's simply a model of enlightened, hardworking goodwill, a man doing his laudable best to advance the human race in his field without meddling in matters outside his domain," Ulrich decided, and then, remembering Hagauer's writing, he descended into thoughts that were not entirely pleasant.

Such people can already be spotted in their school years. They are not conscientious (as is usually said of them, confusing the effect with the cause) so much as methodical and practical in their studies. They lay out every task beforehand the way one must lay out the clothes one will wear the next morning, piece by piece, down to the collar studs and cuff links, if one wants to dress quickly and without fumbling. There is no train of thought they cannot firmly affix to their minds with those five or six buttons they have at the ready, and there is no denying that the results speak for themselves and stand up to scrutiny. In this way they advance to the head of the class without being felt to be morally unpleasant by their classmates, while people like Ulrich, whose nature tempts them to now slightly exceed and then just as slightly fall short of what is required, are left behind in a way that treads as slowly and softly as fate itself, even if they are far more gifted. He noticed that secretly he was in awe of these shining examples, for their intellectual precision made his own romantic enthusiasm for exactness look a little dubious. "They don't have a trace of soul," he thought, "and are thoroughly good-natured. After their sixteenth year, when young people get inflamed over spiritual questions, they seem to fall behind a little and are not really able to understand new ideas and feelings, but here too they work with their ten buttons, and there comes a day when they can demonstrate that they understood everything all along, 'of course without going to untenable extremes,' and in the end it is they who in effect usher these ideas into public life, which for others have become vestiges of their faded youth or the kind of hyperbole one indulges in solitude." And so, by the time Agathe came back into the room, Ulrich, though he still could not imagine what might have happened to her, felt that a battle with her husband, even without just cause, was something that would possess an utterly contemptible inclination to give him pleasure.

Agathe apparently regarded it as futile to explain her decision rationally. Her marriage was in all external respects in perfect order, as was to be expected from a man of Hagauer's character. No quarrels, almost no differences of opinion, not least because Agathe, as she told Ulrich, never confided her opinion to him on any subject. Of course no excesses, neither drinking nor gambling. Not even bachelor habits. Fair distribution of income. Well-ordered household. Quiet routine of social occasions with others and unsocial ones à deux. "So if you simply leave him for no reason at all," Ulrich said, "you will be found at fault in the divorce; provided he sues."

"Let him sue!" Agathe exclaimed.

"Maybe it would be good to grant him a small financial advantage if he agrees to an amicable settlement?"

"All I took with me," she replied, "was what I would need for a three-week trip, and a few childish things and mementos from my time before Hagauer. He can keep all the rest, I don't want it. But he won't get anything more out of me in the future!"

Again she had spoken with surprising vehemence. One possible explanation was that Agathe wanted to avenge herself for having granted this man unfair advantages in the past. Ulrich's pugnacity, competitive spirit, and gift for strategic ingenuity were now aroused, though he felt some misgivings as well; for it was like the effect of a stimulant that agitates the external emotions while the inner ones remain untouched. He changed the course of the conversation, hesitantly seeking a wider perspective: "I've read some of his writing and have heard about him too," he said. "As far as I know, he's considered a rising man in the field of education."

"Yes, he is that," Agathe said.

"Judging by what I know of his work, he's not only well versed in every branch of pedagogy but also took a stand early on for reform in higher education. I remember reading a book of his where there was talk of the irreplaceable value of history and the humanities for a moral education on the one hand and of the equally irreplaceable value of science and mathematics as intellectual disciplines on the other, and thirdly, of the irreplaceable value of harnessing the élan vital through sports and military drill to prepare mind and body for action."

"That may be," Agathe said, "but have you noticed the way he quotes?"

"The way he quotes? Wait a minute: I vaguely remember noticing something. He uses a lot of quotations. He quotes the old masters. He—of course he quotes the moderns as well, and now I know what it is: he quotes in a way that is positively revolutionary for a school-master—he doesn't just quote the eminent scholars but also the aeronautics engineers, politicians, and artists of the day . . . But that's pretty much what I already said, isn't it . . ." he concluded with the sheepish feeling of a memory that has gone off the track and runs up against a buffer.

"The way he quotes," Agathe picked up the thread, "is to go as far as Richard Strauss in discussing music, or as far as Picasso in painting; but he'll never, not even as an example of something that's wrong, bring up a name that hasn't become a fixture in the newspapers at least by attracting their disapproval!"

That was indeed the case. That was what Ulrich had been searching for in his memory. He looked up. He was pleased by the taste and acuity that were revealed in Agathe's reply. "So that's how he became a leader in the course of time, by being one of the first who followed that course in its wake," he added, laughing. "All who come after him see him ahead of them! But do you like our leading figures?"

"I don't know. Anyway, I don't quote."

"Still, let's be humble," Ulrich said. "Your husband's name stands for a program that many people regard as the best there is. His work represents a small piece of solid progress. His rise in the world won't be long in coming. Sooner or later he'll hold a university chair, even though for years he had to eke out a living as a schoolteacher; and I, you see, who had opportunities laid out before me on a straight path, am now in a position where I probably wouldn't even get a lectureship. That's something!"

Agathe was disappointed, which was probably why her face assumed the porcelain-smooth and impassive expression of a lady as she amiably replied: "I don't know, perhaps you need to show consideration for Hagauer?"

"When is he expected?" Ulrich asked.

"Not before the funeral. He has no time to spare. But under no conditions is he to stay in this house. I won't allow it!"

"As you wish!" Ulrich said with unexpected resolution. "I will pick him up and drop him off at a hotel. And if you want, I will say to him: 'Your room is reserved for you here!'"

Agathe was surprised, and suddenly delighted. "That will annoy him tremendously, because it costs money, and I'm sure he expects to stay here!" Her expression had instantly regained a wild and mischievous look, like that of a child contemplating a prank.

"What are the arrangements, by the way?" her brother asked. "Does this house belong to you, to me, or to both of us? Is there a will?"

"Papa left me a big package that's supposed to contain everything we need to know." They went to the study, which was behind the room where the body lay.

Again they glided through candlelight and floral scent, past the horizon of those two eyes that could no longer see. For a second, in the flickering semidarkness, Agathe was no more than a shimmering mist of gold, gray, and rose. They took the package containing the will back to their tea table, where they then forgot to open it.

For as they sat down, Agathe confided to her brother that to all intents and purposes she had been living apart from her husband, though under the same roof. She didn't say for how long it had been that way.

This made a bad impression on Ulrich at first. Often married women, when they think of a man as a possible lover, will tell him this kind of story; and although his sister had made her disclosure with embarrassment, and yet willfully, in an awkward and transparent effort to initiate something or other, it bothered him that she hadn't thought of a more original line; he considered the whole thing an exaggeration. "Frankly," he said, "I never understood how you could live with a man like that."

Agathe replied that their father had wanted it, and what could she have done about it?

"But you were a widow then, not a child!"

"That's exactly why. I had returned to Papa; everybody was saying I was too young to live alone, because even though I was a widow, I was just nineteen years old; and then I just couldn't stand it here."

"But why didn't you find yourself another man? Or study something and start an independent life that way?" Ulrich asked, unrelenting.

Agathe just shook her head. She paused briefly before answering: "I already told you, I'm lazy."

Ulrich felt this was no answer. "So you had a special reason for marrying Hagauer!?"

"Yes."

"You were in love with someone you couldn't have?"

Agathe hesitated. "I loved my deceased husband."

Ulrich regretted that he had used the word "love" so tritely, as though he regarded the importance of the institution it refers to as inviolable. "One wants to give comfort," he thought, "and just that is already like doling out charity." Nevertheless he felt tempted to continue talking in the same vein. "And then you realized what had befallen you and you started to make trouble for Hagauer," he said.

"Yes," Agathe said. "But not right away—quite late," she added. "Very late, in fact."

At this point they got into a little argument.

These confessions were visibly costing Agathe an effort, though she offered them of her own volition and evidently, as was natural at her age, considered the negotiation of sexual life to be an important topic for everyone. She seemed prepared from the start to take the chance of not being understood, sought his trust, and was firmly and not without candor and passion intent on securing her brother's allegiance. But Ulrich, though morally still in a mood of largesse, was not able as yet to meet her halfway. For all his strength of spirit, he was not always free from the prejudices his mind rejected, having too often allowed his life to go one way and his mind another. And because he had too often exploited and abused his influence over women with a hunter's delight in trapping and observing his quarry, he had almost always encountered the corresponding image of woman as game that collapses under the man's love-spear, and his memory was deeply imprinted with the raptures of humiliation to which a woman in love subjects herself, while the man is far from experiencing any comparable surrender. This conception of masculine power and feminine weakness is still quite common today, even though new ideas have evolved with the successive waves of youth, and the naturalness with which Agathe talked about her dependence on Hagauer pained her brother. It seemed to Ulrich that his sister had suffered a degradation without being fully aware of it, by submitting herself to the influence of a man he disliked and persisting in that condition for years. He did not say this, but Agathe must have read something like it in his face, for she suddenly said: "I couldn't very well run away from him right away, once I had married him; that would have been a little overwrought!"

Ulrich—always the Ulrich in the state of older brother and somewhat obtuse dispenser of edifying counsel—jolted upright and cried out: "Would it really be overwrought to suffer revulsion and immediately draw all the necessary conclusions?!" He tried to soften his words by following them with a smile and looking at his sister in as friendly a way as possible.

Agathe was also looking at him; her face was wide open from the effort of trying to read his features. "Surely a healthy person won't be so piqued by an awkward situation?!" she persisted. "What does it matter, after all?"

This had the effect of causing Ulrich to pull himself together, with the resolve to no longer entrust his thoughts to a partial self. He was now once more the man of functional understanding. "You are right," he said, "what do processes as such really matter! What matters is the system of ideas through which we regard them, and the personal system these form a part of."

"How do you mean that?" Agathe asked distrustfully.

Ulrich apologized for putting it so abstractly, but while he searched for a more accessible analogy, his brotherly jealousy returned and influenced his choice of terms: "Suppose a woman we care about has been raped," he said. "Within the framework of a heroic system of ideas we would have to expect revenge or suicide; in a cynical-pragmatic framework, we would expect her to shake it off like a hen; and what would actually happen today would probably be a combination of the two; but this inner incertitude is more loathsome than anything."

But Agathe did not accept this way of putting it either. "Does it really seem so awful to you?"

"I don't know. It seemed to me that it must be humiliating to live with a person one does not love. But now—as you will!"

"Is it worse than when a woman who wants to marry less than three months after her divorce is compelled by the State to be examined by an officially appointed gynecologist to see whether she's pregnant or not, because of the laws of inheritance? I've read that that happens!" Agathe's forehead seemed to bulge with protective anger, and the little vertical furrow between her eyebrows had appeared again. "And every one of them gets over it if she has to!" she said contemptuously.

"I don't disagree with you," Ulrich replied. "All events, once they actually happen, pass like rain and sunshine. You're probably much more sensible than I am in considering these things in a natural way; but a man's nature is not natural, it impinges on nature and alters it and is therefore sometimes overwrought." His smile was a plea for friendship, and his eyes saw how young she was. The skin on her face scarcely creased when she was agitated, but was further tautened and smoothed by the inner tension, like a glove on a clenched fist.

"I never thought about this in such general terms," she now said. "But after listening to you, it seems to me again that the life I've been leading has put me terribly in the wrong."

"It's only because you've already volunteered so much without coming to the point," her brother said, playfully settling the debt implied by their mutual confessions of fault. "How can I hit the mark if you won't tell me anything about the man for whose sake you're finally leaving Hagauer?"

Agathe looked at him like a child or a student who feels misjudged by her teacher. "Does it have to be a man?! Can't it happen by itself? Have I done something wrong by leaving him without a lover? I suppose I would be lying to you if I claimed that I had never had a lover; I don't want to be so absurd; but I don't have a lover now and I would resent it if you thought I couldn't leave Hagauer unless I had one!"

Her brother had no choice but to assure her that passionate women sometimes leave their husbands without having a lover, and that this was the more dignified course. —The tea for which they had met had been converted into an informal early supper, at Ulrich's request. He was very tired and wanted to go to bed early in order to get a good night's sleep, for the next day promised all sorts of business and unrest. Now, as they smoked their last cigarettes before parting, he didn't know what to make of his sister. There was nothing either emancipated or bohemian about her, even though she was sitting there in the wide trousers in which she had received her unknown brother. It was more something hermaphroditic, it seemed to him now; as she gestured and moved in conversation, the light, masculine garment, which was semitransparent, like water, suggested the delicate form underneath, and in contrast to the independent freedom of her legs, her lovely hair was gathered up in decidedly feminine style. But the center of this amphibious impression was still her face, which possessed the charm of a woman to a high degree and yet had something missing or held in reserve whose nature he could not make out.

And that he knew so little about her and was sitting with her so intimately, and yet not at all as he would with a woman to whom he would be a man, this was something very pleasant, in the lassitude to which he was now beginning to surrender.

"A big change since yesterday!" he thought.

He was grateful for that and tried to think of some affectionate brotherly thing to say to her upon parting, but since he lacked any experience with this, nothing occurred to him. So he just put an arm around her and kissed her.

3

DAYBREAK IN A HOUSE OF MOURNING

IT WAS still early when Ulrich woke from dreamless sleep as smoothly as a fish leaping from water. All traces of the previous day's fatigue were gone. He set out in search of breakfast and walked through the house. The mourning rituals were not quite in motion yet; there was merely an aura of sorrow hovering in all the rooms, reminding him of shops that open their shutters at dawn when the street is still empty of people. Then he took the scientific papers he had been working on from his suitcase and went to his father's study. The room, now with its stove lit, looked more human than it had on the previous evening. Even though a pedantic mind had designed it with an obsessive view to weighing *this* on the one hand against *that* on the other, all the way to the plaster busts lined up in parallel rows on top of the bookshelves, still, the many small, personal things that had been left behind—pencils, monocle, thermometer, an open book, boxes of pen nibs, and the like—gave it the touching vacancy of a lifelong abode that had been abandoned by its tenant just a moment ago. Ulrich sat in the midst of it—not far from the window, actually, yet near the room's center of gravity, the desk—and felt a peculiar listlessness. Portraits of his forebears hung on the walls, and some of the furniture dated from their time; the man who had lived here had formed the egg of his life from the shells of theirs; now he was dead, and his furnishings still stood there as clean-cut as if they had been carved out of space with a file, but already the order of things was about to crumble away to adapt itself to his successor, and one felt the longevity of these inanimate objects almost imperceptibly burgeoning with renewed life behind their rigid air of mourning.

In this mood Ulrich spread out his work, which he had interrupted weeks and months ago, and his gaze immediately settled on the equations of hydrodynamics where he had gotten bogged down. He darkly remembered having thought of Clarisse when he had used the three basic states of water as an example to show a new mathematical possibility; and Clarisse had then diverted him from it.* But there is a kind of remembering that recalls not so much the word as the atmosphere in which it was spoken, and so Ulrich suddenly thought: "Carbon..." and then had the impression, as if out of nowhere, that it would help him if he could just instantaneously know in how many states carbon occurred; but he couldn't remember, and instead he thought: "Man occurs in two states, male and female." He dwelled on this thought for quite a while, seemingly stunned with amazement, as if it were God knows how great a discovery that man lives in two different permanent states. But concealed beneath this momentary stopping of his mind, something different was taking place. For one can be hard, selfish, driven, pushed outward in bas-relief, as it were, and suddenly feel oneself to be not only the same Ulrich So-and-so but also the opposite, recessed and inverted, a selflessly happy creature in an ineffably tender and somehow also selfless state of all surrounding things. And he asked himself: "How long has it been since I last felt this?" To his surprise, it was little more than twenty-four hours. The silence that surrounded him was refreshing, and the state he was reminded of did not seem as uncommon as it usually did. "After all, we're organisms," he thought, reassured, "who have to prevail against one another in an unfriendly world with all the vigor and desire we have at our disposal. But each of us, together with all his enemies and victims, is also a particle and child of this world, and perhaps not as separate from the rest or as independent as he imagines." Given that premise, it seemed to him not at all incomprehensible that from time to time an intimation of unity and love arises from the world, almost

*One of the major story lines in *The Man Without Qualities* concerns the marriage of the brilliant and neurotic Clarisse to Walter, and their fraught relationship with Ulrich.

a certainty that the palpable urgencies of life under ordinary circumstances keep us from seeing more than half of the pattern in which all beings are interwoven. There was nothing in this that had to be offensive to a person whose feelings were imbued with the precision of a mathematical-scientific worldview: Ulrich was even reminded of the work of a psychologist with whom he was personally acquainted that dealt with two large opposing groups of concepts, one based on the sense of being encompassed by the contents of experience, the other on the encompassing of these contents by the subject. It proposed that such a state of "being within something" and "looking at something from outside," a "concave" and a "convex" way of feeling, a "spatial" and a "figural" awareness, an "insight" orientation and an "outlook" orientation, occurred in so many other opposite pairs of experience and their corresponding linguistic tropes that it was justifiable to assume a primeval doubleness of human consciousness behind it. It was not the kind of study that is rigorously based on factual research, but was of the imaginative kind that roams slightly in advance of established knowledge and that originates in an impetus that lies outside the scope of everyday scientific activity; but it was built on solid foundations and its deductions were persuasive, edging towards a unity of feeling that was hidden behind primordial mists, and whose myriad scattered fragments, Ulrich now assumed, had produced the present-day mentality that is vaguely organized around contrasting male and female modes of experience and is mysteriously shadowed by ancient dreams.

Here Ulrich sought to secure his footing—literally the way one uses ropes and crampons for a descent down a dangerous rock face—and began a further deliberation.

"The most ancient philosophies, which are almost incomprehensibly obscure to us, often speak of a feminine and a masculine 'principle,'" he thought.

"The goddesses that existed side by side with the gods in primeval religions are in truth no longer accessible to our sensibility. For us a relationship with these superhumanly powerful women would be masochistic!

"But nature," he thought, "gives men nipples and women a male sex organ, which does not necessarily mean that our forebears were hermaphrodites. Nor, then, are they likely to have been psychically androgynous. In which case the double possibility of a giving and a taking vision must once have been received from without, as a two-faced aspect of nature, and somehow all that is much older than the difference between the sexes, who later adapted these modes to complement their psychological wardrobe."

Such was the direction his thoughts took, but subsequently it happened that he remembered a detail from his childhood, and he was distracted by it, because—and this had not happened for a long time—he was finding pleasure in remembering. It must be said in advance that his father had in earlier days been a horseman and had also owned riding horses, to which the empty stable by the garden wall that Ulrich had seen on his arrival still bore witness. Probably that was the only aristocratic fancy his father had arrogated to himself out of admiration for his feudal friends' way of life, but Ulrich had been a little boy at the time, and the infinity, or at any rate the vastness, that a horse's tall, muscular body possessed for an admiring child reestablished itself to his senses as an eerie fairytale landscape, a mountain covered with fields of hair through which the ripples of the skin ran like waves of wind. It was, he realized, one of those memories whose splendor comes from the child's powerlessness to fulfill his wishes; but these words are not adequate to the magnitude of that splendor, which was virtually supernatural, or to the no less miraculous splendor that little Ulrich touched shortly afterward with his fingertips in a quest for the earlier one. For at that time posters announcing a circus had been put up in the town, showing not only horses but also lions and tigers, as well as magnificent large dogs that lived in friendship with the wild beasts, and he had spent a long time staring at these posters before he finally succeeded in getting hold of one of those brightly colored sheets and cutting out the animals, which he now stiffened with little wooden supports so they could stand up. But what happened then can only be compared to drinking that never quenches one's thirst, no matter how long one goes on drinking; for it knew no bounds, nor, as it went on for weeks, did it yield any progress, and was a constant pull drawing him out of himself and into those adored creatures, which now, with the unutterable happiness of a lonely child, he believed he possessed whenever he looked at them, while just as strongly he felt that some ultimate thing was missing, a lack that nothing could fill, which was precisely what gave his longing the immense radiance that suffused his whole body. But then, along with this peculiarly boundless memory, another, slightly later experience emerged from the oblivion of those young days and despite its childishness took possession of the big adult body that was sitting there, dreaming with open eyes. It was the memory of a little girl who had only two qualities: that she had to belong to him and that as a result he got into fights with other boys. And of these two, only the fights were real, for the little girl did not exist. What a strange time that was, setting out like a knight-errant in search of some unknown boy, preferably bigger than himself, preferably on a lonely road that was capable of harboring a mystery, there to leap at the throat of his surprised enemy and, with some luck, wrestle him to the ground. He had received quite a few beatings for this and won great victories, too, but no matter how it turned out, he felt cheated of satisfaction. Nor would his feelings consider the obvious possibility that the little girls he actually knew were the same kind of creatures as the one he went into battle for, because like all boys his age he became rigid and awkward in the presence of girls; until one day something happened that was an exception to the rule. And now Ulrich remembered it as clearly as if he were looking at the image in the circle of a telescope trained across the years on an evening when Agathe was dressed up for a children's party. She was wearing a velvet dress, and her hair flowed over it like waves of lighter velvet, so that suddenly, in much the same way he had yearned for the animals in the posters, he felt an unspeakable longing to be a girl. At that time he knew so little about men and women that he did not regard it as entirely impossible, but he knew enough not to try to enforce the fulfillment of his wishes, as children often will; rather it was a combination of the two, an ambiguous state which if he were to describe it now was as if he were groping in the dark for a door, meeting with a blood-warm or warmly sweet resistance, pressing against it again and again as it tenderly yielded to his urge to push through without actually ever giving way. Maybe it also resembled a harmless kind of vampire passion that sucks the object of its longing into itself, except this little man did not want to draw that little woman into himself but wanted to be entirely in her place; and this happened with that dazzling tenderness that accompanies only the earliest intimations of sex.

Ulrich stood up and stretched his arms, marveling at his reverie. No more than ten steps away, on the other side of the wall, lay his father's body, and only now did he notice that, around them both, the house, which had been dead and desolate, was bustling with people, who seemed to have suddenly risen from the earth. Old women were laying carpets and lighting new candles, there was hammering on the staircase, flowers were delivered, floors were being waxed, and now it appeared that he too was about to be drawn into this bustle, for visitors were announced who were up and about at this hour because there was something they wanted to have or to know, and from that time on the flow of people was unending. The university needed information about the funeral, a peddler came and shyly asked for clothing, a local antiquarian-book dealer announced himself with profuse apologies to present an offer, on behalf of a German firm, for a rare legal tome that was presumed to be in the deceased's library, a chaplain asked to speak with Ulrich regarding some point that was not clear in the parish registry, a man from the insurance company came with a lengthy contestation, someone was looking for a cheap piano, a real estate agent left his card in the eventuality that the family might wish to sell the house, a retired government clerk offered to address envelopes, and so the coming, going, asking, and wanting went on without cease in these favorable early morning hours, each caller making matter-of-fact reference to the death in the family and staking his claim to existence, in speech and in writing, at the front door, where the old servant turned away as many as he could, and upstairs, where Ulrich nonetheless had to receive everyone who slipped through. He had never imagined how many people politely wait for the death of others and how many hearts are quickened the moment one's own heart stops. He was somewhat astonished, and saw: A beetle lies in the forest, and other beetles, ants, birds, and swaying butterflies gather around.

For embedded in all this greedy commotion there was also a flickering and fluttering of forest-deep darkness. Self-interest peered through the windows of mournful eyes like a lantern left burning in broad daylight when a man with black crepe on the sleeve of a black garment that was a blend of condolence and business suit appeared at the door and stopped, apparently waiting for either himself or Ulrich to burst into sobs. But when after a few seconds neither had done so, the man seemed to consider the gesture sufficient, for now he entered the room entirely and introduced himself, in the same manner in which any other tradesman would have, as the director of the funeral parlor. He said he had come to inquire if Ulrich was satisfied with the services that had been rendered thus far, and assured him that everything else would be conducted in a manner that even the blessed Herr Papa, difficult to please as he famously was, would have found absolutely unimpeachable. He pressed into Ulrich's hand a sheet of paper equipped with blocks of small print and rectangles that turned out to be a contract form itemizing all classes of funerals, and forced him to read particular words, such as: . . . eight horses or two horses . . . wreath carriages . . . number of . . . harnesses à la . . . with outriders, silver-plated . . . attendants à la . . . torches in Marienburg style . . . in Admont style . . . number of attendants . . . illumination, style of . . . illumination, duration of . . . coffin woods . . . floral tributes . . . name, date of birth, sex, profession . . . disclaimer of liability for any unforeseen . . . Ulrich had no idea where some of the more antiquated terms came from; he inquired, the funeral director looked at him with surprise, and he too had no idea. He stood in front of Ulrich like a reflex arc in the brain of humanity, a link between stimulus and response that required no consciousness. A centuries-old tradition had been entrusted to this merchant of mourning, who was at liberty to invoke it as his product description. Evidently he felt that Ulrich had loosened a screw that should have been left untouched, and quickly sought to tighten it again with a remark that was intended to expedite the delivery to its destination. He explained that all these distinctions were unfortunately prescribed by the statutes of the national association of undertakers, but that it really didn't matter if they were ignored, as indeed they always were, and if Ulrich would be kind enough to sign—since Madam, his sister, had declined to do so yesterday without first consulting her brother—it would simply indicate that the gentleman was in accord with the instructions left by his father, and he could be assured of a first-class operation.

While Ulrich was signing, he asked the man if he had already seen those electrically driven sausage machines with a picture of Saint Luke as patron of the guild of butchers; he himself, he said, had once seen them in Brussels—but before he could expect to receive an answer, this man had been displaced by another who also wanted something from him and who was a reporter from the leading local newspaper seeking information for the obituary. Ulrich dismissed the undertaker, but as soon as he began to recite to the journalist the most important events in his father's life, he realized he did not know what was important and what wasn't, and his visitor had to come to his aid. Only then, thanks to the precision grip of a curiosity trained to isolate essentials, did the interview get underway, and Ulrich began to feel as if he were present at the creation of the world. The reporter, a young man, asked if the old gentleman had died after a long illness, or unexpectedly, and when Ulrich answered that his father had continued lecturing until the last week of his life, the resulting formulation was: . . . in the full exercise and enjoyment of his powers. Then the chips began to fly off the old gentleman's life until all that was left were some ribs and joints: Born in Protivín in 1844 . . . attended these and those schools and universities . . . appointed to the post of . . . on this and that date . . . appointed as . . . until finally, with five appointments and honorary degrees, the essential facts were nearly exhausted. A marriage in between. A few books. Once he almost became minister of justice, but ran into opposition from some quarters. The reporter took notes, Ulrich checked them, everything was correct. The reporter was pleased, he had the requisite number of lines. Ulrich was astonished at the small heap of ashes that remains of a life. For every piece of information supplied, the reporter had a coach-and-six phrase at the ready: distinguished scholar, wide-ranging sympathies, forward-looking but cautious politician, a Renaissance man, and so forth; apparently no one had died for a considerable time and the long-unused words were hungry for employment. Ulrich reflected: he would have liked to add a kind word about his father, but the chronicler had his facts and was putting his notebook away, and the rest was like trying to take hold of the contents of a glass of water without the glass.

The coming and going had receded in the meantime. The stream of visitors Agathe had referred to her brother the previous day had passed along, and after the reporter had taken his leave, Ulrich found himself alone. Something or other had put him in an embittered mood. Had his father not been right to lug the sacks of knowledge, shovel about in the heaped grains a little, shifting their order, and for the rest simply subject himself to the kind of life he conceived of as powerful? He thought of his own work, which lay untouched in a desk drawer. Probably no one would even be able to say of him, as they could of his father, that he had done spadework! Ulrich went into the small room where the body lay on its bier. This rigidly straight-walled cell amidst the ceaseless bustle that had arisen from it was fantastically uncanny. The dead man floated, stiff as a piece of bark, among the floods of activity, but there were moments when the image was reversed, and then the motions of life seemed rigid while the body appeared to be gliding along with an eerily quiet momentum. "What does the traveler care," it said then, "for the towns left behind at the piers: I lived here and conducted myself as was expected of me, but now I am moving on!"... Ulrich's heart constricted with the unease of a man who lives among others yet wants something different from what they want. He looked into his father's face. What if everything Ulrich regarded as his own personal idiosyncrasy was nothing more than an objection to this face, an opposition childishly developed some time long ago? He looked around for a mirror, but there was none, and only that sightless face reflected light. He searched it for resemblances. Maybe there were some. Maybe everything was in this face: the bonds of blood and ancestry, the impersonal stream of heredity in which one is merely a ripple, the limitations, the discouragements, the eternal repetitions and circulations of the mind, which he hated with all the passion of his deepest will to live!

Suddenly overcome by this discouragement, he thought of packing his bags and leaving before the funeral. If there really was something he could still achieve in life, what was he doing here?

But in the doorway he ran into his sister, who had come looking for him.

4
"I ONCE HAD A COMRADE"

FOR THE first time, Ulrich saw her dressed as a woman, and after his impression of her the previous day, it almost seemed to him that she was in disguise. Through the open door artificial light fell into the tremulous gray of midmorning, and the black apparition with blond hair seemed to stand in a grotto of air that was flooded with radiance. Agathe's hair was drawn back closer to her head, which made her face look more feminine than it had the day before. Her delicate breasts were enfolded in the black of her severe dress in that perfect balance between yielding and resistance that is characteristic of the featherlight hardness of a pearl, and the tall, slender legs resembling his own which he had seen yesterday were now curtained by a skirt. And because her appearance as a whole resembled him less today, he noticed the resemblance of their faces. It was as if he himself had stepped through the door and were walking towards him: only this version was more beautiful and steeped in a radiance in which he never saw himself. For the first time he was seized by the thought that his sister was a dreamlike repetition and variation of himself; but as the impression lasted only a moment, he forgot it again.

Agathe had come to quickly remind her brother of duties that she had neglected to take care of, as she had overslept: she held their father's will in her hands and drew Ulrich's attention to some clauses that needed immediate attention. In particular, there was a somewhat fuzzy stipulation regarding the old man's medals, which Franz, the servant, also knew about. Agathe had zealously, if somewhat irreverently, marked this point in the testament with a red pencil. The deceased had wanted to be buried with his medals, of which he possessed quite a few, but since it was not out of vanity that he wanted this done, he had added a long philosophical explanation, of which his daughter had read only the beginning, leaving it to her brother to explain the rest.

"How can I explain it?" Ulrich said, after reading the passage through. "Papa wants to be buried with his medals because he considers the individualist theory of the state to be wrong. He recommends the universalist idea, because it is only through the creative community of the State that man receives a purpose that goes beyond the personal, and with it goodness and justice. By himself the individual is nothing, and that is why the monarch is a spiritual symbol. That, in short, is the reason why a man at the time of his death should wrap himself up in his medals, so to speak, the way a dead sailor is wrapped in the flag before his body is consigned to the sea!"

"But I've read that the medals have to be given back," Agathe said.

"The heirs must return the medals to the Imperial Chamberlain's Office. That's why Papa had duplicates made. But evidently he doesn't feel that the ones he bought at the jeweler's were authentic enough, so he wants us to leave the originals pinned to his breast and not to replace them with the duplicates until the moment before the coffin is closed: that's the trouble! Who knows, maybe it's a silent protest against the regulation that he didn't want to express in any other way."

"But by that time a hundred people will be here, there'll be too much distraction and we could forget!" Agathe said.

"We might as well do it now."

"There's no time now; you'd better read the next part, what he writes about Professor Schwung. Professor Schwung may show up at any moment. I was already expecting him yesterday."

"So we'll do it after Schwung leaves."

"It bothers me not to carry out his wish," Agathe objected.

"He'll never know it."

She looked at him doubtfully. "Are you sure about that?"

"Oh?" Ulrich exclaimed, laughing. "Do you doubt it?"

"I'm not sure about anything," Agathe answered.

"Even if it were not certain—we could never do anything right for him anyway!"

"That's true," Agathe said. "So let's do it later. But tell me one thing now," she added: "Do you never worry about what's expected of you?"

Ulrich hesitated. "She has a good dressmaker," he thought. "I needn't have worried that she might be provincial." But because her words were somehow related to the previous evening, he wanted to give an answer that would hold true and be useful to her, but couldn't think of a way to begin that would prevent any possible misunderstanding, and finally came out with an undesirably juvenile remark: "Not only is our father dead, the ceremonies around him are dead too. His will is dead. The people who show up here are dead. I'm not trying to be mean; God knows how grateful one probably ought to be to those who contribute to the solidity of the earth: but all that is as limestone is to the ocean!" He caught a puzzled glance from his sister and realized how obscurely he was talking. "Society's virtues are vices to the saint!" he concluded with a laugh.

In a gesture that could be taken as patronizing or playful, he put his hands on her shoulders, purely out of awkwardness. But Agathe stepped back with a serious face and did not play along. "Did you make that up?" she asked.

"No, a man I love said that."

She had something of the sullenness of a child who is being forced to think hard as she succinctly summed up Ulrich's answers: "So you wouldn't call a person good who is honest out of habit? But a thief who steals for the first time, with his heart almost leaping out of his chest, you would call good?"

These odd words took Ulrich aback, and he became more serious. "I really don't know," he said curtly. "There are situations where I myself don't much care whether something is considered right or wrong, but I can't give you a rule to go by."

Agathe slowly detached her searching gaze from him and returned to the will again: "We have to read further, here's another marked passage," she admonished herself.

Before taking to his bed for the last time, their father had written a series of letters, and his will contained notes elucidating their content and instructions as to where they were to be sent. The specially marked passage referred to the letter for Professor Schwung, and Professor Schwung was that former colleague who after a lifelong friendship had galled and embittered the last year of the old man's life by opposing his view on the statute regarding diminished responsibility. Ulrich immediately recognized the familiar long-drawn-out arguments about imagination and will, the sharpness of law and the ambiguity of nature, which his father had summarized for him once again shortly before his death. Nothing seemed to have been as much on his mind in his final days as Schwung's denunciation of the "social school" of jurisprudence which he had joined, as an emanation of the Prussian spirit. He had just begun to outline a pamphlet that was to bear the title "The State and the Law, or Consistency and Denunciation," when he felt his strength beginning to fail and saw, with bitterness, his enemy in sole possession of the field. In solemn words such as are only inspired by the imminence of death and the struggle to preserve the hallowed good of one's reputation, he obliged his children not to let his work fall into oblivion, and imposed on his son in particular the duty to cultivate the influential connections he had gained thanks to his father's tireless exhortations, in order to thoroughly crush Professor Schwung's hopes of realizing his aims.

Once one has written such a missive, it may well happen that, after the deed has been done, or rather earmarked for execution, one may feel the urge to forgive an erstwhile friend such errors as were inspired by lowly conceit. As soon as a man suffers greatly and, while still living, already feels his earthly envelope quietly coming apart at the seams, he is inclined to forgive and ask forgiveness; but when he feels better again, he takes it back, for the healthy body is by nature implacable; evidently the old gentleman had experienced both states of mind during his final vicissitudes, and the one must have seemed as justified as the other. But such a condition is intolerable for a distinguished jurist, and so his logically trained mind had devised a means of leaving his will in such a way that its integrity as a *last* will would remain unimpeachable by any subsequent counterclaims of emotion: He wrote a letter of forgiveness but left it unsigned and undated, instructing Ulrich to date it with the hour of his death and then sign the document together with his sister as proxies, as can be done with an oral will when the dying person does not have the strength to sign his own name. Truly, in his quiet way and without wanting to admit it, he was an odd duck, this little old man who had always subordinated himself to the hierarchies of being and defended them as their zealous servant while harboring all sorts of revolts for which, on the path he had chosen in life, he could find no outlet. Ulrich was reminded of the death notice he had received, which had probably been marshaled in the same frame of mind; indeed he almost saw a kinship with himself in it, though this time it was not with anger but with compassion, at least in the sense that at the sight of this hunger for expression he could understand the old man's rage against a son who had made life easy for himself by indulging in unseemly liberties. For that is how fathers always regard their sons' solutions to the problems of life, and Ulrich felt a twinge of filial piety as he thought of all that was still unresolved inside himself. But he no longer had time to find an adequate and understandable way to express any of this to Agathe, for he had barely begun when with a great surge the half-light in which they stood suddenly swept a man into the room. Propelled by his own momentum, he strode straight up to the halo of candlelight where, one step away from the bier and before the flummoxed servant could catch up to announce his arrival, he raised a hand in front of his eyes with an ample gesture. "Esteemed friend!" the visitor intoned with a solemn voice. The little old man lay with clenched jaws in front of his enemy Schwung.

"Young friends: Above us the majesty of the starry firmament, within us the majesty of the moral law!" the visitor continued, regarding his faculty colleague through misted eyes. "Within this breast, now cold, there once dwelt the majesty of the moral law!" Only then did he turn his body around to shake hands with the brother and sister.

But Ulrich took this first opportunity to acquit himself of his assignment. "Privy Councilor, you and my father were unfortunately adversaries in recent times?" he said, testing the waters.

The white-bearded visitor gave the impression of needing to bethink himself before he understood. "Differences of opinion and not worth mentioning!" he magnanimously replied, gazing soulfully at the deceased. But when Ulrich politely persisted, hinting that his question related to a last will, the room suddenly became as tense as a backstreet dive when everyone knows: Someone has just drawn a knife under the table and hell will break loose at any moment. So even in the act of expiring the old man had found a way to inconvenience his colleague Schwung! Enmity of such long standing had of course ceased to be a feeling and become a habit of thought; unless something stirred up the affects of hostility, they simply were no longer there, and the accumulated substance of countless disagreeable episodes had congealed into a mutual contempt that was as independent of the coming and going of emotions as any unbiased truth could be. Professor Schwung felt this just as his now dead antagonist had felt it; it seemed to him utterly childish and superfluous to forgive, because this one conciliatory impulse before the end, a mere feeling at that, not a professional admission of error, lacked any probative force against knowledge accrued through years of contention, and was, in Schwung's view, quite shamelessly intended to serve no other purpose than to put him in the wrong if he should wish to exploit his victory. It was of course an entirely different matter that Professor Schwung felt the need to take leave of his dead friend. Good lord, we knew each other as graduate students, before we were married! Do you remember that evening in the Burggarten when we drank to the setting sun and argued about Hegel? However many suns have set since then, I remember that one especially! And do you remember our first professional quarrel, which nearly turned us into enemies even back then? How beautiful that was! Now you are dead, and I'm happy to say I am still on my feet, albeit at your bier! Such are the well-known feelings of elderly people when their contemporaries die off. As we come into the ice years, poetry breaks through. Many people who haven't made a poem since they were seventeen will suddenly write one at seventy-seven when drawing up their will. Just as the dead are called forth one by one at the Last Judgment—even though they have rested at the bottom of time along with their centuries like the cargoes of foundered ships!—so, too, in a last will things are summoned by their names, and their personality, which was lost through much handling, is restored to them. "The Bukhara rug with the cigar burn in my study," it may say in such a final manuscript, or "the umbrella with the rhinoceros-horn handle I bought at Sunshine & Winter in May 1887"; even the bundles of stocks and shares are addressed and invoked individually by their numbers.

And it is no coincidence that along with this last lighting-up of each particular object there awakens as well a desire to invoke a moral, an admonition, a blessing, a principle, that would conjure a powerful charm on this unreckoned multitude of things that emerge one last time on the brink of the final descent. That is why, together with the poetry that begins to stir at the time of testamentary contemplation, the spirit of philosophy too is awakened, and not surprisingly it is almost always an old and dusty philosophy that we haul out again after having forgotten it fifty years ago. Ulrich suddenly understood that neither of these two old men could possibly have given in. "Let life do as it will, as long as principles remain intact!" is a very sensible need if one knows that in a few months or years one will have been outlived by one's principles. And the two principles that were still contending with each other in the old privy councilor were plain to see: his romanticism, his youth, and his sense of poetry called for a fine, sweeping gesture and a noble utterance; his philosophy, on the other hand, demanded that he embody the imperviousness of the law of reason to sudden incursions of feeling and sentimental lapses of the kind his dead enemy had laid in his path like a snare. For the past two days Schwung had been thinking: Well, he's dead now, and there's nothing to stand in the way of the Schwungian view of diminished responsibility; and so his feelings had flowed toward his old friend in great surging billows, and he had worked out his scene of farewell like a carefully organized plan of mobilization that needs only a signal to be carried out. But a drop of wormwood had fallen into that plan, and its effect was clarifying. Schwung had begun with a mighty surge, but now he felt like someone who comes to his senses in the middle of a poem and the last lines won't come. So there they were, face-to-face, white stubble beard and white beard stubbles, each with his jaws implacably clenched.

"So what will he do?" Ulrich wondered, keenly intent on the scene before him. In the end Privy Councilor Schwung's happy certainty that ¶318 of the Penal Code would now be adopted in accordance with his proposals prevailed over his wrath, and being freed from resentment, he would almost have liked to intone that old song, "I once had a comrade / You will find no better / The drum called to battle / He walked at my side," so as to give vent to his now entirely benevolent and undivided feelings. And since he could not do that, he turned to Ulrich and said: "Believe me, young son of my friend, it is the moral crisis that leads the way; social decadence follows after!" Then he turned to Agathe and continued: "It was the mark of greatness in your father that he was always ready to support an idealistic view struggling to prevail in the foundations of the legal code." Then he seized one of Agathe's hands and one of Ulrich's, shook them, and exclaimed: "Your father attached far too much importance to minor differences of opinion, which are sometimes unavoidable in long years of collaboration. I was always convinced that he had to do this in order to protect his delicate sense of justice from the barbs of reproach. Many professors will take leave of him tomorrow, but the like of him will not be found among them."

Thus the scene ended on a conciliatory note, and on leaving, Schwung even assured Ulrich that he might count on his father's friends in case he should still decide to take up an academic career.

Agathe had listened, wide-eyed, contemplating the uncanny final form that life gives to a human being. "That was like being in a forest of plaster trees!" she said to her brother afterward.

Ulrich smiled and responded: "I feel as sentimental as a dog in moonlight!"

5

THEY DO WRONG

"Do you remember," Agathe asked him after a while, "Once when I was still little you were playing with other boys and fell into the water up to your waist, and you wanted to hide it, so you sat at the table with your dry upper half, but the chattering of your teeth led to the discovery of the lower half?"

When he had been a boy home from boarding school for the holidays—which over a long period had actually only happened that one time—and when the small, shriveled cadaver was still an almost omnipotent man for both of them, Ulrich would not infrequently balk at admitting some misdemeanor and refuse to show any remorse, even when he could not deny the evidence of what he had done. That was how, on that day, he caught a fever and had to be quickly put to bed. "And all you got to eat was soup!" Agathe said.

'That's true," her brother confirmed, smiling. The memory of his punishment, which had nothing to do with him now, seemed no different than if he saw standing on the floor the small shoes he had worn as a child, which had nothing to do with him either.

"Soup was all you would have got anyway, on account of your fever," Agathe continued, "but all the same it was administered as a punishment for you!"

"True!" Ulrich agreed again. "But of course that was not done out of malice, but in the fulfillment of a so-called duty." He didn't know what his sister was getting at. He himself was still seeing the child's shoes. Not seeing them but seeing them as if he were seeing them. Feeling as well the insults and humiliations he had outgrown. And thinking: "Somehow this 'nothing-to-do-with-me-now' expresses the fact that at no time in our lives are we completely inside ourselves!"

"But you wouldn't have been allowed to eat anything but soup anyway!" Agathe repeated, and added: "I think I've spent my whole life being afraid that I might be the only person who can't understand this!"

Can the memories of two people talking of a past familiar to both not only supplement each other but also meld even before they are uttered? Something of the kind was happening at that moment! A shared state of mind surprised, even bewildered, the siblings, like hands coming out of coats in places one would never expect and suddenly grasping each other. Each of them suddenly knew more of the past than either of them thought they knew, and Ulrich was feeling again the fever light creeping up the walls from the floor, similarly to the glistening of the candles in the room they were standing in now. Then his father had come, waded through the cone of light cast by the table lamp, and sat down by his bed. "If your moral sense was notably troubled by the possible consequences of what you intended to do, a milder view might be taken of the deed, but in that case you will first have to admit it to yourself!" Perhaps those were words from the will or from the letters about ¶318 that had insinuated themselves into Ulrich's memory. Normally he had no memory for detail, nor for the wording of phrases; so it was something quite unusual that suddenly in his recollection entire groups of sentences stood before him, and it had to do with his sister standing before him, as if it were her proximity that was bringing about this change in him. "If you had the strength to decide upon a wicked deed of your own free will, independent of any compelling need, then you must also realize that you acted wrongly!" Ulrich continued aloud. "He must have talked that way to you too."

"Maybe not quite the same way," Agathe replied. "He usually told me my faults were 'mitigated by my inner constitution.' He was always reproaching me for not understanding that will is connected to thought and is not about acting on instinct."

"It is the will," Ulrich quoted, "that, with the gradual development of the faculties of understanding and reason, must subjugate desire, which is to say instinct, by means of reflection and the resolution that follows upon it."

"Is that true?" his sister asked.

"Why do you ask?"

"Probably because I'm stupid."

"You're not stupid."

"I was always a slow learner and never really understood what I learned."

"That doesn't prove much."

"Then I'm probably spoiled, because I don't assimilate what I do understand."

They were standing face-to-face, close to each other, leaning against the posts of the door to the side room, which had been left open when Professor Schwung departed; daylight and candlelight played on their faces, and their voices intertwined as in a responsory, Ulrich intoning his phrases like liturgy and Agathe's lips serenely following. The old ordeal of those admonitions, which consisted in forcing a harsh and alien system into the tender, uncomprehending brain of a child, amused them now, and they were playing with it.

And suddenly, unprompted by anything they had said, Agathe cried out: "Now just imagine all of this extended to everything, and you have Gottlieb Hagauer!" And she began to imitate her husband like a schoolgirl: "Do you really not know that *Lamium album* is the white dead nettle?" "And how else could we make any progress, if not by walking the same arduous path of induction, at the hand of a faithful guide, that brought the human race through many thousands of years of strenuous labor, with many mistakes, to its present state of knowledge?" "Can't you see, my dear Agathe, that thinking is also a *moral* obligation? What is concentration if not a constant conquest of indolence?" "And intellectual discipline is that training of the mind by which man becomes steadily more capable of working out long series of concepts rationally and with constant skepticism toward his own notions, which is to say, by means of flawless syllogisms, by chain inferences and inference chains, by induction or by demonstrations *per signum*, and by submitting the conclusions thus gained to verification until all the concepts have been brought into conformity."

—Ulrich marveled at his sister's feat of memory. Agathe seemed to take enormous pleasure in reciting these pedantries, which she had appropriated God knows where, perhaps from a book, in perfect word order. She claimed that was how Hagauer talked.

Ulrich did not believe her. "How could you have memorized such long, complicated sentences just from hearing them?"

"They stuck in my mind," Agathe replied. "That's how I am."

"Do you even know," Ulrich asked, astonished, "what verification and demonstrations *per signum* are?"

"No idea!" Agathe admitted with a laugh. "Maybe he only read it somewhere too. But he talks that way. And I learned it by heart as a series of meaningless words by listening to him. I think I did it out of anger at him, for talking like that. You're different from me; with me, things just stay inside me because I don't know what to do with them—that's my good memory. It's due to being stupid that I have a frightfully good memory!" She acted as if this state of affairs were a sad truth that she would have to shake off in order to continue in her exuberant manner: "With Hagauer, this even goes on when he plays tennis: 'When, in learning to play tennis, I deliberately for the first time place my racket in a certain position in order to give the ball, which up to that point was sailing across the net to my satisfaction, a particular direction, I am intervening in the course of the phenomenal world: I am experimenting!'"

"Is he a good tennis player?"

"I always beat him six–love."

They laughed.

"Do you realize," Ulrich said, "that Hagauer is factually quite right about everything you have him say? It just sounds comical."

"It may well be that he's right," Agathe replied. "I don't understand any of it. But you know, there was a boy in his school who translated a passage from Shakespeare, 'Cowards die many times before their deaths,' literally, word for word, and Hagauer crossed it all out and replaced it with the old Schlegel-Tieck version, line by line, word for word! And there's another passage I remember, I think it's by Pindar, which went: 'The law of nature, King of all mortals and immortals, reigns supreme, approving the most violent things, with almighty hand!' and he decided to give it a final polish: "The law of nature, reigning over mortals and immortals, rules with almighty hand, approving even violence.' And wasn't it beautiful, the way that little boy he corrected translated the words exactly the way he found them, like a heap of stones spilled out from a mosaic, with such spine-chilling directness?" Raising an arm and wrapping her hand around the doorpost as if around the trunk of a tree, she recited the rough-hewn verses again, hurling out the words with wild and beautiful fervor, her eyes reflecting the pride of youth, undeterred by the hapless shrunken body that lay beneath her gaze.

Frowning, Ulrich stared at his sister. "A person who will not polish an ancient poem, preferring to leave it weather-beaten, with half its meaning destroyed, is the same as the one who will never put a marble nose where a nose is missing on an ancient statue," he thought. "You could call that a sense of style, but that's not what it is. Nor is it a person with such a lively imagination that he doesn't mind when something is missing. Rather, it's the person who attaches no importance at all to completeness and therefore won't demand of his feelings that they be 'whole.' She has probably kissed," he concluded in a sudden turn, "without feeling herself swept away in body and soul." It seemed to him at this moment that those ardent verses were all he needed to know of his sister to realize that she was never "completely inside" of anything, that she too was a person of "passionate incompleteness" like himself. This even made him forget the other half of his nature, which required moderation and control. He could now have told his sister with certainty that none of her actions ever corresponded to her nearest surroundings, but were all dependent on a much vaster surrounding that is highly subject to caution, indeed one could venture to say a surrounding that does not begin or end anywhere, and the conflicting impressions of their first evening would have found a satisfactory explanation. But his customary reserve proved to be stronger, and so he waited, curious and even a little doubtful, to see how Agathe would come down from the high limb she had ventured out on. She was still standing with her arm raised against the doorpost, and just a moment too much could spoil the whole scene. He despised women who behave as if they have been placed into the world by a painter or a stage director, or whose tune fades away in an artful pianissimo after a moment of exaltation like Agathe's. "One possibility," he thought, "would be for her to suddenly let herself slide down from her peak of enthusiasm with the benumbed, somnambulant look of a medium coming out of a trance; she probably has no other option, and even that will be embarrassing!" But Agathe seemed to know this herself, or else she had glimpsed the danger lurking in her brother's eyes: she gaily leapt from the high limb she had ventured out on, landed on both feet, and stuck out her tongue at Ulrich.

But then she was grave and quiet again, and without saying a word went to fetch the medals. And so the siblings set about acting against their father's last will.

It was Agathe who carried out the plan. Ulrich was shy of touching the old man lying there defenseless, but Agathe had a way of doing wrong that did not permit the thought of wrongdoing to arise. The movements of her eyes and hands resembled those of a woman ministering to an invalid, and at times they also had the unspoiled endearing quality of young animals that briefly pause in their play to make sure their master is watching. Ulrich collected the medals as they were removed and handed Agathe the replicas. He was reminded of the thief who steals for the first time with his heart leaping out of his chest. And if it seemed to him that the stars and crosses shone more brightly in his sister's hand than the ones in his own, indeed that they virtually turned into magical devices, perhaps it was really so in the black-green room filled with many reflections of large leafy plants, but perhaps it was also an effect of his sister's will seizing hold of his own, leading hesitantly but with youthful eagerness; and since there was no evident plan in this, there arose again at these moments of unalloyed contact an almost extensionless and therefore intangibly powerful feeling of their joint existence.

Agathe stopped; she was done. But there was something that had not happened yet, and after reflecting a little while she said, smiling: "Why don't we, each of us, write something beautiful on a piece of paper and put it in his pocket?" This time Ulrich immediately knew what she meant, for there were not many such shared memories, and he recalled how at a certain age they had both been very fond of sad poems and stories in which someone died and was forgotten by everyone. Perhaps it was the desolation of their childhood that caused this; and often they made up such stories together. But even then Agathe was already inclined to act the stories out, while Ulrich only took the lead in the more masculine undertakings, which were audacious and heartless. So it was Agathe's idea that each of them cut off a fingernail in order to bury it in the garden, and then she added to the nails a small bundle of her blond hair. Ulrich declared proudly that in a hundred years someone might come across these relics and wonder who it might have been, a notion influenced by his intention to live on in posterity; but for little Agathe, what mattered was the burial as such, for it gave her the feeling of hiding a part of herself and withdrawing it permanently from the supervision of the world, whose pedagogic demands intimidated her even though she did not think highly of them. And because at that time the cottage for the servants was being built by the edge of the garden, they agreed to do something unusual together. They would write some wonderful poems on two pieces of paper and add who they were, and this was going to be bricked up in the walls; but when they set about writing the verses, which were supposed to be especially beautiful, they couldn't think of any, day after day, and the walls were already growing out of the foundations. Then at last, with time pressing, Agathe copied a sentence from her math primer and Ulrich wrote, "I am ——," followed by his name. Nevertheless their hearts were pounding violently when they sneaked up on the two bricklayers who were at work there, and Agathe simply threw her piece of paper into the pit where the workers were standing and ran away. But Ulrich, being bigger and a man, was of course even more afraid of being stopped and questioned by the astonished bricklayers and was so agitated he could move neither arm nor leg. Then Agathe, emboldened by the fact that nothing had happened to her, came back and took his piece of paper from him. Assuming the air of a guileless stroller, she advanced with it, sauntering, to inspect a brick at the far end of a row that had just been laid, lifted it, and pushed Ulrich's name into the wall before someone could send her away. Ulrich himself followed her hesitantly and at the moment of the deed felt the terrible grip of anxiety turn into a wheel with sharp knives whirling inside his chest so fast that at the next moment it became a spurting sun, like those fireworks that spin around as they burn. It was to this, then, that Agathe had alluded, and for the longest time Ulrich gave no answer and only smiled his demur, for to reenact this game with the dead man struck him as not allowable.

But Agathe had already bent down and slid a wide silk garter off her leg, lifted the magnificent shroud, and pushed the garter into her father's pocket.

Ulrich? At first he could not believe his eyes to see this memory returned to life. Then he almost jumped forward to stop her, simply because it was so contrary to all order. But then he caught in his sister's eyes a flash of the pure dewy freshness of early morning before the bleakness of a day's work has set in, and it held him back. "What on earth are you doing?" he said in gentle remonstration. He did not know whether she wanted to conciliate the dead man because he had been wronged, or whether she wanted to give him something good to take with him because he himself had done so much wrong: he could have asked, but the barbaric idea of sending the frigid dead man on his way with a garter still warm from his daughter's thigh constricted his throat and started all sorts of disorder in his brain.

6

THE OLD GENTLEMAN IS FINALLY LEFT IN PEACE

THE SHORT time that was available until the funeral had been filled with countless unaccustomed little tasks and passed quickly; finally, in the last half hour before the departure of the deceased, the steady arrival of callers that had run like a black thread through all the hours became a black gala. The undertaker's men had intensified their hammering and scraping with the same earnestness as a surgeon who cannot be argued with once one has placed one's life into his hands, and had laid, through the otherwise untouched quotidian normalcy of the rest of the house, a pathway of reverent solemnity leading from the entrance up the stairs into the room where the body lay in state. The flowers and potted plants, black cloth and crepe hangings, and silver candelabra with trembling little gold tongues of flame that received the visitors knew their assignments better than Ulrich and Agathe, who were obliged to represent the family and greet all who had come to pay their last respects to the deceased, and who scarcely knew who anyone was except when their father's old servant inconspicuously drew their attention to particularly eminent guests. And all those who appeared glided up to them, glided away, and dropped anchor somewhere in the room, either singly or in small groups, to stand motionless and observe the brother and sister, whose faces in turn assumed masklike demeanors of grave introversion, until finally the owner of the funeral home, who may also have been in charge of the horses—the same man who had presented his printed forms to Ulrich and who during the last half hour had run up and down the stairs at least twenty times—hurried up to Ulrich in a kind of sidelong canter and, with a tactfully modulated display of his own importance, like an adjutant addressing his general on parade, informed him that everything was now ready.

Since the cortege was to be conducted through the town in a solemn procession on foot before the carriages were boarded, Ulrich was charged with leading the way, flanked on one side by the imperial and royal vice-regent, who had appeared in person to honor the final sleep of a member of the House of Lords, and on the other by an equally high-ranking gentleman, the elder in a delegation of three representing the House of Lords; behind them came the two other noblemen, then the rector and the senate of the university, and only after these, but ahead of the seemingly endless river of top hats worn by persons of varying and, in their sequence from front to rear, gradually decreasing dignity, came Agathe, surrounded by women in black and designating the point where private sorrow meted out by fate had its place among the pinnacles of public service. The unregulated attendance of people with "nothing but sympathy" only began behind those appearing in an official capacity, and it was even possible that it consisted of no one but the old servant couple trudging along by themselves behind the procession. So it was on the whole a procession of men, and the person walking at Agathe's side was not Ulrich but her husband, Professor Hagauer, whose apple-cheeked face with the bristly caterpillar of a moustache above his mouth had become alien to her in the meantime, an impression augmented by the dense, black veil that permitted her to observe him in secret, and which made him look blue. Ulrich himself, who had been in his sister's company throughout the many preceding hours, suddenly had the feeling that the ancient protocol of funeral procedure, which dated from the time of the university's founding, had torn her away from him, for he missed her and was not permitted to turn around to see her; he tried to think of a joke to greet her with when they met again, but his thoughts were deprived of their freedom by the vice-regent, who was striding beside him with lordly bearing and for the most part in silence but who occasionally addressed him with a murmured statement he was obliged to catch—a quality of solicitude that had already been shown him by all of their Excellencies, all the way up to their Magnificences and

Worships—for he was reputed to be Count Leinsdorf's shadow, and the mistrust with which the count's patriotic campaign was gradually coming to be regarded conferred distinction upon him.*

There were moreover masses of onlookers crowding the sidewalks and filling the windows, and though Ulrich knew it would all be over in an hour, much like a theater performance, he nevertheless experienced the events of this day with a special vividness, and the universal sympathy with his fate lay like a heavily trimmed cloak around his shoulders. For the first time he felt the upright stance of tradition. The wave of emotion running ahead of the procession, the crowd's chatter quieting, falling silent, and breathing freely again, the ecclesiastical magic, the dull thuds produced by clods of earth dropping on wood, already audible in his anticipation, the pent-up silence of the procession: all this plucked at the vertebrae as if at the strings of a primordial musical instrument, and with astonishment Ulrich felt within himself an indescribable resonance whose vibrations seemed to be raising his body from within, as if the surrounding solemnity were literally bearing him aloft. And as he was closer than usual to others on this day, he went on to imagine how different it might be if at this moment, in accordance with the original meaning of the pomp that was now being enacted as a half-forgotten custom, he were actually striding along as the heir to some great position of power. Sadness vanished at this thought, and death changed from an awful private affair into a transition that was accomplished through a public ceremony; there was no longer the gaping hole, stared at with dread, which every man or woman whose presence one is accustomed to leaves behind after the first days of their disappearance, but already the successor was walking in the place of the deceased, the crowd breathing its fealty to him, the ceremony at once a death rite and a coming of age for the one who would now take up the sword and set forth alone, for the first time without anyone to follow, toward his

---

*For a description of the Great Patriotic Campaign, also known as the Parallel Campaign, and Count Leinsdorf's and Ulrich's role in it, see the introduction, pages ix–x.

own end. "I should have closed my father's eyes!" Ulrich inadvertently thought. "Not for his sake or my own, but—" he didn't know how to finish the thought; but that he had never liked his father, and that his father had not liked him, seemed a petty overestimation of the importance of persons in the face of this order of things; and indeed, faced with death, any personal thoughts had the stale taste of emptiness, whereas all that was meaningful in the moment seemed to emanate from the giant body of the procession as it slowly advanced through the crowd-lined street, however pervaded by idleness, curiosity, and thoughtless compliance that body might be.

But the music played on, it was a light, clear, splendid day, and Ulrich's feelings swayed to and fro like the canopy that is carried in processions above the Holy of Holies. Occasionally Ulrich glanced at the windows of the hearse that was driving in front of him and saw his head with hat and shoulders reflected in them, and from time to time he would notice again on the floor of the hearse, next to the coffin with its armorial decor, the little droppings of candle wax from earlier burials that had not been properly cleaned away, and then, without any thought, he simply felt sorry for his father as he would for a dog that had been run over in the street. His eyes grew moist, and when his gaze moved beyond the black throng to the spectators by the sides of the street, they looked like freshly sprinkled flowers, and the notion that he, Ulrich, was now seeing all this and not the one who had spent all his days here, and who moreover loved ceremony much more than he did, was so strange that it seemed downright impossible to him that his father could not be among those who saw him departing from a world that he had, all in all, regarded as good. It was a deeply moving thought, but it didn't escape Ulrich that the agent or undertaker who was leading this Catholic procession to the cemetery and keeping it in good order was a tall, muscular Jew in his thirties. He was graced with a long blond moustache, carried papers in his pocket like a tour guide, and rushed back and forth, fiddling with a horse's harness or whispering something to the musicians. This reminded Ulrich that his father's corpse had not been in the house on the last day and had only been returned shortly before the funeral, after being placed at the disposal of science, in accordance with a testamentary disposition inspired by the free spirit of humanistic inquiry, and it seemed rather likely that after this anatomical intervention the old gentleman had been only hastily sewed together again; whereupon, behind the windows reflecting Ulrich's image, a haphazardly stitched-up thing rolled along as the focal point of this great, beautiful, solemn act of imagination and illusion. "With or without his medals?!" Ulrich asked himself in dismay; he had forgotten about it and did not know whether his father had even been dressed again before the closed coffin returned to the house. The fate of Agathe's garter, too, was uncertain; it could have been found and he could imagine the jokes the students would have made. All of this was extremely embarrassing, and so the objections of the present again dissolved his feeling into many particulars, after it had, for a moment, nearly attained the smooth round wholeness of a living dream. All he felt now was the absurdity and confused vacillation of all human order and of himself. "Now I'm completely alone in the world," he thought. "A mooring rope has snapped. I'm rising!" It was in this thought, which recalled the sensation he had felt on receiving the news of his father's death, that his feeling now clothed itself as he walked on between the walls of the watching crowd.

7

A FAMILY OF TWO

ULRICH says: "When two men or women have to share a room for some time—while traveling, in a sleeping car or a crowded inn—they often strike up an odd sort of friendship. Everyone has a different way of rinsing his mouth or leaning over to take off his shoes or bending a leg when lying down in bed. Clothes and underwear are the same on the whole, but there are countless small and particular differences that reveal themselves to the eye. At first—probably due to the hypertense individualism of our current way of life—there's a resistance that could be taken for faint aversion, a guardedness against coming too close and suffering a breach of one's personal boundaries. Once that is overcome, a fellowship of feeling forms that bears the mark of its unusual origin like a scar. After this transformation many people behave more cheerfully than usual; most of them more innocuously; many more talkatively; almost all more amiably. The personality is changed, one could almost say, exchanged beneath the skin, for one that is less individual. Something new is taking the place of the I—something that is felt to be distinctly uncomfortable and a diminution, yet irresistible. It is the first, germinal budding of a We."

Agathe answers: "This aversion in close proximity exists between women especially. I've never been able to get used to women."

"It exists between men and women too," Ulrich says. "Only there it's covered over by the obligatory transactions of love, which immediately claim one's attention. But it happens quite often that lovers suddenly wake from their entwinement, and then they see—with astonishment, irony, or panic, depending on type—a totally alien creature basking in comfort at their side; in fact, with some people this goes on for many years. Then it is impossible for them to say which is the more natural: their ties with others or the self's hurt recoil from these ties into its own imaginary uniqueness—because after all, both are in our nature. And both get confounded in the concept of the family! Life in the family is not the full life; young people feel robbed, diminished, not at home with themselves when they are in the family circle. Look at old unmarried daughters: they're sucked dry by their family, drained of their blood. What they have turned into is a very peculiar hybrid of I and We."

Agathe, stretched out on the divan, has raised one knee and responds with animation to his train of thought: "That's why I had to marry again! You yourself explained it by what you just said!"

"And yet there is something to the so-called 'sanctity of the family,' this merging into one another and being at each other's service, this selfless movement in a closed circle," Ulrich continues, taking no notice, and Agathe wonders at the way his words so often move away from her right after coming so close. "Normally this collective self is just a collective egotist, and then a strong sense of family is the most insufferable thing one could imagine; but I can also imagine that absolute willingness to leap into the breach, to fight shoulder to shoulder and bear wounds for each other, as a primordially pleasant feeling that resides in the depths of human time, and in fact is already pronounced in the animal herd," she hears him say, without being able to make much of it. Nor can she do more with his next sentence: "This condition degenerates easily, as is the case with all ancient conditions whose origin has been lost." And it is only when he concludes by saying: "And one probably has to demand of the individuals that they be something quite out of the ordinary if the whole they make up together is not to become a mindless travesty!" that she feels again at ease in his presence and would like to prevent her eyes from blinking as she watches him so that he won't disappear in the meantime, because it is so strange that he sits there saying things that vanish in the heights and suddenly drop down again like a rubber ball that was caught in the branches of a tree.

The siblings had met in the drawing room in the late afternoon. Several days had passed since the funeral.

It was a long room that was not only decorated in bourgeois Empire taste but also furnished with genuine pieces from the period; between the windows hung the tall rectangular mirrors encased in plain gilt frames, and the moderately stiff chairs were ranged along the walls, so that the empty floor seemed to have flooded the room with the darkened sheen of its parquet, filling it like a shallow basin in which one hesitated to set foot. At the edge of this stylishly inhospitable salon—since the study where Ulrich had sat down the first morning had been set aside for him—approximately where, in a niche in the corner of the room, the stove stood like a stern column, bearing a vase on its head (and precisely at the middle of its front, on a shelf that ran around it at waist height, a single candlestick), Agathe had created a highly personal peninsula for herself. She had had a divan moved in and had laid a rug at its feet whose antique red-blue, together with the couch's Turkish pattern, which repeated itself in meaningless infinity, presented a sumptuous challenge to the delicate grays and soberly poised lineaments that were at home in this room by dint of forefatherly will. She further offended against that austere and high-minded will by placing a green, large-leafed, man-size plant, which she had retained from among the funeral decorations along with its pot, at the head of the couch as a "forest"—opposite the tall bright floor lamp that would enable her to read in comfort while lying down, and which in the room's classicistic landscape had the effect of a searchlight or an antenna mast. This salon, with its coffered ceiling, pilasters on the walls, and small pillar cabinets, had not changed much in the last hundred years, because it was rarely used and had never really been included in the lives of its more recent owners; perhaps in their ancestors' day the walls had been covered with delicate fabrics instead of the light gray coat of paint they wore now, and the upholstery on the chairs might have looked different, but since her childhood Agathe had known this salon as it presented itself now, and was not even sure if it was her great-grandparents or strangers who had furnished it like this, for she had grown up in this house and the only specific thing she knew was a memory of always entering this room with the shyness that is instilled into children in regard to something they might easily damage or soil. But now she had put away the last symbol of the past, her mourning clothes, and was dressed again in her lounging pajamas, lying on the rebelliously intruded divan, and had spent most of the day reading good and bad books she had amassed, interrupting herself from time to time in order to eat or fall asleep; and when the day thus spent was waning, she gazed through the darkening room at the pale curtains that, already steeped in twilight, were billowing out from the windows like sails, and this impression made her feel as if, haloed by the lamp's hard glare, she had been voyaging through the stiffly delicate room and had just come to a halt. That was how she had been found by her brother, who registered her illuminated headquarters with one glance; for he too knew this drawing room and could even tell her that the original owner of the house was supposed to have been a rich merchant who later ran into trouble, which enabled their great-grandfather, who was an imperial notary, to acquire the attractive property at a price well within his means. There were all sorts of other things Ulrich knew about this salon, which he had examined thoroughly, and his sister was especially struck by the explanation that in their great-grandparents' time this rigid decor was felt to be particularly natural; she did not find it easy to understand this, because to her the room's furnishings looked like something spawned in a geometry class, and it took a while before she could feel her way into the sensibility of an age that was so satiated with the overbearing forms of the baroque that its own somewhat stiff affectation of symmetrical balance was veiled by the tender illusion of being in accord with a nature conceived to be pure, rational, and unadorned. But when finally, with the help of all the details Ulrich supplied, she had envisioned this shift of ideas, she found it nice to know so much about things that her experience of life up to then had led her to despise; and when her brother wanted to know what she was reading, she quickly covered her hoard of books with her body, even though she boldly insisted that she enjoyed reading bad books just as much as good ones.

Ulrich had worked in the morning and had then left the house. His hope for a period of concentrated study had not been fulfilled so far, and the helpful effect that might have been expected from the interruption of his customary life had been outweighed by the distractions that his new circumstances brought in their wake. Only after the funeral did a change occur, when relations with the outer world, which had started up in such a lively fashion, had been cut off as if at a stroke. For it was only as a kind of representation of their father that the siblings had been the center of sympathetic attention for a few days and come to feel the numerous kinds of connections attendant upon their position, and apart from Walter's old father they knew no one in the town whom they would have wanted to visit;* nor had anyone invited them, in consideration for their mourning; and only Professor Schwung had shown up, not only at the funeral but also the following day, to inquire whether his dead friend had not left a manuscript on the problem of diminished responsibility, which one might hope to see published posthumously. This abrupt transition from ceaseless bubbling activity to leaden stillness produced an almost physical shock. Besides, they were sleeping in the rooms they had occupied as children, as there were no guest rooms in the house, upstairs in the attic on makeshift cots surrounded by the meager trappings of childhood, which have something of the simplicity of a padded cell, crowding the mind with the honorless luster of oilcloth on the tables or the linoleum wasteland on the floor into which the stone block construction kit once spewed its fixed ideas of architecture, and insinuating themselves even into one's dreams. These memories, which were as senseless and limitless as the life for which they were supposed to have been a preparation, made it seem pleasant to the siblings that at least their bedrooms were adjacent, separated only by a closet used for clothes and storage; and because the bathroom was on the floor below, they were dependent on each other after waking as well, encountering each other in the emptiness of the stairs and of the house as soon as they got up in the morning,

*Walter is Clarisse's husband. See footnote on page 23.

forced to take each other's wishes into account, and having to tackle jointly the many problems posed by the unfamiliar household with which they had suddenly been entrusted. Naturally this alliance, as intimate as it was unforeseen, had an element of humor that did not escape them; it resembled the adventurous comedy of a shipwreck that had swept them back to the solitary island of their childhood; and both these circumstances led them after the first few days, over which they had no control, to strive for independence, but each of them did so more out of consideration for the other than for themself.

That was why Ulrich had already gotten up before Agathe built her peninsula in the drawing room, and had stolen quietly into the study, where he took up his interrupted mathematical investigation, actually more as a way of passing the time than with an expectation of success. But to his not inconsiderable surprise, in the few hours of a single morning he brought to completion, except for some insignificant details, the work he had left lying untouched for several months. This unexpected solution came about with the help of one of those ideas that lie outside the norm and of which one might say, not that they show up when one no longer expects them but rather that their startling effulgence reminds one of the sudden radiance of the beloved who has been there all along among the other girls before the perplexed suitor ceases to understand how he could have thought any others her equal. Such inspirations involve more than the intellect—there is always some prerequisite of passion at work—and Ulrich felt that at this moment he should be finished and free, and in fact, as no reason or purpose could be found in the thing, he was positively struck by a sense of having finished prematurely; and now the remaining energy drove outward into reverie. He glimpsed a possibility of applying the idea that had solved his problem to far greater questions, playfully dreamed up an outline of such a system, and in these moments of happy relaxation even felt tempted by Professor Schwung's suggestion that he return to his career and seek the path that leads to success and influence. But when, after a few minutes of intellectual satisfaction, he soberly considered what the consequences would be if he were to yield to his ambition and now, as a laggard, set out on an academic path, it occurred to him for the first time that he was too old for such a venture. Not since his boyhood had he felt this half-impersonal concept of age as something that had inherent substance, nor had he ever known the thought: There is something you can no longer do!

When Ulrich was telling this to his sister afterward, in the late afternoon, he happened to use the word "fate," and that aroused her interest. She wanted to know what "fate" was.

"Something halfway between 'my toothache' and 'King Lear's daughters!'" Ulrich replied. "I'm not one of those people who like to bandy this word around."

"But for young people it's part of the song of life; they want to have a fate and don't know what it is."

"There will come a time when people are better informed, and then the word 'fate' will probably have acquired a statistical meaning," Ulrich responded.

Agathe was twenty-seven, still young enough to have retained some of the hollow forms of feeling that one develops in the beginning of life, and old enough to have intimations of the content reality pours into them later. She replied: "I guess getting old is a fate in itself!" and was very dissatisfied with this answer, which expressed her youthful melancholy in a way that struck her as insipid.

But her brother did not take notice of this and gave an example: "When I became a mathematician," he said, "I wanted to achieve scientific success and applied all my energy to that end, even though I regarded it only as a preliminary to something else. And even though my first papers were of course imperfect, as beginnings always are, they really did contain ideas that were new at the time and either remained unnoticed or even met with resistance, even though my other work was well received. Now I suppose one could call it 'fate' that I lost patience with having to go on driving that wedge with all my strength."

"Wedge?" Agathe interrupted him, as if the mere sound of this industriously masculine word connoted something that could not fail to be unpleasant. "Why do you call it a wedge?"

"Because that was all I wanted to do in the beginning: I wanted to keep driving the investigation further and deeper like a wedge, and then I simply lost patience. And today, when I finished what may be the last work reaching back to that period, I realized that I probably might have been not entirely unjustified in regarding myself as the leader of a movement, if at the time I had been luckier or shown more persistence."

"You could still make up for lost time!" Agathe said. "After all, a man isn't as likely to get too old for something as a woman is."

"No," Ulrich replied, "I don't want to do that. Because it is surprising, but true, that objectively—in the course of things, in the development of mathematical science itself—nothing would have changed. I may have been about ten years ahead of my time, but others, moving more slowly and along different paths, got there without me. The most I could have done was lead them there more quickly; and it's an open question whether such a change in my life would have quickened my imagination enough to give me a new lead and carry me across the finish line. So there you have a piece of what is called personal fate, but it amounts to something remarkably impersonal.

"Anyway, it happens more and more often the older I get," he continued, "that something I used to hate subsequently and in a roundabout way takes the same direction as my own path, so that suddenly I can no longer deny its right to exist; or else it will happen that ideas or events that once brought out my greatest enthusiasm turn out to be faulty. So in the long run it seems to make no difference if one gets excited, nor does it matter what meaning one has invested one's excitement in. It all comes to the same thing in the end. Everything serves a development that is impenetrable and unfailing."

"This used to be attributed to the unfathomable will of God," Agathe answered, frowning, in the tone of one speaking from experience, and not in the most respectful way. Ulrich remembered that she had been educated in a convent. He was sitting at the foot of the divan where she lay in her long trousers gathered at the ankles, and the lamp shone on them both, casting a large leaf of light on the floor that had darkened around them. "Nowadays," he said, "fate gives more the impression of the all-compelling movement of a mass. We are inside it and are rolled along with it, whether we want to or not." He remembered having been struck once by the thought that in our time every truth comes into the world divided into its half-truths, and that nevertheless in this slippery, capricious way, a much greater overall achievement may result than if everyone earnestly strove to do their whole duty, each man by himself. He had once even made a presentation of this idea, which stuck like a barb in his self-esteem but was nonetheless not without the possibility of greatness, and had added the corollary, which he didn't mean seriously, that therefore one could do whatever one liked! For nothing could have been further from his mind than this conclusion, and especially now that his fate seemed to have released him from duty, leaving him nothing further to do, at this moment of danger to his ambition, when he had been so oddly driven to finish this last, laggard work still binding him to his earlier days, precisely at this moment of utter personal blankness, what he felt instead of a waning was the new suspense that had developed since he had left home. It had no name; for the moment, one could say that a young person who was akin to him was seeking his advice, or one could say something different: But he saw with astonishing acuity the radiant mat of bright gold against the black-green of the room, and on it the delicate diamond checks of Agathe's Pierrot costume, and himself, and, framed by an oddly sharp margin, lifted out of the dark, the accident of their being together.

"How did you put that?"

"What we still refer to as a personal fate is being displaced by a collective process that can ultimately be summed up in statistical terms," Ulrich repeated.

Agathe reflected, and then she had to laugh. "Of course I don't understand that, but wouldn't it be wonderful if one could melt in statistics; it's been ages since love could achieve that!" she said.

And this led Ulrich to suddenly tell his sister what had happened to him when, after finishing his work, he had left the house and walked to the center of the town in order to fill the void left in him by the completion of his paper. He hadn't wanted to talk about it, because it seemed too personal. For whenever his travels took him to cities with which he had no connection through business of any kind, he greatly enjoyed the special feeling of solitude it gave him, and seldom had this feeling been as strong as this time. He had seen the colors of the trams, the automobiles, shopwindows, gateways, the shapes of church towers, faces, and facades, and although they all had the usual European resemblance, his gaze skimmed above them like an insect that has flown off course, attracted by the foreign colors of a field where it cannot settle, though it would like to. This walking without aim or purpose in a busily self-preoccupied town, this heightened intensity of experience, which increases as the strangeness of one's surroundings intensifies and is further heightened by the conviction that it is not oneself that matters but only the aggregate of these faces, only these movements wrenched loose from the body and summed up as armies of arms, legs, or teeth, to whom the future belongs—all this can evoke the feeling that to wander about by oneself as a whole self-contained human being is a positively antisocial and criminal activity; but if one yields to this a little more, there can be a sudden shift to such a delightfully foolish and irresponsible sense of physical well-being, as if the body no longer belonged to a world where the sensual self is enclosed in strands of nerves and blood vessels, but belongs instead to a world flooded with somnolent sweetness. With these words Ulrich described to his sister what might have been the result of a frame of mind without goal or ambition, or of a diminished ability to maintain the illusion of personal selfhood; or perhaps it was nothing other than the "primal myth of the gods," that "double face of nature," that "giving" and "taking" way of seeing which he was all but chasing down like a hunter. He now waited curiously to see if Agathe would give a sign of agreement or indicate that she too was familiar with such impressions, and when that did not happen, he explained it again: "It's like a slight split in one's consciousness. One feels embraced, encompassed, pierced to the heart by a pleasantly will-less unselfreliance; but on the other hand one is awake, capable of judgment in matters of taste, and even prepared to start a fight with people and things that are full of unventilated pretension. It's as if there were two relatively autonomous strata of life within us that usually keep each other profoundly in balance. And since we were speaking of fate, it's also as though we had two fates: one that is active and irrelevant and takes its course, and one that is motionless and important that we never get to know."

Now Agathe, who had been listening for a long time without stirring, suddenly said: "It's like kissing Hagauer."

She had propped herself up on an elbow, laughing, her legs still stretched out on the couch. And she added: "Of course it was never as beautiful as the way you describe it!" And Ulrich laughed too. It was not quite clear why they were laughing. Somehow this laughter had come upon them from the air or from the house or from the traces of awe and unease left behind by the solemnities of the last days, which had touched so uselessly on the Beyond, or from the uncommon pleasure they found in their conversation; for every human custom that is developed and refined to its fullest bears within it the seed of change, and every excitement that goes beyond the ordinary is soon misted over by a breath of sadness, absurdity, and satiation.

And so, by this roundabout route, they arrived at last and as if for recreation at the more innocuous exchange about I and We and family, and at the realization, wavering between banter and wonder, that together they formed a family. And while Ulrich speaks of his desire for community—now once more with the zeal of a man mortifying his own nature, though he does not know whether it is his true or an assumed nature he is tormenting—Agathe listens to the way his words come near to her and withdraw again, and he notices that for a long time—as is, regrettably, his habit—he has been looking for something in her appearance, which is defenselessly exposed to his view by the bright light and her whimsical garment, that would repel him, but has found nothing, and for this he is thankful with a pure and simple affection that he otherwise never feels. And he is very delighted by the conversation. But when it ends, Agathe asks ingenuously: "Now, are you actually for what you call the family, or are you against it?"

Ulrich replies that this doesn't really matter, because what he has been talking about is a vacillation in the world, not his personal in-decision.

Agathe thinks about this.

Finally, she says abruptly: "I don't know how to judge that. But I do wish I could be completely at one and in accord with myself for once and also . . . : well, somehow live that way! Wouldn't you like to try it too?"

8

AGATHE WHEN SHE CANNOT TALK TO ULRICH

AT THE moment when Agathe had boarded the train and begun the unexpected journey to her father, something happened that bore every resemblance to a sudden rupture, and the two fragments into which the moment of departure burst flew as far apart as if they had never belonged together. Her husband had taken her to the station, he had raised his hat and held it, the stiff, round, black, steadily diminishing hat, at a slant before him in the air, as is proper on occasions of leave-taking, while she drove off in her train, and it seemed to Agathe as if the station were rolling backwards as fast as the train was rolling forwards. At this moment, though only an instant earlier she had still believed that she would not stay away longer than circumstances absolutely required, she decided never to return, and she felt herself inwardly agitated like a heart that suddenly realizes it has escaped a danger of which it had not been aware.

When Agathe thought about it later, she was by no means completely satisfied. What she disapproved of in her behavior was that its form reminded her of a strange illness that had befallen her as a child soon after she had started school. For more than a year she had suffered from a not inconsiderable fever that neither rose nor subsided, and had become so frail and emaciated that the doctors were worried, as they could not find a cause. Nor was this illness ever explained later. Now, Agathe had doubtless enjoyed seeing how the great doctors from the university, who looked so dignified and full of wisdom when they first entered her room, lost some of their confidence from week to week; and even though she obediently swallowed every medicine that was prescribed for her and really would have liked to get well, because it was expected of her, she was still pleased that the doctors with all their knowledge could not bring about a cure, and felt herself to be in a supernatural or at least extraordinary state as less and less of her remained. She was proud that the grown-ups had no power over her as long as she was sick, and had no idea how her little body was able to do it. But in the end it recovered of its own accord and in a way that seemed just as remarkable.

Almost all she knew about it today was what the servants had told her later. They claimed that a beggar woman who often came into the house but was once rudely turned away had bewitched her; and Agathe had never found out how much truth there was in this story, for the servants liked to indulge in hints but avoided explanations and appeared to be afraid of violating a strict ban Agathe's father was said to have imposed. Her own memory had retained only a single, but vivid, image from that time, in which she saw her father striking out in a flaming rage at an untrustworthy-looking woman and slapping her face several times; it was the only time in her life she had seen that small, almost always painfully fair-minded intellectual so utterly changed and beside himself; but as far as she could recall, that had happened not before but during her illness, for she was fairly certain that she was lying in bed at the time, and that this bed, instead of being in her room in the attic, had been on the floor below, "with the grown-ups," in one of the rooms where the servants should not have allowed the beggar woman to enter, even though she was not a stranger to the kitchen and below stairs. Indeed, it seemed to Agathe that this incident must have occurred toward the end of her illness and that she had suddenly recovered a few days later, roused from her bed by that peculiar impatience with which this illness ended as unexpectedly as it had begun.

Of course she did not know whether these memories stemmed from reality or whether they were fictions produced by the fever. "Probably the only remarkable thing about all of it," she thought with annoyance, "is that these images were able to survive, halfway between truth and fantasy, without my finding them unusual." —The jolting of the taxi that was driving them across badly paved streets prevented them from talking. Ulrich had suggested taking advantage of the dry winter weather for an outing, and he also had an idea of where they should go—not a destination in the usual sense, but rather an advance into half-imagined landscapes they had known. And now they were in a cab that was to take them to the outskirts of the town.—"I'm sure that's the only remarkable thing about it!" Agathe repeated to herself what she had thought a moment ago. That was how she had learned her lessons in school, so that she never knew whether she was stupid or clever, willing or unwilling: the answers expected of her imprinted themselves on her mind with ease, but without her ever discovering the purpose of the questions, against which she felt herself to be protected by a deep-seated indifference. After her illness she had liked going to school as much as she had before, and because one of the doctors had hit on the idea that it might be of benefit if she were removed from her father's house and brought together with children her own age, she had been placed in a convent school. There, too, she was regarded as a cheerful, docile child, and later she attended a secondary school. Whenever she was told that something was necessary or true, she would take her bearings from that and willingly comply with everything that was demanded of her, because that seemed to require the least effort, and it would have seemed pointless to her to undertake anything against institutional arrangements that had nothing to do with her and were clearly part of a world that had been constructed according to the will of fathers and teachers. Nor did she believe a word of anything she had learned, and because, despite her apparent docility, she was far from being a model student, and because wherever her wishes came into conflict with her convictions she casually did what she wished, she enjoyed the respect of her classmates and even that admiring affection that is earned in school by those who know how to get by without undue exertion. It could even be that she had arranged her strange childhood illness for her own comfort, for with this one exception she had always been healthy and not notably nervous. "In short, a dull and useless character," she concluded uncertainly. She remembered how much more vigorously than herself her friends had often mutinied against the rigid discipline of the boarding school, and with what maxims of revolt they had equipped their assaults against law and order; yet as far as she had come into a position to observe, it was precisely those who had been most passionate in their rebellion against details who later came to be on the best of terms with the whole of life; those girls had developed into well-married women who brought up their children not very differently from the way they themselves had been reared. And so in spite of her dissatisfaction with herself, she was not convinced that it was better to be an active and good character.

Agathe detested female emancipation just as much as she despised the female need to raise a brood for which a male must supply the nest. She liked to think back on the time when she had first felt her breasts stretching the fabric of her dress and had borne her burning lips through the cooling air of the streets. But the evolved erotic fuss and bustle that emerges from the protective veils of girlhood like a round knee from pink tulle had aroused her scorn throughout her life. When she asked herself what she was actually convinced of, the answer she received was a feeling that she was destined to experience something extraordinary and different; and this had been the case already back then, when she knew almost nothing about the world and did not believe the little that she had been taught. And it had always seemed to her a mysterious kind of activity, corresponding to this impression, to let everything happen to her as it would, if necessary, without immediately overestimating its importance.

Agathe looked at Ulrich, who was sitting gravely and stiffly at her side, swaying with the movements of the car; she remembered how hard put he had been to comprehend, on their first evening together, that she had not run away from her husband on her wedding night even though she did not like him. She had felt tremendous respect for her big brother while awaiting his arrival, but now she smiled, secretly recalling the impression Hagauer's thick lips had made on her in those first months whenever they rounded amorously beneath the bristles of his moustache: his entire face would be drawn in thick-skinned folds toward the corners of his mouth, and she would feel, as if filled to satiety: "Oh, what an ugly man this is!" She had also endured his mild pedagogic vanity and goodness as merely physical nausea, more outer than inner. After the first surprise was over, she had occasionally been unfaithful to him: "If one wants to call it that," she thought, "when, to an inexperienced young thing whose sensuality is dormant, the advances of a man who is not her husband come like a thunderous knocking at the door!" She had shown little talent for infidelity: Lovers, once she had come to know them, struck her as no more compelling than husbands, and it seemed to her that she could just as well take seriously the ceremonial masks of an African tribe as the romantic masquerades of European men. Not that she had never lost her head: but with the first attempts at repeating the magic, the spell was gone. The enacted fantasy world and theatricality of love left her untransported. These stage directions for the soul, elaborated by men for the most part, all amounting to the notion that life, being hard, should now and then contain an hour of weakness—with one or another variation on the theme of weakening: the enthrallment, the languishing, the being taken, the giving of oneself, the succumbing, the losing of one's senses, and so forth—struck her as cheaply melodramatic and overdone, since she had at no time ever felt herself to be other than weak in a world so superbly constructed by the strength of men.

The philosophy Agathe acquired in this way was simply that of the female human being who refuses to be taken in and cannot help noticing what the male human being is trying to put over on her. In fact, it was not a philosophy at all, but only a defiantly hidden disappointment, still mingled with a cautious readiness for some unknown resolution, a readiness that perhaps increased in the same measure as the outward defiance abated. Since Agathe was well read, but by her nature not inclined to engage in theories, she often had occasion, when she compared her own experiences with the ideals of books and the theater, to wonder why her seducers had never held her spellbound like game caught in a trap, which would have accorded with the Don Juan–like self-image a man of that time would have adopted if, with a woman's consent, he stumbled into an affair; nor had life with her husband assumed the form of a Strindbergian battle of the sexes in which the captive woman, by the rules of this secondary mode, uses her powers of cunning and weakness to torment her despotic and inept lord and master to death. In point of fact her relations with Hagauer, in contrast to her deeper feelings about him, had always remained quite good. On the first evening Ulrich had used big words like "terror," "shock," and "rape" that were completely off the mark. "I very much regret not being able to serve up an angel in my stead," Agathe thought, bristling again at the memory, for in fact everything in her marriage had taken a very natural course. Her father had supported the man's proposal with sensible reasons, she herself had decided to marry again: fine, one does it, one has to put up with whatever is involved; it's neither particularly beautiful nor excessively unpleasant. Even now she was still sorry to be consciously hurting Hagauer, though she absolutely wanted to do just that! She had not entered the marriage with a hope for love; she had thought it would all work out somehow. He was a good man, after all.

Though perhaps it was rather that he was one of those people who always do good; the goodness is not in themselves, Agathe thought. Apparently goodness disappears from people to the degree that it turns into goodwill or good deeds! How had Ulrich put it? A stream that turns factory wheels loses its gradient. Yes, he had said that too, but it wasn't what she was looking for. Now she had it: "It seems that it's really only those people who don't do much good who are able to preserve all their goodness"! But the moment she had the sentence, plausibly the way Ulrich must have said it, it struck her as completely nonsensical. It couldn't be taken out of the forgotten context of their conversation. She tried shifting the position of the words and exchanging them for similar ones; but then it became clear that the first version was the right one, for the others were as if spoken into the wind and there was nothing left of them. So Ulrich had said it that way, but: "How can one call people good who behave badly?" she thought. "This really *is* nonsense!" And she knew: that statement, at the moment when Ulrich pronounced it, though it signified no more then than it did now, had been wonderful! "Wonderful" was not the word for it: she had almost felt sick with joy when she heard that sentence! Such statements explained her whole life. This one, for instance, had been uttered during their last long talk, after the funeral and after Professor Hagauer had left; and suddenly she had realized how carelessly she had always acted, including the time when she had simply thought it would "work out somehow" with Hagauer because he was "a good person"! Ulrich often said things that for a moment would fill her entirely with joy or misery, even though it wasn't possible to "keep" those moments. When was it, for example, that he had said that in some circumstances he might love a thief but never a person who was honest from habit? She couldn't remember at the moment, but the marvelous thing was that she very soon realized it was not he who had said it but herself. As a matter of fact, much of what he said she had already thought: just not with words, for with only herself to rely on, as she had been until now, she would never have made such definite assertions! Agathe, who up to now had been feeling very content among the jolts and bumps of the car as it drove along cobbled suburban streets, wrapping them both in a net of mechanical vibrations that rendered them speechless, had also used her husband's name in the midst of her thoughts with the same placid contentment and merely as a term of reference to a certain time and its contents; but now, slowly and for no particular reason, an infinite horror went through her: Hagauer had actually been there with her in the flesh! The fair-minded way in which she had been thinking of him disappeared, and her throat tightened with bitterness.

He had arrived on the morning of the funeral, had asked, with loving urgency, if despite his lateness he could still see his father-in-law, had gone to the autopsy lab, had delayed the closing of the coffin, had, in a tactful, sincere, restrained way been deeply moved. After the funeral Agathe had feigned exhaustion, and Ulrich had been obliged to dine out with his brother-in-law. As he told her afterward, Hagauer's constant company had made him as frantic as a tight collar, and for that reason alone he had done everything to dispose of him as soon as possible. Hagauer had planned to go to the capital for a conference of educators, to spend another day there calling on people at the ministry and doing some sightseeing, and had as an attentive husband scheduled two days prior to this to spend with his wife and look after her inheritance; but Ulrich, in accordance with the agreement he had made with his sister, had invented a story that made it seem impossible for Hagauer to be put up at the house and informed him that a room was reserved for him at the best hotel in town. As expected, Hagauer had wavered; the hotel would be inconvenient and expensive, and it would be only proper for him to pay for himself; on the other hand, perhaps two days could be devoted to his calls and sightseeing in the capital, and if one traveled by night, one could save the cost of an overnight stay. And so Hagauer, pretending regret, had said he found it very difficult to take advantage of Ulrich's thoughtful provisions, and finally revealed his resolve, which could hardly be modified now, to depart that same evening. Thus all that was left to discuss was the question of the inheritance, and now, remembering that moment, Agathe smiled again, for at her request Ulrich had told her husband that the will was not to be opened for a few days yet. Agathe would be there, after all, he was told, to look after his interests, and he would also receive a proper legal notification; and as for furniture, mementos, and the like, Ulrich, as a bachelor, would make no claim he was not prepared to subordinate to his sister's wishes. Finally he had asked Hagauer whether he would agree in case they decided to sell the house, which was of no use to anyone, of course without committing himself, as none of them had seen the will yet, and Hagauer had replied, without committing himself of course, that he could think of no reason to object for the moment, but that he must reserve the right to determine his position if it came to an actual transaction. All this Agathe had suggested to her brother, and he had passed it on, because he thought nothing of it and because he wanted to get rid of Hagauer. But suddenly Agathe felt miserable again, for after they had managed this so adroitly, her husband had come to her room, together with her brother, to say goodbye to her. Agathe had behaved as unfriendly as she could and said there was absolutely no way of telling when she would return home. Knowing him as she did, she immediately saw that he was unprepared for this and that he resented the way his decision to leave right away was now making him look like the unloving husband; and he was suddenly offended in retrospect by the suggestion that he stay at a hotel, and by the cool reception he had found at the house, but since he was a man who lived according to plan, he said nothing, decided to present his wife with the facts later on, and kissed her, after taking his hat, politely on the lips. And this kiss, which Ulrich had seen, now seemed to demolish Agathe. "How is it possible," she asked herself in dismay, "that I stayed with this man for so long? But then, haven't I put up with things my whole life without resisting?!" She reproached herself passionately: "If I were worth anything at all, it could never have gone this far."

Agathe averted her face from Ulrich, whom she had been watching, and looked out of the window. Low suburban buildings, icy street, heavily muffled people—images of an ugly bleakness rolled past, reproaching her for the desert waste of a life into which she felt she had drifted as a result of her negligence. She was now no longer sitting up straight but had let herself slide down into the cab's upholstery, with its musty smell of old age, in order more comfortably to see out of the window, and remained in this ungraceful position, in which the jolts of the car rudely clutched and shook her belly. This body of hers, tossed about like a rag, gave her an uncanny feeling, for it was the only thing she owned. Sometimes, waking up in her boarding school in the half-darkness of morning, she had felt herself drifting into the future inside her body as if in the shell of a small boat. Now she was about twice the age she had been then, and the same half-darkness pervaded the car. But she still could not imagine her life and had no idea what it should be like. Men were a complement and a completion of one's own body but did not fill it with meaning; one took them as one was taken by them. Her body told her that in just a few years it would begin to lose its beauty: which meant losing the feelings that, coming as they did directly out of its self-certainty, were only to a small degree expressible in words and thoughts. Then everything would be over without anything having been there. It occurred to her that Ulrich had spoken in a similar way about the futility of his gymnastics, and while she forced her face to remain averted from him, still looking out of the window, she resolved to ask him about it.

9

FURTHER COURSE OF THE EXCURSION TO THE *SWEDISH* RAMPART. THE MORALITY OF THE NEXT STEP

THE SIBLINGS had left the cab by the last, low, and already quite rural looking houses on the edge of the town and set off, walking steadily uphill, along a wide, furrowed country road with frozen wheel tracks that crumbled beneath their feet. Soon their shoes were coated with the dismal gray of this parquet for peasants and cart drivers, in sharp contrast with their elegant city clothes, and though it was not cold, a fierce wind blowing down on them from above made their cheeks burn, and the glazed brittleness of their lips made it hard to talk.

The memory of Hagauer urged Agathe to explain herself to her brother. She was convinced that this failed marriage must be incomprehensible to him in every way, even by the simplest social standards; yet, though the words inside her were already prepared, she could not make up her mind to overcome the resistance of the steep incline, the cold, and the air beating against her face. Ulrich was striding ahead, in a broad track left by some object dragged behind a cart, which they were using as a path; she saw his broad, lean shoulders and hesitated. She had always imagined him hard, unyielding, and something of an adventurer, perhaps only because of the disapproving remarks she had heard from her father and occasionally also from Hagauer, and the thought of this brother, estranged and escaped from the family, had made her ashamed of her own acquiescence in life. "He was right not to bother about me!" she thought, and her dismay at having so often put up with unwanted situations repeated itself. But in truth she had in her the same tempestuous, contradictory passion that had made her proclaim those wild lines of poetry standing between the doorposts of the room where her father's dead body lay. Pressing on to catch up with Ulrich, she fell short of breath, and suddenly that serviceable road rang with questions such as it had probably never heard before, and the wind was torn by words that had not yet resounded in any wind among these hills.

"You remember—" she exclaimed, and gave several well-known examples from literature: "You didn't tell me if you would pardon a thief—but these murderers you would find good?!"

"Of course!" Ulrich shouted back. "Well—no, wait: Those may just be people with a good disposition, people of value. They won't lose that, even as criminals. But they don't continue being good!"

"But why do you love them even after their crime?! Surely not because of their former good inclinations, but because you still like them!"

"It's always like that," Ulrich said. "It's the person who gives character to the act, and not the other way around! We distinguish between good and evil, but within ourselves we know they are inseparable!"

Agathe's wind-flushed cheeks burned an even deeper red, because the passion of her questions, which was at once explicit and concealed in her words, had been able to find its examples only in books. The abuse of "cultural matters" is so pervasive that it was possible to feel that they are out of place where trees stand and the wind blows, as if human culture were not the sum of all natural formations! But she had fought with herself bravely, had linked her arm in her brother's, and now replied, close to his ear, so that she no longer needed to shout, her face trembling with a strange, high-spirited glee: "That must be why we exterminate evil people but serve them a hearty breakfast first!"

Ulrich, sensing some of the fervor at his side, leaned down to speak in his sister's ear, albeit loudly enough: "Everyone readily assumes that he himself couldn't do anything evil, because after all he's a good person!"

With these words they had reached the top, where the road no longer climbed but cut through a widespread, treeless plateau. The wind had suddenly abated, and it was no longer cold, but in the pleasant stillness the conversation fell silent and could not immediately be resumed.

"What made you think of Dostoyevsky and Stendhal in the middle of that wind?" Ulrich asked after a while. "If someone had been watching us, he'd have thought we were crazy."

Agathe laughed. "He wouldn't have understood us any more than the cries of the birds! . . . By the way, you talked to me about Moosbrugger just the other day."*

They walked on with long strides.

After a while Agathe said: "But I don't like him!"

"I'd almost forgotten about him myself," Ulrich answered.

After they had again walked on in silence, Agathe stopped. "Tell me," she said, "You've done many irresponsible things, haven't you? For example, I remember you were in the hospital for a bullet wound once. I'm sure you don't think everything out beforehand . . . ?"

"The questions you're asking today!" Ulrich exclaimed. "What do you expect me to say to that?"

"Don't you ever regret what you've done?" Agathe asked quickly. "I have the impression you never regret anything. You once said something like that yourself."

"Good God in heaven," Ulrich answered, walking on again, "there's a plus in every minus. Maybe I did say something like that, but there's no need to take it all that literally."

"A plus in every minus?"

"Something good in everything bad. Or at least in much of what is bad. Usually in a human minus variant there is an unrecognized plus variant: that's probably what I wanted to say. And when you regret something, just that may give you the strength to do something better than you could have done otherwise. The crucial thing is never what one does but always what one does afterward."

"And when you've killed someone, what can you do afterward?"

Ulrich shrugged. He felt like answering, just to follow the thought to its logical conclusion: "Conceivably that could enable me to write a poem that gives thousands of people their inner life, or to make a

---

*Moosbrugger is a psychopath who is on trial for murdering a prostitute. His story, and Ulrich and Clarisse's interest in his case, forms one of the major subplots of the novel.

great invention." But he stopped himself. "That would never happen!" he realized. "Only a lunatic could persuade himself of such a thing. Or an eighteen-year-old aesthete. Such ideas, God knows why, contradict the laws of nature. By the way—" he corrected himself, "it *was* like that for prehistoric man; he killed because human sacrifice was a great religious poem!"

He did not say any of those thoughts aloud, but Agathe continued: "This may be a silly objection, but the first time I heard you say it doesn't matter what step one takes, what matters is always the next step, what I imagined was this: If a person could fly inwardly, fly morally, so to speak, always moving at great speed from one improvement to the next, he wouldn't know any remorse! I envied you tremendously for that!"

"That is absurd," Ulrich said emphatically. "I said that a misstep doesn't matter, what matters is the next step. But what is it that matters after the next step? Obviously the step after that. And after the nth step, the nth-plus-one step? Such a person would have to live without an end or a decision, in fact without any reality at all. And yet, what matters is always only the next step. The fact is, we have no method for dealing adequately with this inexorable sequence. Dear Agathe," he concluded abruptly, "sometimes I regret my whole life!"

"But that's just what you can't do!" his sister said.

"Why absolutely not? Why precisely not that?!"

"I," Agathe replied, "have never done anything and therefore always had time to regret the few things I did undertake. I am convinced you have no experience of this: a state where there's so little light. The shadows come, and what was has power over me. It's present in the smallest details, and I can't forget anything and don't understand anything. It's not a pleasant state . . ."

She said this without emotion, very humbly. Ulrich had in fact never known this backward-streaming movement of life, since his own life had always been set on expansion, and it merely reminded him that his sister had at times sounded noticeably unhappy about herself. But he failed to ask her about it, for they had meanwhile reached a hilltop that he had chosen as their destination and were coming near its far edge. It was a mighty elevation associated by legend with a Swedish siege in the Thirty Years' War because it looked like a fortification, even though it was much too big for that, a green bulwark of nature, without bush or tree, that fell away as a high bright wall of rock on the side overlooking the town. A deep-set, empty world of hills surrounded this promontory; no village, no house was to be seen, only the shadows of clouds and gray pastures. Once again Ulrich felt the spell of this place, which he remembered from his youth; the town still lay far below in the distance, anxiously huddled around a few churches that looked like hens with their chicks, so that one suddenly felt like bounding into their midst with a single leap and wreaking havoc among them, or sweeping them up in the grip of a giant hand. "It must have felt glorious to those Swedish adventurers, coming to a place like this after riding along for weeks and then, from the saddle, catching sight of their quarry for the first time!" he said, after explaining to his sister the significance of the place. "It's only at such moments that the weight of life is ever really lifted from us—the burden of our secret grievance that we all have to die, that everything is so brief and probably so futile!"

"What moments do you mean?" Agathe asked.

Ulrich did not know how to answer. He did not want to answer at all. He remembered that as a young man he had always felt the need in this place to clench his teeth and keep silent. At last he replied: "Those moments of risk and tumult when events run away with us: the meaningless moments, basically!" As he said this, he felt his head perched on his neck like a hollow nut, with old phrases inside it like "the grim reaper" or "My trust in nothing now is placed!" and with them the faded fortissimo of the years when the boundary between the expectations of life and life itself has not yet been established. He thought: "What experiences have I had since then that were unequivocal and happy? None."

Agathe responded: "I've always acted without meaning, that only makes for unhappiness."

She had walked very close to the edge of the cliff; her ears were deaf to her brother's words, she did not understand them and saw before her a somber, barren landscape whose sadness corresponded to her own. When she turned around, she said: "It's a place to kill oneself," and smiled; "the emptiness in my head would dissolve with infinite tenderness into the emptiness of this view." She took a few steps back to Ulrich. "All my life," she continued, "I've been reproached for having no ambition, for not loving anything, not respecting anything, in short for lacking the will to live. Papa used to scold me for it, Hagauer faulted me for it: So now do tell me, for God's sake, tell me finally when, at what moments, does anything in life seem necessary?"

"When one turns over in bed," Ulrich gruffly declared.

"What does that mean?"

"Excuse the mundane example," he said, "but it's true: You're uncomfortable; you keep thinking of changing your position; you form one resolution after the other; and suddenly you've turned over! It's really more accurate to say you've been turned over. Whether you act on the spur of passion or after long reflection, it's always the same pattern." He did not look at her as he said this; he was answering himself. He still felt: "Here I stood and wanted something that was never satisfied."

Agathe smiled again, but the smile that passed over her lips resembled a movement of pain. She returned to where she had stood earlier and stared silently into the unknowable distance. Her fur coat formed a dark silhouette against the sky, and her slender figure formed a striking contrast to the wide stillness of the landscape and the cloud shadows flitting across it. Watching her, Ulrich had an indescribably intense feeling of being in the presence of an event. He was almost ashamed to be standing there in the company of a woman instead of next to a saddled horse. And although he was well aware that the cause of this lay in the tranquil pictorial effect emanating from his sister at that moment, he had the impression that something was happening, not in himself but somewhere in the world, and that he was missing it. He told himself he was being ridiculous. And yet there had been something accurate in his thoughtlessly uttered assertion that he regretted his whole life. Sometimes he longed to be embroiled in events as in a wrestling match, even if they were senseless or criminal, as long as they were decisive. Definitive, not vitiated by the constant provisional quality that events have when people remain superior to their experience. "In other words, ending in themselves, and valid for no other reason," Ulrich reflected, now searching intently for another way to say it, and inadvertently this train of thought no longer wandered off to imagined events but settled on the sight that Agathe herself, mirroring nothing but herself, offered at these moments. Thus brother and sister stood for quite a while, apart and solitary, in a hesitance filled with contradictions that did not permit either of them to introduce a change. But perhaps the strangest thing was that on this occasion nothing was further from Ulrich's thoughts than that something had already happened, since, on Agathe's behalf and out of a wish to get rid of his unsuspecting brother-in-law, he had palmed off on him the lie that there was a sealed will that was only to be opened after several days, and assured him, equally against his better knowledge, that Agathe would look after his interests, actions Hagauer would later characterize as "aiding and abetting."

Somehow they managed to leave the place where each had stood steeped in private reverie, and walked on together without having spoken their minds. The wind had picked up again, and because Agathe seemed tired, Ulrich suggested they pay a visit to a shepherd's cottage he knew of nearby. They soon found it, a stone cabin. They had to stoop as they entered the door, and the shepherd's wife stared at them with defensive embarrassment. In the Germano-Slavic dialect that was spoken in that region and that he still dimly recalled, Ulrich asked if they might warm themselves and eat their provisions in the shelter of the house, and bolstered this request so voluntarily with an offer of money that the involuntary hostess broke out into a horrified lamentation that in her repulsive poverty she was unable to offer "such beautiful guests" better hospitality. She wiped off the greasy table by the window, lit some brushwood in the stove, and put a pot with goat's milk over the flame. Agathe, however, had immediately squeezed past the table to the window without paying attention to the troubles that were being taken, as if it were a matter of course that one would find shelter somewhere, and a matter of indifference where. She looked out through the foggy little square of four panes onto the inland side of the Rampart, an area that, lacking the expansive view offered by the cliff, reminded one more of the feeling of a swimmer surrounded by cresting green waves. Though the day was not yet declining toward evening, it had passed its zenith and begun to lose its light. Agathe suddenly asked: "Why don't you ever talk to me seriously?"

What better answer could Ulrich have given than to glance up at her briefly with a look that was supposed to represent innocence and surprise? He was occupied with spreading out ham, sausage, and eggs on a sheet of paper between himself and his sister.

But Agathe continued: "When one accidentally bumps into your body, it hurts and there's a shock at the enormous difference. But when I want to ask you something important, you dissolve into thin air!" She did not touch the food Ulrich pushed towards her; indeed, in her aversion to concluding the day with a rural banquet she had raised herself up so straight she was not even touching the table. And now something happened that was almost a repetition of their climb up the country road. Ulrich shoved aside the mugs of goat's milk that had just been brought to the table from the stove and were emitting an odor that was very disagreeable to an uninitiated sense of smell; and the slight nausea it caused had the sobering, clarifying effect one sometimes gets from a sudden bitterness. "I have always spoken seriously to you," he retorted. "I can't help it if you don't like what I say, because what you dislike in my responses is the morality of our time." At that moment it became evident to him that he wanted to explain to his sister, as completely as he possibly could, everything she would have to know in order to understand herself, and to some extent her brother as well. And with the resolution of a man who regards any interruption as superfluous, he set out on a lengthy speech.

"The morality of our time, no matter what else may be said about it, is the morality of achievement. Five more or less fraudulent bankruptcies are good so long as the fifth one is followed by a time of blessings and beneficence. Success can make anything be forgotten. When you reach the point where you fund elections and buy paintings, you have also acquired the indulgence of the State. There are unwritten rules: If someone gives money to the Church, to charities, and to political parties, it need not be more than a tenth of what he would have to spend if he came up with the idea of proving his good-will by patronizing the arts. Also, some limits are still imposed on success: one cannot yet achieve every end by every means: some principles of Crown, Aristocracy, and Society still exert a certain retarding influence on the "parvenu." The State, on the other hand, avows, with respect to its own suprapersonal person, the most naked commitment to the principle that one may rob, murder, and cheat so long as the result is power, civilization, and glory. Of course I am not saying that all this is acknowledged in theory as well; on the contrary, theoretically it is all quite murky. But what I just told you sums up the most ordinary facts. Moral reasoning is, in this context, just one more means to an end, a weapon one uses in pretty much the same way as a lie. That is what the world made by men looks like, and I would want to be a woman if only—women did not love men!

"What is considered good nowadays is anything that gives us the illusion that it will get us somewhere: but this conviction is precisely what you called the "flying man without remorse," and what I said is a problem that can't be solved because we lack a method. As a scientifically educated person, I feel in every situation that my knowledge is incomplete and a guideline at best, and that maybe tomorrow I will already possess new experience that will allow me to think differently than today; on the other hand, even a person wholly in the grip of emotion, a "man in ascent," as you imagined him, will experience every one of his acts as a step that is raising him up to the next one. So there is something in our minds and in our souls, a "morality of the next step," but is this merely the morality of the five bankruptcies, does the entrepreneurial morality of our time reach that far into the interior life, or is this seeming correspondence an illusion, or is the careerist's morality a miscarriage—grotesquely disfigured and born before its time—of more profound possibilities? At the moment I wouldn't be able to give you an answer!"

The short breathing space Ulrich admitted into his exposition was entirely rhetorical, for he intended to develop his views still further.

But Agathe, who so far had been listening with the alert impassivity that was sometimes characteristic of her, gave the conversation an unplanned direction with the simple remark that this answer was of no interest to her, because all she wanted to know was Ulrich's position, and she was incapable of taking in all the different possible ways of thinking. "But if you should demand of me that I accomplish something in any way whatsoever, I would rather not have any morality at all," she added.

"Thank God!" Ulrich exclaimed. "It gives me pleasure every time I look at your youth, beauty, and strength and then hear you say that you have no energy! Our era is dripping with vigor and drive as it is. It's had its fill of ideas, all it wants is action. This mania for action comes from having nothing to do. I mean inwardly. But even outwardly everyone spends his whole life just repeating one and the same act: getting ahead in the occupation he started out with. I think this brings us back to the question you asked me earlier, when we were outside. It's so easy to summon the drive for action and so difficult to find a meaning in it! Hardly anyone understands this nowadays. That's why men of action look like competitors in a bowling alley who know how to knock over ten wooden things with the gestures of a Napoleon. It wouldn't even surprise me if they ended up flying at each other's throats, overwhelmed by the incomprehensible fact that all their actions are insufficient!..." He had begun in a lively manner but then became pensive and even fell silent for a while. At last he just looked up with a smile and contented himself with saying: "You say that if I expect you to make a moral effort, you will disappoint me. I say that if you expect me to give you moral advice, I will disappoint you. It seems to me that we ought not to have any specific requirements of each other; I mean all of us: Truly, instead of demanding deeds of one another, we ought to lay the foundations for them; that is my feeling!"

"But how should one do that?!" Agathe said. She was aware that Ulrich had deviated from the big general discourse he had begun and had arrived at more personal considerations, but even these were too general for her taste. She had, as we know, a prejudice against general analyses and regarded any mental effort that extended beyond her own skin, so to speak, as rather pointless; she was certain of this with regard to exertions that might be required of herself, and assumed it was probably true of the generalizing statements of others as well. Still, she understood Ulrich quite well. She noticed that her brother, as he sat there with his head lowered, softly arguing against the spirit of action, was unconsciously carving lines and notches into the table-top with the blade of his pocketknife, and that all the sinews of his hand were taut. The thoughtless but almost passionate activity of this hand, and that he had said so frankly that she was young and beauti-ful, was a purposeless duet above the orchestra of the other words; nor did she give it any significance other than that she was sitting here and watching.

"What should be done?" Ulrich replied in the same tone as before. "Once at our cousin's I suggested to Count Leinsdorf that he should found a world secretariat for precision and soul, so that churchgoers wouldn't be the only people who know what they are supposed to do. Of course I was only joking. We created science for the sake of truth a long time ago, but the idea that something similar might be needed for what is left over seems so foolish in our time that one would be ashamed to propose it in earnest. And yet everything you and I have been talking about would lead us to this secretariat." He had abandoned his speech and leaned back against his bench. "I sup-pose I'm dissolving into thin air again if I add: But how would that turn out today?" Since Agathe did not answer, the room became still. Ulrich said after a while: "By the way, sometimes I myself believe that I cannot stand this conviction! When I saw you earlier," he continued in a lowered voice, "standing there on the Rampart, I don't know why, I had a wild urge to suddenly do something. I've actually done some really rash things in the past; the magic lay in this: after it had happened, there was, besides me, something more. Sometimes I can even imagine a person becoming happy as a result of committing a crime, because it gives him a certain ballast, and with it, maybe, a steadier course."

Again his sister did not immediately answer. He observed her calmly, even searchingly, but the experience he was talking about did not return; in fact, he was not thinking anything. After a little while she asked him: "Would you be mad at me if I committed a crime?"

"Now how do you expect me to answer that?" Ulrich asked. He was again bent over his knife.

"Is there no such thing as a decision?"

"No, there are no real decisions in our time."

After that Agathe said: "I want to kill Hagauer."

Ulrich forced himself not to look up. The words had entered his ear lightly and softly, but after they had passed, they left an imprint in the memory, like a wide wheel track. He had immediately forgotten the tone of her voice; he would have needed to see her face in order to know how her words were to be understood, but he did not want to accord even that much significance to them. "Fine," he said, "and why not?! Could there be a person today who hasn't wanted something like that at some time? Do it, if you really can! It's the same as if you had said: I want to love him for his faults!" Only now did he straighten up again and look his sister in the face. Her expression was stubborn and surprisingly agitated. Still gazing at her, he slowly declared: "You see, something here doesn't add up; on this frontier between what goes on inside us and what happens outside, some kind of intermediary link is missing these days, and transmuting them into each other is not possible without tremendous losses; one could almost say that our evil wishes are the shadow side of the life we are actually living, and the life we are actually living is the shadow side of our good wishes. Just imagine you really did that: it wouldn't be anything like what you thought, and you would at the very least be terribly disappointed . . ."

"I could suddenly become a completely different person: You admitted that yourself!" Agathe interrupted him.

Glancing aside at this moment, Ulrich was reminded that they were not alone: two people were listening to their conversation. The old woman—she might have been no more than forty but her rags and the traces of her humble life made her look older—had sat down by the stove with a friendly look on her face, and sitting beside her was the shepherd, who had come home unbeknownst to his guests, who were too preoccupied with themselves to have noticed his arrival. The two old people rested their hands on their knees and listened, flattered, it seemed, and astonished by such a conversation, even if they did not understand a single word of it. They saw that the milk had not been drunk and the sausage had not been eaten; it was a spectacle, and who knows, maybe an uplifting one. They did not even whisper with each other. Ulrich's gaze dove into their opened eyes, and out of embarrassment he gave them a smile, which only the woman reciprocated, while her husband gravely maintained respectful decorum.

"*We must eat!*" Ulrich said in English to his sister. "*They're wondering about us.*"

Obediently she toyed with some bread and meat, while he resolutely ate and even drank of the milk. Agathe meanwhile said, aloud and unembarrassed: "When I really think about it, I find the idea of seriously hurting him unpleasant. So maybe I don't want to kill him. But I do want to extinguish him! Rip him into little pieces, pulverize them in a mortar, pour the dust into the water: this I would like to do! Completely destroy everything that has happened!"

"You know, it's a little funny, the way we're talking," Ulrich said.

Agathe was silent for a while. But then she said: "Remember, you promised me on the first day that you would support me against Hagauer."

"Of course I will. But not that way."

Again Agathe was silent. Then she suddenly said: "If you bought or rented a car, we could drive to my house via Iglau and come back by the longer route, I think via Tabor. It wouldn't occur to anyone that we were there in the night."

"And the servants? Fortunately I can't drive!" Ulrich laughed, but then he shook his head, annoyed: "Some newfangled notions you've got!"

"You can say that," Agathe said. Pensively she pushed a piece of bacon back and forth with her fingernail, and it looked as if the fingernail, which had acquired a greasy sheen from the bacon, were doing it all by itself. "But you also said: The virtues of society are vices for the saint!"

"Except I didn't say the vices of society are virtues for the saint!" Ulrich corrected her. He laughed, seized Agathe's hand, and cleaned it with his handkerchief.

"The fact is, you always take everything back!" Agathe scolded, smiling ruefully, while the blood rose to her face as she tried to free her finger.

The faces of the two old people by the stove, who were still watching as before, now lit up with wide, beaming smiles.

"When you talk to me like that, first one way, then the other," Agathe said forcefully with a low voice, "it's like seeing myself in the shards of a mirror. With you it's impossible to see all of oneself in one view!"

"No," Ulrich replied, still holding on to her hand, "these days no one sees all of himself, nor does anyone move as a unified whole: that is the problem!"

Agathe gave in and suddenly stopped trying to withdraw her arm. "I'm certainly the opposite of holy," she said softly. "I may have been worse in my indifference than a woman for hire. And I'm certainly not enterprising and probably won't be able to kill anyone. But when you said what you said about the saint the first time, quite a while ago, there was something I saw as a whole ...!" She lowered her head to think or to prevent him from seeing her face. "I saw a saint, he may have been standing on a fountain. To tell the truth, I may have seen nothing at all, but I felt something that would have to be described that way. The water was flowing, and what the saint was doing also flowed over the rim, as if he were the bowl of a fountain brimming over on all sides. That, I think, is how one ought to be, then you would always be doing the right thing, and it wouldn't matter what you did."

"Agathe sees herself standing in the world as a fount of holy profusion, trembling on account of her sins and much astonished to see snakes and rhinoceroses, mountains and chasms lying at her feet, serene and even smaller than she is. But what about Hagauer?" Ulrich said, gently teasing her.

"That's just it. He can't be part of it. He has to go!"

"I'll tell you a story too," her brother said. "Every time I've had to take part in some common venture, some genuine human occasion, I've been like a man who steps out of the theater before the last act for a breath of air, sees the great dark emptiness with the many stars, and leaves hat, coat, and show behind him in order to walk away."

Agathe gave him a searching look. It was and it wasn't a fitting answer.

Ulrich met her gaze. "You too are often plagued by an aversion for which the corresponding attraction does not yet exist," he said, and thought: "Is she really like me?" Again it seemed to him: Maybe she is, in the way a pastel resembles a woodcut. He considered himself the more solid of the two. And she was more beautiful. So pleasing in her beauty. He now released her finger to grasp her whole hand; it was a warm, long hand full of life, which up till now he had held only for greeting. His young sister was agitated, and though there were no actual tears in her eyes, there was a shimmer in them. "In a few days you will leave me too," she said, "and how am I going to cope with everything then?"

"We can stay together, you can join me later on."

"How do you picture that?" Agathe asked, with that pensive little frown on her forehead.

"I haven't pictured it yet; I thought of it only just now." He stood up and gave the sheepherders more money, "for the cuts in the table." Through a haze Agathe saw the peasants grinning and nodding and heard them affirming some joyful sentiment in short words she could not understand. As she passed them, she felt those four hospitable eyes gazing on her face with naked emotion and realized that she and Ulrich had been taken for lovers who had quarreled and made up. "They thought we were lovers!" she said. Exuberantly she slid her arm into his, and all her joy flared into expression. "You ought to give me a kiss!" she demanded, laughing, and pressed her brother's arm against her body as they stood on the threshold of the cottage and the low door opened into the darkness of the evening.

10

HOLY CONVERSATIONS. BEGINNING

During the rest of Ulrich's stay, little more was said about Hagauer, and a long time passed before the siblings returned to the idea of prolonging their renewed relationship by starting a life together. Nevertheless, the flame that had shot forth with Agathe's unrestrained desire to eliminate her husband went on smoldering beneath the ashes. It spread out in conversations that reached no conclusion, then leapt up again; perhaps one should say that Agathe's spirit was seeking another chance to burn freely.

She would usually begin such a conversation with a definite and personal question, the inner form of which was: "Am I allowed or am I not?" The lawlessness of her nature had until then lived by the sad and weary conviction: "I can do whatever I want, I just don't care to," and so his younger sister's questions occasionally, and not without justification, affected Ulrich rather like the questions of a child, which are as warm as the little hands of this helpless being.

His answers were of a different kind, but no less characteristic of him: He was always glad to share with her something of the yield of his life and reflections, and, as was his custom, he expressed himself in a manner as candid as it was intellectually enterprising. He always arrived quickly at "the moral of the story" his sister was talking about, summing it up with a formula, liked to use himself for illustration, and in this way told Agathe a great deal about himself and especially about his earlier, more eventful life. Agathe told him nothing about herself, but she admired his ability to talk about his life like that, and his way of subjecting all her suggestions to moral scrutiny suited her very well. For morality is nothing other than an order of the soul and of things, encompassing both, and so it is not strange that young people whose will to live has not yet been blunted on all sides talk about it a great deal. But with a man of Ulrich's age and experience some explanation is needed; for men talk about morality only in their working lives, if it is part of their occupational lingo; otherwise the word has been swallowed up by the activities of life and never regains its freedom. So when Ulrich spoke of morality, it signaled a deep disorder, which attracted Agathe because it resonated with something in herself. She was ashamed of her somewhat naive confession that she would like to live "in perfect accord with herself," now that she was hearing what intricate preconditions would have to be met; yet she wished impatiently that her brother would arrive at a result more quickly, for often she felt that everything he was saying was moving in that direction, was in fact becoming more and more precise as he neared the conclusion, halting only at the last step, just before the threshold, where, each time, he would abandon the project.

The locus of this turnaround and those final steps could be described in the most general terms—and the paralyzing effect of this did not escape Ulrich—as follows: Every proposition in European morality leads to such a point beyond which there is nowhere further to go; so that a person giving account of himself has at first the gestures of a man wading in shallow waters, as long as he feels some firm conviction underfoot, until suddenly, when he goes a little farther, the gestures are those of a fearful drowning, as if the very foundations of life had fallen abruptly from the shallows to a depth that offers no foothold at all. This manifested itself outwardly in the siblings' conversation as well: Ulrich could talk in a calm and elucidating manner on any subject he started out with so long as his intellect was engaged, and Agathe felt a similar eagerness in listening; but then, when they stopped and were silent, a much more intense alertness came into their faces. And so it happened once that they were led across the boundary at which they had unconsciously halted before then. Ulrich had maintained that "the only distinguishing mark of our morality is that its commandments contradict each other. The most moral of all propositions is this one: The exception proves the rule!" Probably all that provoked him to say this was his aversion to a moral system that pretends to be unbending but in practice has to bend at every turn, which means it is the opposite of an exact procedure that takes account of experience first and obtains the law from those observations. Of course he was aware of the distinction that is made between natural and moral laws, according to which the first are derived from the observation of nature, which knows no morality, while the second must be imposed on the less obstinate nature of man; but in his opinion something about this division was no longer valid, and he had been about to say that moral thought was a hundred years behind the times, and that this was why morals were so difficult to apply to present-day needs. But before he reached that point in his explanation, Agathe interrupted him with an answer that seemed very simple but at that moment took Ulrich by surprise.

"Is being good not good, then?" she asked her brother, and there was something in her eyes that he had seen before, when she was doing something with the medals that would probably not have been good in everyone's estimation.

"You're right," he replied eagerly. "One really does have to start with such a proposition if one wants to feel the original meaning again! But children still love being good the way they love sweets—"

"Being bad too," Agathe added.

"But is being good one of the passions of adults?" Ulrich asked. "It's one of their principles! Not that they *are* good, that would strike them as childish. They *do* good. A good man is a person with good principles who does good works: it's an open secret that he may at the same time be thoroughly loathsome!"

"See Hagauer," Agathe added.

"There is a paradoxical absurdity in these good people," Ulrich said. "They turn a state into a demand, a grace into a norm, a way of being into a goal! This family of the good spends a lifetime eating leftovers. Meanwhile a rumor circulates that there was once a great feast of which these are the scraps! To be sure, from time to time a few virtues come back into fashion, but as soon as that has happened, they lose their freshness again."

"Didn't you once say that the same act can be good or bad, depending on circumstances?" Agathe now asked.

Ulrich agreed. That was his theory, that moral values are not absolutes but functional concepts. But when we moralize and generalize, we detach them from their natural context: "And that," he said, "is probably already the point where something is amiss on the path to virtue."

"How else could moral people manage to be so dreary," Agathe added, "when their intention to be good ought to be the most delightful, the most challenging, and the most engaging thing one could possibly imagine!"

Her brother hesitated; but suddenly he let slip a statement that led their relationship into unusual terrain. "Our morality," he declared, "is the crystallization of an inner movement that is completely different from it! None of what we say adds up! Take any phrase—here's one I just thought of: 'Prison is a place for repentance!' Anyone can say this with a good conscience, but no one takes it literally, because it would amount to hellfire for prisoners! So how is one to take it? I'm sure few people know what repentance is, but everyone can tell you the place where repentance should properly reign. Or just think of something 'uplifting': how did that notion find its way into moral discourse, and where did it come from? When were we ever so prostrate, with our faces in the dust, that it was a blessing to be uplifted? Or imagine being literally in the grip of an idea: the moment you experienced that as a palpable reality, you would already be deep in the realm of lunacy! And so every word needs to be taken literally, otherwise it decays into a lie, but no word should be taken literally, otherwise the world will turn into a madhouse! Some great rapture rises out of this as an obscure memory, and it can be tempting to imagine that our experience consists entirely of fragments torn from an ancient wholeness that was destroyed a long time ago and was then put together again in a way that was all wrong."

The conversation in which this remark was made took place in the room that served as a library and a study, and while Ulrich sat over several books he had brought along on his trip, his sister was rummaging through her father's collection of legal and philosophical books, a bequest of which she was now a co-inheritor, and from which she drew inspiration for some of her questions. Since their outing the siblings had rarely left the house. This was how they spent their time. Occasionally they would stroll in the garden, where winter had peeled the leaves from the naked shrubs, exposing the swollen, rain-soaked earth beneath. This sight was painful. The air was pallid, like something that has long lain in water. The garden was not large. The paths soon turned back upon themselves, and as the siblings followed them, they found themselves in a state of mind that drifted in circular eddies like those of a current rising behind a dam. When they returned to the house, the rooms were dark and sheltered, and the windows were like deep shafts through which daylight entered with the delicacy and brittleness of thin ivory. Agathe had now, after Ulrich's last, spirited words, stepped down from the library ladder on which she had been sitting and laid an arm around his shoulder, without answering. That was an unaccustomed show of tenderness, for apart from the two kisses the one on the evening of their first encounter and the one a few days ago on leaving the shepherds' hut—the modest reserve that naturally obtains between brother and sister had not yet relaxed into more than words and small friendly gestures, and even those two moments of intimate contact had been covered over by the unexpectedness of the first occasion and by the exuberant mischief that prompted the second. But this time Ulrich immediately thought of the garter his sister had warmly bestowed on the deceased in place of a quantity of words. And another thought shot through his head: "There is no question that she has a lover; but she doesn't seem to care about him very much, otherwise she would not be so content to stay here." She was evidently a woman, and had led a woman's life quite independently of him and would continue to do so. His shoulder felt the beauty of the arm that was resting upon it by the distribution of its weight alone, and from the side that was turned toward his sister he had a shadowy sense of the nearness of her blond armpit and the outline of her breast. But in order not to just sit there in passive surrender to this quiet embrace, he took hold of the fingers of the hand resting near his neck, thus muffling the intimacy of her touch with his. "You know, it's a little childish, the way we're talking," he said, not without annoyance. "The world is full of resolution and action, and we're sitting here talking in lazy luxuriance about the sweetness of 'being good' and the theoretical pots we could fill with it!"

Agathe freed her fingers but let her hand return to its place. "What's this book you've been reading all these days?" she asked.

"You know what it is," he replied. "You've peeked into it over my shoulder often enough."

"But I can't make heads or tails of it."

He could not decide whether he should talk about it. Agathe, who had now pulled up a chair, was crouching behind him and was simply and peacefully resting her face in his hair, as if sleeping in it. Ulrich was strangely reminded of the moment when his enemy Arnheim had wrapped an arm around him and the unregulated current of physical contact with another being had poured into him as if through a breach. But this time his own nature did not rise to repel the intruder; instead something was flowing toward it that had been buried beneath the rubble of mistrust and resentment that fills the heart of any man who has lived a fairly long time. Agathe's relationship to him, hovering between sister and woman, stranger and friend, yet not identifiable as any of them, also did not—as he had already quite often concluded—reside in a particularly far-reaching agreement of thought and feeling; and yet, as he noticed at this moment almost with amazement, this highly ambiguous relationship had become indistinguishable from the fact that in the course of relatively few days, in consequence of myriad impressions impossible to review in a moment, Agathe's mouth now rested on his hair without further claim, and that the hair had become warm and moist from her breath. This was something as spiritual as it was physical. For when Agathe repeated her question, Ulrich was overcome by a seriousness such as he had not felt since the days when he was still young and a believer; and by the time this cloud of weightless gravity had vanished—a field extending from the space behind his back through his whole body to the book on which his thoughts were resting—he had given an answer that surprised him more by the complete absence of irony in its tone than by its content. He said: "I'm instructing myself about the ways of the holy life."

He had stood up and walked a few steps, not to move away from his sister but in order to see her from there. "You needn't laugh," he said. "I'm not religious; I'm looking at the road to holiness and wondering if it's possible to drive a car on it!"

"I only laughed," Agathe replied, "because I'm so curious to hear what you're going to say. The books you brought along are new to me, but I have a feeling they're not completely beyond my understanding."

"Does this sound familiar?" her brother asked, already convinced that she would not find it strange: "You can be caught up in the most vehement emotion but suddenly your glance falls on the play of some random thing abandoned by God and the world and you can't tear yourself away from it?! Suddenly you feel yourself wafted aloft by its tiny existence like a feather sailing in the wind, relieved of all weight and all power?!"

"Except for the vehement emotion you make such a point of, I think I know what you mean," Agathe said, and now had to smile again at the fierce embarrassment that showed in her brother's face, not at all in keeping with the delicacy of his words. "Sometimes one forgets seeing and hearing," she said, "and loses the power of speech altogether. And yet it's precisely then that you feel you've come to yourself for a moment."

"I would say," Ulrich went on excitedly, "it's similar to looking across a wide sparkling body of water: everything is so bright it seems like darkness to the eye, and on the opposite shore things don't seem to be resting on the earth but rather hovering in the air with an extreme and delicate distinctness that is bewildering and almost hurts. There's a feeling of intensification and of loss in this, both. You're connected with everything and can't quite make contact with anything. You're standing here and the world is over there, hypersubjective and hyperconcrete, but both sides almost painfully distinct, and what separates and connects these usually mingled elements is a dark flashing pulse, a brimming over and an extinction, a swinging out and in. You are floating like the fish in the water and the bird in the air, but there is no bank and no branch and only this floating!" It was doubtless a kind of poetry he was speaking, but the ardor and firmness of his language stood out in metallic relief against its subtle, hovering content. He seemed to have cast off a caution that usually restrained him, and Agathe looked at him in astonishment, but also with uneasy joy.

"And you think there's something behind it?" she asked. "More than a 'humor,' or whatever vile reassuring term would be applied?"

"I certainly do!" He sat down again in his previous place and leafed about among the books that lay there, while Agathe stood up to make room for him. Then he laid one of them open, saying, "This is how the saints describe it," and read aloud: "During these days I was exceedingly restless. Now I sat a while, now I wandered back and forth through the house. It was like an anguish and yet more to be called a sweetness than an anguish, for there was no vexation in it, but rather a strange, quite supernatural pleasantness. I had risen above all my faculties up to the dark power. There I heard without sound, there I saw without light. There my heart became bottomless, my spirit formless, and my nature insubstantial." It seemed to them both that these words resembled the restlessness by which they themselves were driven through house and garden, and Agathe especially was surprised that saints, too, call their heart bottomless and their spirit formless; but Ulrich soon appeared to be wrapped in his irony again.

He explained: "The saints say: Once I was shut inside, then I was drawn out of myself and immersed in God without understanding. The emperors out hunting, about whom we read in our storybooks, describe it differently: they say a stag appeared to them with a cross between his antlers, causing the murderous spear to drop from their hands; and then they raised a chapel on that spot so they could go on hunting. And the rich, clever ladies with whom I associate will answer you immediately, if you ask them about it, that the last one who painted such experiences was Van Gogh. Maybe instead of a painter they will talk about Rilke's poetry; but generally they prefer Van Gogh, who represents an excellent capital investment and cut off his ears because his painting didn't do enough for him compared to the rapture of things. The majority of our people, on the other hand, will say that cutting off ears is not a German way of expressing one's feelings. The lofty German way is found in the unmistakable void one experiences in mountain panoramas. For them solitude, little flowers, and babbling brooks are the epitome of human exaltation: but even in that bovine enjoyment of uncooked nature at her wholesome best there lies concealed the misunderstood final residue of a mysterious second life, and all in all something like it must exist or have existed at some time!"

"Then you really shouldn't make fun of it," Agathe objected, grim with the thirst for knowledge and shining with impatience.

"I only make fun of it because I love it," Ulrich curtly retorted.

11

HOLY CONVERSATIONS. CHANGEFUL DEVELOPMENTS

In the days that followed, there were always numerous books on the table, some of which he had brought with him and others he had bought since. He would either speak extemporaneously or else quote from one of many passages he had marked with slips of paper, either to prove a point or because he wanted an exact citation. The books before him were mostly biographies of mystics or scholarly works about them, or collections of their personal utterances, and usually he would deflect the conversation from these texts with the words, "Now let's look at what is going on here as soberly as possible." This was a cautious stance that he was not prepared to give up voluntarily, and so once he said to Agathe: "If you could read straight through all these descriptions that men and women of past centuries have left about their state of divine rapture, you would find truth and reality between all these letters, and yet your will to be of the present would be loath to accept the assertions that were formed with these letters." And he went on: "They speak of an overflowing radiance. Of an infinite expanse, an infinite abundance of light. Of an ethereal 'oneness' of all things and all the soul's capacities. Of a marvelous and indescribable exaltation of the heart. Of insights that come so swiftly that everything is simultaneous and that are like drops of fire falling into the world. And on the other hand they speak of a forgetting and no longer understanding, and even of a perishing of things. They speak of an immense peace that is far removed from the passions. Of a muteness that befalls them. A vanishing of thoughts and intentions, a blindness in which they see clearly, a clarity in which they are both dead and supernaturally alive. They call it an 'annihilation,' yet claim to be living more fully than ever: Are these not the same feelings, shimmering through the veils woven in the attempt to express them, that one still has in our time when the heart—'ravenous and sated,' as they say!—finds itself suddenly in those utopian regions that lie somewhere and nowhere between an infinite tenderness and an infinite solitude?!"

As Ulrich briefly paused to think, Agathe's voice joined in: "This is what you once called two layers that are inside us, one on top of the other."

"I did—when?"

"You'd gone into town without any goal or purpose, and you felt as if you were dissolving into it, but at the same time you didn't like the town; and I told you that this happens to me often."

"Oh yes! You even went on to say 'Hagauer!'" Ulrich exclaimed. "And we laughed: I remember it now. But we didn't really mean it. I've told you on other occasions about the giving and the taking kinds of seeing, about the male and the female principle, about the hermaphroditism of the primal imagination, and the like: I can go on and on about these things! As though my mouth were as far from me as the moon, which is also always available for a confidential nighttime chat if one needs it. But what these pious people have to tell about their soul's adventure," he continued, and as he spoke, a tone of objectivity and also of admiration mingled with the bitterness of his words, "is written in a way that is at times comparable with the ruthless rigor and conviction of a Stendhalian analysis. However," he now injected a qualification, "this is only the case as long as they stick to the phenomena and leave their judgment out of it, because their judgment is warped by the flattering conviction that they are singled out by God to have direct experience of Him. And, of course, as soon as that happens, they stop telling us about their perceptions, which have no nouns or verbs and are therefore very hard to describe, and speak instead in sentences with subject and object, because they believe in their soul and in God as if these were two doorposts between which the miraculous will open. And so they arrive at these statements about the soul being drawn from the body and immersed in the Lord, or that the Lord penetrates them like a lover; they are captured, devoured, dazzled, plundered, ravaged by the Lord, or their soul expands to meet Him, enters into Him, tastes Him, embraces Him with love and hears Him speak. The earthly model for this is unmistakable; and these descriptions now no longer resemble tremendous discoveries, but merely the rather monotonous imagery with which an erotic poet embellishes his subject, about which only one opinion is permissible. For someone like me, at least, who was brought up to maintain reserve, the effect is one of being stretched on a rack, because the elect, at the moment when they assure me that God spoke to them or that they understood the speech of the trees and the beasts, neglect to tell me what was imparted to them; and if they ever do, all that comes out is personal business or church news. It is an everlasting pity that there are no trained scientists who have visions!" he concluded his long reply.

"Do you think they could?" Agathe tempted him. Ulrich hesitated for a moment. His answer came out like a confession.

"I don't know. Maybe it could happen to me!" When he heard his words, he smiled in order to limit their meaning.

Agathe also smiled; she now seemed to have the answer she had been craving, and her face reflected the little moment of baffled disappointment that follows the sudden cessation of a state of suspense. And perhaps she now raised an objection only to spur her brother on. "You know," she declared, "I was educated in a very pious school. Because of that, as soon as someone starts talking about religious ideals, I feel a simply scandalous urge to lampoon these things. Our teachers wore a habit whose two colors formed a cross, and to be sure, that was a reminder of one of the most sublime ideas, which we were supposed to be mindful of all day long; but we didn't give that a moment's thought and only called our Sisters the cross-spiders, because of the way they looked and because of their silky smooth way of talking. That's why, while you were reading aloud, I didn't know whether to laugh or cry."

"Do you know what that proves?" Ulrich exclaimed. "Nothing more or less than this: That the power for good, which really does seem to exist within us, immediately eats its way through the walls if it gets shut up into a solid form and escapes straightaway through the hole into its opposite! It reminds me of the time when I was in the army, upholding throne and altar together with my fellow officers: at no other time in all my life have I heard people speak so loosely about those two as we did in our circle! Feelings don't like being put on a leash, but some feelings in particular can't put up with it at all. I'm sure your worthy Sisters believed what they were preaching: but faith must never be more than an hour old! That's it!"

Even though Ulrich had expressed himself too hurriedly for his own satisfaction, it was clear to Agathe that the faith of those nuns who had robbed her of the joy of believing was a "canned" faith, preserved in its own juices, so to speak, not lacking any of the qualities of faith but no longer fresh; indeed, in some indeterminable way it had entered a condition that was different from what it had been at its source. And perhaps, at this moment, the nature of that original faith was dawning on the truant and rebellious pupil of holiness.

This, among all the other things they had already said about morality, was one of the poignant doubts her brother had implanted in her mind, and it played a part in an inner reawakening she had been feeling since, without having a clear idea of what it was. For the state of indifference she pointedly displayed and encouraged within herself had not always ruled her life. Something had happened once that caused this need for self-punishment to emerge directly from a deep despondency that had made her regard herself as a worthless person because she believed she had not been granted the capacity to keep faith with lofty emotions, and since then she had despised herself for the apathy of her heart. This episode lay between her life as a girl in her father's house and her incomprehensible marriage to Hagauer and occupied such a narrow span of her life that even Ulrich, for all his sympathy, had not thought of asking her about it. What happened does not take long to tell: At the age of eighteen Agathe had married a man who was only slightly older than herself, and on a trip that began with their wedding and ended with his death, he was torn away from her within a few weeks by a sickness he contracted while traveling before they had even decided upon their future home. The doctors called it typhus, and Agathe repeated the word after them and found a semblance of order in it, for this was the side of the event that was polished smooth for the use of the world; but on the unpolished side it was different: until then Agathe had lived with her father, who was universally respected, so that she came to doubt herself and, worse, presume herself unjust in not loving him, and the long, uncertain waiting for herself at school, with its attendant self-mistrust, had not stabilized her relationship to the world either; later, on the other hand, when her spirits were suddenly stirred into life, and in a joint effort with the companion of her youth she managed in a few months to surmount all obstacles to a marriage arising from their age, even though the lovers' families had no objection to each other, she had all at once ceased to be lonely and just for that reason become herself. This, then, could well be called love; but there are lovers who gaze into love as into the sun and are merely blinded, and there are lovers who behold life with amazement for the first time when it is illuminated by love. It was to the second kind that Agathe belonged, and before she even knew whether she loved her companion or something else, there came already what the language of the unilluminated world called an infectious disease. It was a storm of horror that burst in upon them with elemental suddenness from the alien regions of life, a flaring up of desperate refusal, a guttering descent, a snuffing out, a ghastly visitation upon two human beings clinging to each other and the drowning of an innocent world in vomit, excrement, and fear.

Agathe had never accepted the event that had annihilated her feelings. Deranged by despair, she had lain on her knees at her dying friend's bedside and convinced herself that she could conjure up again the strength with which she had overcome her own illness as a child; and when his decline advanced nonetheless and his consciousness was already waning, she had, in the rooms of a foreign hotel, stared into that vacant face, incapable of understanding, holding the dying body in her arms without considering the danger and without considering the reality to which an indignant nurse was attending, and done nothing but murmur into his ear for hours: "You can't, you can't, you can't!" But when it was all over she had stood up in amazement, and without believing or thinking anything in particular, simply out of a solitary nature's self-will and capacity to dream, from that moment of empty astonishment on she had treated what had happened as if it were not final. One can see the first signs of such a tendency in anyone who refuses to believe disastrous news or paints the irrevocable in soothing colors; but the special quality in Agathe's behavior was the force and extent of this reaction, evident from the start in the eruptive suddenness of her disdain for the world. Since then, when encountering anything new, her mind was set on receiving it less as something that was presently the case than as something highly uncertain, an attitude that was greatly facilitated by the mistrust with which she had long regarded reality; the past, on the other hand, had become petrified by the blow she had suffered, and was worn away by time much more slowly than usually happens with memories. But this had nothing of the fog of dreams, the one-sidedness and skewed proportions that cry out for a doctor. On the contrary, Agathe went on with her life, outwardly perfectly lucid, unassumingly virtuous, and merely a little bored, in a slightly elevated state of unwillingness to go on living that was now really quite similar to the fever she had suffered with such peculiar willingness as a child. And the fact that in her memory, which never easily dissolved its impressions into generalizations, the horror of the past remained present hour after hour, like a corpse wrapped in a white sheet, made her blissfully happy, despite all the torment of remembering so exactly, for it had the effect of a mysteriously belated hint that all was not yet over, and kept alive, in the derelict state of her inner being, a vague but exalted tension. Of course all this really amounted to was merely that she had lost the meaning of her life and was deliberately putting herself in a condition that did not suit her years; for only old people live by dwelling on the experiences and successes of the past and are no longer affected by the present. But fortunately, at the age Agathe was then, even as one forms resolutions for all eternity, a single year has nearly the weight of half an eternity, and so it was only to be expected that after a while repressed nature and fettered imagination would forcibly reclaim their freedom. The details of how this happened are unimportant; a man whose advances under different circumstances would never have caught her off balance succeeded in becoming her lover, and this attempt at a reenactment ended, after a very short time of fanatical hope, in passionate disenchantment. Agathe now felt herself reviled by both her real life and her unreal life and unworthy of lofty aspirations. She was one of those intense people who are capable of remaining still and watchfully waiting for a long time until at some point they suddenly fall prey to total confusion; and so in her disappointment she soon made another ill-considered decision that consisted, in short, of punishing herself in a manner opposite to the way in which she had sinned, by condemning herself to share her life with a man who instilled in her a slight revulsion. And this man whom she had sought out for her punishment was Hagauer.

"I have to say that was neither fair nor considerate toward him," Agathe confessed to herself, and it must be admitted that this was the first time she did so, for fairness and consideration are not popular virtues among young people. Still, her self-punishment in this marriage was not inconsiderable either, and Agathe now examined this matter further. She had gone far afield in her ruminations, and Ulrich too was searching for something in his books and had apparently forgotten their conversation. "In earlier centuries," she thought, "a person who felt as I did would have entered a convent"—and the fact that she had married instead was not without an innocent comedy that had previously escaped her. This comical aspect, however, which had not been apparent to her youthful mind, was none other than that of our present time, which satisfies the need for escape from the world at worst in a tourist inn, but usually in an Alpine hotel, and even aspires to equip its prisons with attractive furniture. This exemplifies the deep European need not to overdo anything. No European scourges himself any longer, or smears himself with ashes, cuts out his tongue, truly abandons himself, or even just withdraws from all human company, pines away with passion, racks or impales, but everyone does feel an occasional urge to do these things, and so it is hard to tell which is more worth avoiding, the wanting or the not doing. Why then should an ascetic, of all people, starve himself? It will only encourage disturbing fantasies. Rational asceticism consists in having an aversion to eating while maintaining a healthy diet. This kind of asceticism holds out a promise of longevity and permits the spirit a freedom it does not have when it is bound to the body in passionate rebellion! Such bitterly amusing observations, adopted from her brother, now had a fortifying effect on Agathe, for they dissected the "tragic," which she had long believed in with a kind of fixity to which, in her inexperience, she thought herself obliged, into irony and a passion that had neither a name nor a goal and for that reason alone was not aborted by what she had experienced.

In this way, ever since she had been with her brother, she was becoming aware that a quickening current was flowing into the great split she had suffered between irresponsible living and spectral imaginings, a freeing and at the same time a recombining of what had been released. Now, for instance, in the silence, deepened by books and memories, that reigned between her and her brother, she remembered Ulrich's description of how, leaving the house for an aimless walk, he had entered into the town and the town had entered into him: it reminded her very precisely of the few weeks of her happiness; and it had been right, too, that she laughed, madly and for no reason, when he told her about it, because she realized that there was something of this inversion of the world, this blissful and comical inside-out gesture even in Hagauer's thick lips when they puckered for a kiss. That thought made her shudder, admittedly; but there is a shudder, she thought, even in the bright light of noon, and somehow that gave her the feeling that all possibilities were not yet exhausted for her. Some Nothing, a vacancy that had always lain between past and present, had recently flown away. She secretly looked around. The room she was in was one of the rooms in which her destiny had taken shape; this occurred to her now for the first time since she had arrived. For it was here that she had met with her childhood playmate when she knew her father was out, and where they made the great decision to love each other; it was here that she had also sometimes received the one she had called "unworthy," and had stood by the windows with furtive tears of rage or despair, and where finally, under paternal auspices, Hagauer's courting had taken place. After having so long served merely as the unnoticed backdrop to human activities, the furniture, the walls, the oddly shut-in light now at this moment of recognition became oddly tangible, and the life that had so strangely come and gone in this setting formed as corporeal and unequivocal a past as if it were ash or charcoal. All that was left was the comically shadowlike sense of things over and done with, the peculiar tingle one feels when coming upon old traces of oneself that have turned to dust, a sensation that, at the moment it comes, is impossible either to grasp or dispel; and that sensation became almost unendurably strong.

Agathe made sure that Ulrich was not paying attention, and carefully opened the top of her dress, where she kept next to her skin the locket with the little picture that she had not ceased to wear through the years. She went to the window and pretended to look out. Cautiously, she snapped open the sharp edge of the tiny golden scallop and furtively gazed at her dead beloved. He had full lips and soft, thick hair, and the brash look in the eyes of the twenty-year-old sprang from a face that had only half emerged from the eggshell. For a long time she did not know what she was thinking, but suddenly she thought: "My God, a twenty-one-year-old!"

What do such young people talk about to each other? What significance do they give to their concerns? How comically presumptuous they often are! How the vividness of their ideas misleads them as to their soundness! Curiously Agathe unwrapped from the tissue paper of memory some remarks she had preserved there because she had thought them marvelously clever: My God, she thought, that was almost profound; but even that couldn't really be said with assurance unless one had a picture of the garden where these things were spoken, with the strange flowers whose names they didn't know, the butterflies that settled on them like tired drunkards, and the light that flowed over their faces as though heaven and earth were melted together in it. If she measured herself against that, she was now an old and experienced woman, even though not many years had passed, and with some confusion she noticed the incongruity in the fact that she, the twenty-seven-year-old, was still in love with the twenty-one-year-old: he had grown much too young for her! She asked herself: "What feelings would I have to have if, at my age, this boyish man were really to be the most important thing in the world to me?" No doubt they would have been rather peculiar feelings, but she could not even form a clear conception of them. In the end it all dissolved into nothing.

Agathe acknowledged with a great, swelling emotion that in the one and only proud passion of her life she had fallen prey to an error, and the core of that error consisted in a fiery mist that could not be touched or grasped, whether by saying that faith must not grow an hour old or by any other set of words; and it was always this that her brother had been talking about since they were together, and always it was she herself of whom he was speaking, even if he took all sorts of detours into abstraction and his caution was frequently much too slow for her impatience. They always came back to the same conversation, and Agathe herself burned with desire that its flame should not diminish.

When she now spoke to Ulrich, he had not even noticed how long the interruption had lasted. But whoever has not already picked up the clues to what was developing between this brother and sister, let him put aside this account, for it describes an adventure he will never be able to approve of: a voyage to the edge of the possible, leading past, and perhaps not always steering clear of, the dangers of the impossible and the unnatural, indeed of the repulsive; a "limit case," as Ulrich later called it, of restricted and special validity, reminiscent of the freedom with which mathematics occasionally employs the absurd in order to arrive at truth. He and Agathe came upon a path that had much in common with the business of the God-possessed, but they walked it without piety, without believing in God or the soul, or even in a Beyond or a Once Again; they had come upon it as human beings belonging to this world and walked it as such: and just that was the remarkable thing about it. Ulrich, who at the moment when Agathe spoke again was still occupied with his books and the problems they set him, had nevertheless not for a moment forgotten the conversation that had broken off at her resistance to the piety of her teachers and his own demand for "exact visions," and he replied immediately: "There's absolutely no need to be a saint in order to experience something of the kind! You can be sitting on a fallen tree or a bench in the mountains watching a herd of grazing cows and already you're participating in something that seems nothing less than a transport into another life! You lose yourself and suddenly come to yourself: you yourself have talked about this!"

"But what is it that happens there?" Agathe asked.

"First you need to get clear about what the usual is, Sister Human!" Ulrich declared, trying to put a brake on the all too rapid momentum of the thought with a quip. "The usual is that a herd of cattle means nothing to us but grazing beef. Or it's a picturesque subject with a background. Or we hardly notice it at all. Herds of cattle beside mountain paths are part of what mountain paths are, and what one experiences at the sight of them would be noticed only if an apartment building or a giant electrical clock appeared in their place. Otherwise, one's thoughts turn to the question of whether to stand up or remain seated; one finds the flies that swarm around the herd annoying; one looks to see if there's a bull among the cows; one wonders where the path leads: these are countless little intentions, worries, calculations, and perceptions that form the paper, as it were, on which the picture of grazing cows can be seen. One isn't aware of the paper at all, one is only aware of the cows that are on it."

"And suddenly the paper tears!" Agathe interjected.

"Yes. That is, some network of habit in us tears. Now there is no longer anything edible grazing; or anything paintable; nothing gets in your way. You can no longer even form the words 'grazing' or 'pasture,' because that involves a great many purposeful, useful ideas which you've suddenly lost. What's left on the picture plane is almost unnamable; maybe the closest one can get is to call it a surge of sensations that rises, sinks, breathes, or glitters, as if filling your whole field of vision without any contours. Of course innumerable individual perceptions are included in this: colors, horns, movements, smells, and everything that makes up reality; but this is already no longer acknowledged, even if it may still be recognized. I'm tempted to say: The details lose their egotism, by which each one claims our attention for itself, and are instead deeply and fondly attuned to each other, like kindred souls. And of course there is no longer a 'picture plane.' Instead everything flows into you, without bounds or limits."

Again Agathe eagerly took up the description: "Now all you need to say instead of the 'egotism of the details' is the 'egotism of people,'" she exclaimed, "and you've got what is so hard to express: 'Love thy neighbor!' doesn't mean love him as you and he are. It refers to a kind of dream state!"

"All moral propositions," Ulrich confirmed, "refer to a kind of dream state that has already escaped the rules that are supposed to define it!"

"Basically, then, there is no good and evil but only faith—or doubt!" cried Agathe, to whom the self-sustaining original state of faith now seemed so close, as did its disappearance in morality, of which her brother had spoken when he said that faith cannot live longer than an hour.

"Yes, the moment one slips out of the inessential life, everything is in a new relationship to everything else," Ulrich agreed. "I would almost say, in no relationship at all. Because this kind is completely unknown to us, we have no experience with it, and all other relationships are extinguished; but this one is so obvious, despite its obscurity, that it can't be denied. It is strong, but it is inconceivably strong. And there's also this: Usually one looks at something, and that glance or gaze is like a fine rod or a taut thread by which the eye and what is seen mutually support each other, and every moment is supported by some great weaving of that sort; but at this other moment it's more as though something painfully sweet were drawing our eye-beams apart."

"One owns nothing in the world, one no longer holds on to anything, one is not held by anything," Agathe said. "It's all like a tall tree with no leaf stirring. And one can't do anything base in this condition."

"It has been said that nothing can happen in this condition that is not in harmony with it," Ulrich added. "A desire 'to be part of it' is the sole reason, the loving purpose, and the only form, of all doing and thinking that take place within it. It is something infinitely tranquil and encompassing, and everything that happens within it increases its quietly mounting significance. Or else it doesn't increase it, in which case it's bad, and yet the bad cannot happen, because at the instant it happens the stillness and clarity are torn and the miraculous condition ceases to be."

Ulrich gave his sister a searching look which she was not meant to notice; he had a persistent feeling that they ought to stop soon. But Agathe's face was expressionless; she was thinking of things long past. She answered: "I'm surprised at myself, but there really was a brief period when I knew nothing of envy, malice, vanity, greed, and things like that; it's hard to believe, but it seems to me that all of a sudden they disappeared not only from my heart but from the world! In that state it's not just oneself who can't do anything base, but others can't either. A good person makes everything that comes in contact with him good, no matter what action others may take against him: the moment that action enters his sphere, it's already transformed!"

"No," Ulrich interjected, "it's not quite like that; on the contrary, the way you put it is one of the oldest misconceptions! A good person doesn't make the world good in the least, he doesn't affect the world at all, he just separates himself from it!"

"But he doesn't leave the world, does he? He stays right in the midst of it!?"

"He stays in the midst of it, but he feels as if space had been drawn out of things or as if something imaginary were happening: it's difficult to say!"

"Still, I have the feeling that nothing base ever crosses the path of a 'high-hearted' person—that word just came to me! It may sound like nonsense, but it's an experience."

"It may be an experience," Ulrich retorted, "but there is also the opposite experience! Or do you think the soldiers who crucified Jesus did not have base emotions? And yet they were instruments of God! Besides, according to the testimony of the ecstatics themselves, there are bad feelings: they lament that they fall from the state of grace and feel unspeakable distress, they're well acquainted with fear, anguish, shame, maybe even hatred. It's only when the quiet burning starts again that remorse, wrath, fear, and anguish turn into bliss. It's all so hard to make sense of!"

"When were you that much in love?" Agathe asked abruptly.

"Me? Oh! I already told you about it. I fled a thousand miles from the woman I loved, and once I felt safe from any possibility of her actual embrace, I wailed for her like a dog howling at the moon!"

Now Agathe confided to him the story of her love. She was excited. Her last question had already sped off as if plucked on an overly taut string, and the rest now followed in the same fashion. She trembled inwardly as she revealed what had been kept secret for years.

But her brother was not notably shocked by her account. "Usually memories age along with people," he expounded, "and the most passionate experiences become comical in the perspective of time, as if one were seeing them at the end of ninety-nine successively opened doors. But sometimes there are memories that don't age because they are associated with very strong emotions and hold entire strata of the self in bondage, as it were. That was the case with you. There are such points in almost everyone that slightly distort one's psychic equilibrium; one's behavior flows over their invisible presence the way a river flows over a boulder; and with you this just happened to be very strong, so it almost resembled a standstill. But in the end you freed yourself and you're in motion again!"

He said this calmly, almost in the manner of a professional evaluation; how easily he was diverted! Agathe was upset. Stubbornly she said: "Of course I'm in motion, but that's not what I'm talking about! I want to know where I almost arrived at back then!" She was also annoyed, without meaning to be, simply because her excitement had to express itself somehow. Nevertheless, she went on talking in the direction her feelings had originally taken, and she felt quite dizzy between the tenderness of her words and the anger in the background. She spoke about that wondrous state of heightened receptivity and sensitivity that produces a welling up and subsiding of sense impressions, giving rise to a feeling of being in touch with all things, an effortless giving and receiving as if afloat in the soft mirror of a sheet of water; that marvelous sense of outer and inner boundlessness and self-abandonment that love and mysticism have in common! Of course Agathe did not say it in such words, which already entail an explanation, but merely strung passionate fragments of memory into a sequence. But though Ulrich had given much thought to these things, he too was unable to explain such experiences. Above all he did not know whether to attempt an explanation in the terms of the experience itself or by the usual procedures of rational thought. Both were equally natural to him, but not to his sister's evident passion. What he said in reply, therefore, was merely a mediation, a kind of testing of the possibilities. He pointed out how, in the exalted state they were speaking of, a remarkable affinity exists between thinking and moral feeling, such that every thought is felt as a joy, an event, and a gift and does not wander off into the storage rooms nor attach itself to the sentiments of acquisition and mastery, retention and observation, so that, in the head no less than in the heart, the pleasure of self-possession is replaced by a limitless giving of oneself and intertwining of oneself and others. "Once in your life," Agathe replied then with rapturous conviction, "everything you do is done for someone else. You see the sun shining for him. He is everywhere, you yourself are nowhere. And yet this is not 'egotism à deux,' because the same thing must be happening with the other person. In the end the two hardly exist for each other anymore, and what's left is a world for people all in twos, which consists of mutual recognition, surrender, friendship, and selflessness!"

In the darkness of the room her cheek glowed with ardor like a rose standing in the shadow. And Ulrich pleaded: "Let us speak more soberly now; there tends to be far too much humbug in these matters!" And that too seemed right to her. Maybe it was due to her anger, which had still not dissipated, that her delight was somewhat dampened by the reality he was invoking; but it was not an unpleasant sensation, this unsteady trembling of the borderline.

Ulrich began to speak of the mischief of interpreting the kind of experiences they were talking about not only as if they involved a peculiar mental shift but as if some superhuman way of thinking were taking the place of the ordinary kind. Whether one called it divine illumination or, in the modern fashion, merely intuition, he considered it the main hindrance to real understanding. In his view nothing could be gained by yielding to fantasies that could not withstand the test of careful investigation. It's like Icarus, he exclaimed, with his wings of wax that melt in the upper regions; if one wants to fly in reality, not just in dreams, one must learn to do it on metal wings.

And pointing to the books, he continued after a little while: "Those are Christian, Jewish, Indian, and Chinese testimonies, some of them separated by more than a thousand years. And yet in all of them one finds the same pattern of inner movement, diverging from the ordinary but consistent in itself. They differ among each other, almost precisely, only in particulars that stem from their connection with this or that school of theology and cosmic wisdom under whose protective roof they took shelter. Therefore, we may assume the existence of one specific additional, extraordinary condition of great importance, of which man is capable and which has deeper origins than the religions.

"The churches, on the other hand," he added, "which is to say, the civilized communities of religious people, have always treated this condition with the kind of mistrust a bureaucrat has for the spirit of private enterprise. They have never recognized this rapturous mode of experience without reservation; on the contrary, they have directed great and apparently justified efforts toward replacing it with a regulated and intelligible morality. So the history of this condition resembles a progressive denial and dilution, something like the draining of a swamp.

"And when the spiritual dominion of the Church and its vocabulary became outdated, this condition of ours understandably came to be regarded as a chimera. Why should bourgeois culture have been more religious than the religious culture it replaced?! Under its aegis, the other condition has gone to the dogs, or rather it's been reduced to the status of a dog that retrieves insights. A lot of people nowadays complain about rationality and want us to believe that in their wisest moments they think by means of a special faculty that is higher than reason. That is the last vestige, itself already a perfectly rationalistic, public thing; what's left of the drained swamp has turned into hot air! And so, aside from a tolerated existence in poems, the only life granted to the ancient condition is during the first weeks of love among uneducated persons, where it is regarded as a passing confusion. Those are belated green leaves, so to speak, that occasionally sprout from the wood of beds and lecterns: but where it threatens to revert to its original luxuriant growth, it gets dug up and rooted out without mercy!"

Ulrich had spoken for about the length of time a surgeon takes to wash his hands and arms to prevent germs from being carried into the operating field; and also with the patience, dedication, and equanimity that contravene the excitement that will come with the work at hand. But after he had thoroughly sterilized himself, he thought almost with longing of a little infection and fever, for he did not love sobriety for its own sake. Agathe was sitting on a ladder that served to reach books on high shelves and gave no sign of participation, even when her brother fell silent; she gazed out into the infinite, sea-like gray of the sky and listened to the silence as much as to the words. So Ulrich went on talking with a touch of defiance that was barely concealed beneath a jocular tone.

"Let's go back to our bench in the mountains with the herd of cows," he requested. "Imagine some municipal councilor in brand-new lederhosen sitting there, with the words 'Grüß Gott' embroidered on his green suspenders: he represents real life, with its true worth, on vacation. Naturally his consciousness of his own existence is temporarily altered. Looking at the grazing cows, he doesn't count them, doesn't classify them, doesn't estimate their live weight, forgives his enemies, and thinks indulgently of his family. The herd has turned from a practical subject into a quasi-moral one for him. It's possible, of course, that he's still estimating and classifying just a bit and doesn't wholly forgive, but even so these feelings will at least be surrounded by a murmuring forest, a babbling brook, and sunshine. One could sum it up by saying: The usual content of his life now seems 'far away' and 'not really important.'"

"It's a holiday mood," Agathe added mechanically.

"Quite right! And if just now his nonholiday life seems 'not really important,' it means only: for as long as he's on vacation. So that is the truth today: Man has two states of existence, of consciousness, and of thought and saves himself from the deadly fright of meeting his own spectral otherness by regarding one condition as a vacation from the other, an interruption, a respite, or something about them that he thinks he knows. Mysticism, on the other hand, would entail the intention of going on a permanent vacation. The municipal councilor is bound to call that dishonorable and instantly feel, as he always does toward the end of his vacation, that real life resides in his orderly office. And do we feel any differently? Whether something needs to be put in order or not will always ultimately determine whether one takes that something completely seriously or not; and here these experiences have not had much luck, because over thousands of years they have not gone beyond their primordial disorder and incompleteness. And this is just the kind of thing for which the term "mania" lies readily at hand—religious mania, erotomania, take your pick. You can be assured: nowadays even the majority of religious people are so infected with the scientific way of thinking that they don't dare to look at what is burning deep inside their hearts and would always readily speak of this ardor in medical terms as a mania, even if officially they use a different language!"

Agathe looked at her brother, and there was a quality in her eyes like the crackling of fire in the rain. And when he fell silent, she reproached him: "Now you've managed to manoeuver us out of it!"

"You are right," he admitted. "But here is the strange thing: Even though we've boarded it all up like an unsafe well, some remnant drop of this uncanny miracle water is still burning a hole into all our ideals. Not one of them is quite right, not one of them makes us happy; they all point to something that is not there; you know what I mean, we've talked enough about that today. Our civilization is a temple of what would be called mania if it were unconfined, but at the same time it is the prison of its confinement, and we don't know if we are suffering from an excess or a deficiency."

"Maybe you never dared to give yourself over to it all the way," Agathe said regretfully, and stepped down from her ladder; for they had let themselves be distracted, first by the books and then by their conversation, from their task of sorting their father's papers, which had become pressing as the days went by. Now they went back to perusing the instructions and notes concerning the distribution of their inheritance, for the day to which Hagauer had been put off was approaching; but before they had seriously begun doing this, Agathe sat up straight and asked him once more: "To what extent do you yourself believe everything you've been telling me?"

Ulrich answered without looking up. "Imagine that in that herd, while your heart is turned away from the world, there is a dangerous bull! Try to really believe that the deadly illness you told me about would have taken a different course if your feelings had not weakened for a second!" Then he raised his head and pointed at the papers beneath his hands. "And law, justice, right proportion? Do you think all that is completely superfluous?"

"So to what extent do you believe?" Agathe repeated.

"Yes and no," Ulrich said.

"That means no," Agathe concluded.

Here chance intervened in their talk. At the moment when Ulrich, who was neither inclined to resume the discussion nor calm enough to think about practical matters, gathered up the papers that were spread out before him, something fell to the ground. It was a loose packet of all sorts of things that had been inadvertently pulled out, together with the will, from a corner of the desk drawer, where it might have lain for decades without its owner's knowing. Ulrich looked at it distractedly as he picked it up, and recognized his father's handwriting on several pages; it was not the script of his old age but that of his prime. Looking more closely, he saw that in addition to handwritten pages, the bundle contained playing cards, photographs, and various knickknacks, and now he quickly realized what he had found. It was the desk's "poison drawer." Here were painstakingly recorded jokes, most of them smutty; nude photographs; postcards, to be sent sealed, of plump dairymaids whose panties could be opened at the back; decks of cards that looked quite proper but, when held against the light, showed horrid things; manikins that produced offensive language when their belly was squeezed; and more of that kind. No doubt the old gentleman had forgotten the things lying in that drawer, or else he would have destroyed them in time. They obviously dated from those years in which quite a few aging bachelors and widowers warm themselves with such indecencies, but Ulrich blushed at this exposure of his father's unprotected fantasies, now severed from the flesh by death. Their relevance to the conversation that had just broken off was immediately clear to him. Nevertheless, his first impulse was to destroy these documents before Agathe had seen them. But Agathe had already noticed that something unusual had come into his hands, so he changed his mind and called her over.

He wanted to wait and hear what she would say. But suddenly he was again acutely aware that she was, after all, a woman who must have had her experiences, a fact of which he had been completely unaware during their more profound conversations. But her face gave no sign of what she was thinking; she looked gravely and calmly at her father's illicit legacy. From time to time she smiled openly, but without much animation. So Ulrich himself spoke, despite his resolve. "There you have it, the last vestige of mysticism!" he said with angry amusement. "Sharing the same drawer, the testament with its stern moral admonitions and this swill!" He had stood up and was walking back and forth in the room. And no sooner had he begun to talk than his sister's silence spurred him on to new words.

"You asked me what I believe," he began. "I believe that all the precepts of our morality are concessions to a society of savages.

"I believe none of them are right.

"There's another meaning glimmering behind them. A fire that ought to melt them down so they can be recast. I believe that nothing is final.

"I believe there is no equilibrium, but everything wants to rise by the leverage of everything else.

"That's what I believe: that was born with me or I with it."

After each sentence he had halted, for he was speaking softly and needed somehow to give emphasis to his confession. His eye was now caught by the classical plaster figures that stood on top of the book shelves; he saw a Minerva, a Socrates; he remembered that Goethe had placed an over-life-size plaster head of Juno in his room. This predilection felt alarmingly remote to him: what had once been a flourishing idea had since withered into a dead classicism. Had become the rearguard righteousness and duty-bound constriction of his father's contemporaries. Had been in vain.

"The morality that has been handed down to us," he said, "is like being sent out on a swaying rope that's slung across an abyss with no other advice than 'At all times keep a rigid posture.'

"It seems that, without any action on my part, I was born with a different morality.

"You asked me what I believe! I believe I can receive a thousand proofs that something is good and beautiful, it will leave me indifferent, and I will take my bearings solely from one indication: Does this make me rise or sink?

"Does it breathe life into me or not?

"Is it merely my tongue and brain that speak of it or the radiant shudder in my fingertip?

"But I can't prove anything either.

"And I'm even convinced that a person who gives in to this other morality is lost. He will end up in twilight. In fog and inane nonsense. In spineless ennui.

"If you remove the unequivocal from life, what remains is a carp pond without a pike.

"I believe, then, that our meanest, nastiest trait is the good angel that protects us!

"And so, I don't believe!

"Above all I do not believe in the constraint of evil by good, which is the hallmark of our cultural farrago: I find this repugnant!

"So I believe and do not believe!

"But maybe I believe that in a not-too-far-off future human beings will on the one hand become highly intelligent, and on the other hand be mystics. Maybe it is already happening, and our morality is splitting into these two components. I could also say: into mathematics and mysticism. Into practical melioration and adventuring in the unknown!"

He had not been so openly excited in years. He did not notice the "maybes" in his speech; they seemed only natural to him.

Agathe meanwhile had kneeled down in front of the stove; she had placed the packet of pictures and writings on the floor beside her, looked at each object one more time, and then pushed it into the fire. She was not entirely unsusceptible to the crude sensuality of the obscenities she was looking at. She felt her body being aroused by them. It seemed to her that this was no more herself than if in some barren solitude one sees a rabbit flitting past. She did not know if she would be ashamed to tell her brother about this; but she was profoundly tired and did not want to talk. She was no longer listening to what he was saying; her heart had by now been too shaken by these ups and downs and could no longer follow. Others had always known better than she what was right; she thought of this, but because she was ashamed, she thought it with secret defiance. To walk a forbidden or secret path: in this she felt superior to Ulrich. She heard how, again and again, he took back everything he allowed himself be carried away into saying, and his words struck against her ear like big drops of happiness and grief.

12

THE WILL

Ulrich has temporarily taken leave of Agathe and gone to Vienna to take care of various business, but finds himself preoccupied with recent developments involving his sister.

ULRICH ... no longer wanted to put off a decision and tried to recall the "incident" as precisely as he possibly could. That was his mitigating term for what had taken place during his last hours with Agathe and a few days after their big conversation.

Ulrich had packed and was ready to leave on a sleeper train that came through the town late in the evening, and the siblings had met for a final supper. They had agreed earlier that Agathe was to follow him after a short time, and they had somewhat vaguely estimated this separation at five days to two weeks.

At the table Agathe said: "But there's something we still have to do before you leave."

"What?" Ulrich asked.

"We have to change the will."

Ulrich remembered looking at his sister without surprise: despite all their previous discussions he had assumed she was leading up to a joke. But Agathe was gazing down at her plate and had the familiar wrinkle above the root of her nose that always appeared when she was mulling something over. Slowly she said: "He shouldn't keep as much of me between his fingers as would be left if a woolen thread had burnt away between them ... !"

Something must have been furiously at work in her over the last few days. Ulrich was about to tell her that he regarded these deliberations on how to damage Hagauer as impermissible and that he didn't want to talk about it again: but just then the old servant came in to bring them their meal and they could go on talking only in allusions.

"Aunt Malvina," Agathe said, smiling at her brother, "do you remember Aunt Malvina? She had intended to leave her entire estate to our cousin; that was all settled and everyone knew about it! Consequently, all that the girl was left in her parents' will was the minimum she was entitled to by law, while the rest went to her brother. That way neither of the children, whose father loved them both equally, would receive more than the other. Surely you remember this? The annuity that cousin Agathe—I mean Alexandra," she corrected herself, laughing, "has been receiving since she got married was discounted against this obligatory inheritance until further notice. It was a complicated business, to give Aunt Malvina time to die . . ."

"I don't understand what you're saying," Ulrich had muttered.

"But it's easy to understand! Aunt Malvina is dead today, but she had already lost everything she had before she died; she even had to be supported. Now Papa only needs to have forgotten to revoke that change he himself made in his will, and Alexandra gets absolutely nothing, even if her marriage contract stipulates joint ownership of property!"

"I don't know, I think that would be far from certain," Ulrich said impulsively. "Also, Father must have given certain assurances. He couldn't have done all this without discussing it with his son-in-law!"

Yes, he remembered only too well having answered like that, because he simply couldn't keep silent listening to his sister's dangerous mistake. He remembered vividly, too, the smile with which she had looked at him then: "That's how he is!" she seemed to be thinking. "All you need to do is present a case to him as if it weren't flesh and blood but some general state of affairs, and you can lead him around by the nose!" And then she had curtly asked: "Were any of these assurances left in writing?" and answered herself: "I never heard anything about it, and if it were the case, I certainly should have known. The fact is, Papa was strange about everything."

At this moment food was being served, and she took advantage of Ulrich's helplessness to add: "Verbal agreements can always be reneged. But if the will was in fact changed again after Aunt Malvina had lost her money, there is every indication that this second codicil has been lost."

And again Ulrich let himself be gulled into correcting her: "But there's still the obligatory inheritance, which is a considerable amount; this can't be taken away from biological children!"

"But I already told you that this was paid out during the father's lifetime! Alexandra was married twice, after all!"

They were alone for a moment, and Agathe hastily added: "I looked at that passage carefully. Only a few words need to be changed, then it looks as if the obligatory inheritance was already paid out to me earlier. Who knows anything about it now?! When Papa went back to leaving us equal shares after our aunt's losses, it was put in a codicil, which can be destroyed; besides, who's to say I couldn't have waived my legal share to leave it to you for some reason!"

Ulrich looked at his sister dumbfounded and missed his chance to counter her inventions as he felt duty-bound to do; by the time he was ready, they were no longer alone, and he had to veil his words:

"One really shouldn't," he began hesitantly, "even think such things!"

"Why not?" Agathe retorted.

Such questions are very simple when they are at rest; but as soon as they rear their heads, what was previously a harmless-looking smudge becomes a monstrous serpent: Ulrich remembered answering: "Even Nietzsche obliges 'free spirits' to respect certain outer rules for the sake of inner freedom!" He had said it with a smile, but at the same time with the feeling that it was cowardly to hide behind someone else's words.

"That's a lame principle!" Agathe curtly determined. "I was married according to this principle!"

And Ulrich thought: "It really is a lame principle." It seems that people who have new and revolutionary answers to particular problems strike a balance by making a compromise with everything else, which allows them to live a respectable morality in slippers; the more so as such an approach, which aims at keeping all conditions constant except for the one that is to be changed, corresponds entirely to the creative economy of thought they are at home with. Ulrich himself had always regarded this as a rigorous rather than lax way of going about things, but when that conversation took place between himself and his sister, he felt she had touched a nerve; he could no longer bear the undecidedness he had loved, and it seemed to him it was precisely Agathe's mission to bring him to this point. And while he nonetheless continued to expostulate with her about the "rule of free spirits," she laughed and asked him whether he didn't notice that the moment he tried to set up general rules, a different man stepped into his place.

"And even though I'm sure you're right to admire him, basically you couldn't care less about him," she asserted, giving her brother a willful and challenging look. Again he felt himself prevented from answering her and remained silent, expecting an interruption at any moment, yet he couldn't make up his mind to break off the conversation. This situation gave her courage. "In the short time we've been together," she continued, "you have given me such wonderful advice about how I should live, things I would never have dared to imagine on my own, but then, every time, you've asked whether what you said was really true! It seems to me that the truth, the way you use it, is a force that abuses people!"

She did not know what gave her the right to reproach him in this way; her own life seemed so worthless to her that she really should have kept silent. But she drew her strength from Ulrich himself, and that was such a curiously feminine state, this leaning on him even as she attacked him, that he felt it too.

"You don't understand the desire to combine ideas into large, articulated masses," Ulrich said. "The combat experiences of the mind are unknown to you; all you see in them are columns marching in some kind of formation, the impersonal lockstep of many feet whirling up truth like a dust cloud!"

"But didn't you yourself describe to me, more clearly and precisely than I ever could, the two states in which you can live?" she answered.

A glowing cloud with swiftly changing outlines passed over her face. She longed to bring her brother to a point where he could no longer turn back. The thought of it filled her with fervor, but she did not know yet whether she would have enough courage, and so she postponed finishing her meal.

All this Ulrich knew, he guessed it; but now he had roused himself and addressed her resolutely. Sitting opposite her with an absent gaze, forcing his mouth to speak, he had the impression that he was not really in himself but had been left somewhere behind himself and was now calling out to himself the words he was saying. "Imagine," he said, "that while traveling it occurs to me to steal a stranger's golden cigarette case. Now I ask you, isn't that simply unthinkable?! So I don't even want to discuss whether the kind of decision you have in mind can be justified on the grounds of some higher freedom of the mind. It may even be right to do Hagauer an injury. But imagine me in a hotel, neither penniless nor a professional thief, nor a mental defective with a deformed head or body, nor do I have a hysteric for a mother or a drinker for a father, nor am I confused or stigmatized by anything else, but I steal nonetheless: I tell you again, this is a case that does not exist anywhere in the world. It simply doesn't happen! It can be ruled out with positively scientific certainty!"

Agathe laughed out loud: "But Ulo! What if one does it anyway?!"

Ulrich himself had to laugh at this answer, which he had not expected; he leapt to his feet and hastily pushed back his chair, for he did not want to encourage her with his compliance. Agathe rose from the table. "You can't do this!" he begged her.

"But Uli," she replied, "Do you think even when you dream, or do you dream that something is happening?"

This question reminded him of the assertion he had made a few days ago, that all the demands of morality point to a kind of dream state that has fled by the time they are formulated. But Agathe had already gone into her father's study, which could now be seen, lamp lit, behind two opened doors, and Ulrich, who had not followed her, saw her standing in this frame. She was holding a sheet of paper to the light and reading it. "Does she have any idea what she is taking upon herself?" he wondered. But none of the diagnostic keys that were in current use, such as nervous inferiority, neurological deficit, emotional debility and the like, seemed to fit, and in the lovely picture Agathe presented while committing her crime not a trace of greed or vengefulness or any other inner ugliness could be seen. And though with the aid of such concepts even the actions of a criminal or semi-psychotic would have seemed relatively tame and civilized to Ulrich, for there the distorted and displaced motives of ordinary life glimmer in the depths, his sister's gently savage resoluteness, in which purity and crime were indistinguishably mixed, had a stunning effect on him. He was unable to accommodate the thought that this person, who was about to commit a bad act, could be a bad person, and had to watch while Agathe took one paper after another from the desk, read it, and placed it aside as she earnestly searched for a specific document. Her determination gave the impression of having descended from another world to the plane of ordinary decisions.

As he made these observations, Ulrich was additionally disturbed by the question of why he had talked Hagauer into leaving without suspecting anything. It seemed to him that he had acted from the start as an instrument of his sister's will, and to the very last, even when he contradicted her, he had given her answers that helped her to move forward. The truth abuses people, she had said: "Very well put, but she has no idea what truth means!" Ulrich mused. "With advancing years, it gives you the gout; when you're young it's all hunting and sailing." He had sat down again. Suddenly it struck him that not only had Agathe somehow got from him what she said about truth, but also that what she was doing in the room next door was something for which he had prepared the outlines. Hadn't he said that in the highest state attainable to man there is no good and evil but only faith and doubt? That inflexible rules are inimical to the innermost nature of morality and that faith must never be more than an hour old? That in the state of faith it is not possible to do anything base? That intuition is a more passionate state than truth? And now Agathe was about to leave the sanctuary of moral constraint and venture into that boundless depth where the only choice is that between rising and sinking. She was carrying out her plan in the same way as, earlier, she had taken the medals from his hesitant hand in order to exchange the originals for the replicas, and at this moment he loved her despite her lack of conscience with the strange feeling that his own thoughts had gone from him to her and were now returning from her to him, having become poorer in deliberation but all the more redolent of the balsamic scent of freedom, like a creature of the wild. And trembling from the effort to restrain himself, he cautiously made a suggestion: "I will stay another day and consult a notary or a lawyer. What you're doing may be terribly transparent!"

But Agathe had already found out that the notary her father had employed was no longer alive. "No one knows about this any longer," she said. "Don't touch it!"

Ulrich noticed that she had taken a piece of paper and was making an attempt to imitate her father's handwriting.

Attracted by this, he had stepped closer to stand behind her. There, in a pile, lay the sheets of paper on which his father's hand had lived, its movement still palpable; and there was Agathe conjuring something almost identical onto fresh sheets of paper, like an inspired actress. It was strange watching this. The purpose for which it was happening, the thought that it was forgery, vanished. And in truth Agathe had not given this any thought at all. An aura of justice with flames instead of logic surrounded her. Goodness, decency, and law-abidance, as she had experienced these virtues in the people she knew, Hagauer in particular, had always seemed to her as if a stain had been removed from a dress; but the wrong that hovered around her at this moment was like the drowning of the world in the light of a rising sun. It seemed to her as if right and wrong were no longer general terms and a compromise arranged for millions of people, but the magical encounter of Me and You, the madness of a first creation, not yet comparable with any thing, not measurable by any standard. Essentially she was making Ulrich the gift of a crime, by placing herself in his hands, fully trusting that he would understand her rashness, much as children will come up with the most unexpected solutions when they want to give a present and have nothing to give. And Ulrich guessed most of this. As his eyes followed her movements, he experienced a pleasure he had never known, for there was an enchanting absurdity in succumbing, for once entirely and without caution, to what another being was doing. Even as the memory that harm was being done to a third person intervened, it merely flashed by for a second like an ax, and he quickly reassured himself that it really wasn't anyone's business what his sister was doing there; it was by no means certain that these handwriting experiments would actually be used, and what Agathe did inside her own four walls remained her own affair as long it had no effect beyond them.

She now called out to her brother, turned around, and was surprised to find him standing behind her. She awoke. She had written everything she wanted to write, and now resolutely held the page over the candle flame in order to make the document look old. She held out her free hand to Ulrich, who did not take it, but he was also unable to shroud his face entirely in a dark frown. Thereupon she said: "Listen! When something is a contradiction and you love it for both its sides—really love it!—doesn't that already resolve the contradiction, like it or not?!"

"This question is much too frivolously posed," Ulrich grumbled. But Agathe knew how he would judge it in his "second way of thinking." She took a clean sheet of paper and cheerfully wrote in the old-fashioned script she was so good at imitating: "My bad daughter Agathe provides no reason for changing the above provisions to the disadvantage of my good son Ulrich!" Not yet satisfied with this, she wrote on a second sheet: "My daughter Agathe is to be educated by my good son Uli for some time."

—————

So that was how it had happened, but after Ulrich had resurrected it with all its details, he ended up knowing just as little what to do as he had before he began.

He should not have left without straightening the situation out: no doubt about that! And obviously the present-day superstition that one must not take anything too seriously had played a trick when it prompted him to withdraw for the time being and not increase the value of that contentious episode with sentimental resistance. Things are never as bad as they seem; the most overblown situations, left to themselves, eventually level off to a new mediocrity; you couldn't board a train or walk in the street without having a loaded gun at the ready if you couldn't count on the law of averages, which automatically makes extreme possibilities improbable: this was the European faith in empirical knowledge that Ulrich had obeyed when, despite all his scruples, he had taken the trip home. At bottom he was even glad that Agathe had shown a different side of herself.

All the same, the conclusion of this matter, if it was to be legally unimpeachable, could only be that Ulrich now, and without delay, make up for what he had neglected. He ought to have sent his sister an immediate special delivery letter or telegram, and he realized it should have said something like, "I refuse to have anything to do with you unless . . . !" But he was not at all minded to write anything of the kind; it was simply impossible for him to do so at the moment.

Moreover, that fateful performance had been preceded by a decision to live together or at least share his house in the coming weeks, and the short time that was left before Ulrich's departure had constrained them to talk primarily about that. They had agreed provisionally on "however long it will take to work out the divorce," so that Agathe would have counsel and protection. But now, as Ulrich recalled that conversation, he also remembered an earlier remark his sister had made, that she wanted "to kill Hagauer," and evidently this "plan" had been working in her and taken on a new form. She had vigorously insisted on selling the family property quickly, which might very well have had the purpose of causing the estate to dissolve, though the sale might have seemed advisable for other reasons as well; in any case, the siblings had hired a broker and set their terms. And so Ulrich now had to consider as well the question of what would happen to his sister after he had returned to his carelessly provisional life, which he himself could not approve of. The situation she was in could not possibly continue. Surprisingly close though they had grown in the brief time they had been together—a fated crossing of their paths it seemed, though no doubt the result of all sorts of unrelated details; while Agathe perhaps had a more far-fetched view of it—they knew so little of each other in the many and various superficial respects on which a shared life depends. Indeed, when he thought of his sister impartially, Ulrich found many unresolved questions, and he could not even form a clear conception of her past; the most revealing light seemed to be shed by the conjecture that she had a very lax way of treating everything that happened through her or to her and that she lived very precariously and perhaps fantastically in expectations that ran alongside her actual life, for this at least could plausibly explain her having lived with Hagauer for so long and then broken with him so suddenly. It would also explain the indifference with which she treated the future: she had left home, that seemed to satisfy her for the time being, and as for the question of the next step, she simply avoided it. And Ulrich himself was unable either to picture her now living without a husband and waiting indefinitely like a young girl, or to imagine the man for whom his sister would be the right woman; and this he had also said to her shortly before he left.

But she had looked into his face with alarm—though probably she was clowning a bit, pretending to be alarmed—and then calmly answered with a question: "Can't I just stay with you for the time being, without our having to decide everything?"

It was in this vague way, without any more definite notion, that the idea of living together was confirmed. Ulrich realized that this experiment would put an end to his experiment of a "life on vacation." He did not want to think of the possible consequences, but the fact that his life would from now on be subject to certain restrictions was not unwelcome, and for the first time he thought again of the circle of people, and especially the women, involved in the Parallel Campaign. The prospect, entailed in this change, of cutting himself off from everything was wonderfully appealing. Just as it often takes only a small alteration in a room to turn its dull reverberations into glorious resonance, so now in his imagination his little house was transformed into a shell in which one could hear a muted echo of the city's noise, like the murmur of a distant river.

And then, toward the end of that conversation, there had been one other special little conversation:

"We will live like hermits," Agathe said with a happy smile, "but in matters of love we're both free, of course. For you at least nothing stands in the way!" she assured him.

"Do you realize," Ulrich said in reply, "that we will be moving into the Millennium?"

"What's that?"

"We've talked so much about a love that's not like a stream flowing toward a destination but is a state of being like the ocean. Now let's be honest: When you were told in school that the angels in Paradise do nothing but praise the Lord and glory in His presence, were you able to imagine this blissful state of doing nothing and thinking nothing?"

"I always imagined it must be a little boring, which is surely due to my imperfection," was Agathe's answer.

"But after everything we've agreed on," Ulrich explained, "you now have to imagine this ocean as a state of motionlessness and seclusion that is filled with everlasting crystal-clear events. In ancient times people tried to imagine such a life here on earth: that is the Millennium, the Kingdom of a Thousand Years, formed in our own image and yet not among any of the kingdoms that we know! And that is how we will live! We will cast off all self-interest, we will treasure neither goods nor knowledge, nor lovers, nor friends, nor principles, nor even ourselves. Accordingly, our spirit will open, dissolve its separation from man and beast, and thus disclose itself in such a manner that we can no longer continue as 'we' and will only maintain ourselves by being interwoven with all that is!"

This little interlude had been a joke. He had been sitting with paper and pencil, making notes and sporadically talking with his sister about what she could expect from the sale of the house and furniture. He was also still angry, and he himself didn't know whether he was blaspheming or fantasizing. And due to all this they had not got around to grappling with the matter of the will in a responsible way.

It was probably due to this confluence of multiple currents that Ulrich, still on this day, had by no means arrived at active contrition. There was much about his sister's coup de main that appealed to him, even though he himself was defeated by it. He had to admit to himself that the man living at ease "by the rule of free spirits," to whom he had granted all too much comfort within himself, had thereby with a single blow been brought into dangerous conflict with the profoundly undefined person from whom real seriousness emanates. Nor did he want to dodge the consequences of such an act by redressing it quickly and in an ordinary way: But then there was no rule, and events had to be allowed to unfold as they would.

13

DIFFICULTIES OF A MORALIST IN WRITING A LETTER

Two days later, toward evening, Ulrich sat down at his desk and began writing a letter to Agathe.

It was clear to him—as light and clear as a windless day can sometimes be—that her ill-considered venture was extremely dangerous; what had happened so far could still be regarded as a risky bit of foolishness that concerned only the two of them, but this depended completely on its being undone before it gained relationships with reality, and the danger was growing with each passing day. Ulrich had written thus far when he stopped, feeling uneasy at the thought of entrusting to the mail a letter that discussed this in undisguised terms. He told himself that it would be more suitable in every way if he himself went with the next train instead of the letter; but of course that also made little sense, since he had let days go by without doing anything about the matter, and then he knew he would not go.

He noticed there was something beneath these vacillations that was almost as firm as a resolution: he felt like simply letting things take their course and waiting to see what would come of the incident. So the problem he was faced with was merely that of determining to what extent and how consciously he could really want this, and now all sorts of far-ranging thoughts went through his head.

Right at the start he made the observation that until now, whenever he conducted himself "morally," he always found himself in a less resourceful state than when he was doing or thinking something one would usually call "immoral." This is a universal phenomenon: for when people are brought into conflict with their surroundings, they deploy all their faculties, while in situations where they are merely doing their duty they understandably behave no differently than while paying their taxes; from which we may conclude that everything bad is carried out with some degree of imagination and passion, whereas the good is distinguished by an unmistakably joyless and affectless demeanor. Ulrich remembered that his sister had expressed this moral predicament very ingenuously by asking whether being good was no longer good. It ought to be difficult and breathtaking, she had claimed, and wondered at the fact that moral people nevertheless were almost always boring.

He smiled contentedly and carried that thought forward with the observation that Agathe and he both stood in a special kind of contrast to Hagauer that could be roughly described as that of people who are bad in a good way to a man who is good in a bad way. If one leaves out of account the great middle range of life, which is, reasonably enough, occupied by people in whose thinking the general terms "good" and "evil" have simply ceased to occur ever since they let go of their mothers' apron strings, then the marginal strata, where deliberate moral efforts still exist, are indeed left to such bad-good and good-bad people, of which the former have never seen the good fly or heard it sing and therefore call on all their fellow men to share their enthusiasm for a moral landscape where stuffed birds perch on lifeless trees; whereupon the latter, the good-bad mortals, vexed by their rivals, assiduously cultivate at least in their thoughts a penchant for evil, as though they were convinced that only in bad deeds, which are not quite as shopworn as the good ones, some tremulous remnant of moral vitality still survives. And so—of course without Ulrich's being quite conscious of this foreknowledge—the world at that time had the choice between being ruined either by its lame morality or by its nimble immoralists, and probably still does not know which of the two it finally decided on with overwhelming success; unless, perhaps, the teeming many, who never have time to concern themselves with morality in general, did concern themselves with it in one particular instance, because they had lost confidence in the state of the world they lived in and of course subsequently lost a number of other things as well. For bad-bad people, whom one can so easily blame for everything, were as rare then as they are now, and the good-good represented an ideal as remote as a distant nebula. But it was precisely of them that Ulrich was thinking, while everything else he appeared to be thinking about was a matter of complete indifference to him.

And he gave his thoughts an even more general and impersonal form by putting the relationship that exists between the injunctions "Do!" and "Do not!" in the place of good and evil. For as long as a morality is in the ascendancy—and this is as true of the spirit of neighborly love as it is of the spirit of a horde of vandals—"Do not!" is merely the reverse and a natural corollary of "Do!": the doing and the not-doing are a burning passion, and whatever faults they entail hardly matter, because these are the faults of heroes and martyrs. In this condition good and evil are identical with the happiness and unhappiness of the whole person. But as soon as the contested ethos has come to power and has spread, and there are no particular obstacles to its fulfillment, the relationship between commandment and prohibition necessarily passes through a decisive stage where duty is no longer born anew and alive each day but needs to be kept at hand, leached of its substance and dissected into ifs and buts, for every kind of use and application; and thus begins a process in the course of which virtue and vice, due to their provenance in the same rules, laws, exceptions, and restrictions, come to look more and more like each other, until in the end that strange but basically unbearable self-contradiction comes about that was Ulrich's point of departure: that the distinction between good and evil loses all meaning when compared with the delight of a pure, deep, spontaneous mode of action—a thrill that can leap like a spark from sanctioned as well as from forbidden activities. Indeed, anyone inquiring into this without prejudice will probably recognize that the proscriptive part of morality is more highly charged with this tension than the prescriptive one: While it seems relatively natural that certain actions that are thought of as "bad" must not be performed, or, if one performs them nonetheless, at least should not have been performed, such as appropriating other people's property or unrestrained sensual indulgence, the corresponding affirmative moral conventions—in this case, unlimited devotion to giving or the mortification of fleshly desire—have almost been lost, and where they are still practiced, they are the business of fools and crackpots or bloodless prigs. And in such a condition, where virtue is decrepit and moral behavior consists mainly in avoiding what is immoral, it can easily happen that the latter appears to be not only more spontaneous and vigorous than the former, but actually more moral, if one may use that term not in the sense of law and justice but as a gauge of whatever passion can still be aroused by matters of conscience. But could anything be more contradictory than cultivating an inward predilection for evil because, with whatever remnants of a soul one still possesses, one is seeking the good?!

Ulrich had never experienced this contradiction more strongly than he did at the moment when the rising arc his reflections had traversed led him back to Agathe. Her innate readiness to resort to (and here again he used that cursory term) a good-bad form of expression, which had manifested itself so momentously in her tampering with their father's will, offended the same readiness in his own nature, which had taken the merely speculative form of, one might say, a pastor's admiration for the devil, while in his personal life he was not only capable of living fairly and squarely in accord with the times but, as he could see, did not wish to be disturbed in doing so. With equal degrees of melancholy satisfaction and ironic lucidity he noted that his entire theoretical preoccupation with evil amounted to wishing that he could protect evil incidents from the evil people who are itching to exploit them, and he suddenly felt a longing for goodness, as a man who has uselessly roamed about in foreign parts might imagine coming home someday and going straight to the village well to drink its water. But if this simile had not occurred to him first, he might have noticed that his entire effort to form an idea of Agathe as a morally hybrid person such as the present age produces in large numbers was only a pretext serving to shield him from a prospect that frightened him far more. For oddly enough, his sister's behavior, which could not be condoned if one examined it consciously, exerted a beguiling allure as soon as one joined her in her dream; because then all discord and division vanished, and in their stead arose an impression of a passionate, affirmative, eagerly resolute goodness that, in comparison with its enfeebled everyday forms, could very easily be mistaken for an ancient vice.

Ulrich did not easily permit himself such an exaltation of his feelings, least of all when faced with the task of writing this letter, so he now directed his thoughts back out into generalities. These reflections would have been incomplete had he not remembered how easily and how often, in the times he had lived through, the longing for a duty drawn from the fullness of life had led to now one, now another virtue being selected from the available supply and made the focus of noisy veneration. National, Christian, humanistic virtues had all taken their turn; at one point it was steely strength, then it was kindness, individuality came next, soon thereafter community, one day it was the ethos of the split second, while the day before it was historical serenity: the shifting moods of public life basically derive from the exchange of such guiding ideals; but this had always left Ulrich indifferent and only made him feel that he was standing on the sidelines. Even now, all it meant to him was a complement to the general picture, for it is only a partial understanding that can lead one to believe it possible to tackle the moral uninterpretability of life, which sets in at a level of complexity that has become too great, with interpretations that are already part of the problem. Such attempts merely resemble the movements of a sick man restlessly changing his position while the paralysis that ties him to his bed advances inexorably. Ulrich was convinced that the condition that gave rise to these efforts was inevitable and that it defined the stage at which every civilization had begun to decline, because none so far had been able to generate a new inner excitement in place of the one it had lost. He was also convinced that what had happened to every moral system in the past lay in store for every future one. For the slackening of moral intensity has nothing to do with the domain of commandments and the following of them, it is independent of their distinctions, it is not amenable to external rigor, it is an entirely inner process, marked by a lessening of the meaning of all actions and of faith in the unity of responsibility for them.

And so, without his having previously intended it, Ulrich's thoughts returned to the idea he had once jokingly characterized, in a remark to Count Leinsdorf, as the "general secretariat for precision and soul"; and even though on other occasions he had only brought it up playfully and in jest, he now realized that all his adult life he had consistently behaved as if such a "general secretariat" lay within the realm of possibility. Perhaps—he could tell himself this by way of excuse— every thinking person carries such an idea of order within himself, just as grown men still wear beneath their clothes the pictures of saints which their mothers hung around their necks when they were children, and this icon of order which no one dares to either take seriously or discard must look more or less like this: on one side it vaguely symbolizes the longing for a law of right living, an iron and natural law that allows no exception and is proof to every objection, that is as freeing as a rapture and as sober as the truth; the other side, however, represents the conviction that one's own eyes will never behold such a law, that one's own thoughts will never conceive it, that no single man's gospel and authority but only an exertion by all will bring it about, if it is not altogether a chimera. For a moment Ulrich hesitated. Undoubtedly he was a believer who just didn't believe anything: his greatest dedication to science had never succeeded in making him forget that the beauty and goodness of people comes from what they believe and not from what they know. But faith had always been bound up with knowledge, even if only an imagined knowledge, ever since the primordial days of its magical origin. And this ancient component of knowledge has long since rotted and has pulled faith down with it into the same decay: the task now, therefore, is to establish that connection anew. And, of course, not simply in a manner that raises faith "to the level of knowledge"; but rather in such a way that it takes wing from that height. The art of rising above knowledge must be practiced again. And since this cannot be done by any one person, all human beings would have to turn their minds to it, whatever else their minds might be occupied with; and when Ulrich at this moment thought of a ten-year, a hundred-year, or a thousand-year plan humanity would have to adopt in order to direct its efforts toward that goal, he did not have to inquire very far to realize that this was what he had long imagined, under all sorts of names, as the truly experimental life. For what he meant by the word "faith" was not that stunted wanting-to-know, that credulous ignorance that generally goes by the name of faith, but rather an intuitive knowing that is neither knowledge, nor imagination, nor belief either, but precisely that "other" quality that eludes all these terms.

With a quick movement he pulled the letter toward himself, but immediately pushed it away again.

The austere fervor that had lit up his face just a moment ago was extinguished, and his dangerous pet idea struck him as ridiculous. As though with a glance through a suddenly opened window he sensed what was really around him: the guns, the commerce of Europe. The notion that people who lived in this fashion could ever join together for a deliberate navigation of their spiritual destiny was simply impossible to conceive, and Ulrich had to admit that historical development had also never been the result of any planned association of ideas such as may, in a pinch, be possible in the mind of an individual, but was always prodigal in spirit and hence wasteful in effect, as if scattered onto the table by the fist of an uncouth gambler. He even felt a little ashamed. Everything he had thought in this hour was suspiciously reminiscent of a certain "Survey for the Drafting of a Guiding Resolution and to Ascertain the Wishes of Participant Circles of the Population,"* and the very activity of moralizing, this theoretical way of thinking that observes nature by candlelight, struck him as utterly unnatural, unlike the operations of the simple man, who, accustomed to seeing things in the clear light of day, always reaches only for what is nearest at hand and never troubles himself with any question other than the particular one of whether his grasp will succeed in holding that object securely.

At this moment, Ulrich's thoughts streamed back from generalities to himself, and he felt the importance of his sister. It was to her that he had shown that strange, unconditional, incredible, and un-

---

*This is the title of one of the Parallel Campaign's eccentric resolutions.

forgettable state in which everything is a yes. The state in which one is capable of no spiritual movement other than that of morality, and hence also the only condition in which there is a morality without interruption, even if it should only consist in all actions hovering groundlessly within it. And all that Agathe had done was reach out for this possibility. She was the person whose hand reaches out, and into the place of Ulrich's reflections there now entered the bodies and forms of the real world.

Everything he had been thinking now appeared to him as mere delay and transition. He decided to "chance it" and see what would come of Agathe's whim, and at this moment it was a matter of complete indifference to him that the mysterious promise it held had begun with what by ordinary standards was a disgraceful act. It remained to be seen whether the morality of "rising and sinking" would turn out to be as applicable to this state of affairs as the simple morality of honesty. And he remembered his sister's passionate question of whether he himself believed what he was telling her; but even now he was as unable to answer it with a simple "yes" as he had been at the time. He admitted to himself that he was waiting for Agathe in order to answer this question.

The telephone rang shrilly and Walter, at the other end of the line, was suddenly flooding him with rushed explanations and hastily bundled words. Ulrich listened indifferently and obligingly, and when he had put the receiver down and stood up, it was as if the ring tone were still fading in his ear; depth and darkness streamed back into his surroundings. The effect was soothing, but he would not have been able to say if it happened in sounds or in colors. It was like a depth of all the senses. Smiling, he took the sheet of paper on which he had begun writing to his sister and tore it slowly into small pieces before leaving the room.

14

THROW EVERYTHING YOU HAVE INTO THE FIRE, INCLUDING YOUR SHOES

DURING this time and from the moment when she had stayed behind alone, Agathe had been living completely at ease, released from the tension of all relationships, in a serenely melancholy suspension of the will, as if at a great height where there was nothing to be seen but the wide blue sky. Every day she strolled for her pleasure through the town; she read when she was at home; she attended to her affairs: she experienced this mild, aimless activity of living with grateful appreciation. Nothing troubled the state she was in, no clinging to the past, no straining for the future; when her gaze fell on any of the objects in her vicinity, it was as if she were coaxing a young lamb to come near; it would either gently approach her, or else simply take no notice of her—but she never took mental possession of it with that motion of inner grasping that imbues every act of cold recognition with something violent and yet futile, for it scares away the happiness that is in things. And so it seemed to Agathe that everything around her was much more understandable than usual, but it was her conversations with her brother that mainly occupied her mind. In keeping with her unusually exact memory, which did not deform its material with intentions and prejudices, there now rose up around her again the living words, the surprising little inflections of voice and gesture accompanying the talk; but these came out of sequence and rather the way they had been before Agathe had quite understood them and realized what they wanted. Nevertheless, it was all in the highest degree meaningful; her memory, which had so often been haunted by remorse, was now full of quiet affection, and the recent past lay sensuously close to the warmth of the body, instead of losing itself, as it usually did, in the frost and darkness that lie in wait for what has been lived in vain.

And in this way, wrapped in invisible light, Agathe also spoke with the lawyers, notaries, and businessmen her path led her to. Nowhere did she meet with rejection; everyone was happy to oblige the charming young woman, who came recommended by her father's name, with everything she desired. She conducted herself with an air that combined assurance and absence in equal measure: what she had resolved upon was outside herself, as it were, and the experience she had gained in life—something else that can be distinguished from the essential person—continued working on that resolution like a hired agent who calmly and cleverly exploits opportunities that offer themselves to his task; that she was preparing to commit a fraud— which to a neutral observer would be the most obvious meaning of her actions—did not penetrate to her own perception at the time. The unity of her conscience excluded it. The radiance of her conscience outshone this dark point, which nevertheless, like the core of a flame, formed its center. Agathe herself did not know how to express it: As a result of her intent she found herself in a state that was as far from that ugly intent as the sky is from the earth.

Already in the morning after her brother left, Agathe had observed her appearance very closely: it had begun by accident with her face, when her glance had fallen on it and not come back out of the mirror. She was held fast the way sometimes one may not feel like walking at all, yet walks another hundred steps and then another hundred and a hundred more all the way to some object that comes into view only now, at which point one really decides to turn back, but again does not do so. In this way, without vanity, she was captivated by the landscape of her self that lay before her behind a vaporous film of glass. She moved on to her hair, which was still like light velvet; she opened the collar of her reflection's dress and slipped the dress off its shoulders; finally, she undressed it completely and examined it down to the rosy nails, where the body ends in hands and feet and scarcely belongs to itself anymore. Everything was still like the sparkling day approaching its zenith: ascendant, pure, exact, and afloat on that slowing arc of becoming that is the time before noon and that manifests itself in a human being or a young animal as it does in a ball that has almost, but not quite, reached its highest point in the air. "Maybe it's passing through that point at this moment," Agathe thought. This notion frightened her. But actually it could take a while yet: she was only twenty-seven. Her body, as uninfluenced by athletic coaches and masseurs as it was by childbearing and the tasks of motherhood, had been formed by nothing but its own growth. If it could have been set naked into one of those grand and lonely landscapes that are formed by the sky-facing side of a high mountain range, the vast, infertile, billowing swell of such an elevation would have carried her like a pagan goddess. In nature of this kind, noon does not pour down swaths of light and heat, it merely seems to rise beyond its zenith for a while and imperceptibly shades into the sinking, hovering beauty of the afternoon. From the mirror came the slightly uncanny sense of that imponderable hour.

Just then it occurred to Agathe that Ulrich too was letting his life go by as if it would last forever. "Maybe it's a mistake that we didn't meet as old people," she said to herself, and had a melancholy vision of two banks of fog sinking to the ground in the evening. "They're not as beautiful as a radiant noon," she thought, "but what do these two shapeless gray things care how people feel about them! Their hour has come and is as soft as the most glowing noonday hour!" She had nearly turned her back to the mirror, but there was a taste for hyperbole in her mood that suddenly provoked her to turn around again, and now she had to laugh at the memory of a fat couple at a Marienbad spa she had observed years ago, sitting on a green bench and caressing each other with the utmost tenderness and delicacy of feeling. "Their hearts are slim too, beating under all that fat, and because they're entranced by the inner view, they don't know how amusing they look from outside," Agathe told herself in self-reproach and made the face of someone swooning in rapture, trying at the same time to make herself look fat by squeezing her body and squashing it into pudgy folds. When this bout of exuberance had passed, it looked just as though tiny tears of anger had risen to her eyes, and coolly pulling herself together, she returned to a dispassionate, objective scrutiny of her appearance. Although she was considered slender, she detected in her limbs the interesting possibility that they could become heavy. Also her chest was possibly too broad. The very white skin of the face was dimmed by blond hair as though by candles burning in daylight; the nose stood out a little too far, and on one side its almost classical line was dented at the tip. Indeed, it might well be that everywhere in the flame-like basic form a second form was hiding that was broader and more melancholic, like a linden leaf that has fallen among laurel branches. Agathe became curious about herself, as if she were looking at herself for the first time. This could very well be how the men she had become involved with had seen her, and she herself had known nothing about it. There was something unsettling about this feeling. But by some vagary of the imagination, before she could call her memories to account about this, she heard behind everything she had experienced the ardent, long-drawn-out mating cry of the donkey, which had always strangely excited her: it sounds utterly foolish and ugly, but just for that reason there may be no second heroism of love as disconsolately sweet as his. She shrugged her shoulders at the life she had led and turned back to her image with the firm intention of finding a place in it where her appearance was already yielding to age. There were the little areas near the eyes and ears that are the first to develop fine wrinkles that make them look as if something had slept on them, or the round beneath the inner side of the breasts, which so easily loses its definition: it would have given her satisfaction at this moment and a promise of peace to observe a change of this kind, but there was still none to be perceived anywhere, and the beauty of the body floated almost eerily in the depth of the mirror.

At this moment it struck Agathe as really strange that she was Frau Hagauer, and the difference between the densely defined relationship that was constituted thereby and the inward wake of uncertainty that flowed back to her from it was so strong that she herself seemed to be standing there without a body, while the body in the mirror seemed to belong to Frau Hagauer; and it was up to

Frau Hagauer to come to terms with that body, since it had pledged itself to circumstances that were beneath its dignity. Even in this there was something of that buoyant delight in being alive that can sometimes resemble fright, and the first thing Agathe decided, after hastily getting dressed, led her into her bedroom to look for a capsule that had to be in her luggage. This small airtight capsule, which had been in her possession for almost as long as she had been married to Hagauer, and from which she never parted, contained a tiny amount of a drab-looking substance she had been promised was a deadly poison. Agathe remembered certain sacrifices she had needed to make in order to acquire this forbidden substance, about which she knew only what she had been told about its effect, along with one of those chemical names that sound like a magic formula which the uninitiated must memorize without understanding it. But apparently all the devices that bring the end a little closer, like the possession of poison or weapons or the pursuit of survivable adventures, belong to the romanticism of joie de vivre; and it may be that the course of most people's lives is so depressed, so erratic, with so much darkness in the light and altogether so perverse that life's indwelling joy can only be released by a far-off possibility of putting an end to it. Agathe felt reassured when her eyes lit on the small metal object that appeared to her, in the uncertainty that lay ahead, as a bringer of luck and a talisman.

So this did not at all mean that Agathe at that time already intended to kill herself. On the contrary, she feared death exactly the way every young person does when the thought occurs, for instance before falling asleep after a wholesomely spent day: "It can't be avoided: there will be a day just as fine as today, and I will be dead." Nor does it make one feel like dying when one has to watch someone else die, and her father's demise had tormented her with impressions whose horrors had reemerged ever since she had stayed behind in the house after her brother's departure. But: "I am a little dead"—this was a feeling Agathe had often. And especially at moments like this, just after she had been conscious of her young body's shapeliness and health, of this taut beauty that in its mysterious composition is as groundless as the decomposition of the elements at death, she could easily fall from a state of happy security into one of trepidation, awe, and silence such as one feels when stepping out of a room full of lively activity and suddenly finding oneself beneath the glitter of the stars. Despite the resolutions that were stirring inside her, and despite her satisfaction at having rescued herself from a failed life, she now felt at a slight remove from herself, and only tenuously connected to herself. Coolly she thought of death as a condition of being released from all toils and illusions, and pictured it as an intimate, gentle lulling to sleep: one lies in God's hand, and this hand is like a cradle or a hammock slung between two tall trees and faintly swaying in the wind. She imagined death as a great tranquility and fatigue, free of all wanting, all effort, all attention and thought, rather like the pleasant feebleness one feels in one's fingers when sleep carefully loosens their hold on some last thing in the world they were still holding on to. Without question this indolent and casual conception of dying was consistent with the needs of a person who is not fond of the exertions of living, and in the end she amused herself with the observation that this reminded her of the divan she had brought into her father's austere drawing room so that she could lie on it, reading—the only change she had made in the house on her own initiative.

Nevertheless, the thought of giving up life was anything but a game for Agathe. It seemed profoundly believable to her that after so much fruitless agitation a state of blissful repose should follow, which inadvertently assumed a kind of corporeal substance in her imagination. She experienced it this way because she felt no need for the stirring illusion that the world can be improved, and because she was at all times prepared to relinquish her share in the world completely, so long as that could be done in a pleasant fashion; besides, she had already had a special encounter with death in that unusual sickness that had befallen her on the borderline between childhood and girlhood. That was when—in a scarcely perceptible depletion of her strength, which seemed to inject itself into each tiniest span of time even while, as a whole, it advanced with irresistible speed—more and more parts of her body fell away from her and vanished into the void; but in step with this decline and this turning away from life, there had been an unforgettable new striving toward a goal that banished all the agitation and fear that came with her illness, a curiously meaningful state in which she was even able to exert a certain domination over the adults around her, while they became increasingly unsure of themselves. It is not inconceivable that this advantage, which she had come to know under such impressive circumstances, later formed the nucleus of her spiritual readiness to withdraw from life in a similar fashion if, for some reason, the excitements it offered did not correspond to her expectations; but more probably it was the other way around and the illness that enabled her to escape the demands of school and home was the first expression of her transparent relationship to the world, which made her permeable, as it were, to a ray of feeling she could not explain. For Agathe felt herself to be of a spontaneous, simple disposition, warm, lively, even fun-loving and easily satisfied, and indeed she had adapted herself amicably to many very different kinds of situations; nor had she ever experienced that collapse into indifference that befalls women who can no longer bear their disillusionment: but in the midst of the laughter or the tumult of sensual adventuring that still continued, there was a sense of debasement that made every fiber of her body tired and nostalgic for something else, the most nearly accurate name of which would probably have to be Nothing.

This Nothing had a definite, albeit undefinable, content. For a long time, on many occasions, she had recited to herself a saying by Novalis: "What, then, can I do for my soul, which dwells within me like an unsolved riddle, granting the visible man the utmost license, because it cannot govern him in any way?" But always the flickering light of these words fell back into darkness after a lightning-swift flash of recognition, for she did not believe in a soul, as that seemed too presumptuous and also too definite a notion to apply to herself. But neither could she believe in the earthly domain. To understand this rightly, one need only to realize that this turning away from the earthly order without a belief in a supernatural order is something profoundly natural, for in every mind, the strict and simple order of logic, which mirrors the outer conditions, is accompanied by an affective order whose logic, if one may call it that, corresponds to the nature of feelings, passions, and moods. The laws governing these two bear roughly the same relationship to each other as those of a lumberyard where chunks of wood are hewn into rectangular blocks and stacked ready for transport and the laws of the forest in their dark convolutions and mysterious rustling commotion. And since the objects of our thinking are by no means independent of the state our thinking is in, these two modes of thought not only mingle in each person, but can to a certain degree confront him with two worlds, at least immediately before and after that "first occult and indescribable instant" that, according to a famous religious thinker, occurs in every sense perception before feeling and view separate and occupy the places where one is accustomed to find them: as a thing in space and a contemplation that is now locked into the observer.

Whatever the relationship between things and feelings in the mature weltanschauung of civilized man may be, everyone knows those moments of ardor in which a split has not yet occurred, as though the waters had not yet been divided from the land and the waves of feeling still shared the same horizon with the heights and valleys that form the appearance of things. One need not even assume that Agathe experienced such moments unusually often or with uncommon intensity; she just apprehended them more vividly, or if one prefers, more superstitiously, for she was always prepared to believe the world and then again not to believe it, just as she had done since her school days, nor had she unlearned this habit after coming into closer contact with the logic of men. In this sense, which is far removed from whim and caprice, Agathe, had she been more self-confident, would have been entitled to claim that she was the most illogical of women. But it had never occurred to her to regard the averted feelings she experienced as more than a personal idiosyncrasy. It was only the encounter with her brother that brought about a change in her. In those cavernous rooms, hollowed out in the shadows of solitude and just recently filled with talk and a fellowship that touched the innermost core of the soul, the distinction between physical separation and spiritual presence fell away, and as the days glided along without a mark or a trace, Agathe felt, more intensely than ever before, the peculiar attraction of omnipresence and omnipotence that arises when the felt world crosses over into the world of perceptions. Her attention now seemed to be not with the senses but wide open deep within her heart, which could and would not receive anything as true that did not shine with the same radiance as its own, and as she remembered the words she had heard from her brother, she reckoned that, in spite of the ignorance of which she usually accused herself, she understood everything that mattered without having to think about it. And now that her spirit was so filled with itself that even the liveliest insight had something of the soundless floating quality of a memory, everything that came her way expanded into a limitless presence; even when she did something, all that actually happened was that some difference between herself as the agent and the act that was being performed melted away, and her movement seemed to be the path by which things came toward her of themselves when her arm reached out to them. But this gentle power, her knowing, and the speaking presence of the world were, when she smilingly asked herself what she was doing, hardly distinguishable from a complete absence of power and a wordless silence of the mind. With only a slight exaggeration of what she was experiencing, Agathe could have said that she no longer knew where she was. On all sides she was in a state of suspension in which she felt herself to be simultaneously lifted up and vanished from the scene. She might have said: I am in love, but I don't know with whom. She was filled with a clear will, which she had always felt a lack of, but she could not imagine what she could possibly do in this clarity, for all the good and evil there had been in her life had no meaning.

So it was not only while contemplating the capsule with the poison but every day that Agathe thought that she would like to die, or that the happiness of death must be something like the happiness in which she was spending these days while she was waiting to go and join her brother and meanwhile doing precisely what he had begged her to refrain from doing. She had no idea what would happen once she was with her brother in the capital. Almost reproachfully she remembered that from time to time he would casually intimate that he expected she would be successful there and soon find a new husband or at least a lover; but that was precisely how it was not going to be, this she knew! Love, children, happy days, lighthearted company, trips and a little art—: the good life was so simple, she understood and was not unresponsive to its appeal. But ready though she was to regard herself as useless, Agathe harbored all the born rebel's contempt for such homespun simplicity. She recognized it as an imposture. The life supposedly lived to the full is in reality "without rhyme or reason," and in the end, and truly at the real end, death, something is always missing in it. It is—she searched for a way to express it—like lots of things heaped together, instead of being ordered by a higher aspiration: unfulfilled in its fullness, the opposite of simplicity, just a jumble that one accepts with habitual pleasure! And suddenly going off on a tangent, she thought: "It's like a crowd of unknown children you look at with conventional friendliness, filled with growing anxiety because you can't find your own child among them!"

It calmed her that she had resolved to put an end to her life if the new turn that was still in store for her did not bring about a change. Like the fermentation in wine, there was a streaming anticipation in her that death and terror would not be the last word of truth. She felt no need to think about it. She even felt afraid of this need, to which Ulrich so readily yielded, and it was a belligerent fear. For she sensed that everything that took hold of her with such power was not entirely free of a persistent hint that it was merely an illusion. But it was just as certain that within the illusion there was a flowing, diffuse reality: perhaps a reality that had not yet become earth, she thought: and in one of those wonderful moments when the place where she stood seemed to dissolve into the unknown, she was able to believe that behind her, in the space one could never see, maybe God was standing. It was too much, and it frightened her. An immense vastness and emptiness suddenly flooded her, a shoreless radiance darkened her mind and instilled terror in her heart. Her youth—easily given to the anxieties of inexperience—whispered warnings that she was in danger of allowing an incipient madness to grow: She struggled to turn back. Fiercely she remonstrated with herself that she did not believe in God at all. And in fact she had not believed in God ever since she had been taught to do so—a subdivision of the mistrust she had developed toward everything she had been taught. She was not in the least religious in that concrete sense that suffices for an otherworldly or even just a moral conviction. But, exhausted and trembling, she had to admit after a while that she had felt "God" as clearly as she would a man standing behind her and placing a coat around her shoulders.

After she had thought about it enough to regain her boldness, she discovered that the meaning of what she had experienced did not lie in that "solar eclipse" of her physical sensations; rather, its meaning was mainly a moral one. A sudden transformation of her innermost condition and consequently of all her relations with the world had for a moment lent her that "unity of the conscience with the senses" that she had previously only known through intimations so faint that its evidence in her ordinary life amounted to little more than a tinge of something desolate and dolefully passionate, no matter if Agathe tried to act in a good way or a bad way. It seemed to her that this transformation had been an incomparable surging flow that emanated both from her surroundings toward her and from herself toward them, a oneness of the most exalted meaning with the slightest movements of the mind, which were scarcely distinguishable from the things around her. Things had become pervaded by feelings and feelings by things in such a convincing manner that Agathe felt she had never been so much as touched by anything to which previously she would have applied the word "conviction." And this had happened in circumstances that by ordinary standards ruled out the possibility of being convinced.

So the meaning of what she experienced in her solitude did not lie in the psychological role it might have played as a sign of a high-strung or fragile personality, for it did not lie in the personal sphere at all, but in something universal, or in the nexus between the personal and the universal, which Agathe not unjustly regarded as a moral one, in the sense that it seemed to this young woman who was so deeply disappointed in herself that if she were granted the ability to always live as she did in those minutes of exception, and if she were not too weak to persist in that state, she would be able to love the world and comply with its ways in good grace; and that otherwise she would not be able to do so! Now she was filled with a passionate longing to return there, but such moments of supreme intensity cannot be recovered by force; and it was only when her tempestuous efforts proved futile that she realized, with the clarity a pale day assumes after the sun has gone down, that the only thing she could hope for, and was in fact waiting for with an impatience that had merely concealed itself beneath her solitude, was that strange prospect her brother had once half-jokingly proclaimed as the Thousand-Year Kingdom, or the Millennium. He could just as well have chosen a different word for it, for what it meant to Agathe was only the convincing and confident ring of something that is on its way. She would not have said this out loud. After all, even now she was not sure yet if it was truly possible. She did not even know what it was. At this moment she had forgotten all the words her brother had used to prove that beyond what was imbuing her spirit with mere shining nebulae, the realm of possibility extended beyond measure. But for as long as she had been with him she had always had the feeling that a country was taking shape from his words, and that this land was not forming in her head, but truly beneath her feet. The very fact that he often only talked about it ironically, and in general his alternations between coolness and emotion, which had often confused her in the past, now gladdened Agathe in her solitude as a warrant that he meant it in earnest, which is an advantage all unfriendly states of mind have over moods of rapture. "I was probably only thinking of death because I'm afraid he doesn't mean it seriously enough," she admitted to herself.

The last day she had to spend in absentia took her by surprise; suddenly everything in the house was tidied up and cleared out, and all that remained was to hand over the keys to the old couple, who were being pensioned off under the provisions of the will and would stay behind in the servants' cottage until the property found a new owner. Agathe had refused to move into the hotel and wanted to stay at the house until it was time to go to the train station between midnight and morning. The whole house was packed up and shrouded. A single bulb was lit. Some crates had been pushed together to serve as a table and a chair. At the edge of a ravine, on a terrace of crates, a tablecloth and cutlery had been laid out for dinner. Her father's old servant balanced a loaded tray through light and shadow; he and his wife had insisted on helping from their own kitchen, so that the "gracious young lady," as they put it, should be properly served when dining for the last time in her parental home. And suddenly Agathe thought, completely outside the spirit in which she had spent these days: "Could they have noticed something after all?" It was not in-conceivable that she had neglected to destroy all the sheets of paper on which she had practiced before changing the will. She felt cold terror, the nightmare weight of fear that clings to every limb, the miserly fear of reality that gives nothing to the spirit but only depletes it. At that moment she became fiercely aware of her newly awakened desire to live. It rebelled violently against the possibility of her being prevented from doing so. When the old servant returned, she searched his face. But the old man went unsuspectingly to and fro with his cautious smile, steeped in a silent and solemn emotion of his own. She could not peer into him any more than she could see the inside of a wall; impossible to know whether there was anything else behind that blank glitter. She too now felt a mute solemnity and sadness. He had always been her father's confidant, always ready to betray every one of his children's secrets to him: but Agathe had been born in this house, and everything that had happened since was coming to an end today, and it moved her that she and he were now solemn and alone. She formed the resolution to give him a special small gift of money, and in sudden weakness decided to say it was from Professor Hagauer— not out of cunning, but as an act of atonement and with the intention of leaving nothing undone, even though it was clear to her that this was as inexpedient as it was superstitious. Before the old man returned, she also took out her two little containers, the poison capsule and the locket with the image of her unforgotten beloved. The locket she pushed, after a last frowning look at the young man, under the cover of a loosely nailed crate destined to go into storage indefinitely and apparently filled with kitchenware or lighting fixtures, for she heard metal clinking against metal, like branches falling from a tree; but the capsule with the poison she put in the place where she had formerly worn the portrait.

"How unmodern I am!" she thought with a smile as she did so. "I'm sure there are more important things than experiences with love!" But she didn't believe it.

At this moment it could no more be said that she rejected the thought of entering into illicit relations with her brother than that it was something she wished for. That might depend on the future; but nothing in her present state of mind was definite enough to formulate such a question.

The light painted the crates surrounding her a glaring white and deep black. And a thought came, wearing a similar tragic mask that gave its otherwise simple meaning an uncanny expression, that she was now spending her last evening in the house where she had been born of a woman she had never been able to remember, and of whom Ulrich had also been born. An impression crept up on her from her earliest days, that clowns with deadly serious faces and strange instruments were standing around her. They began to play. Agathe recognized it as a waking dream from her childhood. She could not hear this music, but all the clowns were looking at her. She told herself that at this moment her death would be no loss to anyone or anything, and that for herself it might mean no more than the outer conclusion of an inner extinction. So she thought while the clowns made their music swell all the way up to the ceiling, and she seemed to be sitting on a circus floor covered with sawdust, and tears dropped onto her fingers. It was a feeling of profound futility that she had often felt as a young girl, and she thought: "I suppose I never stopped being childish," which however did not prevent her from thinking, as of something that looked immeasurably great through her tears, that right at the start of their reunion she and her brother had come face-to-face wearing clown garments much like these. "What does it mean that what

I have inside me should have attached itself to my brother, of all people?" she asked herself. And suddenly she was really weeping—out of sheer happiness, it seemed: she could not have given any other reason for it. She shook her head violently, as though there were something inside it that she could neither pull apart nor bring together.

All the while she imagined with natural naivete that Ulrich would surely find an answer to all questions, until the old man came back into the room and was moved by the sight of her emotion. "The gracious young lady…," he said, likewise shaking his head. Agathe looked at him in confusion, but as soon as she realized the misunderstanding that underlay this expression of sympathy, which had gone out to what he took be her childlike grief, her youthful exuberance returned. "Throw everything you have into the fire, down to your shoes. When you have nothing more, think not even of a shroud and throw yourself naked into the fire," she said to him. It was an ancient saying which Ulrich had read aloud to her with great delight, and the old man bared his damaged teeth in a smile that betokened understanding of the grave and gentle sweep of the words, which she recited to him with eyes that glowed beneath her tears, and following the movement of his mistress's hand, which was intended to facilitate his understanding by misdirecting it, he looked at the steep tower of crates that were heaped up almost like a pyre. At the mention of the shroud, he had nodded comprehendingly, eager to follow, though the path the words took seemed to him not quite level; but at the word "naked" he stiffened, and when Agathe repeated her saying, his face had reverted to the mask of the well-trained servant whose expression conveys assurance that he will neither see, hear, nor judge.

For as long as he had served his old master, this word had not once been uttered in his presence; if the need had ever arisen, "undressed" might have been the word. But young people were different nowadays, and most likely he would no longer be able to serve to their satisfaction. With the serenity of the hour when the day's work is done, he felt that his career was at an end. But Agathe's last thought before leaving was: "Would Ulrich really throw everything into the fire?"

15

FROM KONIATOWSKI'S CRITIQUE OF DANIELLI'S THEOREM TO THE FALL OF MAN. FROM THE FALL OF MAN TO THE EMOTIONAL RIDDLE OF THE SISTER

THE STATE in which Ulrich stepped into the street when he left Count Leinsdorf's palace resembled the matter-of-fact feeling of hunger; he halted in front of a billboard and sated his hunger for bourgeois normality by sampling the various announcements and advertisements. The board was several meters wide and covered with words. "Actually," it occurred to him, "it's not unreasonable to suppose that these words, which are repeated at every corner of the city, could be enlightening." They seemed akin to the stock phrases uttered by the characters of popular novels at significant junctures of their lives. He read: "Have you ever worn anything as pleasant and practical as the Tropinam silk stocking?" "His Excellence enjoying himself." "Saint Bartholomew's Night, revised." "Convivial Cheer at the Black Knight." "Erotic Panache and Dancing at the Red Knight." Next to that notice was a political attack on "nefarious machinations": it didn't refer to the Parallel Campaign, though, but to the price of bread. He walked on and looked into a bookstore window. THE GREAT AUTHOR'S LATEST WORK, it said on a cardboard sign next to a row of fifteen copies of the same book. In the opposite corner of the display window, another sign drew attention to a second work: LADIES AND GENTLEMEN ALIKE ARE ENTHRALLED BY 'LOVE'S TOWER OF BABEL' BY...

"Great author?" Ulrich thought. He remembered reading one of his books and concluding that he did not need to read a second one: the man had become famous since. And in view of this showcase of the German mind and spirit, Ulrich remembered an old joke from his army days: "Mortadella." That had been the nickname of an unpopular general, after the popular Italian cold cut, and if someone asked for the solution to the riddle, the answer was: "Half pig, half donkey." Ulrich was inclined to spin variations from this intriguing analogy, but was prevented from doing so by a woman who addressed him with the words: "Are you waiting for the streetcar too?" at which point he realized that he was no longer standing in front of the bookshop, and that moreover he had walked on and now stood motionless by a streetcar stop.

The lady who brought this to his attention was wearing a knapsack and spectacles; she was an acquaintance of his, a member of the Astronomical Institute and one of the few women who make important contributions to this masculine discipline. His gaze settled on her nose and the bags beneath her eyes, which had come to resemble gutta-percha sweat shields from the habitual strain of intellectual labor; then he noticed beneath these foci her short loden skirt, and above them a grouse feather on a green hat that hovered above her learned features, and he smiled. "Off to the mountains?" he asked.

Dr. Strastil was indeed going to the mountains for three days of "recreation." "What do you think of Koniatowski's paper?" she asked Ulrich. Ulrich said nothing. "It will infuriate Kneppler," she said. "But Koniatowski's critique of Kneppler's deduction from Danielli's Theorem is interesting, don't you agree? Do you think this deduction is tenable?"

Ulrich shrugged. He was one of those mathematicians, called logicians, for whom nothing was ever correct and who were building a new fundamental theory. But he considered the logicians' logic to be not quite right either. Had he continued his work, he would have fallen back on Aristotle; he had his own views about that.

"Even so, I don't think Kneppler's deduction is off the mark, it's just wrong," Dr. Strastil confessed. She could just as well have emphasized that she considered the deduction to be off the mark but nevertheless, in its basic tenets, not wrong; she knew what she meant, but in ordinary language, where words are not defined, no one can express himself unequivocally: as she made use of this vacation language, something beneath her sightseer's hat stirred with the kind of nervous hauteur that might be aroused in a cloistered monk when he carelessly comes into contact with the sensual world of the laity.

Ulrich got into the streetcar with Fräulein Strastil: he didn't know why. Maybe because Koniatowski's critique of Kneppler seemed so important to her. Maybe he wanted to talk with her about literature, which she knew nothing about. "What will you do in the mountains?" he asked.

She wanted to climb the Hochschwab.

"There'll still be too much snow there," he said, for he knew the mountains. "It's too late to get up there on skis, and too early to go up without them."

"Then I'll stay at the bottom," Fräulein Strastil declared. "I once spent three days in one of the huts at the foot of the Färsenalm. All I want is a bit of nature!"

The face this worthy astronomer made while pronouncing the word "nature" provoked Ulrich to ask what it was that nature had to offer her.

Dr. Strastil was sincerely indignant. She could lie on that pasture for three days straight without moving: "Like a boulder!" she pro claimed.

"That's only because you're a scientist!" Ulrich interjected. "A peasant would be bored!"

Dr. Strastil did not agree. She spoke of the thousands who sought nature every holiday on foot, on wheels, or by boat.

Ulrich spoke of rural migration, the peasants' attraction to city life.

Fräulein Strastil doubted that he was feeling at a sufficiently elemental level.

Ulrich asserted that the only elemental requirement, next to food and love, was comfort, not a trek to an Alpine meadow. The supposedly natural feeling that drove people to do such things, he said, was a modern Rousseauism, a complicated and sentimental attitude. He did not feel that he was expressing himself well at all, he did not care what he was saying, he only went on speaking because it was still not whatever it was he wanted to bring out from within himself. Fräulein

Strastil cast a mistrustful glance at him. She could not make him out; her great experience with abstract concepts was not of the slightest use to her, she could neither distinguish nor fit together the notions he seemed to be merely tossing around with a certain alacrity; she assumed he was talking without thinking. That she was listening to such words with a grouse feather in her hat was her only satisfaction and increased the pleasure with which she looked forward to her solitary retreat.

At that moment Ulrich's glance fell on his neighbor's newspaper, and he read the bold headline of an advertisement: "Our Time Provokes Questions—And Answers Them": it could have been a recommendation of a new arch support or a lecture, there's really no way of telling these days, but his thoughts suddenly jumped into the track he needed. His companion made an effort to be objective: "Unfortunately," she confessed hesitantly, "I don't know much about literature, our like never has enough time. And maybe I haven't even read the right things. But X, for instance"—she mentioned a popular name—"X is unbelievably rich for me. I find that when a writer can make us feel things so intensely, this is greatness!" However, since Ulrich felt he had already received enough benefit from Dr. Strastil's combination of extraordinarily developed capacity for abstract thought with noticeably stunted emotional intelligence, he stood up cheerfully, gave his colleague an extravagant compliment, and hastily got off under the pretext of having already gone two stops too far. Standing on the street, he raised his hat to her once more, and Fräulein Strastil, remembering that she had recently heard disparaging remarks about his contributions, felt humanly moved by a wave of blood that had been aroused by his gracious parting words, an effect that to her way of thinking did not exactly speak for him; he, however, now knew, without yet quite knowing completely, why his thoughts were revolving around the subject of literature and what they were after, from the interrupted Mortadella comparison to the way he had unconsciously led good Dr. Strastil to make those confessions. After all, literature had ceased to be of any concern to him since he had written his last poem, at the age of twenty; even so, there had been a period before that when writing in secret had been a fairly regular habit, and he had given it up not because he had grown older or because he had realized he lacked sufficient talent, but for reasons that now, given his current impressions, he would most likely have characterized with a word that expresses a great deal of effort flowing into the void.

For Ulrich was one of those book lovers who do not like reading anymore because they feel that the whole business of writing and reading is a plague. "If the rational Strastil wants to be 'made to feel,'" he thought ("And she's right about that! If I had contradicted her, she would have invoked music as her crown witness!"), and, as often happens, his thinking partly took place in words and partly impinged on the mind as a wordless objection: so if the sensible Dr. Strastil wanted to be made to feel, what it amounted to was what everyone wants from art, which is to be moved, overwhelmed, entertained, surprised, to be granted a whiff of noble ideas, in short to be given a "vital experience" by a work that itself brings something "to life." Not that Ulrich was at all opposed to that. In a subsidiary train of thought that ended as a mixture of faint sentimentality and reluctant irony, he reflected: "Feeling is rare enough. Protecting a certain temperature of feeling from cooling down probably helps to maintain the brooding conditions for every kind of cognitive development. And when a person is lifted out of the hodgepodge of intelligent intentions that enmesh him with innumerable foreign objects, and finds himself for a few moments in a condition that is wholly without purpose—for example, while listening to music—he is almost in the state of being of a flower on which rain and sunshine fall." He was ready to admit that there is a more eternal eternity in the human mind's pauses and quiescence than in its activity; but now he noticed that his thoughts had moved from "feeling" to "experiencing," and this entailed a contradiction. For there were, after all, experiences of the will! There were experiences of climactic action! True, one could probably assume that when every one of these experiences reaches its highest point of radiant bitterness, it is nothing but feeling; but that would bring up another contradiction, namely that feeling, in a state of perfect purity, would be a quiescence, a dying away of all action! Or was it not a contradiction after all? Was there some strange coherency in which the highest activity was motionless at the core? But here it became apparent that this sequence of reflections was not so much a side thought as an unwanted one, for with a sudden stirring of resistance against the emotive turn it had taken, Ulrich repudiated the entire view he had stumbled into. He was not disposed to meditate on certain states of mind and, when he thought about feelings, fall prey to emotion himself.

In a flash it occurred to him that what he was getting at could be described, without further ado, as the futile actuality or eternal momentariness of literature. Does it result in anything? Either it is an enormous detour from experience to experience, leading back to itself, or it is an epitome of stimulus and response, without any particular outcome whatsoever. "A puddle," he thought, "has given everyone the impression of depth more often and more strongly than the ocean, for the simple reason that there are many more opportunities to experience puddles than oceans." It seemed to him that it was the same with feelings, and that trivial feelings were thought to be deep for no other reason than this. For the habit of favoring the activity of feeling over feeling itself, which is the hallmark of all emotional people, as well as the wish to make others feel and to be made to feel that is common to all institutions serving the emotional life, amounts to a degradation of the rank and nature of feelings in favor of their fleeting moment as a personal state, and leads to that shallowness, stunted development, and utter irrelevance for which there is no dearth of examples. "Of course such a view can only be repugnant," Ulrich continued, "to all those people who wear their feelings as a cock wears his feathers and even preen themselves on the idea that eternity begins anew with every 'unique individual!'" He had a clear mental image of an enormous perversity of nearly humanity-wide proportions but was unable to express it in a way that would have satisfied him, probably because the ramifications were too complex.

While he was occupied with these thoughts, he watched the streetcars going past, waiting for one that would take him back as close as possible to the center of town. He saw the people climbing in and out, and his technically trained eye absently considered the interplay between welding and casting, rolling and bolting, engineering and hand finishing, historical development and current state of the art, of which the invention of these rolling barracks consisted. "In the end a committee from the department of streetcars comes to the factory and decides on the veneer, the coating, the upholstery, the mounting of armrests and hand supports, the placement of ashtrays and the like," he thought idly, "and it's precisely these minuscule details, and the red or green color of the box, and the buoyancy with which one can climb in, using the running board, that for tens of thousands of people make up what they remember and what remains, in their experience, of all that genius. This is what shapes their character, endows it with swiftness or comfort, makes them perceive red cars as home and blue ones as foreign, and is the source of that unmistakable odor of small facts that the centuries wear on their clothes." So there was no denying—and this unexpectedly fell in line with Ulrich's principal train of thought—that to a large extent life itself peters out into trivial actuality, or, to put it technically, that in life's balance of energy, the effective coefficient of spirit is very small.

And suddenly, as he felt himself swinging onto the streetcar, he said to himself: "I must impress this on Agathe: Morality is the subordination of every momentary state in our life to a single steady state!" This sentence had suddenly occurred to him in the form of a definition. But the overly polished and honed formulation had been preceded and followed by intuitions that, though less fully developed and articulated, enlarged his understanding. A rigorous conception and discipline for the harmless activity of feeling, an austere hierarchy of values, now appeared, vaguely foreshortened, in the prospective future: Feelings must either serve or belong to a state that extends to the ultimate and is as vast as the coastless sea, and that has not been described yet at all. Should that be called an idea, should it be called a longing? Ulrich had to let the matter rest, for at the moment when his sister's name occurred to him, her shadow had darkened his thoughts. As always when he thought of her, he felt that in her company he had shown himself in a different frame of mind than usual. He also knew that he wanted passionately to return to that condition. But the same memory covered him with shame at having behaved in a presumptuous, ridiculous, intoxicated manner, no better than a drunk who throws himself to his knees in front of spectators whom he won't be able to look in the face the next day. Given the temperate restraint that governed the siblings' relationship, that was a grotesque overstatement, and if it was not completely unfounded, it was probably no more than a reaction to feelings that were as yet unformed. He knew that Agathe would be arriving in a few days, and he was putting no obstacles in her way. Had she actually done anything wrong? Conceivably she had gone back on it all when her mood cooled off. But a very vivid premonition assured him that Agathe had not abandoned her intention. He could have tried to find out from her. Once again he felt it was his duty to warn her in a letter. But instead of taking that impulse seriously for even a moment, he imagined what might have impelled Agathe to behave in such an unusual way: he saw it as an unbelievably vehement gesture meant to show her trust in him and to put herself in his hands. "She has very little sense of reality," he thought, "but a wonderful way of doing what she wants. Rash, one could say; but just for that reason, not tepid! When she's angry, she sees the world ruby red!" He smiled amicably and looked around at the people traveling with him. Every one of them had wicked thoughts, this could be taken for granted, and everyone suppressed them, and no one reproached himself unduly for having them: but no one had these thoughts outside himself, in a person who gives them the enchanting inaccessibility of a dreamed experience.

For the first time since he had left his letter unfinished, Ulrich realized that he no longer had to choose, and that he was already in the state he was still hesitant to enter. According to his laws—he allowed himself the arrogant ambiguity of calling them sacred—Agathe's error could not be repented but only be made *good* by succeeding developments—which, incidentally, corresponded to the original meaning of repentance, which is, after all, a purifying fire and not a state of corruption. To re-compense or in-demnify Agathe's inconvenient husband would have meant nothing but a taking-back of damage done; in short, merely that double and paralyzing negation of which ordinary good behavior consists, which inwardly cancels itself out to zero. But to reduce to nothing what was going to happen to Hagauer, lift it from him, as it were, like a hovering load, would involve summoning up a great surge of feeling toward him, and that could not be contemplated without trepidation. Thus, according to the logic that Ulrich was seeking to embrace, all that could ever be made good was something other than the damage done, and he had not a moment's doubt that this other was to be his and his sister's whole life. "Putting it presumptuously," he thought: "Saul did not make good each single consequence of his previous sins; he became Paul!" To this peculiar logic, however, feeling and conviction raised the habitual objection that it would be more decent, and in any case no deterrent to later exaltations, to straighten out accounts with one's brother-in-law first and only then turn one's sights on the new life. After all, the kind of morality that appealed to him so strongly was completely inadequate for the settling of financial affairs and the conflicts they give rise to. Unsolvable and contradictory problems were bound to turn up on the borderline between that other life and ordinary existence, so it was probably best not to let these develop into borderline cases but instead clear them away sooner rather than later in the normal, passionless way of ordinary decency. But here Ulrich felt again that one could not take one's bearings from the normal requirements of goodness if one wanted to venture into the realm of unconditional goodness. The task imposed on him, to step into the unknown, seemed to brook no subtraction.

The last redoubt still holding out in his defense was guarded by a strong aversion to the fact that notions like "self," "feeling," "goodness," "the other goodness," "evil," of which he had made a great deal of use, were so personal and at the same time so high-flown and rarified that they really befitted the moral speculations of much younger people. He fared as doubtless many who follow his story will fare: he irritably picked out individual phrases, asking himself such questions as: "'Production and results of feelings'? What a mechanical, rationalistic idea, what ignorance of human nature! 'Morality as the problem of a permanent state to which all individual states are subordinate,' and that's it? How perfectly inhuman!" If one looked at this through the eyes of a reasonable person, it all seemed tremendously perverse. "The very essence of morality has as its foundation that the important feelings always remain the same," Ulrich thought, "and the only thing required of the individual is that he act in harmony with them!" But just at that moment the lines, drawn with T square and compass, that defined the rolling locality that enclosed him came to a halt at a spot where his eye, peering out from the body of a modern means of transport and still involuntarily participating in its equipment and furnishings, lit on a stone pillar that had been standing at the edge of the street since the baroque period, so that the unconsciously registered technical comfort of a rational creation suddenly stood in contrast to the eruptive passion of that ancient gesture, which suggested something not unlike a petrified stomachache. The effect of this optical collision was an uncommonly intense confirmation of the ideas from which Ulrich had just been trying to escape. Could anything have made the aimlessness of life more obvious than that accidental glance? Without taking sides with either the Now or the Then in matters of taste, as one usually does when such juxtapositions occur, his mind did not hesitate for a moment in feeling left out by both modernity and tradition, and saw only the grand demonstration of a problem that is likely at bottom a moral one. He could not doubt that the transitoriness of what is regarded as style, culture, the will of the times or the spirit of the age, and is admired as such, is a moral defect. For on the vast scale of the ages this means the same as if, on the smaller scale of one's own life, one were to develop one's faculties in a completely one-sided way, squandering oneself in excess and dissolution, never attaining a measure of one's will, never quite forming a full-fledged character, swept along by one haphazard passion after the other. For that reason it seemed to him also that what is called the "changes" or even the "progress" of historical periods is just a term for the fact that none of these experiments ever arrives at a point where all of them would unite on the way to a conviction that would embrace the totality and thereby provide, for the first time, a possible basis for steady development, lasting enjoyment, and that gravity of great beauty of which nowadays scarcely more than a shadow occasionally falls into our life.

Of course it struck Ulrich as an outrageous presumption to assume that everything had amounted to nothing. And yet it was nothing. As existence, immeasurable; as meaning, a muddle. Measured by its result, at least, it was no more than that from which the soul of the present day had evolved—in other words, little enough. But even as Ulrich thought this, he was abandoning himself to this "little" with relish, as if it were the last meal at the table of life that his intentions permitted him. He had left the streetcar and taken a route that would lead him quickly to the center of town. He felt as if he were emerging from a cellar. The streets shrieked with gaiety, prematurely filled with the warmth of a summer day. The sweet, toxic taste of soliloquy faded from his mouth; everything was frank and outgoing and glad to be in the sun. Ulrich stopped at almost every shopwindow. These little flasks in so many colors, these bottled fragrances and countless variants of the nail scissor: what a sum of genius there was even in a hairdresser's salon. A glove shop: what connections and inventions are needed before a goatskin is drawn over a lady's hand and the animal's hide has become more refined than her own! He marveled at the matter-of-course assemblage of countless accoutrements and dainty belongings that make up the carefree life, as though he were seeing them for the first time. What a delightful word, he felt: belonging. And what happiness, this tremendous concord of living together! There was nothing here to remind one of the earth crust of life, the unpaved roads of passion, the—he was actually feeling this: *uncivilized* aspects of the soul! The attention, a bright and narrow thing, glided across a flower garden of fruits, gems, fabrics, shapes, and enticements that opened their gently penetrating eyes in every color. Since at that time whiteness of skin was prized and protected from the sun, a few gaily colored parasols were already floating above the crowd and laying silky shadows on the pale faces of women. Ulrich's gaze was even enchanted by the matte golden beer he saw in passing through the plate-glass windows of a restaurant, standing on tablecloths that were so white that they formed blue planes at the boundary of shadow and light. Then the archbishop drove past him; a smooth-rolling, heavy barouche, with red and purple in its darkness: it had to be the archbishop's carriage, for this horse-drawn vehicle Ulrich was following with his eyes looked quite ecclesiastical, and two policemen stood at attention and saluted the follower of Christ without thinking of their predecessors who had run a lance into his predecessor's side.

He gave himself over to these impressions, which just a short while ago he had called "the futile actuality of life," with such eagerness that little by little, as he took his fill of the world, he began to feel sated, until his earlier antagonism returned. Now Ulrich knew exactly where the weakness of his speculations lay. "What would be the point," he asked himself, "in the face of this self-sufficient glory, of looking for some outcome above, behind, or beneath it all?! What would that be: a philosophy? An all-encompassing conviction, a law? Or God's finger? Or rather the assumption that morality has until now lacked an 'inductive ethos,' that it is much harder to be good than has generally been supposed, and that it will require an endless collaborative effort similar to the kind practiced everywhere in scientific research? I assume there is no morality because it cannot be deduced from anything constant, that there are only rules for the useless maintenance of transient conditions; and I assume there is no deep happiness without a deep morality: but even so it strikes me as a pallid, unnatural state of affairs that I'm pondering over this, and it isn't at all what I want!" Indeed, he might well have asked himself far more simply: "What have I taken upon myself?" And now he did that. But this question touched his sensibility more than his intellect; indeed it interrupted his thinking, and even before he apprehended it as a question, it had already eroded, bit by bit, Ulrich's always alert delight in strategic planning. It had begun like a dark tone close to his ear, accompanying him; then the tone was inside himself, just an octave deeper than everything else; and now Ulrich was finally at one with the question and seemed to himself like a strangely deep sound in the bright hard world, surrounded by a wide interval. So what had he actually taken upon himself, what had he promised?

He thought hard. He knew that though his use of the term "the Millennium" had been for comparison only, it had not been a mere offhand joke. If one took this promise seriously, what it amounted to was the wish to live, by means of mutual love, in a secular condition so exalted that one can only feel and do whatever heightens and preserves this state. That there are intimations of such a disposition in man was something he had felt as a certainty as far back as he could remember. His own first encounter with it had been "the affair with the major's wife," and though his subsequent experiences had not been many or great, they had all been the same. If one summed it all up, one would almost have to conclude that Ulrich believed in the "fall of man" and "original sin." That is, he was strongly inclined to assume that at some time or other there had been a fundamental change in man's attitude, which would have had to be more or less like falling out of love: the lover, no longer in love, now sees the whole truth, but something greater has been torn to pieces, and truth, wherever he looks, consists of nothing more than fragments that have been left over and patched together again. Maybe it really was the apple of "knowledge" that wrought this change in consciousness and cast the human race out of a primordial state to which it might find its way back only after having grown wise through sin in the aftermath of an infinity of experience. But Ulrich did not believe in such stories in the form in which they are handed down, but only in the form in which he had discovered them: he believed in them like a man accustomed to reckoning with numbers who applies his skills to the system of feelings spread out before him and, finding that not a single one of them is justified, concludes upon the necessity of introducing a fantastical hypothesis whose properties can be intuitively discerned. This was no small matter! He had entertained similar thoughts often enough, but never before had he been in the position of having to decide within a few days whether to take it seriously as a matter of consequence for his life. A faint sweat broke out under his hat and collar, and he was bothered by the proximity of the people jostling past him. What he was thinking of amounted to taking leave of most living relationships; he had no illusions about that. For people live compartmentalized lives today, and it is as parts of ourselves that we find ourselves linked with others; what one dreams has to do with dreaming and with what others are dreaming; what one does coheres in itself, but to a much greater degree it is bound up with what others are doing; and what one is convinced of is bound up with convictions of which only a fraction are one's own: so it is completely unrealistic to insist upon acting out of the fullness of one's own reality. And he of all people had all his life been steeped in the idea that one must impart one's conviction to others, that one must have the courage to live in the midst of moral contradictions, because that was the price of great achievement. Was he at least convinced of what he was thinking about the possibility and significance of another way of living? Not at all! Nevertheless, he could not prevent his feelings from responding as though faced with the unmistakable signs of a fact for which it had been waiting for years.

Now, of course, he had to ask himself what on earth entitled him to resolve, like one who has fallen in love with himself, never again to do anything that left the soul indifferent. It runs counter to the spirit of the active life, which is second nature to every man of our time; and even though there were God-persuaded times in the past that were able to give rise to such an endeavor, it had faded away like the light of dawn in the growing strength of the sun. Ulrich felt a scent of reclusiveness and sweetness in himself that he was finding more and more distasteful. And so he sought to restrain his extravagant thoughts as fast as possible and admonished himself, though not quite sincerely, that the promise of a Thousand-Year Kingdom he had so oddly held out to his sister was, if one considered it reasonably, nothing more than a kind of charity; for no doubt living with Agathe would require of him a concerted deployment of delicacy and selflessness, qualities that had hitherto been all too lacking in him. He recalled, in the way one recalls an uncommonly transparent cloud sailing across the sky, certain moments of their time together that had already been of that kind. "Maybe the content of the Millennium is nothing but the burgeoning of this power that shows itself first in two people at a time, until eventually it becomes a resounding communion of all?" he wondered, slightly embarrassed. Once again he sought counsel from his own "affair with the major's wife," which he now set himself to remembering: Leaving aside the illusions of love, whose immaturity had been the cause of that mistake, he focused all his attention on the tender sensations of goodness and adoration he had been capable of in his solitude at the time, and it seemed to him that to feel utter trust and affection, or to live for another person, must be a happiness that would move one to tears, as beautiful as the luminous sinking of the day into the peace of evening, and, also to the point of tears, somewhat poor in pleasure and mentally uneventful. For at moments his plan was already striking him as comical, rather like an arrangement between two old bachelors to move in together, and such sudden glints of parody gave him a sense of how little the notion of a life of service in brotherly love was likely to bring him fulfillment. With relative dispassion he admitted to himself that from the beginning there had been a large measure of the asocial in the relationship between Agathe and himself. Not only the business with Hagauer and the will, but the whole emotional tone that prevailed between them pointed to something hard, not to say violent, and without a doubt their bond as brother and sister did not entail more love for each other than repulsion of the rest of the world. "No!" Ulrich thought. "Wanting to live for another person is nothing but the bankruptcy of an egotism that opens a new shop next door, with a partner!"

In point of fact, despite this deftly chiseled remark, his inner exertion had already passed its peak at the moment when he had been tempted to contain in a small earthly lamp the light that had been filling him; and when it turned out now that this had been a mistake, his thought already lacked the will to attempt a decision, and he readily let himself be distracted. Two men had just bumped into each other near him and were shouting unpleasant remarks at each other as if preparing for a fight, a spectacle he followed with refreshed attention, and no sooner had he turned away from it than his glance collided with that of a woman whose gaze met his like a fat flower nodding on its stem. In that pleasant mood that is an equal blend of emotion and extroverted attention, he took note of the fact that, among real people, the ideal obligation to love one's neighbor is obeyed in two parts, the first consisting in not being able to stand the human race, and the second in compensating for that by engaging in sexual relations with one half of it. Without stopping to reflect, he turned after a few steps to follow the woman; it was still a mechanical consequence of being touched by her glance. He saw her figure beneath the dress like a large white fish near the surface of the water. He felt the masculine wish to harpoon it and see it flap and flail, and there was as much aversion in this as desire. Some barely perceptible signs made him certain this woman knew he was prowling after her and did not object. He tried to determine her place on the social scale and guessed at the upper reaches of the middle class, where it is difficult to define the exact position. "Merchant's family? Civil servants?" he wondered. But several images arbitrarily obtruded, among them that of a pharmacy: he felt the pungently sweet smell of the husband coming home; the compact atmosphere of the home itself betraying no sign of the quick darting beam of an intruder's flashlight that had only recently moved through it. The thought was without question repugnant, and yet dishonorably enticing.

And while Ulrich continued to walk behind the woman, in reality afraid that she might stop in front of a shopwindow and force him to either stumble foolishly past her or start up a conversation, something inside him was still undistracted and wide awake. "I wonder what Agathe actually wants from *me*?" he asked himself for the first time. He did not know. He assumed it must be similar to what he wanted of her, but his reasons for thinking that were purely emotional. Wasn't it rather astonishing how quickly and unexpectedly it had all happened? Except for a few childhood memories, he had known nothing about her, and the little he had heard, for instance about her connection with Hagauer over several years, had not disposed him favorably toward her. Now he also remembered the peculiar hesitation, almost reluctance, with which he had approached his father's house on the day of his arrival. And suddenly the idea embedded itself in his mind: "My feeling for Agathe is nothing but imagination!" In a man who constantly wanted something other than his surroundings, he thought, now in a serious vein again, in such a man, who always only gets to feel dislike and never arrives at liking, the usual "humane" combination of goodwill and lukewarm kindliness must disintegrate into a cold hardness with a mist of impersonal love hovering above it. Seraphic love, he had once called it. Or, he thought, one could also say: love without a partner. Or just as well: love without sex. Nowadays people only loved in sexual terms: those of the same sex couldn't abide each other, and in the cross-pollination from one sex to another, mutual love went along with a growing revolt against the overestimation of this compulsion. But seraphic love was free of both of these. It was love liberated from the countercurrents of social and sexual aversions. This love, which could be sensed everywhere side by side with the cruelty of contemporary life, could truly be called the sisterly love of an age that has no room for brotherly love, he told himself, wincing in irritation.

But even though these were his thoughts in the end, alongside them and intermittently he dreamed of a woman who cannot be attained at all. His vision of her was like late autumn days in the mountains, where the air is as if drained of its blood and dying, but the colors burn with the fiercest intensity of passion. He saw the blue vistas extending without end in mysteriously rich gradations. He completely forgot the woman who was walking in front of him, was far from all desire and perhaps near to love.

He was distracted only by the lingering gaze of another woman, who resembled the first one though she was neither brash nor fleshy, but well-bred and delicate like a pastel stroke, which nonetheless impresses itself in a fraction of a second: He looked up and in a state of utter inner exhaustion beheld a very beautiful lady in whom he recognized Bonadea.*

---

*Bonadea is Ulrich's on-again, off-again mistress, who is obsessed with Ulrich and by whom Ulrich is bored.

The glorious day had lured her out onto the street. Ulrich looked at his watch: he had been strolling for just a quarter of an hour, and no more than forty-five minutes had passed since he had left Count Leinsdorf's palace. Bonadea said: "I'm not free today." Ulrich thought: "How long, by this measure, is a whole day, a year, or even a resolution for a lifetime!" It was beyond calculation.

16

AGATHE IS REALLY HERE

THAT EVENING a telegram arrived, and the next afternoon, Agathe.

Ulrich's sister came with only a few suitcases, just the way she had envisioned leaving everything behind. Not that the quantity of her bags was wholly in keeping with the injunction: Throw everything you have into the fire, including your shoes. When Ulrich heard of this resolution, he laughed: there were even two hatboxes that had escaped the fire.

Agathe's forehead assumed its charming expression of piqued dignity and futile rumination over the offense.

Whether Ulrich was right in finding fault with the incomplete expression of a vast and transporting emotion remained uncertain, for Agathe did not raise this question; the unavoidable gaiety and disorder aroused by her arrival whirled in her eyes and ears like the swaying undulations of dancers around a brass band: she was very cheerful and felt slightly disappointed, even though she had not expected anything definite and had even deliberately abstained from all expectations during her trip. It was only when she remembered the previous night, when she had not had any sleep, that she suddenly became very tired. She didn't mind that Ulrich had to confess after a while that when he received the news of her arrival, it had been too late to postpone an appointment he had for that afternoon; he promised to be back in an hour and, with an elaborate fussiness that made them both laugh, prepared a bed for his sister on the divan in his study.

When Agathe woke up, the hour was long over, and Ulrich was nowhere to be seen. The room was sunk in deep dusk light and was so unfamiliar that the thought of now being in the midst of the new life she had been looking forward to frightened her. As far as she could make out, the walls were lined with books just as her father's had been, and the tables were covered with papers. She curiously opened a door and entered the adjacent room: there she encountered wardrobes, a shoe tree, a boxing ball, barbells, a Swedish ladder. She walked on and found more books. She came to the bathroom, with its cologne, aromatic essences, brushes, and combs, then to her brother's bed, to the hall with its hunting decor. Her path was marked by the flaring up and dying down of gaslight, but as chance would have it, Ulrich noticed nothing of this, even though he was already in the house; he had put off waking her in order to let her have a longer rest, and now he ran into her on the landing as he came up from the rarely used basement kitchen. He had gone there in search of refreshment for her, since on this day of unforeseen demands the house lacked even the most basic help. Now that they were standing side by side, Agathe felt the jumble of impressions she had received coalesce into an unease and despondency that made her feel it would be best to run away as soon as possible. There was something about the indifference and haphazardness with which things had been heaped together in this house that alarmed her.

Ulrich noticed this and apologized, offering some facetious explanations. He told her how he had come to acquire his house and recounted its history in detail, beginning with the antlers, which he owned without having ever gone hunting, and ending with the boxing ball, which he set dancing for Agathe's benefit. Agathe looked at everything again with disquieting seriousness and even turned her head when they left a room, as if to confirm her impression. Ulrich tried to be amused by this examination, but as it went on he began to feel embarrassed about his house. Something that was usually concealed by habit now became apparent: he occupied only the most necessary rooms, so that the other rooms hung off them like disheveled finery. When they were sitting down together after the tour of the house, Agathe asked: "But why did you do it, if you don't like it?"

Her brother provided her with tea and everything the house had

to offer, and insisted on giving her a hospitable welcome, belated
though it was, so that this second reunion should not be inferior to
the first with respect to creaturely comfort. Hurrying back and forth,
he assured her: "I did it all haphazardly, incorrectly, and in such a
way that the place has nothing to do with me."

"But it really looks very nice," Agathe now consoled him.

Ulrich remarked that if he had done it differently, it would probably have been even worse. "I can't stand homes that are custom-made
to match their owner's personality," he declared. "It would make me
feel as if I had ordered myself from an interior decorator!"

And Agathe said, "Homes like that scare me too."

"Even so, it can't stay like this," Ulrich corrected himself. He was
sitting with her at the table now, and the mere fact that from now on
they would always be having their meals together raised a number of
questions. The realization that all sorts of things would have to be
different took him by surprise; he felt that he was required to exert
himself in an utterly unfamiliar way, and at first he had the zeal of a
beginner. "A person alone," he said, countering his sister's indulgent
readiness to leave everything as it was, "can have a weakness: it will
blend in with his other qualities and disappear among them. But
when two share a weakness, its weight doubles in comparison with
the qualities they don't have in common and comes to look like a
deliberate avowal."

Agathe could not see that.

"In other words, as brother and sister we can't do some things that
each of us have felt free to do on our own; which is precisely why we
have come together."

That appealed to Agathe. Still, his negative way of putting it, that
they were together only in order not to do something, felt incomplete
to her, and after a while, returning to the subject of his furnishings
and how they had been sent piecemeal by a number of elegant firms,
she asked: "I still don't quite get it. Why did you furnish your house
like this if you didn't think it was right?"

Ulrich received her cheerful gaze and let his eyes rest on her face,
which, above the slightly wrinkled dress she had traveled in, suddenly

appeared smooth as silver and so wondrously present that it could just as well be close or far away; or rather, far and near canceled each other out in this presence, just as the moon in its depthless sky will suddenly appear behind a neighbor's roof. "Why I did it?" he replied with a smile. "I don't remember. Probably because it could just as well have been done differently. I felt no responsibility. I would be on less certain ground if I were to tell you that the irresponsibility with which we lead our lives today could be a step toward a new sense of responsibility."

"How so?"

"Oh, in many ways. As you know: An individual life may be no more than a slight divergence from the most probable average value in a series. And so on."

Agathe had heard only what made sense to her. She said: "What this adds up to is 'quite nice' and 'very nice.' Pretty soon one no longer has any sense of how abominably one is living. But it can get gruesome sometimes, sort of like waking up on a slab in a morgue!"

"So what was your home like?" Ulrich asked.

"Philistine. Hagauerish. 'Quite nice.' Just as fake as yours."

Ulrich meanwhile had picked up a pencil and was sketching the floor plan of the house on the tablecloth and reassigning the rooms. That was easy and so quickly done that Agathe's housewifely gesture in defense of the tablecloth came too late and aimlessly ended with her hand settling on his. The difficulties arose again only when it came to the principles by which the house was to be furnished. "We happen to have a house," Ulrich argued, "and need to rearrange things for the two of us, but by and large it's an outdated and idle question. 'Setting up house' is setting up a facade with nothing behind it. Social conditions and personal relations are no longer solid enough for houses. Putting on an appearance of permanence and continuity no longer gives anyone genuine pleasure. People used to do this, showing who they were by the number of their rooms, servants, and guests. Now almost everyone feels that a formless life is the only form that is in keeping with the diverse purposes and possibilities life is filled with, and young people either love bare simplicity, which is like a theater without props, or else they dream of wardrobe trunks and bobsled championships, of tennis cups and a luxury hotel by a highway jammed with cars and golf-course scenery and music in the rooms that can be turned on and off like running water." He was making conversation, as if entertaining a stranger; but actually he was talking himself up to the surface, because the combination of finality and dawning in their being together made him uneasy.

But after she had let him finish, his sister asked: "So are you suggesting that we live in a hotel?"

"Definitely not!" Ulrich hastened to assure her. "Except maybe now and then while traveling."

"And for the rest of the time we'll build ourselves an arbor on an island or a log cabin in the mountains?"

"We'll settle in here, of course," Ulrich replied, more seriously than this conversation warranted. They fell silent for a little while. He had stood up and was walking back and forth in the room. Agathe pretended to be fixing something on the hem of her dress, bending her head below the line on which their eyes had been meeting. Suddenly Ulrich stopped and said with a voice that came out with difficulty but was forthright and sincere: "Dear Agathe, there exists a circle of questions with a large circumference and no center: and all of these questions mean 'How shall I live?'"

Agathe had also risen, but still did not look at him. She shrugged. "One has to try it!" she said. A rush of blood had risen to her brow; but when she raised her head, her eyes were bright with exuberant high spirits, and the blush lingered briefly only on her cheeks like a passing cloud. "If we're going to stay together," she declared, "you will have to help me unpack, put my things away, and change, because I haven't seen a maid anywhere!"

Now her brother's bad conscience galvanized his arms and legs to make good, under Agathe's direction and with her assistance, for his inattentiveness. He cleared out closets like a hunter disemboweling an animal and abandoned his bedroom with a pledge that it was now Agathe's and that he would find himself a couch somewhere. Eagerly he carried back and forth the objects of daily use that had hitherto lived in their places as quietly as flowers in a flowerbed, awaiting the selecting hand as the only variation in their destiny. Suits piled up on chairs; on the glass shelves in the bathroom, all implements of personal hygiene were carefully partitioned into a gentleman's and a lady's department; by the time order had been more or less turned into disorder, only Ulrich's shiny leather slippers still stood deserted on the floor, looking like an offended lapdog evicted from its basket, by the very pleasantness and triviality of their nature a perfect emblem of disturbed comfort. But there was no time to be touched by this, for Agathe's suitcases were next, and however few of them there had seemed to be, the abundance of delicately folded things that spread out as they emerged from their confines, blossoming in the air much like the hundred roses a magician pulls from his hat, was all but inexhaustible. These garments had to be hung up and laid down, shaken out and neatly stacked, and since Ulrich assisted in this task as well, it was accompanied by accidents and laughter.

But actually, amidst all these activities, Ulrich could think of only one thing, constantly, over and over: that all his life and still a few hours ago he had been alone. And now Agathe was here. This little sentence: "Agathe is here now," repeated itself in waves, like the astonishment of a little boy who has just been given a present; something about it had an inhibiting effect on the mind, but on the other hand also an utterly incomprehensible fullness of presence, and all in all it kept coming back to that little statement: "Agathe is here now." "So she's tall and slender?" Ulrich thought, observing her secretly. But that didn't describe her at all: she was shorter than he was, and she was broad-shouldered. "Is she attractive?" he wondered. You couldn't say that either: her proud nose, for example, was slightly turned upward when viewed from one side, which exerted a far more potent charm than mere attractiveness. "Is she actually beautiful?" Ulrich asked himself in an oddly whimsical way. For the question was not an easy one for him, even though as a woman, if one left convention aside, Agathe was a stranger to him. After all, there is no such thing as an inner prohibition against looking at a blood relation with sexual desire; that is mere custom, or it can be explained along the detours of morality and social hygiene; besides, the fact that Ulrich and Agathe had not grown up together had prevented them from developing the sterilized brother-sister feeling that prevails in the European family: nevertheless, convention alone initially sufficed to rob the feelings they had for each other, even the harmless feeling in the mere thought of her beauty, of an ultimate keenness whose absence Ulrich sensed at that moment by his own distinct surprise. To find something beautiful probably means, first of all, to *find* it: whether it is a landscape or a woman, there it lies, gazing back on the charmed finder and appearing to have been waiting solely and exclusively for him; and so, with this delight in the fact that she now belonged to him and wanted to be discovered by him, he felt immensely fond of his sister, but still he thought: "One can't find one's own sister truly beautiful; at the most, one can be flattered that others fancy her." But then, where in the past there had been silence, he heard her voice for minutes at a time, and what was her voice like? Waves of fragrance accompanied the movement of her clothes, and what was this scent like? Her motions were now a knee, now a delicate finger, now an unruly lock of hair. The only thing one could say about it was that it was there. It was there where before there had been nothing. The difference in sheer intensity between the most vivid moment of thinking about the sister he had left behind and the emptiest present moments was still as great and as distinctly pleasant as when a shaded spot is filled with the scent of wild herbs opening to the light and warmth of the sun.

Agathe was aware that her brother was watching her, but she did not let him know that. During lulls in their talk, when she felt his gaze follow her movements, in the pauses between one remark and the response to it, which were not so much a suspension as a glide through silence, like a car coasting over a deep and treacherous spot with its motor turned off, she too enjoyed the hyperimmediacy and calm intensity of their reunion. And when all the unpacking and putting away was done and Agathe was alone in the bath, an adventure ensued that threatened to burst like a wolf into this gentle pasture for the eyes, for she had undressed down to her underwear in a room where Ulrich now, smoking cigarettes, kept watch over her belongings. With the water swirling around her, she wondered what she should do. There was no maid, so ringing or calling out was not going to be of much help. Apparently her only recourse was to wrap herself in Ulrich's bathrobe, which was hanging on the wall, knock on the door, and send him out of the room. But Agathe cheerfully doubted whether, in view of the grave familiarity that, if not already full-fledged, had just been born between them, it was permissible for her to conduct herself like a young lady and beg Ulrich to withdraw, so she decided not to acknowledge any equivocal femininity and to appear before him as the natural friend and companion he must see in her even in scanty clothing.

But when she resolutely entered the room, they both felt an unexpected stirring of the heart. Both tried not to be embarrassed. For a moment they were unable to divest themselves of the inconsequence that allows near nudity at the beach but in a room turns the hem of a chemise or panties into the secret path of romantic fantasy. Ulrich smiled awkwardly as Agathe, with the light of the antechamber behind her, stood in the open door looking like a silver statue lightly veiled in a smokelike shroud of batiste; whereupon, with a voice that was much too emphatically casual, she asked for her stockings and dress, which turned out to be in the next room. Ulrich showed her the way, and to his secret delight she strode off a little too boyishly, savoring the difference with a kind of defiance, as women tend to do when they don't feel themselves protected by their skirts. A little later there was a new development when Agathe found herself half-sheathed in her dress and half-caught in it and had to call Ulrich for help. As he was fiddling with the hooks and fastenings at the back of it, she felt, without sisterly jealousy, but rather with a sense of convenience, that he was quite adept at finding his way around women's clothes, and she herself moved nimbly when the nature of the procedure required her to do so.

Bent close over the supple, tender, and yet firm skin of her shoulders, intently given over to the unaccustomed task, which raised a flush on his brow, Ulrich was courted by a feeling that could not be quite put into words, unless one were to say that his body was equally assailed by a sense of having a woman and not having a woman very close to him; but one could just as well have said that though he was doubtlessly standing in his own shoes, he nevertheless felt drawn out of himself and over to her as if he had been given a second, far more beautiful body for his own.

That was why the first thing he said to his sister after standing up straight again was: "Now I know what you are: You are my self-love!" No doubt it sounded strange, but it really described what moved him. "In a certain sense, I've always lacked true self-love, which other people have so strongly," he explained. "And now evidently, by mistake or by fate, that self-love was embodied in you, instead of in myself!" he added without further ado.

It was his first attempt that evening to form a judgment on the meaning of his sister's arrival.

17

THE SIAMESE TWINS

LATER that evening he returned to this.

"You should know," he began to tell his sister, "that there is a kind of self-love I have never experienced, a certain tender relationship to oneself that seems to come naturally to most other people. I'm not sure how to describe it. I could say, for example, that I have always had lovers with whom I was mismatched. They were illustrations of some sudden whim, caricatures of my mood of the moment: in other words, basically just examples of my inability to enter into natural relationships with other people. Even that has to do with one's relationship to oneself. Basically I always chose women I didn't like—"

"But you were perfectly justified in doing so!" Agathe interrupted him. "If I were a man, I would have no qualms treating women as irresponsibly as I pleased. And I would desire them out of distraction and wonder, nothing more!"

"Really? You would? That's nice of you!"

"They're ridiculous parasites. They share a man's life together with his dog!" She said this without even a hint of moral indignation. She was pleasantly tired and was keeping her eyes closed, having gone to bed early, and Ulrich, who had come to say good night, saw her lying in his place in his bed.

But it was also the bed in which Bonadea had lain only thirty-six hours earlier. That was probably why Ulrich returned to the subject of his mistresses. "All I was trying to describe," he repeated, smiling, "was my own inability to arrive at a mildly reasonable relationship with myself. In order for me to experience anything with real interest, it has to be part of some context, it has to be controlled by an idea. The experience itself I'd really prefer to have behind me, as a memory; the emotional effort it calls for strikes me as unpleasant and absurdly misplaced. That's how it is when I describe myself ruthlessly to you. And the simplest, most primal idea, at least in one's younger years, is that you're a hell of a guy, completely without precedent, and the world has been waiting for you. But once you've turned thirty, this is no longer sustainable!" He reflected a moment and then said: "No! It's so hard to talk about oneself: What I really ought to say is that I've never been ruled by a lasting idea. There was nothing like that to be found. One should love an idea like a woman. It should be sheer joy to return to it. And one always has it inside oneself! And looks for it in everything outside oneself! I never found any ideas like that. I've always had a man-to-man relationship to the so-called great ideas, maybe even to the ones that are rightly so-called. I think I was not born to subordinate myself: ideas provoked me to overthrow them and put others in their place. Perhaps it was precisely this jealousy that drove me to science, whose laws are sought through collaboration and are not regarded as immutable either!" Again he paused and laughed, either at himself or at his self-portrayal. "But at any rate," he continued earnestly, "because of this way I have of associating no idea or every idea with myself, I lost the ability to take life seriously. I find life much more exciting when I read about it in a novel, where it's wrapped up in some conception; but when I'm expected to live it in all its particulars, I always find it outdated, crammed with detail in an old-fashioned way, and intellectually passé. I don't think it's just me, either. Most people are like this nowadays, even though many put on a charade of intense joie de vivre, rather like schoolchildren who are taught to skip merrily through the daisies. There's always something deliberate about it, and they feel that. Actually they're as capable of murdering each other in cold blood as they are of cheerfully getting along. Our time really doesn't seem to take seriously the events and adventures it's filled with. When they happen, there's a stir. Before you know it, that sets off new happenings, one after the other, like a vendetta, a compulsive recital of the alphabet from *B* to *Z* because one has said *A*. But these events in our life have less life than a book, because they don't have a coherent meaning."

That was how Ulrich spoke. Loosely. Shifting in tone and mood. Agathe did not answer; her eyes were still shut, but she was smiling.

Ulrich said: "I no longer know what I'm telling you. I don't think I can get back to the beginning."

They were silent for a while. He was able to contemplate his sister's face at leisure, since it was not defended by the gaze of her eyes. It lay there as a piece of naked body, like women when they are alone with each other in a bathhouse. The feminine, unguarded, natural cynicism of this sight, not intended for men's eyes, still exerted an unaccustomed effect on Ulrich, even though it was no longer as intense as in their first days together, when Agathe had immediately claimed her sisterly right to talk to him without hiding her soul behind veils of decorum, since for her he was not a man like others. He remembered the mixture of surprise and fright he had felt as a boy when he had seen a pregnant woman on the street, or a mother breastfeeding her baby: secrets carefully withheld from the boy suddenly bulged, full-blown and unembarrassed in the sun. And perhaps he had been carrying vestiges of such impressions about with him for a long time, because suddenly it seemed to him that he felt entirely free of them. That Agathe was a woman with all sorts of experiences in her past was a pleasant and comfortable thought; there was no need to guard one's speech as with a young girl, indeed it struck him as touchingly natural that with a mature woman everything was already morally less constrained. He also felt a need to protect her, to make up to her for something or other by being kind to her in some way. He resolved to do everything he possibly could for her. He even resolved to find her another husband. And this need for kindness recovered for him, though he barely noticed, the lost thread of the conversation.

"Probably our self-love changes during the years of sexual maturation," he said without transition. "Because there, a meadow of tenderness in which one had been playing suddenly gets mowed down to produce fodder for one particular instinct."

"To make the cow give milk!" Agathe supplemented after the slightest pause, mischievously and with dignity, but without opening her eyes.

"Yes, I suppose it's all connected," Ulrich said, and continued: "So there is a moment when our life loses almost all its tenderness and contracts into that one particular operation, which then remains supercharged with it: Doesn't it seem to you too as if there were a horrible drought that prevails everywhere on earth, except for one place where it never stops raining?!"

Agathe said: "It seems to me that as a child I loved my dolls more fiercely than I've ever loved a man."

"What did you do with them?" Ulrich asked. "Did you give them away?"

"Who could I have given them to? I laid them to rest in the kitchen stove."

Ulrich responded with animation: "When I recall my earliest years, I'm tempted to say that outside and inside were scarcely distinguishable. When I crawled toward something, it came toward me on wings; and when something happened that was important to us, it wasn't just we who were excited by it, but the things themselves began to seethe. I wouldn't claim that we were happier then than we were later. We weren't in possession of ourselves yet; in fact, we didn't really exist, our personal states were not yet distinctly separated from those of the world. It sounds strange, and yet it is true when I say that our feelings, our volitions, our very selves were not yet entirely inside ourselves. What is even stranger is that I could just as well say: were not yet entirely apart from ourselves. Because if today, when you feel you're entirely in possession of yourself, if you ask yourself the unusual question, "Who am I really?" you will make this discovery. You will always see yourself from the outside, like a thing. You will notice that at one moment you get angry, at another sad, just as your coat will at one time be wet and at another time hot. No matter how closely you observe yourself, you will at best find unknown sides of yourself, but your inner self will remain hidden. Whatever you do, you remain outside yourself, except for those rare moments when someone would say of you that you're beside yourself. As adults, of course, we've compensated by being able to think, 'I am,' whenever we wish, if we care to do so. You see a car, and somehow in a shadowy way you also see: 'I see a car.' You're in love or you're sad and you see that you're sad or in love. But in a full sense neither the car nor your sadness or your love, nor you yourself, are completely there. Nothing is as completely there as it once was in childhood. Instead, everything you touch, down to your innermost self, is more or less petrified from the moment you have succeeded in being a 'personality,' and what is left over, enveloped in a wholly external existence, is a spectral thread of misty self-certainty and murky self-love. What has gone wrong there? One has a feeling that somewhere, something could still be reversed! Surely no one can claim that a child's experience is totally different from a man's! I don't have a definitive answer to this question, even though there may be this or that idea about it. But for a long time my answer has been that I've lost my love for this manner of selfhood and this kind of world."

Ulrich was pleased that Agathe had listened without interrupting him, for he was not expecting an answer from her any more than from himself and was convinced that for the present no one could give the kind of answer he had in mind. Nevertheless, he did not fear for a moment that what he was talking about might be too difficult for her. He did not regard it as philosophizing or even as an unusual subject for conversation, any more than a very young person, whom he resembled in this situation, will allow difficulties of expression to dissuade him from finding everything simple when he is prompted to exchange views on the eternal question "Who are you? This is how it is with me." He derived his conviction that his sister could follow him word for word not from thought but from her presence. His gaze rested on her face, and he felt unaccountably happy. This face with closed eyes gave not even a hint of recoil. It exerted a bottomless attraction on him; also in the sense of drawing him into a depth without end. Sinking into contemplation of this face, he found nowhere that ground sludge of dissolved resistances from which a man who has dived into love can push off to rise back up to the dry surface.

But since he was accustomed to experience inclination toward a woman as a violently reversed dislike of the person, which—even though he disapproved of it—does offer a certain guarantee of not losing oneself, he was now alarmed by the pure inclination with which he was leaning curiously and ever more deeply toward her, almost as if yielding to the pull of vertigo, so that he soon drew back and from sheer happiness took refuge in a somewhat boyish prank to recall Agathe to everyday life: with the most gingerly touch he was capable of, he tried to open her eyes. Agathe opened them, laughing, and exclaimed: "Considering I'm supposed to be your self-love, you're treating me rather roughly!"

This response was just as boyish as his attack, and their looks pressed against each other with playful exaggeration, like two boys who are ready for a scuffle but are laughing too hard to go through with it. But suddenly Agathe dropped this and asked seriously: "Do you know the myth Plato tells, based on some ancient tradition, that the gods divided the original human being into two parts, man and woman?" She had raised herself on an elbow and unexpectedly blushed, feeling a little foolish for having asked Ulrich whether he knew this story, which was probably widely known. So she quickly decided to forge ahead: "Now the unfortunate halves do all sorts of foolish things in order to join together again: This is written in all the schoolbooks for the higher grades; unfortunately, they don't tell you why it can't be done!"

"I can tell you that," Ulrich joined in, happy to realize how exactly she had understood. "No one knows which of the many halves that are running around is the one he is lacking. He or she will grab one that seems to fit and make the most futile efforts to become one with it, until in the end it's clear that this will not happen. If a child is born as a result, both halves will believe through several years of their youth that they've at least become one in their child; but that's just a third half, which soon shows signs of trying to get away as far as possible from the other two and set out in search of a fourth. Thus the human race keeps on bisecting itself physiologically, and the intrinsic oneness stands like the moon outside the bedroom window."

"You'd think siblings should have already gone at least halfway!" Agathe interjected in a voice that had become husky.

"Twins, perhaps."

"Aren't we twins?"

"Certainly!"

Ulrich suddenly veered away. "Twins are rare. Twins of different sexes are extremely rare. If in addition they are not the same age and have hardly known each other for the longest time, it adds up to a phenomenon that's truly worthy of us!" he declared, striving to get back to the shallows of amusement.

"But it was as twins that we met!" Agathe insisted, undeterred.

"Because we happened to be wearing similar clothes?"

"Maybe. And anyway! You can say it was chance, but what is chance? I believe chance is precisely fate or destiny or whatever you want to call it. Didn't it ever seem like chance to you that you were born precisely as you and nobody else? Our being brother and sister is the same thing, doubled!" That was how Agathe explained it, and Ulrich submitted to this wisdom. "So we declare ourselves twins!" he agreed. "Symmetrical creatures of nature's whim, we will from now on be the same age, the same height, have the same hair, wear identically striped clothes with the same ribbon tied under our chins as we follow our path through the throngs of humanity; but let me point out that people watching us as we pass will find us both touching and somewhat absurd, as always when something reminds them of the mysteries of their becoming."

"We could dress in an opposite way," Agathe retorted, amused. "One in yellow when the other one's in blue, or red next to green, and we could dye our hair violet or purple, and I'll make myself a hump and you give yourself a belly: and still we'll be twins!"

But the joke was depleted, its pretext worn out, and they fell silent for a while.

"Do you realize," Ulrich said suddenly then, "that this is a very serious matter we're talking about?" No sooner had he said this than his sister again lowered the fan of her lashes over her eyes and, hiding her interest, let him go on talking by himself. Maybe it only looked as if she had closed her eyes. The room was dark, and what lamplight there was did not clarify so much as submerge all contours beneath planes of pale light. Ulrich had said: "There's not only the myth of the human being who was divided in two; we could also think of Pygmalion, Hermaphroditus, or Isis and Osiris: beneath the differences, it always remains the same. This desire for a double of the opposite sex is very ancient. It seeks the love of a being who is completely the same as oneself and yet an other, distinct from oneself, a magical creature who is oneself and yet remains a magical creature and who, above all, has the advantage over anything we merely imagine of possessing the breath of autonomy and independence. This dream of a quintessential love, free of the limitations of the bodily world, meeting itself in two beings that are the same unsame self, has risen countless times in solitary alchemy from the alembic of the human skull—"

Then he had halted in mid-speech; evidently something disturbing had occurred to him, and he had concluded with the almost unfriendly words: "Even under the most ordinary everyday conditions of love, traces of this can be found: in the charm of every change of clothing, every disguise, in the significance of mutual correspondences or repetitions of oneself in another. The little magic is always the same, whether one sees a lady naked for the first time, or a naked girl for the first time in a high-necked dress, and the great, ruthless passions are all due to someone imagining that his most secret self is peering out from behind the curtains of a stranger's eyes."

It sounded as though he were asking her not to overestimate what they were saying. But Agathe thought once again of the lightning flash of surprise she had felt when they first met, disguised, as it were, in their lounging suits. And she replied: "So this has been around for thousands of years; does it make it any easier to understand if one explains it as a meeting of two illusions?"

Ulrich was silent.

And after a while Agathe said delightedly: "But it's like that in sleep! There you see yourself sometimes transformed into something else. Or you meet yourself as a man. And then you're nicer to him than you ever are to yourself. You'll probably say those are sexual dreams; but to me it seems they're much older."

"Do you often have dreams like that?" Ulrich asked.

"Sometimes; rarely."

"I almost never do," he confessed. "It's ages since I've had that kind of dream."

"And yet you once declared to me," Agathe now said, "—I think it must have been right at the beginning, still in the old house—that thousands of years ago people really had different kinds of experiences!"

"Oh, you mean the 'giving' and the 'receiving' kind of seeing?" Ulrich replied and smiled, even though Agathe could not see him. "The spirit's modes of 'being embraced' and 'embracing'? Yes, of course I must have talked about this mysterious bisexuality of the soul, too. And who knows what else! There are hints of this in everything. Even in every analogy there's a remnant of the magic of being the same and not the same. But haven't you noticed: In all the patterns of behavior we've mentioned—in dream, myth, poem, childhood, even in love— the increase in feeling is purchased at the expense of understanding, and that means: at the expense of reality."

"So you don't really believe in it"? Agathe asked.

To this Ulrich gave no answer. But after a while he said: "Translated into the disastrous idiom of our time, one could call this value, which is in such terrifyingly scarce supply for everyone today, the percentage share of a person in his experiences and actions. In dreams it seems to be a hundred percent, in waking life it doesn't even amount to half of one percent! This is something you noticed immediately in my home today; but my relationships with the people you will meet are no different. Once—and really, if I'm not mistaken, I ought to add that it happened in conversation with a woman where it was very apropos—I called it the "acoustics of the void." If a pin drops in an empty room, the resulting noise has something disproportionate, even exorbitant, about it; but it's the same when there's emptiness between people. Then one no longer knows: Are we screaming, or is there a deathly silence? Because everything that's unaligned or off-kilter acquires the magnetic power of an enormous temptation as soon as it turns out that one has nothing to counteract it with. Don't you agree? But I'm sorry," he interrupted himself, "you must be tired, and I'm not letting you rest. It seems, I'm afraid, there are some things in my surroundings and in my social life that won't be to your liking."

Agathe had opened her eyes. After being hidden so long, her gaze expressed something extremely hard to define, though sympathy was a part of it, which Ulrich now felt spreading over his whole body. Suddenly he began to talk again: "When I was younger, I tried to regard just that as a sign of strength. So one hasn't got anything with which to oppose life? Fine, then life will run away from man and into his works! That's more or less how I thought. And there's no denying the colossal power that resides in the lovelessness and irresponsibility of today's world. At the very least there's a kind of adolescent rowdiness in it. Surely centuries go through growing pains? And like every young man I started by throwing myself into work, adventure, and amusement; it seemed all the same to me what one did, as long as one did it wholeheartedly. Do you remember we once talked about the 'morality of achievement'? That's the inborn image in us by which we orient ourselves. But the older one gets, the more clearly one learns that this apparent exorbitance, this independence and mobility in everything, this sovereignty of the driving parts and the partial drives—sovereignty of your own parts and drives against yourself, as well as your own sovereignty against the world—in short, that everything we, as 'people of today,' have regarded as a strength and a distinction of our species is basically nothing but a weakness of the whole with respect to its parts. Passion and willpower can do nothing against this. The moment you want to be entirely at the center of anything, you find yourself flushed back to the periphery: that's the experience in all experiences today!"

Agathe, with her eyes now open, was waiting for something to happen in his voice; when that did not occur and her brother's talk simply stopped like a path that has branched off from a road and come to a dead end, she said: "So according to your experience one can never really act with conviction, and will never be able to do so.

What I mean by conviction," she corrected herself, "is not some kind of science, or the moral dressage we were put through, but feeling completely present within oneself, and feeling one's presence in everything else as well; where something that is now empty is fulfilled and complete. I mean something one starts out from and to which one returns. Oh, I myself don't know what I mean," she broke off vehemently. "I was hoping that you would explain it to me!"

"You mean exactly what we have been talking about," Ulrich gently replied. "And you're the only person with whom I can talk about it like this. But there wouldn't be any point in my starting over again just in order to add a few enticing words. I should say, rather, that finding oneself in the absolute middle of life, in a state of unimpaired 'inwardness'—if one doesn't understand the word in a sentimental sense, but with the meaning we just gave it—is probably not a demand that can be made in a rational state of mind." He had leaned forward, touched her arm, and looked into her eyes for a long time. "It may be contrary to human nature," he said softly. "But the reality is that we are painfully in need of it! Because this must be where the desire to be like brothers and sisters comes from, which is a complement to ordinary love, in the imaginary direction of a love without any elements of exclusion and not-love." And after a while he added: "You know how popular the brother and sister theme is in bed; people who could murder their real siblings put on silly charades of being naughty little brothers and sisters conspiring under a blanket."

In the half darkness his face quivered in self-mockery. But Agathe's trust was in this face and not in the confusion of the words. She had seen faces twitching like this a moment before they swooped down; this one did not come nearer; it seemed to be moving at infinitely great speed over an infinitely long distance.

Her answer was curt: "Being brother and sister just isn't enough!"

"Well, we've already made it 'twin brother and sister,'" Ulrich retorted, now soundlessly rising, for he had the impression that fatigue had at last overcome her.

"We ought to be Siamese twins," Agathe added.

"Agreed, then, Siamese twins!" her brother repeated, carefully detaching her hand from his and laying it on the quilt, and his words sounded buoyant, their weightlessness still expanding after he had left the room.

Agathe smiled. Gradually she descended into a lonely sorrow whose darkness, imperceptible to her weariness, soon blended with that of sleep. Ulrich meanwhile tiptoed into his study and there, for two hours during which he was unable to work, until he too grew tired, he made his first acquaintance with the experience of being cramped by consideration for another person. He marveled at the number of things he would have liked to do during that time and that had to be suppressed on account of the noise they would make. This was new to him. And it almost irritated him a little, although he did his utmost to imagine sympathetically what it would be like to be physically conjoined with another person. He had little information about how two such nervous systems function together, like two leaves on a single stalk, connected not only through their blood but even more through the effect of their complete interdependence. He assumed that every excitement in one psyche would also be felt by the other, while the process that evoked it took place in a body that was not, in the main, one's own. "An embrace, for instance: you're embraced in the other," he thought. "You may not even consent to it, but your other self floods you with an overwhelming wave of consent! What business is it of yours who kisses your sister? But her arousal, you can't help loving it together with her! Or it's you who are making love, and now you must somehow involve her in it, you can't just flood her with senseless physiological processes . . . !?" Ulrich felt a strong appeal and a great discomfort in this train of thought; it was difficult to draw an accurate distinction between new points of view and a distortion of the ordinary ones.

18

TOO MUCH GAIETY

AGATHE proved naturally adept at making use of the advantages social life offered her, and her brother was pleased with her assured bearing in a circle of extremely arrogant individuals. The years she had spent as the wife of a secondary-school teacher in the provinces seemed to have fallen off her without leaving a trace. For the time being, however, Ulrich summed it all up with a shrug, saying: "The high nobility find it amusing that we should be called the Siamese Twins: they've always been more interested in menageries than, for example, in art."

Tacitly they agreed to treat everything that happened as a mere interlude. There was a great deal that needed to be changed or rearranged in their household, which had been clear to them on the very first day, but they did nothing about it, because they shied away from resuming a discussion whose limits could not be foreseen. Ulrich, who had given up his bedroom to Agathe, had settled himself in the dressing room, with the bathroom between them, and had subsequently ceded most of his closet space to her. An offer of sympathy on this account he rejected with a reference to Saint Lawrence and his grill; but it never seriously occurred to Agathe that she might have disrupted her brother's bachelor existence, because he assured her that he was very happy and because she had only a very vague conception of the degrees of happiness he might have enjoyed previously. She now liked this house, with its unbourgeois layout, the useless extravagance of reception rooms and anterooms around the few usable and now overfilled rooms; it had about it something of the elaborate civility of a bygone age that is defenseless against the self-indulgent boorishness of the present, but sometimes the silent objection of the elegant rooms against the invad-

ing disorder was sad, too, like torn and tangled strings on the beautifully carved hull of an ancient instrument. Agathe saw then that her
brother had not really chosen this secluded house without feeling or
interest, even though he wanted to give that impression, and from its
old walls came a language of passion that was neither quite mute nor
quite audible. But neither she nor Ulrich admitted to anything more
than that they rather enjoyed disarray. They lived with a certain amount
of inconvenience, ordered food from a hotel, and derived from all this
the somewhat excessive high spirits that can ensue at a picnic where
one eats less well on the green earth than one would at the table.

Nor could adequate domestic service be found under these circumstances. The experienced servant whom Ulrich had taken in
when he moved into the house had been hired for a brief period only,
as he was an old man who was ready to retire and was only waiting
for some matter to be settled first; not much could be expected of
him, and Ulrich gave him as little to do as possible. The role of
chambermaid fell to Ulrich himself, for the room where a decent
maid might have been put up was, like everything else, still at the
planning stage, and a few attempts to get over this state of affairs had
not led to good results. Thus Ulrich was making great progress as a
squire arming his lady knight to set forth on her social conquests. In
addition, Agathe had begun to shop for new clothes to supplement
her wardrobe. And as the house was nowhere equipped for the needs
of a lady, she had developed the habit of using the entirety of it as a
dressing room, so that Ulrich, whether he wished to or not, took part
in her new acquisitions. The doors between the rooms stood open, his
gymnastics equipment served as clotheshorses and hangers, and at times
of decision he would be called away from his desk like Cincinnatus
from his plow.* This thwarting of his will to work (which, though in
abeyance, was still ready to be called upon) was something he put up

---

*Lucius Quintius Cincinnatus (born ca. 519 BC) was a Roman statesman who, ac-
cording to legend, was working a plow on the farm to which he had retired when he
was approached by a delegation from Rome begging him to assume the reins of
government at a time of crisis for the republic.

with not only because he assumed it would pass but also because it brought him a pleasure that was new to him and was having a rejuvenating effect. His sister's seemingly idle vivacity crackled in his solitude like a small fire in a long-unused stove. Bright waves of charming gaiety, dark waves of human trust, filled the rooms in which he lived, which as a result lost their nature of a space in which their sole inhabitant moved at the dictates of his own will. But what astonished him above all in this inexhaustible presence that was not his own was that the uncountable trifles of which it consisted added up to something incalculable and utterly different in kind: his impatience with anything that wasted his time, this unquenchable feeling that had been with him all his life, no matter what he had seized on that was considered to be great and important, had to his amazement completely disappeared, and for the first time he was loving his daily life without thinking at all.

He even gasped, a little too obligingly, when Agathe, with the earnestness women bring to such matters, offered for his admiration the thousand dainty things that she had bought. There is a droll oddity in the nature of the human female that renders her, though equal in intelligence, more sensitive than the male and precisely for that reason more receptive to the idea of resorting to the brutal ploys of self-adornment, by which she deviates even further from rationally ordered humanity than he does in his masculine way. Ulrich acted as if this trait irresistibly compelled his sympathetic engagement. And perhaps that was really the case. For the many small, endearingly silly inspirations he was presented with: wreathing oneself in glass beads, crimping one's hair with a curling iron, enlisting the inane patterns of lace and embroidery, applying seductive colors with a determination that is nothing short of ruthless—these baits so akin to the aluminum stars one can win at a fairground shooting gallery that every intelligent woman sees through them without in the slightest losing her taste for them—began to enmesh him in the threads of their gleaming lunacy. For the moment one takes anything, no matter how foolish or lacking in taste, seriously on an equal footing, it begins to display its own harmonious order, the intoxicating scent of its amour propre, its innate urge to play and to please. This was what happened to Ulrich in the course of the operations that were required of him as he assisted Agathe with her regalia. He fetched and carried, admired, appraised, was asked for advice, helped with trial fittings. He stood with Agathe in front of the mirror. Nowadays, when a woman's appearance resembles that of a well-plucked chicken that offers no inconvenience, it is difficult to imagine her earlier appearance in all its allure to a long-deferred appetite, a charm that has in the meantime fallen prey to ridicule: the long skirt, seemingly stitched to the floor by the tailor and yet miraculously ambulant, enclosed a second layer of other, secret light skirts beneath it, pastel-colored silken petals whose gently swaying movement then suddenly gave way to white, even softer tissues, and it was only the delicate foam of those ultimate garments that finally touched the body; and if this attire resembled waves in that it wed an undertow of enticement with a firm rebuff to the eye, it was also an ingenious system of way stations and fortifications ranged around expertly defended wonders and with all its unnaturalness an artfully curtained theater of love, whose breathtaking darkness was lightened only by the dim lamp of the imagination. Ulrich was now seeing this epitome of preliminaries dismantled daily, deconstructed, as it were, from the inside. And though a woman's secrets had long since ceased to be a mystery to him, or perhaps rather because he had always only hurried through them like vestibules or front yards, they took on a completely different importance now that there was no gateway for him and no goal. The tension that lay in all these things rebounded. Ulrich would have been hard put to say what changes it wrought in him. He rightly regarded himself as a man of masculine temperament, and it seemed reasonable to him that such a man might be tempted to see what he has so often desired from its own side, but at times it became almost eerie and he would rebel against it with a laugh.

"As though the walls of a girl's boarding school had risen up around me overnight, completely shutting me in!" he protested.

"Is that so terrible?" Agathe asked.

"I don't know," Ulrich replied.

Then he called her a carnivorous plant and himself a poor insect that had crawled into her luminous calyx. "You've closed it around

me," he said, "and now that, against my nature, I've become part of
you, I'm sitting here surrounded by colors, perfume, and radiance,
waiting for the males we're going to attract!"

And the effect on him—given his concern to "find her a husband"—of witnessing the effect Agathe had on men was indeed rather
strange. He was not jealous—in what capacity could he have been
that?—and subordinated his own welfare to hers. What he wished
for her was that a man worthy of her would soon free her from the
state of transition her separation from Hagauer had placed her in:
and nevertheless, when he saw her standing at the center of a group
of men vying for her attention, or when on the street a man, attracted
by her beauty and heedless of her escort, looked her in the eye, he did
not know what to make of his feelings. Here too, since the simple
way out—male jealousy—was forbidden to him, he often felt enclosed
in a world he had never entered before. From his own experience he
knew as much about male posturing as he did about women's more
guarded procedures in love, and when he saw Agathe exposed to the
one and engaged in the other, he suffered; he felt as if he were attending the courtship of horses or of mice; the snorting and neighing, the
pursing and spreading of lips with which strangers display their
smugness and deference to each other filled him, observing it as he
did without sympathy, with a faint disgust, like a dense anesthetic
torpor spreading up from the depths of his body. And if nevertheless,
in accordance with a deep emotional need, he put himself in his sister's
place, he was afterward not far from feeling, along with bewilderment
at such acquiescence, the shame that a normal man feels when approached under false pretenses by a man who is not. When he confessed
this to Agathe, she laughed. "Well, there happen to be some women
in our circle who are very interested in you," was her answer.

What was going on here?

Ulrich said: "Basically it's a protest against the world!"

And Ulrich said further: "You know my friend Walter: it's been
a long time since we liked each other; but even though he irritates
me and I know that I get on his nerves as well, often at the mere sight
of him I feel affection toward him, as if he and I were in perfect ac-

cord, which in fact we are not. Look, in life one understands so much without having come to an understanding with it; that's why being in agreement with another person from the outset, before one has understood him, is as fabulously, beautifully senseless as when water streams into a valley from all sides in the spring!"

And he felt: "It's that way now!" And he thought: "As soon as I manage to no longer have any self-centered, egotistic thoughts toward Agathe or even a single ugly feeling of indifference, she draws all qualities out of me the way the Magnetic Mountain draws the nails out of a ship! Morally, I am dissolved into a state like that of the primal atom, where I am neither myself nor her! Could it be that beatitude is like this?!"

But all he said was: "It's such fun to watch you!"

Agathe blushed and said: "Why is it 'fun'?"

"Oh, I don't know. Sometimes you're self-conscious in my presence," Ulrich said. "But then you remember that I'm 'only your brother.' And at other times when I catch you in circumstances that would be very appealing to a strange man, you're not embarrassed at all, but then suddenly it occurs to you that this is not for my eyes and tell me to look away..."

"And what's fun about that?" Agathe asked.

"Maybe it makes one happy to follow someone else with one's eyes without knowing why," Ulrich said. "It's like a child's love for his things; without the child's mental powerlessness..."

"Maybe it's only fun for you," Agathe replied, "to play brother and sister because you're sick of playing man and woman?"

"That too," Ulrich said, watching her. "Love, at its origin, is simply the drive toward closeness and the grasping instinct. It has been divided into two poles, lady and gentleman, with all sorts of mad tensions, frustrations, spasms, and perversions arising in between. We've seen enough of this bloated ideology, which is almost as ridiculous as a gastrosophy. I'm convinced most people would be happy if this connection between an epidermal stimulus and the whole of human nature could be canceled out, Agathe! And sooner or later there will come an age of simple sexual companionship, where boy and girl will stand, like-minded and perplexed, before an old heap of broken springs that once drove the mechanisms called Man and Woman!"

"But if I were to tell you that Hagauer and I were pioneers of that age, you would hold it against me!" Agathe replied with a smile as astringent as good unsugared wine.

"I no longer resent anything," Ulrich said. He smiled. "A warrior unbuckled from his armor. For the first time in ages he feels the air of nature instead of hammered iron on his skin and sees his body becoming so wan and frail that the birds might carry it away!"

And thus, smiling, and simply forgetting to stop smiling, he contemplated his sister sitting on the edge of a table, swinging one leg dressed in a black silk stocking; except for her chemise, all she was wearing was a pair of short panties: but these impressions had detached themselves from their intrinsic meaning, as it were, and become separate, isolated images. "She is my friend who, adorably, represents a woman to me," Ulrich thought. "What a realistic complication it is that she really is one."

And Agathe asked: "Is there really no love?"

"There is!" Ulrich said. "But it's an exceptional case. We need to make some distinctions: First, there is a physical experience that belongs to the class of epidermal stimuli; this can be aroused without any moral paraphernalia, even without emotions, as something purely agreeable and pleasant. In the second case there are usually emotions that become intensely associated with the physical experience, but only in ways that, with small variations, are the same for everyone; these peak moments of love I would be inclined to regard as belonging to the physical-mechanical domain rather than that of the soul. And finally there is the soul's own experience of loving: but that has no necessary connection with the two other parts. One can love God, one can love the world; and maybe one can only love God or the world. At any rate, love of a human being is not necessarily involved. But if it is, the physical side pulls the whole world in toward itself, turning it inside out, so to speak—" Ulrich interrupted himself.

Agathe had flushed a deep red.

If Ulrich had deliberately selected and arranged his words with the intention of surreptitiously suggesting to Agathe the act of physical love they inescapably connoted, he would have achieved his purpose.

He looked around for matches, merely to interrupt the unintended shift in their relationship that had occurred.

"At any rate," he said, "love, when it is love, is an exceptional case and can't serve as a model for everyday behavior."

Agathe had reached for the corners of the tablecloth and wrapped it around her legs. "Wouldn't strangers, if they could see and hear us, think there was something perverse in our feelings?" she suddenly asked.

"Nonsense!" Ulrich maintained. "What each of us feels is the shadowy doubling of one's own self in the other's opposite nature. I am a man, you are a woman; it's widely believed that every human being bears within himself or herself the shadowlike or repressed opposite of each of his or her qualities: at any rate one possesses the longing for it, if one is not hopelessly satisfied with oneself. So here my counterself has come to light and slipped into you, and yours into me, and they feel grand in their transposed bodies, simply because they don't have a great deal of respect for their former environs and the view to be had from there."

Agathe thought: "He's said a lot more about all this before. Why is he diluting it?"

What Ulrich said was, of course, consistent with the life they were leading as companions who occasionally, when the company of others leaves them free, marvel at the fact that they are a man and a woman but at the same time twins. When such an understanding exists between two people, their separate relations with the world take on the charm of an invisible game of hide-and-seek involving swapped clothes and bodies and a cheerful hoodwinking of those who do not suspect their two-in-one, one-in-two duplicity. But this playful and all-too-emphatic merriment—the way children sometimes deliberately amplify the noise they are naturally making!—belied the gravity that sometimes, from a great height, laid its shadow on the hearts of brother and sister, making them fall inadvertently silent. One evening, for instance, when by chance they encountered each other again before going to bed and Ulrich saw his sister in a long nightgown, he wanted to make a joke and said: "If this were a hundred years ago, I would have wanted to cry out: 'My angel!' Too bad that expression is out of fashion!" Then he fell silent, taken aback, and thought: "Isn't that the only word I should use for her?! Not friend, not woman! Also: 'Heavenly creature'! People used to say that. Ridiculously high-flown, but it's still better than not having the courage to believe oneself."

And Agathe thought: "A man in pajamas doesn't look like an angel!" But he looked fierce and broad-shouldered, and she was suddenly ashamed of the wish that this powerful face framed by dense hair would darken her sight. She had, in a carnal and innocent way, been sensually aroused; her blood rushed through her body in vehement waves and spread out into her skin, robbing her inner self of all its strength. Since she was not such a fanatical person as her brother, she felt what she felt. When she felt tenderness, she was tender, not lit up with ideas or moral inspirations, although that was something she loved in him as much as she shied away from it. And again and again, day by day, Ulrich summed it all up in the idea: Basically it's a protest against life! They walked arm in arm through the city. Matched in height, matched in age, matched in their views and values. Strolling along side by side, they could not see much of one another. Tall figures, pleasing to each other, they took to the street out of pure enjoyment, feeling at every step the breath of their contact in the midst of alien surroundings. We belong together! This feeling, which is far from uncommon, made them happy, and half given over to it, half against it, Ulrich said: "It's funny that we're so content to be brother and sister. For the rest of the world it's an ordinary relationship, and we're making something special out of it, aren't we?"

Perhaps he had hurt her by saying this. He added: "But it's what I always wished for. When I was a boy, I made up my mind to marry only a woman I had already adopted as a little girl and brought up myself. I'm fairly sure many men have such fantasies, they're downright banal. But as an adult I once actually fell in love with such a child, even though it was only for two or three hours!" And he went on to tell her about it: "It happened on a streetcar. A young girl got on, maybe twelve years old, together with her very young father or an older brother. The way she steps in, sits down, casually hands the conductor the fare for both of them, she's a lady; but totally, and without any childish affectation. There was the same quality in the way she spoke with her companion or silently listened to him. She was stunningly beautiful; suntanned, full lips, strong eyebrows, a slightly upturned nose: maybe a dark-haired Polish girl or a southern Slav. I believe she was wearing a dress that suggested some national costume, but with a long, narrow-waisted jacket that had corded trim and ruffles at the throat and hands and was in its way just as perfect as that whole little person. Maybe she was Albanian? I was sitting too far away to hear what she was saying. It struck me that the features of her serious face were mature beyond her years, so that she seemed fully adult. And yet this was not the face of a dwarfishly small woman. It was a child's face, without question. On the other hand, this child's face was not at all the immature preliminary to an adult's face. It seems that sometimes a woman's face is complete at the age of twelve, even spiritually, fully formed as if by masterful brushstrokes in a first draft, so that everything added by subsequent touches only spoils the original greatness. It's possible to fall passionately in love with such an apparition, mortally, and essentially without desire. I remember looking around shyly at the other passengers, because I felt as if all order was shrinking away from me. When the little girl got out, I followed her, but I lost sight of her in the crowded street," he said, ending his little account.

After resting with this in silence for a while, Agathe asked, smiling: "And how does this fit in with the age of love being over and only sex and comradeship being left?"

"It doesn't fit in with that at all!" Ulrich exclaimed, laughing as well.

His sister, after some reflection, remarked with startling harshness—it seemed to be an intentional repetition of the words he had used on the evening of their reunion: "All men want to play little brother and little sister. There really must be something stupid behind it. These little brothers and sisters call each other Daddy and Mommy when they're a little tipsy."

Ulrich was taken aback. It was not merely that Agathe was right: Gifted women are also merciless observers of the men they love; they just don't have theories and hence make no use of their discoveries unless provoked. He felt somewhat affronted. "This has been explained psychologically, of course," he said hesitantly. "And it couldn't be more obvious that the two of us are psychologically suspect. Incestuous tendencies, demonstrable in early childhood, along with an antisocial mentality and a rebellious stance toward life. Maybe even insufficiently stable monosexuality, though in my case—"

"Mine too!" Agathe interrupted, laughing again, though not entirely willingly. "I don't like women at all!"

"It makes no difference," Ulrich said. "Psychic entrails, in any case. You can also say there's a sultanic need to be the only one who adores and is adored, to the exclusion of the rest of the world; in the ancient Orient this brought forth the harem, and today we have family, love, and the dog. And I can say that the craving to possess a person so exclusively that no one else can come near is a sign of personal loneliness in the human community that even socialists rarely deny. If you want to see it that way, we are nothing but a bourgeois abnormality. —Oh look, how magnificent!" he broke off, pulling on her arm.

They were standing at the edge of a small marketplace surrounded by old houses. Round about the neoclassical statue of some mental giant they could see the many-colored vegetables, the large canvas umbrellas above the market stands, pieces of fruit rolling on the ground, baskets being dragged, dogs being chased away from the splendors in their crates, the red faces of rough-hewn men and women. The air rumbled and shrilled with the industrious clamor of voices and smelled of sun shining on the welter of earthly things. "Just seeing and smelling the world, how can one not love it?" Ulrich asked exuberantly. "And we can't love it, because we are not in agreement with what is going on in their heads," he added.

This separation was not exactly to Agathe's taste, and she did not respond. But she pressed her body against her brother's arm, and they both understood that to mean the same as if she had gently put her hand on his mouth.

Ulrich said laughing: "Look, I don't like myself either! This is what happens when one always finds fault with other people. But even I have to be able to love something, and so a Siamese sister who is neither me nor herself, and just as much me as herself, is clearly the only point where everything intersects!"

He had cheered up again. And as often happened, his mood swept Agathe along. But they never again talked as they had on the first night of their recent reunion or before. That had disappeared like castles in the clouds: when they loom above city streets teeming with life instead of over the solitary countryside, they are hard to believe in. Perhaps the cause of this was only that Ulrich did not know what degree of solidity might be ascribed to the experiences that moved him; but Agathe often believed that all he saw in them was a fantastical aberration. And she could not prove to him that it was not so: for she always spoke less than he did, never struck the right note, and did not feel confident enough to try. She merely felt that he was evading the decision, and that he must not do that. And so in effect they were both hiding in their amusement and pleasure without depth or weight, and Agathe grew sadder day by day, even though she laughed just as often as her brother.

19

PROFESSOR HAGAUER PUTS PEN TO PAPER

BUT THIS changed, thanks to Agathe's husband, to whom all along they had given so little consideration.

On a morning that put an end to those days of mirth, she received a heavy letter in a foolscap envelope stamped with a large round yellow seal bearing the white imprint of the Imperial and Royal Rudolfsgymnasium in ——. Instantly, even while she still held the missive unopened in her hand, out of nothing there arose houses, two-storied: with the mute mirroring of well-polished windows; with white thermometers on the outside of their brown frames, one on each floor, for reading the weather; with Greek pediments and baroque scallops over the windows, heads projecting from the walls and other such mythological sentinels that looked as if they had been made in a cabinetmaker's workshop and painted to look like stone. The streets ran through the town the way they had entered, as brown and wet country roads with deep ruts, and the stores standing on either side with their brand-new window displays looked like ladies of thirty years earlier who have lifted their long skirts but cannot make up their minds to step from the sidewalk into the dirt of the street. The provinces in Agathe's head! Ghosts inside Agathe's head! Incomprehensible not-quite-disappearedness, even though she had thought herself unmoored from it forever! Even more incomprehensible: that she had ever been bound to it in the first place! She saw the way leading from her front door past the walls of familiar houses to the school, a route she had often taken when she accompanied Hagauer from his home to his place of work in the early days, when she was still intent on not missing a single drop of the bitter healing potion. "Is Hagauer now eating lunch at the hotel?" she wondered. "Does he now tear the pages off the calendar the way I used to do every morning?" All this had suddenly assumed again such mindless hyperreality that it seemed it could never die, and with quiet horror she saw awakening within her the familiar feeling of intimidation, consisting of indifference, lost courage, satiation with ugliness, and the state of her own tenuous, aerial nature. With a kind of avidity she opened the thick letter her husband had addressed to her.

When Professor Hagauer had returned to his home and workplace from his father-in-law's funeral and a brief visit to the capital, his environment received him exactly as it always did after his short trips, and he in turn, pleasantly conscious of having properly settled a matter and now exchanging his traveling shoes for the house slippers in which a man works twice as well, turned his attention to his surroundings. He betook himself to his school; he was deferentially greeted by the janitor; he felt himself welcomed when he encountered the teachers subordinate to him; in the principal's office the files and problems no one had dared to tackle in his absence awaited him; as he hastened along the corridors, he was accompanied by a sense that his steps lent wings to the building: Gottlieb Hagauer was a personage and knew it; encouragement and good cheer beamed from his brow throughout the institution of learning he was in charge of, and whenever outside the school someone asked him how his wife was doing or where she was, he would answer with the serenity of a man who knows himself to be respectably married. It is well known that so long as a man is capable of procreation, he experiences brief interruptions of his married life as if a light yoke has been lifted, even when he has no intentions of taking illicit advantage of his freedom, and that after the period of respite has elapsed, he takes up his happiness once more refreshed. That was how Hagauer, too, at first guilelessly accepted Agathe's absence, for a while not even noticing how long his wife was staying away.

What actually drew his attention to it was the same wall calendar, with the page to be torn off day after day, that had appeared in Agathe's memory as an appalling symbol of life; it hung in the dining room as a spot that did not belong on the wall—persisting there as a New Year's gift from a stationery store ever since Hagauer had brought it home from school, and because of its dreariness not only tolerated but maintained by Agathe. Now, it would have been entirely in Hagauer's nature if after his wife's departure he had taken over the task of tearing the sheets off this calendar, for it was contrary to his habits to let that part of the wall run wild, as it were. But on the other hand he was a man who knew at all times on what latitude of the week or month he was situated in the ocean of infinity; moreover, he already had a calendar in his office in school anyway; and finally, just as he was about to raise his hand to regulate the measurement of time in his home, he had felt a strange smiling reluctance, one of those impulses through which, as it later turned out, fate announces itself, but which at that moment he merely took for a tender, chivalrous sentiment that took him by surprise and made him pleased with himself: he decided that the page marking the day when Agathe had left the house should remain untouched, as a token of homage and a souvenir, until her return.

And so in the course of time the wall calendar became a festering wound, reminding Hagauer at every glance how long his wife had avoided coming home. Thrifty with his emotions as with his house-keeping, he wrote her postcards, giving her news of himself and asking her, with gradually mounting urgency, when she expected to return. He received no answer. Soon he no longer beamed when acquaintances asked him sympathetically whether his wife would be away much longer in fulfillment of sad obligations, but fortunately he always had a great deal to do, since apart from the demands of school and of the clubs he belonged to, each day brought him through the mail a plethora of invitations, inquiries, avowals of approval, attacks, proofs to be corrected, magazines and important books: for while Hagauer's human self resided in the provinces, forming part of the unappealing impression these were capable of making on a stranger passing through, his mind was at home in Europe, and this prevented him for a long time from grasping the full significance of Agathe's prolonged absence. But one day there arrived with the mail a letter from Ulrich dryly informing him of the facts: that Agathe had no intention of returning to him and was requesting his consent to a divorce. Despite its polite form, this letter was so curt and so inconsiderate in tone that Hagauer indignantly realized Ulrich was about as concerned with his, the recipient's, feelings as if he intended to remove an insect from a leaf. His first movement of inner defense was: Nothing serious, a whim! The message lay like a mocking specter in the bright daylight of pressing correspondence, tributes, and honorable mentions. It was only that evening, when Hagauer saw his empty house again, that he sat down at his desk and informed Ulrich with dignified brevity that it would be best to regard his note as not having ever been written. But soon a new letter from Ulrich arrived rejecting this view, repeating Agathe's wish (without her knowing about it), and asking Hagauer, in somewhat more courteous detail, to do all that he could to facilitate the necessary legal steps, as befitted a man of his moral stature, and as was desirable, too, if the deplorable concomitants of a public dispute were to be avoided. Now Hagauer grasped the seriousness of the situation and allowed himself three days' time to come up with an answer that would leave nothing to be either desired or regretted afterward.

For two of those three days he suffered from a feeling as if someone had struck him a blow to the heart. "A bad dream!" he plaintively said to himself several times, and whenever he did not take himself very firmly in hand, he forgot to believe in the reality of what was being demanded of him. During these days he felt a deep discomfort in his breast that was very much like injured love, and in addition an indefinable jealousy that was directed, certainly not against a lover whom he suspected of being the cause of Agathe's behavior, but against an intangible Something that had in effect demoted him. It was a kind of humiliation, similar to that of a very orderly man who has shattered or forgotten something: as if something that has had its fixed place in the mind since time immemorial, that one no longer notices but upon which a great deal depends, was suddenly broken. Pale and distraught, in a genuine torment that must not be underestimated because it lacked beauty, Hagauer walked about avoiding people, shrinking from the explanations he would have to give, the humiliations he would have to endure. It was not until the third day that his condition arrived at some stability. Hagauer had a natural aversion to Ulrich that was as great as Ulrich's dislike of him, and though this had never quite shown itself before, it did so now when with a sudden leap of intuition he imputed all the blame for Agathe's behavior to that footloose gypsy brother of hers, who must have completely turned her head; he sat down at his desk and with a few sparse words demanded the immediate return of his wife, declaring with iron resolve that as her husband he would discuss all further matters only with her.

Ulrich sent a refusal, equally brief and equally iron in its resolution.

Now Hagauer decided to work on Agathe directly; he made copies of his correspondence with Ulrich and added a long, carefully reasoned letter, and it was all of this that Agathe saw before her when she opened the large envelope with the official seal.

Hagauer himself had felt as if all of what seemed intent on happening could not be true. After discharging his professional obligations, he had sat in the "deserted house" in the evening facing a blank sheet of paper, just as Ulrich had earlier, not knowing how to begin. But in Hagauer's life the well-known "buttons technique" had proved successful more than once, and he resorted to it this time as well. It consists in taking a methodical approach to one's thoughts, even when faced with an unsettling challenge, much as a man will have buttons sewn to his clothes because to assume that clothes can be removed from the body more quickly without buttons would actually entail a loss of time. The English author Surway, for instance, whose book on the subject Hagauer now consulted, because even in his distress it remained important to compare Surway's views with his own, distinguishes five such buttons in a successful reasoning process: (a) observations of an event that immediately give rise to a sensation of difficulty in interpreting that event, (b) closer ascertainment and definition of these difficulties, (c) arriving at a conjecture as to a possible solution, (d) rational development of conclusions to be drawn from this conjecture, (e) further observations, leading to the acceptance or rejection of the hypothesis and thereby to the success of the reasoning process. Hagauer had already profitably applied a similar method to such a worldly subject as lawn tennis when he learned to play it at the Civil Service Club, and the game had acquired considerable intellectual charm for him as a result, but he had never yet made use of it in purely emotional matters; for his everyday affective life consisted largely of professional relations and, under more personal circumstances, of that "right feeling" that is a compound of all the feelings that are possible and in circulation among members of the white race in any given instance, with a certain premium on those that most nearly correspond with one's locality, profession, and class. Applying the buttons to his wife's extraordinary desire to divorce him was therefore not easy given his lack of practice, and as for the "right feeling," it has a tendency to split in two where personal difficulties are concerned. It told Hagauer, on the one hand, that a man of the times like himself is obligated on many accounts not to put obstacles in the way of dissolving a relationship based on trust; but on the other hand, if one does not want a divorce, that same right feeling will also have a great deal to say that absolves one of such obligation, for the recklessness that has come to the fore in this domain can certainly not be condoned. In a case like his own, Hagauer knew, a modern man must "relax," in other words disperse his attention, loosen up physically, and listen to whatever speaks to him from his innermost depths. Cautiously he put a halt to his deliberations, stared at the orphaned wall calendar, and listened into himself; and after a while a voice did indeed respond from a depth beneath his conscious mind, and told him precisely what he had already been thinking: that there was no reason why he should put up with anything so arbitrary as Agathe's demand.

But at this point, Professor Hagauer's mind was already unexpectedly confronted with buttons *a* to *e* in Surway's or some equivalent series of buttons and freshly cognizant of the difficulties of interpreting the event under observation. "Am I, Gottlieb Hagauer," Hagauer asked himself, "to blame for this embarrassing episode?" He examined himself and could not find a single fault in his own comportment. "Is the cause another man she's in love with?" was his second surmise in the direction of a possible solution. But he found this assumption difficult to make, because when he forced himself to consider the question objectively, it was hard to imagine what another man could offer Agathe that was better than what he gave her. Nevertheless, as this question was more easily clouded by personal vanity than any other, he subjected it to the most exacting scrutiny and, in doing so, found vistas opening out that he had never considered, and suddenly Hagauer felt himself transported to point *c* in Surway's scheme and on the trail of a possible solution via *d* and *e*: For the first time since his marriage, he was struck by a number of phenomena reported, as far as he knew, only in women whose love of the other sex is not in the slightest deep or passionate. It was painful for him that he could not find any evidence in his memory of that wide-open, dreamswept surrender he had become acquainted with earlier, during his bachelor years, in females about whose sensual way of life there could be no doubt, but whose example now offered him the advantage of being able to rule out, in complete scientific calm, the destruction of his matrimonial bliss by a third party. Thus Agathe's behavior was automatically reduced to a purely idiosyncratic revolt against this happiness, all the more so because she had left without the slightest premonitory indication; and because in the short span of time that had elapsed since then no rationally motivated change of mind could have occurred, Hagauer came to the firm and final conclusion that Agathe's incomprehensible conduct could only be explained as one of those gradually gathering temptations to deny life that are said to occur in personalities that do not know what they want.

But was Agathe's nature really of that kind? This still remained to be investigated. Hagauer thoughtfully stroked his beard with the end of his pen. True, she did usually give the impression of being an "agreeable companion," as he put it, but even when faced with matters that held the liveliest interest for him, she tended to show a marked indifference, not to say inertia! There was in fact something about her that was not in harmony with himself or with other people and their interests; it wasn't contrariness; she always laughed or became serious at appropriate moments; but now that he thought about it, she had always, through all the years, given a somewhat distracted impression. She seemed to listen to whatever was being conveyed or explained to her, but she never seemed to believe it. Now that he thought about it more closely, her indifference seemed downright unhealthy. Sometimes one got the feeling that she was not aware of her surroundings at all . . . : And suddenly, before he himself knew it, his pen had begun to run swiftly, covering the page with his characteristically upright script. "Who knows what it is," he wrote, "that makes you think you are too good to love the life I am in a position to offer you, and which I can say in all modesty is a pure and full life: you have always handled it as though with tongs, it seems to me now. You have denied yourself the riches of human and moral values that even a modest life has to offer, and even if I had to assume that there might have been something that made you feel justified in doing this, you would have shown yourself lacking in the moral will to effect a change and would have chosen an artificial and fantastical solution instead!"

He thought it over once more. He mustered the schoolboys who had passed through his guiding hands, looking for a case that might cast a light on the matter; but before he was quite underway with this, there popped into his mind the missing piece in his deliberations that he had been looking for with vague discomfort. At this moment Agathe was for him no longer a purely individual case that could not be approached through a general rule; for when he considered how much she was prepared to give up without being blinded by any particular passion, he was led inescapably, and with delight, to the basic assumption, familiar to modern pedagogy, that she lacked the capacity for suprasubjective reflection and stable mental contact with her environment. Quickly he wrote: "Probably even now as you set about doing whatever it is you have in mind, you have only the vaguest idea of what it is; but I am warning you, before you make a lasting decision! You may well be the most extreme opposite of a self-knowing and life-oriented person such as myself, but just for that reason you should not thoughtlessly divest yourself of the support I am offering!"—Actually Hagauer had wanted to write something else. For human intelligence is not a self-enclosed and isolated faculty, its defects entail moral defects—hence the expression "moral idiocy"—just as moral flaws (though this is more rarely considered) may move the intelligence in whatever direction they choose, or blind it altogether! Thus Hagauer saw in his mind's eye a distinct type that he was inclined to characterize, on the basis of conclusions already arrived at, as "an on the whole adequately intelligent variety of moral idiocy that expresses itself only in certain deficient forms of behavior." But he could not bring himself to use this illuminating expression, partly because he wanted to avoid further provoking his runaway wife, partly because a layperson usually misunderstands such terms when they are applied to him- or herself. Factually, however, it had to be acknowledged that the objectionable manifestations belonged in the broad category of substandard mentality, and at last Hagauer hit on a way out of this tension between conscience and chivalry: by subsuming the irregularities in his wife's behavior in a widespread pattern of female underperformance, he could classify them as social imbecility! Having formed this conception, he rounded off his letter in moving words. With the prophetic wrath of the scorned lover and pedagogue, he described Agathe's asocial nature, so precariously lacking in a sense of community, as a "minus variant" that never grapples vigorously and creatively with the problems of life in the way that "our modern age" requires of "its people," persisting instead in obstinate self-chosen isolation, "separated from life by a pane of glass," constantly on the brink of pathological danger. "If there was something about me you didn't like, you should have opposed it," he wrote; "but the fact is that your mind is no match for the energies of our time and therefore dodges their demands! Having warned you about your character," he concluded, "I repeat: You need reliable support more urgently than others do. In your own interest I urge you to come back immediately, and declare furthermore that the responsibility I bear as your husband forbids me to accede to your wish."

Before signing this letter, Hagauer read it through once more, found its analysis of the psychological type in question very incomplete, but refrained from altering anything, except that at the end—expelling through his moustache with a vigorous exhalation the unaccustomed, proudly accomplished effort to reflect on his wife, and pondering how much still needed to be said on the question of the "modern age"—he interpolated, above the word "responsibility," a chivalrous locution about his venerated father-in-law's precious bequest to him.

After Agathe had read all this, a strange thing happened: the content of these remarks did not leave her unaffected. Slowly, after reading it again word for word—standing all the while, without taking the time to sit down—she let the letter sink and handed it to Ulrich, who had been observing his sister's agitation with surprise.

20

ULRICH AND AGATHE LOOK FOR A
REASON AFTER THE FACT

WHILE Ulrich read, Agathe watched the play of expressions on his
face and was disheartened. He had bowed his head over the letter,
and his response seemed irresolute, as though undecided between
mockery, gravity, sorrow, or contempt. At that moment a heavy weight
descended on her; it encroached on her from all sides, as if the air
were becoming dense and unbearably stale after having just recently
been unnaturally, deliciously light. What Agathe had done with her
father's will was for the first time oppressing her conscience. But it
would be insufficient to say that she suddenly realized the full measure
of the guilt she had incurred in actual fact; rather, what she felt was
the full measure of her guilt in relation to everything, including her
brother, and the sum of it all was an indescribable disillusionment.
Everything she had done seemed incomprehensible. She had spoken
of wanting to kill her husband, she had forged a will, and she had
attached herself to her brother without asking him if she would be
disrupting his life: she had done this in a kind of imaginative delirium.
And what she was especially ashamed of at this moment was that the
most obvious and natural thought had never occurred to her, for any
other woman wanting to free herself from a husband she does not
like will either look for a better one or compensate herself by some
other, equally natural action. Ulrich himself had pointed this out
often enough, but she had not listened. Now she stood there and did
not know what he would say. Her behavior seemed to her so obviously
that of someone who is really not of sound mind that she thought
Hagauer was right to hold up a mirror to her in the way that he had;
and the sight of his letter in Ulrich's hand mortified her, much as a

person might feel when, already accused of a crime, he receives a letter from a former teacher assuring him of his contempt. Of course she had never allowed Hagauer to have any influence over her; nevertheless, the effect was as though he were in a position to say: "I had the wrong idea about you!" or "Unfortunately I was never mistaken about you and always had the feeling you would come to a bad end!" In her need to shake off this ridiculous and sorrowful feeling, she interrupted Ulrich, who was still attentively reading the letter and, it seemed, finding it hard to read all the way through.

"He's actually describing me very accurately," she said with seeming equanimity but with a touch of provocation that clearly betrayed a wish to hear the opposite. "And even though he doesn't explicitly say so, it's true nonetheless: either I must have been non compos mentis when I married him for no compelling reason, or I am now, when I'm leaving him for just as little reason."

Ulrich, who was reading for the third time those parts of the letter that made his imagination an involuntary witness of her close relationship with Hagauer, distractedly muttered something she could not make out.

"Please just pay attention," Agathe requested. "Am I the economically or intellectually active, up-to-date woman? No. Am I the woman in love? I'm not that either. Am I the good, harmonizing, simplifying, nest-building helpmeet and mother? That least of all. So what is left then? What am I in the world for? The social circles we move in, I might as well tell you, basically mean nothing to me. And I almost think I could do without the music, literature, and art that educated people find so enchanting. Hagauer, for example, can't do without them; he needs them, if only for his quotations and allusions. He at least always has at his fingertips the pleasure and orderliness of a collection. So is he not right when he reproaches me with not accomplishing anything, with denying myself 'the wealth of the beautiful and the moral,' and when he tells me the most I can still hope for is sympathy and tolerance from Professor Hagauer?!"

Ulrich handed her back the letter and replied calmly: "Let's face it: You really are socially feebleminded!" He was smiling, but there was in his tone a hint of residual irritation from having looked into this intimate letter.

But Agathe did not appreciate her brother's answer. It made her feel worse. Shyly, she mocked him in turn: "Why then, if that is the case, did you insist, without telling me anything, that I get divorced and lose my only protector?"

"Oh," Ulrich said evasively, "probably because it's so beautifully easy to adopt a firm manly tone with another man. I banged my fist on the table, he banged his fist on the table; and of course then I had to bang twice as hard: I think that's why I did it."

Up to now, though her depression prevented her from realizing it, Agathe had been very glad, indeed wildly elated, that her brother had secretly done the opposite of what he had professed to be doing during the time of their playfully flirtatious brother-and-sister game; for offending Hagauer could only have one purpose: to set up a barrier behind her that would make it impossible for her to return. But now, even here in this place of hidden joy, there was only a hollow sense of loss, and Agathe fell silent.

"We must not overlook," Ulrich continued, "how well Hagauer manages in his own way to misunderstand you with, I'm tempted to say, point-blank accuracy. Watch out, he may yet, in his own fashion, without hiring a detective, merely by starting to think about the weaknesses in your relationship with the human race, ferret out what you did with Father's will. How are we going to defend you then?"

And so, for the first time since they had been together again, the damnably blessed prank Agathe had played on Hagauer became a subject of their conversation. She vehemently shrugged her shoulders and made a vague gesture of defense.

"Hagauer is in the right, of course," Ulrich offered, gently and emphatically, for her consideration.

"He is not in the right!" she replied with emotion.

"He is partly right," Ulrich compromised. "In a situation as dangerous as this we must start out with a completely clear and honest view of what has happened and where we stand. What you did could land us both in jail."

Agathe's eyes widened in alarm. She basically knew this already, but it had never before been stated as a matter of fact.

Ulrich responded with a sympathetic gesture. "That's not the worst of it," he continued. "But how do we protect what you've done, and also the way in which you did it, from the reproach that—" He searched for an adequate expression and found none: "So let's just say it's a little bit like what Hagauer says; that it tends towards the shadow side, nervous disorders, defects born of a deficit? Hagauer represents the voice of the world, even if it does sound ridiculous in his mouth."

"Now comes the cigarette case," Agathe said with a small voice.

"That's right, here it comes," Ulrich said insistently. "There's something I have to tell you that has been bothering me for a long time."

Agathe tried to stop him. "Isn't it better if we undo the whole thing?!" she asked. "Maybe I should talk with him on amicable terms and somehow offer him an apology?"

"It's too late for that. Now he could use it as a tool to force you to go back to him," Ulrich declared.

Agathe was silent.

Ulrich returned to his example of the wealthy man who steals a cigarette case in a hotel. He had developed a theory according to which there could only be three grounds for such a theft: poverty, profession, or, if neither applies, some psychological defect. "Once when we spoke about this you objected that one could do it out of conviction," he added.

"I said one could simply do it!" Agathe interjected.

"Well, yes: on principle!"

"No, not on principle!"

"That's just it!" Ulrich said. "If one does such a thing, there has to be at least some conviction involved! I can't get over this! One doesn't 'simply' do anything, there has to be a reason for it, a ground, either an external one or an internal one. The two may not be easy to tell apart, but let's not philosophize about this; I'm just saying: If one considers something that is completely gratuitous to be right, or if, say, some decision springs out of the void for no reason at all, one comes under suspicion of being pathological or defective."

That was of course far more, and much worse, than what Ulrich had meant to say; but it coincided with the direction of his misgivings.

"Is that all you have to say to me about it?" Agathe quietly asked.

"No, it isn't," Ulrich answered grimly: "If one has no reason, one must find one!"

Neither of them was in any doubt as to where they must look. But Ulrich was after something else, and after a brief span of silence he continued thoughtfully: "The moment you venture away from harmony with everyone else, you will for all eternity cease to know what is good and what is evil. So if you want to be good, you must be convinced that the world is good. And this neither of us are. We live in a time when morality is either disintegrating or going through convulsions. But for the sake of a world that may yet come, one must keep oneself pure!"

"Do you believe this has any influence on whether that world comes or not?" Agathe demurred.

"No, unfortunately I don't believe that. At the most, the way I believe it is like this: If even the people who see this don't act rightly, it will certainly not come, and the decay is unstoppable!"

"What's in it for you if in five hundred years everything will be different, or not?"

Ulrich hesitated. "I do my duty, you see? Maybe like a soldier."

Probably because on that unhappy morning Agathe was in need of a different and more affectionate consolation than Ulrich was giving her, she replied: "So in the end, you're no different from your general?!"*

Ulrich was silent.

Agathe was not inclined to stop. "But you're not even sure it's your duty," she continued. "You do it because that's the way you are and because you enjoy it. And that's all I did!"

Suddenly she lost her self-control. Something in all this was very sad. All at once there were tears in her eyes, and a violent sob constricted her throat. In order to hide this from her brother, she threw

---

*Agathe is referring to Ulrich's loquacious friend General Stumm von Bordwehr, a member of the Parallel Campaign who occasionally visits Ulrich to apprise him of the most recent goings-on there.

her arms around his neck and hid her face against his shoulder. Ulrich could feel her weeping and the trembling of her back. An annoying embarrassment came over him: he felt himself turning cold. No matter how many tender and happy feelings he believed he had for his sister, at this moment, which should have touched him, these feelings were not there; his sensibility was distraught and immobilized. He stroked Agathe and whispered some words of consolation, but did so against strong resistance. And because he felt no reciprocal intellectual excitement in her, the contact of their two bodies seemed to him like that of two bundles of straw. He put an end to it by leading Agathe to a chair and sitting down in another chair at some distance from her. As he did that, he responded to what she had said: "You're not enjoying the business with the will at all! And you never will, because it was a disorderly thing to do!"

"Order?" Agathe exclaimed through her tears. "Duty?!"

She was quite beside herself because Ulrich had behaved so coldly. But she was already smiling again. She realized that she would have to deal with herself unassisted. She felt the smile she had managed to produce hovering outside her, far from her icy lips. Ulrich, on the other hand, was now free of embarrassment; he was even pleased that he had not felt the usual physical responsiveness; it was clear to him that this too must be different between them. But he did not have time to think about it, for he saw that Agathe had been grievously affected, and so he began to talk. "Don't be hurt by the words I used," he begged her, "and don't hold them against me! I'm probably wrong to choose words like "order" and "duty"; that really does sound like a sermon. But why," he said, changing course, "why the devil are sermons contemptible? Shouldn't they be our greatest joy?!"

Agathe had no desire to answer this at all.

Ulrich abandoned his question.

"Please don't think I'm trying to set myself up as being on the side of the angels!" he pleaded. "I did not mean to suggest that I never do anything bad. I just don't like having to do it in secret. I love the bandits of morality, not the thieves. So I want to make a moral bandit out of you," he joked, "and I won't allow you to offend out of weakness."

"For me, there's no point of honor in this!" his sister said from behind her smile, which was very far removed from her now.

"It's really terribly funny that there are times like ours where all the young people are so in love with the bad!" he interjected with a laugh, in order to move the conversation to a less personal plane. "The current passion for the morally gruesome is of course a weakness, probably due to a surfeit of the good among middle-class people; they've had enough of it. I too used to think one should say no to everything. Everyone who's between twenty-five and forty-five today thought this way; but of course that was just a kind of fashion; I could imagine a reversal happening soon, and with it a younger generation that pins morality instead of immorality to its lapel. Then the oldest fools, who have never in their life felt the excitement of morality and merely spouted moral platitudes here and there, will suddenly be the precursors and pioneers of a new character!"

Ulrich had stood up and was walking restlessly back and forth. "Maybe we could say it like this," he suggested. "The good is almost a commonplace by its very nature, whereas evil is still a critique! The immoral attains its divine right as a drastic critique of the moral! It shows us that life has other possibilities. It gives the lie to hypocrisy. We are grateful for this; in exchange we show it some forbearance! The fact that there are forgers of wills who are unquestionably charming should prove that something is amiss with the sanctity of private property. Maybe no proof is needed; but that's where the task begins: because for every kind of crime we must conceive of the possibility of pardoned criminals, even for infanticide and whatever other horrors there may be—"

He had been trying to catch his sister's eye, without success, despite his teasing reference to the will. Now she made an inadvertent gesture of resistance. She was no theoretician, she could only find her own crime excusable; basically his comparison felt like a new affront.

Ulrich laughed. "It looks like a silly game, but it means something that we can juggle like this," he assured her. "It proves there's something wrong with the way we evaluate our actions. And something really is skewed there. In a society of will-forgers, you would doubtless be in favor of the sanctity of the law; but in a society of the righteous these things get blurred and turned inside out. I'd even say that if Hagauer were a scoundrel, you would be fervently righteous: it's truly calamitous that even he is a decent fellow! This is how we all get pushed and pulled!"

He waited for an answer, which did not come; so he shrugged and repeated: "We're looking for a reason that would justify what you did. We have established that respectable people are only too happy to involve themselves in crime, of course only in their imagination. We might add that criminals, to judge by what they themselves say, would all like to be regarded as respectable people. So a definition virtually proffers itself: Crimes are the coming together, in the bodies and minds of sinners, of what other people discharge in small irregularities. Which is to say, in fantasies and in thousands of everyday acts and attitudes of nastiness and spite. One could also say: Crimes are in the air and are merely seeking the path of least resistance that leads them to certain people. One could even say that, while they are the acts of individuals who are incapable of any morality, in the main they are the concentrated expression of some universally human misconduct in the distinction between good and evil. That is what filled us from our early youth with the critical spirit our contemporaries have never got beyond!"

"But what are good and evil, exactly?" Agathe tossed out the question without Ulrich's noticing how he was tormenting her with his impartiality.

"How would I know?" he answered with a laugh. "I'm noticing only now for the first time that I loathe evil. I really didn't know how much until today. Oh, Agathe, you have no idea what it's like," he lamented pensively; "Science, for example! For a mathematician, to put it very simply, minus five is no worse than plus five. A research scientist mustn't loathe anything and will under certain circumstances feel more pleasurable excitement over a beautiful cancer than a beautiful woman. A man of knowledge knows that nothing is true and that the whole truth will not be revealed until the end of days. Science is amoral. This whole glorious business of penetrating into the unknown has weaned us off the habit of being personally concerned with our conscience. In fact, it doesn't even give us the satisfaction of taking such concern entirely seriously. And art? Doesn't it amount to a continual creation of images that don't correspond to the image of life itself? I'm not talking about bogus idealism or the painting of voluptuous nudes at a time when everyone goes around covered all the way up to their nose," he said, joking again. "But think of a real work of art: Have you never had the feeling that something about it reminds you of the scorched smell that rises from a knife you're whetting on a grindstone—a cosmic, meteoric, lightning-storm smell, divinely uncanny!?"

This was the only point at which Agathe interrupted him of her own volition. "Didn't you use to write poems yourself?" she asked him.

"You still remember that? When did I confess that to you?" Ulrich asked. "Yes; well, we all write poems at some stage. I was still doing it even when I was a mathematician," he admitted. "But the older I got, the worse they became; and I don't believe it was due to lack of talent so much as a growing distaste for the disorder and roving romanticism of this emotional digression—"

His sister shook her head almost imperceptibly, but Ulrich noticed it. "Yes, really!" he insisted. "A poem should not be any more of an exceptional event than an act of kindness is! But, if I may ask this, what becomes of the elation the moment after? You love poetry, I know: but what I want to say is that it's not enough to just have the scent of fire in one's nostrils until it fades away. This fragmentary behavior is exactly equivalent to a morality that exhausts itself in half-baked criticism." And suddenly returning to the main subject, he replied to his sister: "If my response to this Hagauer business were what you expect it to be today, then I should be skeptical, casual, and ironic. Then the doubtlessly very virtuous children that you or I may yet have would truthfully say of us that we belonged to a time of middle-class security that entertained no worries, except maybe useless ones. And yet we've gone to such great pains with our conviction!"

Ulrich probably wanted to say a great deal more; he was actually only preparing the plan of action he had in mind for his sister, and it would have been good if he had let her know that. For suddenly she stood up and on a vague pretext made herself ready to go outside.

"So it remains the case that I'm a moral imbecile?" she asked in a forced attempt to make a joke of it. "I can't keep up with everything you're saying to refute that!"

"We're both moral imbeciles!" Ulrich assured her politely. "Both of us!" And he was somewhat annoyed by the haste with which his sister left him without telling him when she would come back.

21

AGATHE WANTS TO COMMIT SUICIDE AND MAKES THE ACQUAINTANCE OF A GENTLEMAN

ACTUALLY she had rushed off because she did not want once again to present her brother with the sight of tears she could scarcely restrain. She was as sad as a person who has lost everything. Why, she did not know. It had started while Ulrich was talking. Why, she did not know either. He should have done something other than talk. What, she did not know. He was right, of course, not to take seriously the "silly coincidence" of her agitation with the arrival of the letter, and to keep on talking in the way he always did. But Agathe had to run away.

At first she felt only a need to run. She ran headlong away from the house. Where the layout of the streets forced her to change course, she hurried on in that direction. She was fleeing; in the same way that animals and humans flee from a disaster. Why, she did not ask herself. Not until she got tired did she realize what she intended to do: Never to go back!

She wanted to walk until evening. Further from home with every step. She assumed that by the time she was stopped by the barrier of evening, her decision would be made. It was the decision to kill herself. It was not exactly the decision to kill herself but the expectation that the decision would be final by evening. A desperate seething and whirling in her head was behind this expectation. She did not even have anything to kill herself with. Her little poison capsule was in a drawer somewhere or in a suitcase. The only thing that was final about her death was the yearning never to have to go back again. She wanted to walk out of life. Of that wish, the walking was already there. With every step, already, she was leaving her life.

When she grew tired, she began to feel a longing for meadows and woods, for walking in silence and open air. But there was no way to get there on foot. She took a streetcar. She had been raised to control herself in front of strangers. So when she bought a ticket and asked for directions, her voice betrayed no agitation. She sat upright and still, with not a quiver in so much as a finger. And as she sat like this, the thoughts came. She would no doubt have felt better if she could have given vent to her feelings; with her limbs fettered, these thoughts were like big bundles she tried in vain to force through an opening. She resented what Ulrich had said. She did not want to hold it against him. She denied herself the right to do that. What good was she to him?! She took up his time and gave him nothing in return; she disturbed his work and his way of life. At the thought of his way of life she felt a pang. In all the time she had lived with him, no other woman seemed to have entered the house. Agathe was convinced that her brother always needed to have a woman. So he was depriving himself for her sake. And as she was unable to compensate him in any way, she was selfish and wicked. At this moment she would have liked to turn around and tenderly beg his forgiveness. But then she remembered how cold he had been. Obviously he regretted having taken her in. All the things he had planned and said before he had gotten sick of her—he no longer mentioned any of them! Once again Agathe's heart was tormented by the great disillusionment that had come with the letter. She was jealous. Senselessly and vulgarly jealous. She wished she could force herself on her brother, and felt the passionate and impotent friendship of one who rushes headlong into the path of rejection. "I could steal for him, walk the streets for him!" she thought, and though she realized this was ridiculous, she could not help it. Ulrich's talk, with its joking manner and apparently impartial superiority, felt like a mockery. She admired his aplomb and all those intellectual needs surpassing her own. But she could not see why all ideas should always apply to all human beings equally. What she needed in her shame and humiliation was personal comfort, not general edification! She did not want to be brave!! And after a while she reproached herself for being the way she was, and increased her pain by imagining that she deserved nothing better than Ulrich's indifference.

This self-belittlement, for which neither Ulrich's behavior nor even Hagauer's painful letter had provided sufficient cause, was a temperamental outburst. Everything that Agathe, in the not very long time since she had been a child, had felt to be her failure to meet the demands of society had been brought about by her living, throughout that period, in disregard or even in opposition to her deepest inclinations. These inclinations were towards devotion and trust, for she had never become as much at home in solitude as her brother; and if until now she had found it impossible to give herself wholeheartedly to a person or a cause, it was because she bore within herself the possibility of a greater devotion, whether it stretched out its arms to the world or to God! One well-known path of devotion to all of humanity consists in not getting along with one's neighbors; in the same way a hidden and fervent longing for God may arise when a social misfit is endowed with great love. The religious criminal, in this sense, is no more absurd a phenomenon than the religious old woman who never found a husband, and Agathe's behavior toward Hagauer, which had the completely senseless form of a self-serving action, was just as much the outburst of an impatient will as was the violence with which she accused herself of having been awakened to life by her brother and now losing it because of her weakness.

She soon lost patience with sitting in the sedately rolling streetcar; when the houses by the side of the road became lower and more rural, she got out and continued on foot. The courtyards were open; through gateways and across low fences she saw artisans, animals, and children at play. The air was filled with a peace in whose vastness voices spoke and tools tapped; these sounds stirred in the bright air with the irregular, soft movements of a butterfly, while Agathe felt herself gliding past them like a shadow toward the nearby rising ground of vineyards and woods. But she halted at one point, outside a yard where coopers were at work, and listened to the good sound of mallets knocking against barrel staves. All her life she had felt pleasure in watching the modest, sensible, well-thought-out actions of hands performing such labor. This time, too, she could not have enough of the rhythmic thuds and the slow striding motions of the men circling the barrel. It allowed her to forget her grief for a moment and plunged her into a pleasant unthinking accord with the world. She always felt admiration for people who could do things like this that had evolved so variously and naturally out of a need that was universally acknowledged. Only she herself did not wish to be active, even though she had a number of mental and practical talents. Life was already complete without her. And suddenly, before the connection became clear to her, she heard bells ringing and could barely prevent herself from weeping again. The two bells of the little suburban church had probably been tolling all along, but Agathe noticed them only now and was instantly overcome by how these useless sounds, shut out from the good, abounding earth and flying passionately through the air, were related to her own existence.

She hastily resumed walking, and accompanied by the tolling of the bells, which now would not leave her ears, she swiftly advanced between the last houses onto the hills, whose lower slopes were studded with vineyards and, here and there, bushes lining the paths, while from above the bright green of the forest beckoned. And now she knew where she was being drawn, and it was a lovely feeling, as though with every step she were sinking more deeply into nature. Her heart pounded with delight and effort when she sometimes stopped and assured herself that the bells were still going with her, though hidden high in the air and hardly audible. It seemed to her that she had never before heard bells ringing like this in the middle of an ordinary day, for no apparent festive reason, democratically mingled with the natural, self-assured business of life. But of all the tongues of this thousand-voiced city, this was the last one that spoke to her, and there was something about it that seized hold of her, as though it wanted to lift her high and swing her up the mountain, but then each time it would let go of her again and lose itself in a small metallic sound that was in no way an exception to the chirping, buzzing, or rustling of all the other sounds of the countryside. So Agathe climbed and walked on for perhaps another hour, when she suddenly found herself facing the little wilderness of shrubs she had carried in her memory. It enclosed a neglected grave by the edge of the forest, where a poet had killed himself nearly a hundred years ago and where, in accordance with his last wish, he had been laid to rest. Ulrich had said he was not a good poet, though a famous one, and the rather shortsighted lyricism that expresses itself in the wish to be *buried* at a site that serves as a scenic view had found a sharp critic in him. But Agathe had loved the inscription on the big stone slab since the day they had come upon it on a walk and together deciphered the rain-worn beautiful Biedermeier letters, and she leaned over the black chains with the big angular links that defined the limit separating the rectangle of death from life.

"I was as nothing to you all" were the words the life-weary poet had asked to be inscribed on his tombstone, and it occurred to Agathe that they could apply to her too. This thought, by the edge of a forest lookout, above the verdant vineyards and the alien, immeasurable city with its slowly stirring plumes of smoke in the morning sun, moved her once again. On a sudden impulse, she kneeled down and leaned her forehead against one of the stone pillars to which the chains were attached; the unaccustomed position and the cool touch of the stone conjured up for her the somewhat rigid and will-less peace of the death that awaited her. She tried to collect herself. But she did not succeed right away: birdcalls intruded into her hearing; she was surprised by how many different birdcalls there were; branches moved, and as she did not feel the wind, it seemed to her that the trees themselves were moving their branches; in a sudden hush, a faint scurrying could be heard; the stone she was resting her forehead against was so smooth that it felt as if there were a piece of ice between her skin and the stone that kept her from quite reaching it. Only after a while did she know that what was distracting her was the very thing she was trying to recall, that fundamental sense of being utterly superfluous, which, reduced to its simplest terms, could only be expressed with the words that life was so complete without her that she had no business meddling with it. This cruel feeling was at bottom neither despairing nor aggrieved; rather, it was a listening and a watching that Agathe had always known, now merely devoid of any impulse, indeed any chance, to include herself. There was almost a quality of being sheltered in this banishment, just as there is an awe that forgets to ask questions. She could just as well go away. But where? There had to be some place, somewhere. Agathe was not one of those people in whom even a conviction of the vanity of all imaginings can take the form of a kind of satisfaction akin to belligerent or spiteful austerity as a way of accepting one's unsatisfactory lot. She was generous and incautious in such matters and not like Ulrich, who put every conceivable difficulty in the way of his feelings, in order to disallow them if they did not pass the test. She was stupid! That was it, she told herself. She did not want to think things through. Defiantly she pressed her deeply lowered brow against the iron chains, which gave a little and then firmly resisted. In these last weeks she had somehow begun to believe in God again, but without thinking of Him. Certain states in which the world had always seemed different to her from the way it appears, and in such a way that she too was no longer shut out but entirely flooded by a radiant conviction, had almost, under Ulrich's influence, been brought close to an inner metamorphosis and a complete transformation. She would have been prepared to conceive of a God who opens his world like a hiding place. But Ulrich said this was not necessary, it could only do harm to imagine more than one could experience. And it was up to him to decide such things. But then he must also guide her without abandoning her. He was the threshold between two lives, and all the longing she felt for one of them, and all her flight from the other, led to him first. She loved him as shamelessly as one loves life. When she opened her eyes in the morning, it was he who awoke in all her limbs. Even now he was looking at her from the dark mirror of her anguish: And only at this moment did Agathe remember that she wanted to kill herself. She had the feeling that to spite him she had run away from home to God when she left the house with the resolve to kill herself. But now that resolve seemed to be exhausted and to have sunk back to its source, which was that Ulrich had hurt her. She was angry at him, that feeling was still with her, but the birds were singing, and she heard them again. She was just as bewildered as before, but now joyfully bewildered. She wanted to take some kind of action, but it should be directed at Ulrich, not just at herself. The infinite torpor in which she had lain on her knees gave way to the warm and lively sensation of blood streaming into her limbs as she rose to her feet.

When she looked up, a man was standing near her. She was embarrassed, for she did not know how long he had been watching her. When her glance, still darkened by excitement, slid across his, she noticed that he was observing her with unconcealed sympathy and apparently wanted to instill her with hearty confidence: The man was tall and gaunt, wore dark clothes, and a short blond beard covered his chin and cheeks. Beneath this beard one could discern soft, slightly pouting lips whose youthfulness contrasted oddly with the gray hair that was already mingling with the blond, as if age had overlooked them beneath the growth of facial hair. This face was altogether difficult to decipher. The first impression suggested a secondary-school teacher; the sternness in this face was not carved out of hard wood but was rather like something soft that had been toughened amid daily little vexations. But if one took as one's point of departure this very softness, in which the manly beard appeared like a thing implanted to satisfy a convention its wearer believed in, one realized that in this perhaps somewhat womanish foundation there were hard, almost ascetic details, evidently shaped out of that soft material by a ceaselessly active will.

Agathe did not know what to make of this face, which held her in suspension between attraction and repulsion. She understood only that this man wanted to help her.

"Life offers as much opportunity to strengthen the will as it does to weaken it," the stranger said, wiping his fogged eyeglasses in order to see better. "One should never flee from difficulties but should seek to master them!" Agathe looked at him in astonishment. Clearly he must have been watching her for a long time, for these words came from the midst of an inner conversation. Suddenly startled, he lifted his hat, making good his failure to perform that indispensable courtesy earlier; but he quickly regained his composure and proceeded straightforwardly. "Pardon my asking if I can help you," he said. "It seems to me that emotional pain, indeed often even a shocking injury to the self, such as I am witnessing here, is more easily confided to a stranger!"

It appeared that the stranger was not speaking without effort; he seemed to have been fulfilling a charitable duty in engaging with this beautiful woman, and now that they were walking side by side, he was positively struggling with his words. For Agathe had simply stood up and begun slowly walking away from the grave, and he with her, out from among the trees into the open space by the edge of the hills, undecided whether they would now take one of the paths leading downward, or if they did, which one. Instead they walked a considerable way along the hillside in conversation; then they turned around, and then they walked again in the first direction, neither of them knowing where the other had intended to go, and each willing to yield to the other's choice. "Won't you tell me why you were weeping?" the stranger repeated with the mild voice of a doctor asking where it hurts. Agathe shook her head. "It wouldn't be easy to explain," she said, and suddenly asked him: "But I have a question for you: What makes you so sure that you can help me without knowing me? I should think that one can't help anyone!"

The man by her side did not answer right away. He opened his mouth to speak several times, but it seemed he was forcing himself to wait. Finally, he said: "Probably one can only help someone who is suffering from something one has lived through oneself."

He fell silent. Agathe laughed at the thought that this man could suppose that he might have experienced what she was suffering, which would fill him with revulsion if he knew what it was. The man seemed not to hear this laugh or else to regard it as bad manners due to nervous agitation.

After a moment's reflection he said calmly: "Of course I don't mean that anyone has a right to imagine that he can show anyone else how to go about his life. But you see: In a catastrophe, fear is infectious, and—escape is infectious too! I mean the mere fact of having escaped, as from a burning house. All the others have lost their heads and are running into the flames: What a tremendous help if a single person stands outside and waves, nothing more than that: waving and shouting that there is a way out, though his words may be unintelligible to them . . . !"

Agathe nearly laughed again at the dreadful thoughts this kindly man harbored in his imagination; but just because they were so incongruent with his appearance, their expression molded his wax-soft face almost uncannily from within.

"My, you talk like a fireman!" she replied, deliberately adopting the teasing superficial manner of a fashionable lady in order to hide her curiosity. "But surely you must have formed some idea of what kind of catastrophe I am involved in?!" —Unwittingly, the seriousness in her mockery came through, for this man's simple notion of wanting to help her aroused her indignation by the equally simple gratitude that arose in her. The stranger looked at her with astonishment. Then he collected himself and retorted almost in the manner of a rebuke: "You are probably still too young to know that our life is very simple. It is insurmountably confusing only when one thinks of oneself; but the moment one does not think of oneself and asks oneself how one can help another person, it is very simple!"

Agathe considered this and did not respond. And whether because of her silence or because of the encouragingly wide-open space into which his words sailed out, the stranger went on talking without looking at her: "The overestimation of the personal is a modern superstition. These days there is so much talk of a culture of personality, living life to the fullest, life affirmation, and the like. But these murky, ambiguous terms only betray their users' need to veil the true meaning of their revolt. What is it that one is supposed to affirm? Everything and anything, with no discrimination? Development always involves opposition, an American thinker has said. We can't very well develop one side of our nature without holding back the growth of the other side. And what is it that should be lived to the full? The mind or the instincts? Our whims or our character? Selfishness or love? If our higher nature is to be lived to the full, our lower nature must learn renunciation and obedience."

Agathe was wondering why it should be simpler to attend to others' needs than to one's own. She was one of those not at all egotistic natures whose thoughts always revolve around themselves but who never look after their own interests, and this is much further removed from the usual, self-serving sort of selfishness than is the contented unselfishness of those who look after their fellow men. And so what her neighbor was saying was at bottom foreign to her, but somehow it affected her nonetheless, and particular words, wielded with such energetic emphasis, danced before her eyes unsettlingly, as if their meaning was more to be seen in the air than heard. They happened to be walking along a ridge that gave Agathe a wonderful view of the deeply sunken valley, while her companion evidently experienced the site as akin to a pulpit or lectern. She stopped, and with her hat, which she had all along been carelessly swinging in her hand, she drew a line through the stranger's speech. "So you did form an image of me," she said. "I see it shining through, and it's not flattering!"

The tall gentleman was dismayed, for he had not meant to offend her, and Agathe gave him a friendly smile. "You seem to be confusing me with the rights of the free personality. And what's more, with a rather neurasthenic and quite unpleasant personality!"

"I was only speaking of the essential foundation of the personal life," he said apologetically, "and admittedly, the situation in which I found you gave me the feeling that you might be in need of counsel. The essential foundation of life goes frequently unrecognized these days. All the neurosis of modern life, with all its excesses, only comes from a slack inner atmosphere where there's a lack of will, because without a special effort of the will no one can gain that unity and constancy that raise one above the dark tumult of the organism!"

Here again two words, "unity" and "constancy," came up like a memory recalling Agathe's yearning and self-reproaches. "Explain to me what you mean by that," she said. "Surely one can only have a will if one already has a goal?!"

"It doesn't matter what I mean," he replied in a tone that was as mild as it was curt. "Don't all of humanity's great scriptures tell us with unsurpassable clarity what we must and must not do?"

Agathe was baffled.

"Establishing fundamental ideals for living," her companion

explained, "demands such a penetrating knowledge of life and of man, and at the same time such a heroic mastery of the passions and of one's own selfish nature, as has only been granted to very few people in the course of thousands of years. And these teachers of humanity have at all times professed the same truth."

Agathe involuntarily resisted, as would any young person who values his or her flesh and blood more highly than the bones of dead sages. "But laws made for all of humanity thousands of years ago can't possibly apply to conditions today!" she exclaimed.

"They are far more timely than is acknowledged by skeptics who have lost touch with living experience and self-knowledge!" her chance companion replied with bitter satisfaction. "The deep truths of life are not arrived at through debate, as Plato already said; man hears them as the living exegesis and fulfillment of himself! Believe me, what makes man truly free, and what robs him of his freedom, what gives him true felicity, and what destroys it: this is not subject to progress, every person with an honest conscience knows this in his heart, if he will but listen!"

The words "living exegesis" appealed to Agathe, but now an unexpected thought occurred to her: "Are you by any chance religious?" she asked. She looked at him with curiosity. He did not answer. "You don't happen to be a priest?!" she continued, but was reassured by his beard, for the rest of his appearance suddenly seemed capable of delivering such a surprise. It must be said to her credit that she would not have been more astounded if the stranger had casually referred to "our sublime ruler, the divine Augustus": she knew that religion plays a great role in politics, but one is so used to not taking seriously the ideas that serve public discourse that to expect the religious parties to consist of believers can seem as far-fetched as it would be to require of a mail clerk that he be a philatelist.

After a long, somehow vacillating pause the stranger replied: "I would rather not answer your question; you are too far removed from all this."

But Agathe had been seized by a lively desire. "Now I want to know who you are!" she demanded, and that was of course a feminine privilege that could not be flatly denied. Again the stranger showed the same somewhat comical insecurity as before, when he had hastened to make good his failure to salute her properly; he appeared to be feeling an itch in his hand to lift his hat again, but then something stiffened in him; one mental army seemed to be battling another until it finally won.

"My name is Lindner and I am a teacher at the Franz-Ferdinand-Gymnasium," he said. After a moment's reflection he added: "I also lecture at the university."

"Then perhaps you know my brother?" Agathe asked eagerly and went on to give him Ulrich's name. "If I'm not mistaken, he recently gave a lecture at the Pedagogical Society on mathematics and the humanities, or something like that."

"I know who he is. And yes, I attended that lecture," Lindner admitted. Agathe thought this answer involved some rejection, but she forgot it in the course of what followed:

"Your father was the well-known lawyer?" Lindner asked.

"Yes, he died recently, and I am now staying with my brother," Agathe said blithely. "Wouldn't you like to come and see us sometime?"

"I'm afraid I have no time for social calls," Lindner replied brusquely, his eyes downcast in evident unease.

"In that case you must not object to my visiting you," Agathe continued, ignoring his reluctance. "I need some advice." And since he had been addressing her as Fräulein, she added: "I'm married. My name is Hagauer."*

"Could it be, then," Lindner exclaimed, "that you are the wife of that accomplished educationalist, Professor Hagauer?"

He had begun the sentence on a note of sheer delight and ended it in a hesitant, muted register. For Hagauer was two things: he was an educationalist, and he was a progressive educationalist; Lindner was actually opposed to his ideas, but how bracing it is when, in the unsteady mists of a female psyche, moments after she has conceived the impossible whim of visiting a stranger in his house, one discerns

---

*"*Ich bin Frau und heiße Hagauer*"—"I am a woman" or "I am to be addressed as Frau" (in acknowledgment of her married status) "and my name is Hagauer"—involves both a subtle piquancy and an indication of Agathe's inner divorce from Hagauer that can't be reproduced in English.

such a familiar enemy; it was the drop from the second to the first of these sentiments that was echoed in the tone of his question.

Agathe had noticed it. She did not know if she should tell Lindner what the status of her relationship with her husband was. Telling him might put an immediate end to everything between herself and this new friend: she had that impression very clearly. And she would have been sorry; for precisely because there was much about Lindner that provoked her to mock him, he also made her feel she could trust him. The impression, credibly supported by his appearance, that this man seemed to want nothing for himself strangely compelled her to be sincere: he put all desire to rest, and then sincerity rose unprompted of its own accord. "I'm about to get a divorce," she finally admitted.

A silence followed; Lindner looked despondent, and Agathe now found him just a bit too pathetic.

Finally, Lindner said with an aggrieved smile: "I already thought it might be something like that when I first saw you!"

"Don't tell me you're an enemy of divorce as well?!" Agathe cried, giving free rein to her annoyance. "Of course, how could you not be! But you know, you're really a little behind the times!"

"At least I don't think it's as unquestionable as you do," Lindner pensively said in defense, took off his glasses, polished them, put them on again, and contemplated Agathe.

"I think you have too little willpower," he concluded.

"Willpower? My will is precisely to get a divorce!" Agathe exclaimed, well aware that she was missing the point.

"That is not the sense in which I am using this term," Lindner gently corrected her. "I'm prepared to believe that you have good reasons. I just happen to think differently: the free and easy morals people allow themselves nowadays never amount to more, in practice, than a sign that an individual is immovably chained to his ego and not capable of living and acting from a wider perspective. Our gentle poets," he added jealously, attempting a jibe at Agathe's impassioned pilgrimage that turned slightly sour in his mouth, "who flatter the sensibilities of the ladies, for which the ladies overrate them in return, are of course in an easier position than I am when I tell you that marriage is an institution of responsibility and mastery over the passions! But before an individual divests himself of the external safeguards that the human race has erected in true self-knowledge against its own unreliability, he would do well to tell himself that isolation from and disobedience to the higher totality constitute worse damage than the body's disappointments we are so afraid to countenance!"

"That sounds like a martial code for archangels," Agathe said, "but I can't see that you're right. I'll walk with you a little way. You must explain to me how one can think as you do. Where are you going now?"

"I have to go home," Lindner replied.

"Would your wife have something against my accompanying you to your house? We can take a cab in town. I still have time!"

"My son will be coming home from school," Lindner said, fending her off with dignity. "We always eat punctually; that is why I must go home. My wife, by the way, died suddenly several years ago," he said in correction of Agathe's mistaken assumption, and with a glance at his watch he added, anxiously and annoyed: "I must hurry!"

"Then you must explain it to me another time, it's important to me!" Agathe eagerly insisted. "If you won't come to see us, I can look you up."

Lindner gasped for air, but nothing came of it. Finally, he said: "But you as a woman can't pay me a visit!"

"Yes, I can!" Agathe assured him. "You'll see, one day I'll show up. I don't know when yet. And I assure you there's no harm in it!"

With this she said goodbye and started down a path that diverged from his.

"You have no willpower!" she said under her breath, trying to imitate Lindner, but the word "will" was fresh and cool in her mouth. It evoked feelings like pride, toughness, confidence; a proud tonality of the heart. The man had done her good.

22

A CONVERSATION ON MORALITY

That same evening Ulrich attends a gala reception for the Parallel Campaign at his cousin Diotima's house, where a large panoply of characters from The Man Without Qualities, *along with a number of new ones—fashionable members of the social elite, pillars of industry and finance, influential journalists, military men, reputed possessors of literary genius, and elegant ladies—mingle and converse. Beneath the polite chatter an ideological polarity can be discerned, pitting those who trust in the good and pacific nature of man against those who hold that only the most modern weaponry and a strong leader can establish lasting peace. Agathe arrives late, and the siblings' private conversation soon turns from her still unresolved legal predicament to the general subject of ethics. Morality, according to Ulrich, comes into being, like every other form of order, through force and compulsion; and if after centuries of social development the moral law seems to span all human life as autonomously as the vault of heaven, that sovereignty itself is without moral foundation: "Everything is moral, but morality itself is not moral." His sister is not convinced.*

"THAT is charming of morality," Agathe said. "But do you know that I met a good man today?"

Ulrich was taken aback by this interruption, but when Agathe started telling him about her meeting with Lindner, he first tried to find a place for it in his train of thought. "You can find good people here by the dozen as well," he said, "but I'll show you why the bad ones cannot fail to be among them, if you'll let me continue."

As they talked, they tried to get away from the party's commotion and had reached the anteroom, where they remained for the time being among the uninhabited coats that were hanging in the lobby. Ulrich could not find a way to resume his thoughts. "I really should start again from the beginning," he said with an impatient and helpless gesture. And suddenly he said: "You don't want to know whether you've done something good or bad; rather you are unsettled by the fact that you do both without any solid reason."

Agathe nodded.

He had taken both her hands in his.

The faint glow of his sister's skin, with its fragrance of plants unknown to him rising from her slight décolleté, lost for a moment all earthly conception. The thrust of the blood throbbed from one hand to the other. A deep moat of unworldly origin seemed to enclose her and him in a nowhereland.

He suddenly lacked the ideas to describe it. He could not even find formulations he had often made use of before. "We don't want to act out of the intuition of particular moments, but out of the state that endures to the end." "In such a way that it takes us to the center from which one cannot return to take anything back." "Not from the periphery with its constantly changing conditions, but out of the one, immutable happiness." Such phrases did come to his lips, and he might well have found it possible to use them if it were just a matter of conversation. But applying them to the immediacy of this moment between him and his sister was suddenly impossible. This left him helplessly agitated. But Agathe understood him clearly. And it should have made her happy that for the first time the shell encasing her "hard brother" had cracked open entirely, exposing what was inside, like an egg that had fallen to the floor. To her surprise however, her feelings this time were not quite ready to go along with his. Between the morning and the evening lay her curious encounter with Lindner, and although this man had merely aroused wonderment and curiosity in her, even that small grain was enough to prevent the infinite mirroring of eremitic love from coming into being.

Ulrich felt it in her hands even before she responded, and Agathe—did not respond.

He guessed that this unexpected self-renunciation had something to do with the experience he had been obliged to hear about moments ago. Abashed and confused by the rebound of his unreciprocated emotion, he said, shaking his head: "It really is annoying how much you seem to expect from the goodness of such a man."

"You're probably right," Agathe conceded.

He looked at her. He realized that this encounter meant more to his sister than any of the courting she had experienced since she had been under his protection. He even knew this man slightly. Lindner was a public figure; he was the man who at the very first session of the Parallel Campaign had made that brief speech, received with embarrassing silence, concerning the "historic occasion" or something like that: awkward, sincere, and mediocre . . . Inadvertently Ulrich looked around; but he did not recall having noticed the man among the guests, and now he realized that Lindner had never been invited back. He must have run into him elsewhere from time to time, probably at some learned society, and have read one or another of his publications, for as he collected his memory, ultramicroscopic traces of images from the past condensed like a viscous, repulsive drop into the verdict: "That insipid ass! If one wants to maintain a certain elevation in one's state of being, one cannot take such a person any more seriously than Professor Hagauer!"

He said this to Agathe.

Agathe responded with silence. She even pressed his hand.

He had the feeling: Something here makes no sense at all, but there's no way to stop it.

At this moment people came into the anteroom, and the siblings drew apart.

"Shall I go back inside with you?" Ulrich asked.

Agathe said no and looked around for an escape.

It suddenly occurred to Ulrich that the only way they could avoid the other guests was by retreating to the kitchen.

There they found the cook and the servants Rachel and Soliman filling batteries of glasses and loading trays with cakes. Rachel dropped a curtsy as they came in, and Ulrich said: "It's too hot in there, can we get some refreshment here?" He sat down on a window ledge with Agathe and put a glass and a plate down for show so that if anyone should see them it would look as if two friends of the house were permitting themselves an amusing breach of decorum. When they were seated, he said with a little sigh: "So it's merely a matter of feeling whether one finds such a Professor Lindner good or insufferable!"

Agathe was occupying her fingers with a wrapped sweet.

"Which is to say," Ulrich continued, "that feeling is neither true nor false. Feeling has remained a private matter! It has been left at the mercy of suggestion, fantasy, persuasion! You and I are no different from those people in there. Do you know what those people want?"

"No, but does it matter?"

"It may very well matter. Because they are forming two parties, each of which is as right or as wrong as the other."

Agathe said it seemed to her somewhat better to believe in human goodness than only in guns and politics, even if the manner of the belief was risible.

"What is he like, this man you met?" Ulrich asked.

"Oh, that's impossible to say. He's good!" his sister replied, laughing.

"You can no more rely on what appears good to you than on what appears good to Count Leinsdorf," Ulrich retorted testily.

Both their faces were tensed with excitement and laughter: the flow of polite and lighthearted humor was restrained by deeper countercurrents.

"For centuries," Ulrich continued, "the world has known truth in the realm of thought and accordingly, to a certain degree and on a rational plane, freedom of thought. But during the same time, feeling has not known the stern school of truth, nor has it been schooled in freedom of movement. For every morality in its time has regulated feeling only insofar—and rigidly at that, even within this perimeter—

as certain basic tenets and basic emotions were needed for whatever action that morality favored; the rest was left to discretion, to the private play of emotions, to the ambiguous efforts of art, and to academic discussion. So morality has adapted feelings to the needs of morality and in doing so neglected to develop them, even though it is itself dependent on feelings: morality is, after all, the order and integrity of the emotional life."

Here he paused, feeling Rachel's fascinated stare on his zealously animated face.

"I suppose it's funny that I talk about morality even here in the kitchen," he said, embarrassed.

Agathe was looking at him intently and thoughtfully. He leaned in closer to his sister and added softly, with a quick, jocular smile: "But it's only another manifestation of a state of passion that takes up arms against the whole world!"

Without intending to, he was reenacting their confrontation of the morning, in which he had performed the unappealing part of the would-be preceptor. He could not help it. For him morality was neither social authority nor philosophic wisdom, but living the infinite wholeness of what is possible. He believed in morality's capacity for intensification, in stages of moral experience, and not merely in the usual notion of stages of moral understanding, as if morality were something already complete for which man was just not pure enough. He believed in morality without believing in any specific morality. Morality is generally understood to be a set of police regulations for keeping life in order; and since life does not obey even these, they come to seem not quite possible to live up to and in this paltry way gain the status of an ideal. But morality must not be brought to this level. Morality is imagination. That was what he wanted Agathe to see. And his second point was: Imagination is not arbitrary. Once the imagination is given over to whim, there is a price to pay. The words twitched in Ulrich's mouth. He was on the verge of talking about the neglected difference between the way various historical epochs developed the rational mind in their own fashion, and the way, also in their own fashion, they fixed and closed off the moral imagination. He was on the verge of saying this because the consequence, however much one may doubt it, has been a more or less steadily rising line, through all the mutations of history, of rational thought and its creations, as against a heap of feelings, ideas, and vital possibilities that are piled up in stratified layers like shards of eternal side issues just the way they were left when they came into being and were then abandoned. Because a further consequence is that there are countless possibilities of having an opinion one way or another as soon as one enters the realm of fundamentals, without there ever being any possibility of bringing these possibilities together. Because one consequence is that these opinions come to blows, as there is no possibility of their coming to an understanding. Because consequently, all told, the affective life of mankind slops back and forth like water in a tub that lacks a firm foundation. And Ulrich had an idea that had been haunting him all evening, an old idea of his, incidentally, but everything that had happened this evening had simply continuously confirmed it, and he wanted to show Agathe where the fault lay and how it could be remedied if everyone wanted it, and in truth, all that he had wanted to express with that thought was the painful intention to prove that one could not any more readily trust the discoveries of one's own imagination either.

And Agathe said, with a little sigh, the way a woman subjected to amorous pressure might quickly resist one more time before she surrenders: "So it boils down to having to do everything 'on principle' after all?" And she looked at him, returning his smile.

But he answered: "Yes, but only on *one* principle!" And this now was something quite different from what he had intended to say. It again came from the realm of the Siamese Twins and the Millennium, where life grows in magical stillness like a flower, and while it may not have been plucked from thin air, it did point directly to frontiers of thought that are solitary and treacherous. Agathe's eye was like a burst agate. If at this instant he had said only a little more or laid his hand on her, something would have happened which, soon after, she was unable to name, as it was already gone. For Ulrich did not want to say any more. He took a knife and a piece of fruit and began to peel it. He was happy because the distance that had separated him from his sister only a short while ago had melted into an immense closeness; but he was also glad that at this moment they were interrupted.

The social demands of the party engulf them. Ulrich gets drawn into conversation with several guests, all of them oddly preoccupied with the same subject of morality, albeit in decidedly worldly terms. ("That was virtually the whole agenda this evening!" sighs Ulrich's friend General Stumm von Bordwehr, who was hoping for a more productive, historically significant meeting of minds.) Agathe listens to her brother from a distance, herself caught up in obligatory chatter.

"Why is he talking with everyone? He should have left with me! He's cheapening what he said to me!" She liked some of the things she could hear him say through the hubbub, but they hurt her nonetheless. Everything that came from Ulrich was hurting her again, and for the second time that day she suddenly felt the need to get away from him. She despaired of ever being able, with her one-sided nature, to be what he needed, and the prospect that after a while they would be going home like any two people, gossiping about the evening behind them, was unbearable.

Not long after, she goes home by herself, leaving word for Ulrich that she had not wanted to disturb him.

23

AFTER THE ENCOUNTER

AS PROFESSOR August Lindner, the man who had entered Agathe's life by the poet's grave, climbed down towards the valley, what he saw before him were images of salvation.

If Agathe had looked back at him after they parted, she would have been struck by the man's ramrod-stiff, prancing gait, for he had a peculiarly buoyant, proud, and yet anxious manner of walking. Lindner carried his hat in one hand and occasionally passed the other hand through his hair; such a free and cozy feeling had come over him.

"How few people," he said to himself, "have a truly empathic soul!" He imagined a soul that is able to put itself completely in the place of a fellow human being, suffer his most hidden sorrows with him, and descend into his profound weakness. "What a prospect!" he cried out to himself. "What a miraculous proximity of divine mercy, what consolation, what a feast day for the soul!" But then he recalled how few people were even able to listen attentively to their neighbors; for he was one of those well-meaning ramblers who free-associate from the solemn to the trite without noticing the difference. "How rarely, for instance, is the question 'How are you?' meant seriously," he thought. "One needs only to answer in detail how one feels in one's heart, and soon enough one finds oneself looking into a bored and distracted face."

Well, he had not been guilty of this error! According to his principles, protecting the weak was the particular and indispensable hygienics of the strong, who without such benevolent self-limitation would all too easily lapse into brutality; and culture, too, needed works of mercy to protect against the dangers inherent within itself.

"Anyone wishing to enlighten us about 'universal education,'" he confirmed for himself through inner acclamation, deliciously refreshed by a sudden lightning bolt hurled at his fellow pedagogue Hagauer, "should truly first be advised: Experience how another person feels! Knowing through empathy means a thousand times more than knowing through books!" It was evidently an old difference of opinion he was now venting on the liberal concept of education on the one hand, and on the wife of his colleague on the other, for Lindner's glasses were peering about like two shields of a doubly puissant warrior. He had been inhibited in Agathe's presence, but if she had seen him now he would have appeared to her like a commander, and in charge of troops that were anything but frivolous. For a truly manly soul is prepared to help, and it is prepared to help because it is manly. He raised the question of whether he had acted correctly when faced with that beautiful woman, and answered himself: "It would be wrong if the high challenge of subordination to the law were left to those who are too weak for it; and it would be a disheartening spectacle if only mindless pedants were permitted to be the protectors and shapers of moral norms; that is why the vital and strong have the obligation, out of their very instinct for health and strength, to call for discipline and limits; they must support the weak, shake the thoughtless, rein in the unbridled." He had the impression that he had done so.

Just as the pious soul of the Salvation Army employs uniforms and military customs, Lindner had taken certain soldierly forms of thought into his service; indeed, he did not even shy away from concessions to Nietzsche's "man of power," who was still a stumbling block for civil society at that time but was for Lindner a whetstone as well. He liked to say of Nietzsche that he could not be characterized as a bad man, but that his doctrine was quite extreme and life-denying, the reason for this being that he rejected pity; for thus he had failed to recognize the wonderful reciprocal gift of the weak, which is to make the strong man gentle! And opposing to this his own experience, he thought, full of joyful aspiration: "Truly great souls do not pay homage to a barren cult of the self; instead they awaken in others a sense of their own majesty by bending down to

them and, if need be, sacrificing themselves for them!" Two young
lovers were coming up the path towards him, closely entwined; he
looked into their eyes, confident of victory and with an expression
of friendly reproof that was meant to encourage virtue. But it was a
rather ordinary couple, and the young lout who formed its male
component pinched his eyes together and said: "Boo!" Lindner, who
was not prepared for this vulgar and derisive threat, was taken aback:
but he acted as if he did not notice. He loved decisive action, and
looked around for a policeman, who ought to be nearby to guarantee
the public safety of honor; but his foot struck against a stone, the
hasty stumbling movement scared up a swarm of sparrows that had
been feasting at God's table on a heap of horse manure, and the sparrows' rustling flight warned Lindner, enabling him, an instant before
falling ignominiously, to clear the double obstacle with a balletically
disguised leap. He did not look back, and after a while he was very
satisfied with himself. "One must be hard as a diamond and tender
as a mother!" he thought, finding happy support in that seventeenth-
century maxim.

Since he also valued the virtue of modesty, he would at no other
time have made such a pronouncement in regard to himself, but
Agathe had aroused such a tumult in the blood! Then again, his
emotions were negatively grounded, as it were, in the knowledge that
this divinely tender female he had found in tears, as the angel had
found the maiden in the dew—oh, he did not want to be presumptuous, and yet how presumptuous indulging in poetry makes one!—and
so he continued in a more severe manner: that this miserable woman
was on the verge of breaking an oath placed in the hands of God; for
that was how he regarded her desire for a divorce. Regrettably, he had
not impressed this upon her with the necessary resoluteness when
they were standing face-to-face—God, what nearness again in these
words!—no, he had not said it strongly enough; he merely remembered
talking to her in general terms about loose morals and ways of protecting oneself against them. The name of God, by the way, had
certainly not passed his lips when they spoke, except maybe as an
empty figure of speech; and the casualness, the candid—one was

tempted to say disrespectful—seriousness with which Agathe had asked him if he believed in God offended him even now as he remembered it. For a truly devout person does not permit himself to simply follow a whim and think about God in a crude, direct way. Indeed, the moment Lindner recalled this impertinence, he detested Agathe as if he had stepped on a snake. He resolved that if he should ever be in the position of repeating his admonitions to her, he would definitely employ only the powerful language of reason, which is suitable to earthly concerns and exists in the world so that not every ill-bred person may trouble God with his long-established confusions; and so he began to employ reason straightaway, and many a phrase occurred to him that might be offered to a woman who has stumbled. For example, that marriage is not a private affair but a public institution; that it has the sublime mission of developing feelings of responsibility and empathy, and the task, so conducive to strengthening a nation's mettle, of training the individual to countenance even the greatest difficulties; perhaps indeed, though this could only be advanced with the greatest discretion, that precisely by lasting a fairly long time, marriage also constitutes the best protection against the limitlessness of desire. He had an image of humanity, perhaps not wrongly, as a sack full of devils that had to be firmly tied shut, and he saw unshakable principles as the tie. How this sympathetic man, whose corporeal part could not be said to have exceeded its bounds in any direction but height, had arrived at the conviction that one must constrain oneself at every step was indeed a riddle, which could only be easily solved if one knew its benefit. When he had already reached the foot of the hill, a train of soldiers crossed his path, and he looked with tender commiseration at the sweat-soaked young men, who had pushed their caps back on their heads and, with faces dulled by exhaustion, looked like a procession of dusty caterpillars. At their sight, his revulsion at the frivolity with which Agathe had treated the question of divorce was dreamily softened by joy that such a thing was happening to his freethinking colleague Hagauer, and this stirring, though not commendable, at least served to remind him how indispensable it was to mistrust human nature. He therefore resolved to make uncompromisingly clear to Agathe—should the occasion actually, and without any fault of his own, present itself again—that in the end the forces of self-interest have only a destructive effect, and that she must subordinate her personal despair, however great it might be, to the moral insight that the true touchstone of life is found in living together.

But whether this occasion was to present itself once again was apparently just the point toward which Lindner's mental powers were so excitedly pressing. "There are many people with noble qualities that are just not yet concentrated in an adamant conviction," he thought of saying to Agathe; but how should he do so if he did not see her again; and yet the thought that she might pay him a visit clashed with all his notions of chaste and tender womanhood. "One would have to confront her with it unequivocally, and right away!" he decided, and now that he had actually formed this resolution, he also no longer doubted that she would really come. He exhorted himself to selflessly endure with her the reasons she would submit to excuse her behavior before he went on to convince her of her errors. With unwavering patience, he would aim at the innermost core of her heart, and after he had envisioned that too, a noble feeling of fraternal vigilance and solicitude descended into his own heart, a consecration as between brother and sister, which he noted, should rest altogether upon the relations the sexes maintain with each other. "Hardly any men," he cried out, uplifted, "have the slightest notion how deep a need noble feminine natures have for the noble man who consorts with the human being in the woman without being immediately unbalanced by coquetry and sexual allure!" These thoughts must have given him wings, for he did not know how he had got to the streetcar terminal, but suddenly there it was; and before stepping in, he took off his glasses in order to cleanse them of the mist with which the heat of his inner processes had coated them. Then he swung himself into a corner, glanced around the empty car, got his fare ready, looked into the conductor's face, and felt quite on his mettle, ready to begin his return voyage on that admirable communal institution called the municipal streetcar. With a pleasurable yawn he discharged the fatigue of his walk, the better to ready himself for new duties, and summed up in one sentence the astonishing digressions to which he had abandoned himself: "Forgetting oneself is surely the healthiest thing a human being can do!"

24
THE DO-GOODER

THERE is only one reliable remedy against the incalculable stirrings of a passionate heart: adherence to schedules, carried out to the last detail; and it was to this practice, which he had adopted in good time, that Lindner owed the successes in his life as well as the belief that he was by nature a man of strong passions and hard to discipline. He got up early in the morning, at the same hour in summer and winter, washed his face, hands, and one-seventh of his body—a different seventh each day, of course—at a small iron washstand, whereupon he rubbed the rest with a wet towel, so that the full bath, that time-consuming and voluptuous procedure, could be limited to one evening every two weeks. This constituted a clever victory over matter, and whoever has had occasion to consider the inadequate washing facilities and uncomfortable beds personalities who have become historical made do with will hardly be able to dismiss the conjecture that there must be a connection between iron beds and iron men, although we must not put too fine a point on this, lest we all immediately proceed to sleep on beds of nails. So here reflection was tasked with an additional, educative function, and after Lindner had washed himself in the reflected glow of inspiring examples, he also (but only within measure) made adroit use of the towel to give the body some movement while drying himself at the same time. It is after all a fateful misunderstanding to base health on the animal part of the person; rather, it is spiritual and moral nobility that produce the body's powers of resistance; and though that does not always apply to the individual case, it applies most certainly on a large scale, for the strength of a people is a consequence of the right spirit, and not the other way around. That is why Lindner had bestowed on his rubdowns a special, meticulous discipline that avoided the crude gripping and grabbing involved in the usual male idolatry but instead engaged the participation of the whole personality by associating the body's movements with beautiful inner tasks. He particularly detested the worship of the dashing daredevil, a foreign import that many in his fatherland were already holding up as an ideal, and distancing himself from this was an integral part of his morning exercises. He substituted for it, with great circumspection, a more statesmanlike attitude in the gymnastic use of his limbs, combining exertion of willpower with properly timed indulgence, mastery over pain with humane common sense, and if, as a concluding exercise for the practice of bravery, he leapt over an upside-down chair, he would do so with as much reserve as self-confidence. Such development of the whole wealth of human capacity made his calisthenics, ever since he had taken them up a few years ago, true exercises in virtue.

But as much could also be said in passing, against the bane of ephemeral self-assertion that under the slogan of body culture has taken possession of the intrinsically healthy idea of sports, and still more could be said against the particular feminine form of this evil, beauty culture. Lindner flattered himself that here, too, he was one of the few who knew how to properly allot light and shadow, and just as he was always prepared to detect an unspoiled core in the spirit of the times, he also recognized the moral obligation of appearing as healthy and agreeable as he possibly could. He himself carefully groomed his beard and hair every morning, kept his nails short and meticulously clean, sprinkled some brilliantine on his head and put protective lotion on his feet, to offset the stress they endured on his daily rounds: but who, on the other hand, would wish to deny that the amount of attention lavished on the body in the course of a worldly woman's day is exorbitant? But if there really was no other way—he gladly made gentle concessions to women, not least because there might be wives of important men among them—than having baths and facials, ointments and wraps, manicures and pedicures, masseurs and coiffeurs succeed one another in almost unbroken sequence, he advocated as a counterweight to such one-sided care of the body the concept of inner beauty culture, *inner beauty* for short, which he had formulated in a public speech. Let the cleansing of the body, for instance, remind us of inner purity; its anointing, of our obligations to the soul; the masseur's manipulations, of the hand of fate; and let the filing of toenails remind us that even in our lowlier aspects, we should be a beautiful sight. Thus he transferred his image to women, but left it to them to adapt the details to the needs of their sex.

Of course it might have happened that someone unprepared for the sight Lindner presented with his ministrations to health and beauty, and even more while he was washing and drying himself, would be moved to laughter: for seen merely in their physical aspect, his movements conjured the image of a multifariously turning and twisting swan's neck, which moreover did not consist of curves but of the sharp element of knees and elbows; his shortsighted eyes, freed from their glasses, looked into the distance with a martyred expression, as if their gaze had been cut off close to the eye, and beneath the beard his soft lips pouted with the pain of exertion. But an observer gifted with spiritual perception might well experience the spectacle of inner and outer forces engaged in a carefully choreographed dance of mutual begetting; and when, while performing that ritual, Lindner thought of those poor women who spend hours in their bathrooms and dressing rooms heating up their imagination with a one-sided cult of the body, he could rarely refrain from considering how much good it would do them if just once they could watch him. Harmless and pure, they welcome modern body culture and go along with it, because in their ignorance they do not suspect that such great attention devoted to the animal part all too easily awakens expectations in it that could destroy life if not strictly held in subservience to higher purposes!

Indeed, Lindner turned everything he came into contact with into a moral imperative; and whether he was in clothes or not, every hour of the day until he entered dreamless sleep was filled with some important content for which that hour had been permanently reserved. He slept seven hours; his teaching obligations, which the ministry had limited in consideration of his well-regarded literary activity, claimed three to five hours a day, which already included the lecture on pedagogy he held twice a week at the university; five consecutive hours—that amounts to almost twenty thousand in a decade!—were devoted to reading; two and a half hours served for the penning of his own works, which flowed like a clear spring from the rocky terrain of his inner being; mealtimes claimed an hour of each day; one hour was dedicated to a walk and simultaneously to edifying reflection on professional matters and important questions of life, while another was dedicated to a work-related change of location and simultaneously to what Lindner called "little cogitations," focusing the mind on the contents of the activity that had just transpired and the one that was about to begin; other units of time were designated, some permanently, others alternating in the framework of the week, for dressing and undressing, gymnastics, letters, household matters, official business, and useful socializing. And it is only natural that this life plan was not only carried out in conformity with its large and rigorous overall design but also entailed all sorts of unique particulars, such as Sunday with its unworkaday obligations, the longer cross-country walk that took place every fourteen days, or the full bath, and additionally entailed daily double-tasking activities that we have not yet had the opportunity to mention, including, for example, Lindner's association with his son during the four meals, or the character training involved in patiently overcoming unforeseen difficulties while getting dressed quickly.

Such exercises for building character are not only possible but also exceedingly useful, and Lindner was instinctively drawn to them. "In the small things I do right I see an image of all the great things that are done right in the world" was something Goethe had already said, and in this sense a mealtime can serve as well as any task set by fate to cultivate self-control and gain victory over desire; indeed, in the resistance of a collar button, inaccessible to all reflection, a more deeply probing mind may even learn how to deal with children. Lindner did not by any means regard Goethe as a model in everything; but what exquisite humility had he not gained just by attempting to drive a nail into a wall with a hammer, undertaking to mend a torn glove himself, or repairing a doorbell that was out of order: if in doing so he banged his fingers or pricked himself, the resultant pain was vanquished, if not right away then after a few horrible seconds, by joy at humanity's industrious spirit, evident even in such trifling skills and their acquisition, which the educated person of our time, much to his general disadvantage, considers beneath him! Then he had felt the Goethean spirit resurrected within himself, a pleasure that was further enhanced when, thanks to the methods of a more advanced age, he felt himself raised above the classic poet's practical dilettantism and occasional delight in prudently exercised manual dexterity. Lindner was in fact free of idolatry toward the old writer, who lived in a world that was only halfway enlightened and therefore overestimated the Enlightenment, and he took Goethe as a model more in charming small things than in his grandeur and gravity, to say nothing of the seductive state minister's notorious sensuality.

His veneration was therefore carefully weighed and balanced. Nevertheless, a peculiar displeasure had entered into it for some time, and this frequently moved Lindner to reflection. He had always believed that he had a more correct understanding of the heroic than Goethe. He did not think highly of Scaevolas who hold their hands in the fire, Lucretias who run themselves through with a dagger, or Judiths who chop the heads off those who attack their honor—"motifs" Goethe would have found meaningful at any time, though he did not treat them in his own works; indeed Lindner was convinced, despite the authority of the classics, that these men and women, who had committed crimes for their personal convictions, would nowadays belong not on a pedestal but rather in the courtroom. Against their inclination to inflict severe bodily harm he set an "internalized and social" conception of courage. In discourse and in thought, he even went so far as to place a carefully considered entry on the subject into his classbook, or a judiciously pondered reflection on how his housekeeper needed to be chided for being a bit too forward in her zeal, because in pursuit of one's duty one ought not only to follow one's own passions but must take the other person's motives into account.

And when he uttered such things, he had the impression of looking back in the well-fitting everyday clothes of a later century on the bombastic moral costume of an earlier one.

The touch of the ridiculous that attended such examples did not escape him, but he called it the laughter of the intellectual rabble; and for this he had two solid reasons. First, he not only maintained that all situations were equally suited to strengthen or weaken human nature, but also that ordinary circumstances were better suited to this than more exalted occasions, since the human inclination to arrogance and vanity is unwittingly encouraged by the shining exercise of virtue, while its inconspicuous everyday exercise consists of pure unseasoned virtue itself. But second, the planned cultivation of a people's moral heritage (Lindner loved this expression, along with the soldierly concept of *Zucht*—discipline and breeding—because of the way it evokes both the rustic and the factory-fresh) must not despise "small occasions" for an additional reason, namely that the godless belief advanced by "liberals and freemasons" that great human accomplishments arise as it were from a void, even if that void is called genius, was already at that time falling out of fashion. The sharpened focus of public attention had already caused the "hero," whom earlier times had portrayed as an arrogant figure, to be recognized as a tireless toiler over details who, if he is to become an explorer, must prepare himself through unremittent diligence in learning; if an athlete, treat his body with the same anxious care as an opera singer training his voice; and as a political rejuvenator of the people, always reiterate the same thing at countless meetings. And of this, Goethe—who all his life had remained a comfortable citizen-aristocrat—had had no idea, but Lindner saw it coming! It was understandable, therefore, that he thought he was protecting Goethe's better part against his ephemeral aspects when he preferred the considerate and cordial Goethe—qualities the poet possessed in such gratifying measure—to his tragic persona; it could also be argued that it did not happen without reflection when, for no other reason than that he was a pedant, the professor considered himself to be a man threatened by dangerous passions.

Indeed, not long afterward it became one of the most popular human possibilities to subject oneself to a "regimen," which may be applied with the same success to obesity as to politics and intellectual life. In a regimen, patience, obedience, regularity, equanimity, and other very tidy qualities become major components of a human being in his private condition, while everything that is unbridled, violent, intemperate, and dangerous, all qualities that he, as a wild romantic, cannot dispense with either, has its own excellent place in the regimen. Probably this strange inclination to subject oneself to a regimen, or to lead a strenuous, unpleasant, and paltry life according to the prescription of a doctor, athletic coach, or some other tyrant (even though one could ignore their dictates with equally unsuccessful results) is a by-product of the worker, warrior, and anthill state toward which the world is moving: but there lay the boundary Lindner was unable to cross, nor could he envisage it in his mind's eye, because his Goethean heritage forbade it. To be sure, his piety was not of a sort that could not have been reconciled to this development; after all, he left the divine to God and undiluted saintliness to the saints; but he could not conceive of renouncing his personality, and the ideal he yearned for was a community of fully responsible moral personalities that, as God's civil army, would of course struggle against the inconstancy of the lower nature and make a sanctum of everyday life, but would also decorate this sanctum with the great works of art and science. If someone had tallied the schedule of his days, he would have noticed that in every instance it added up to only twenty-three hours, so that sixty minutes of a full day were missing, and of these sixty minutes forty were invariably earmarked for conversation and kindly engagement with the aspirations and nature of other human beings, an endeavor that comprised visits to art exhibitions, concerts, and entertainments. He hated these events. Almost every time, their content offended his sensibility, and in his opinion these chaotic and overrated diversions were occasions for the notorious nervous disorder of the age, with its superfluous stimulants and genuine suffering, its insatiable appetite and its inconstancy, its curiosity and its unavoidable moral decay, to let off steam. He would even smile into his thin beard with dismay at the sight of flush-cheeked couples paying homage to the idols of culture. They did not know that the life force is enhanced by restriction and not by fragmentation. They all suffered from the fear of not having time for *everything*, and did not know that having time means precisely *not* having time for everything. Lindner had realized that the poor condition of people's nerves is not due to the excessive pace of work, which in this age is presumed to be the culprit, but on the contrary to culture and humanitarianism, to breaks in routine, to interruptions in the day's work, to the minutes of respite during which the individual wants to live his own life, looking for something he might regard as beautiful, or fun, or important: it is from these minutes that the miasmas of impatience, unhappiness, and meaninglessness arise. That was what he felt, and if he—or, more precisely, the visions that rose in his mind at such moments—had held sway, he would have swept all these temples of culture with an iron broom, and festivals of labor and edification, tightly bound to daily activities, would have taken the place of those supposed celebrations of mind and spirit; it really would have required no more than eliminating from an entire age a few minutes a day that owe their sick existence to a falsely understood liberality. But aside from making a few allusions, he had never summoned up the determination to advocate this seriously and in public.

And suddenly Lindner looked up, for while dreaming his thoughts he was still riding in the streetcar; he felt irritable and vaguely anxious, as one does from being irresolute and inhibited, and for a moment he had the confused impression that all along he had been thinking of Agathe. She was accorded the additional honor that a vexation that had innocently begun with pleasure in Goethe now fused with her, even though no reason for this could be discerned. From habit, Lindner admonished himself, whispering with mute lips: "Dedicate part of your solitude to quiet reflection on your fellow man, especially if you are not in accord with him; perhaps then you will learn to better understand and utilize what repels you, and will know how to be forbearing toward his weaknesses and encourage his virtue, which may simply be intimidated!" It was one of the key statements he had coined against the dubious activities of so-called culture and in which he usually found the composure to bear them; but the words failed to achieve their purpose, and righteousness was apparently not what he lacked this time. He pulled out his watch. It confirmed that he had granted Agathe more time than he had been allotted. But he would not have been able to do so if his daily schedule had not allowed twenty minutes for unavoidable slippage; and it turned out that this deficit account, this emergency supply of time, whose precious drops were the oil that lubricated his daily work, would even on this unusual day still hold a reserve of ten minutes when he stepped into his house. Did this cause his courage to grow? He remembered another of his life maxims, for the second time today: "The more unshakable your patience becomes," Lindner said to Lindner, "the more surely you will strike to the other's heart!" And to strike to the heart, this gave him a pleasure that corresponded to the heroic in his nature; the fact that people struck in this manner never strike back was immaterial.

25

THE SIBLINGS THE NEXT MORNING

ULRICH and his sister came to speak of this man again when they saw each other after Agathe's sudden disappearance from the party at their cousin's house they had attended together the night before. Ulrich had left the excited and quarrelsome gathering soon after she had, but had not been able to ask her why she had left him so abruptly; for she had locked her room and was either already sleeping or purposely ignoring the listener at her door with his hushed question as to whether she was still awake. Thus the day she had met with the curious stranger had closed as capriciously as it had begun. Nor was any information to be had from her in the morning. She herself did not know her true feelings. She had not been able to bring herself to read her husband's letter again, even though now and then she saw it lying beside her. Thinking back to the morning when it had intruded into her life, it seemed incredible to her that hardly a day had passed since she had received it; so often had her condition changed in the meantime. Sometimes she thought the cliché "ghosts of the past" fit it perfectly; nevertheless, it really frightened her, too. And at times it merely aroused a small unease in her, such as one might feel at the unexpected sight of a stopped clock; but at other times she was plunged into fruitless brooding that the world from which this letter had come was claiming to be the real world for her. Something that did not even slightly touch her inside surrounded her outside as an invisible force, and it still held as firm as ever. Inadvertently, she compared this with the events that had transpired between her brother and herself since the arrival of this letter. These had been mainly conversations, and though one of them had even brought her to think of suicide, she had forgotten its subject, though likely enough it lay within her, waiting to come back to life. So it really did not matter what they had talked about, and when she weighed her heart-stirring present life against the letter, she had the impression of a deep, steady, incomparable, but powerless movement. From all this she felt partly faint and sobered, partly tender and restless, like a fever patient after his temperature has gone down.

In this state of animated helplessness, she suddenly said: "To empathize with another person to the point where one actually experiences how he feels must be incredibly hard!" To her surprise, Ulrich replied immediately: "There are people who imagine they can do that." He said it in a tone that was both insinuating and ill-humored, and he had only half taken in what she had said. Her words had caused something to move aside and give way to an anger that had been left behind the day before. And so, notwithstanding that he really ought to find such resentment contemptible, that debate was over for the time being.

The morning had brought a rainy day and confined the siblings to their house. The leaves of the trees gleamed drearily outside the windows like wet linoleum; the pavement behind the gaps in the foliage was as shiny as a rubber boot. One's eyes were almost loath to touch the wet view. Agathe regretted her remark and no longer knew why she had made it. She sighed and began again: "Today the world reminds me of the rooms we had as children." She was referring to the bare upper rooms in their father's house and the bemused reunion with them they had both celebrated. Perhaps that comparison was far-fetched; but she added: "It's a person's first sadness, surrounded by his toys, that comes back again and again!"

Unwittingly, after the recent period of sustained good weather, expectations had been directed toward another beautiful day, and this filled the mind with thwarted desire and impatient melancholy. Now Ulrich looked out of the window as well. Behind the gray, streaming wall of water, will-o'-the-wisps of outings never taken, fenceless meadows and an infinite world, danced and beckoned; and perhaps, too, a spectral wish to be alone some day and free again to move in any direction, the sweet pain of which is the story of the Passion and also already the Resurrection of love. He turned to his sister with something of this still in the expression of his face and body, and asked her almost fiercely: "I suppose I'm not one of those people who can respond empathically to others?"

"No, you really aren't!" she replied, and smiled at him.

"But precisely what such people imagine," he continued, for it was only now that he understood how seriously her words had been meant, "that one can suffer together, is as impossible for them as it is for anyone else. What they have, at best, is the skill nurses have at guessing what someone in need likes to hear."

"In that case they must know what would help him," Agathe objected.

"Not at all!" Ulrich asserted more stubbornly. "Probably the only comfort they give is by talking: someone who talks a lot discharges another person's grief drop by drop, the way rain discharges the electricity in a cloud. This is the well-known alleviation of sorrow by talking!"

Agathe was silent.

"Maybe people like your new friend," Ulrich now said ingenuously, "work the way some cough remedies do: they don't get rid of a sore throat, but they soothe its irritation, and then it often heals by itself!"

In any other situation he could have expected his sister's consent, but Agathe, who since yesterday had been strangely disposed because of her sudden weakness for a man whose worth Ulrich doubted, smiled implacably and toyed with her fingers. Ulrich jumped up and said urgently: "But I know him, even if it's just a passing acquaintance: I've heard him lecture a few times!"

"You even called him a vapid fool," Agathe interjected.

"And why not?" Ulrich defended it. "People like him know less than anyone how to empathize with another person. They don't even know what it means. They simply don't feel the difficulty, the enormously questionable nature of this aspiration!"

Now Agathe asked with almost passionate insistence: "Why do you think it's a questionable aspiration?"

Ulrich was silent. He even lit a cigarette to confirm that he was not going to answer; after all, they had talked about it enough the night before! Agathe knew this too. She did not want to provoke any new explanations. These explanations were as enchanting and as devastating as gazing into the sky and seeing cities of marble in gray, pink, and yellow clouds. She thought: "How lovely it would be if all he said was: 'I want to love you as myself, and I can love you better that way than I can love any other woman, because you are my sister!'" And because he did not want to say that, she took a small pair of scissors and carefully cut off a thread that was sticking out somewhere, as if for the time being this were the single thing in the whole world that deserved her full attention. Ulrich watched with the same attention. She was at that moment more seductively present to all his senses than ever, and some of what she was hiding he was able to guess, though not everything. For meanwhile she had had time to come to this resolution: If Ulrich could forget that she herself was laughing at the stranger who presumed he could help her, he didn't deserve to be reminded of it now. And besides, she had a hopeful presentiment about Lindner. She did not know him. But that he had offered to help her selflessly and with conviction must have inspired trust in her, for a joyous tonality of the heart, hard trumpet blasts of will, confidence, and pride, beneficently opposed to her own state, seemed to be sending their refreshing music from behind all the comedy of that encounter. "No matter how great difficulties may be, they amount to nothing if one meets them with an earnest will!" she thought, and was suddenly seized by remorse, so that she now broke the silence more or less the way one breaks off a flower so that two heads can bend over it, and added a second question to her first: "Do you still remember that you always said 'love thy neighbor' is as different from an obligation as a cloudburst of bliss is from a drop of satisfaction?"

She was astonished by the vehemence with which Ulrich answered her: "I'm not unaware of the irony of my situation. Since yesterday, and probably always, I have done nothing but rouse an army of reasons why this love of one's neighbor is not a joy, but a hugely sublime, all but impossible undertaking! So nothing could be more understandable than your seeking protection from this with a man who hasn't a clue about any of this, and in your position I would do the same."

"But it's not true at all that I'm doing that!" Agathe retorted curtly.

Ulrich could not help casting a glance at her that expressed as much gratitude as mistrust. "It's hardly worth talking about," he assured her. "I didn't really want to bring it up." He hesitated a moment and went on: "But look, given that one must love another person as one loves oneself, no matter how much one loves him it remains a deception and a self-deception, because one simply cannot feel with him how his head hurts, or his finger. It is absolutely unbearable that one cannot really share the experience of a person one loves, and it's something utterly simple. This is how the world is arranged. We wear our animal skin with the hair inside and cannot shed it. And this terror in the midst of tenderness, this nightmare of perpetually thwarted communion—this is something the properly good, the 'well and good' people never experience. Their so-called empathy is actually a substitute to spare them the sense of a lack!"

Agathe forgot that she had just said something that resembled and did not resemble a lie. She saw shining through the disillusionment in Ulrich's words the vision of a sharing in each other next to which the usual proofs of love, goodness, and sympathy lost their meaning; and she understood that this was why he spoke of the world more than of himself, for if it was to be more than idle dreaming one would have to dislodge oneself along with reality like a door from its hinges. At this moment she was far away from the man with the sparse beard and timid severity who wanted to do her good. But she couldn't say it. She just looked at Ulrich, then looked away without speaking. Then she distracted herself with something, then they looked at each other again. After the shortest time the silence gave the impression of having lasted for hours.

The dream of being two people and one—: in truth the effect of this fable was at some moments not unlike that of a dream that has stepped outside the boundaries of night, and now again she found herself suspended between belief and denial, in a state of feeling in which reason had nothing more to say. It was only the body's constitution, impervious to all influence, that relegated feeling back to reality. These bodies, loving each other as they did, displayed their existence before the searching gaze with surprises and delights that renewed themselves like a peacock's fan poised amid the streams of desire; but as soon as the gaze no longer dwelt on the hundred eyes of the spectacle that love offers to love but sought to penetrate into the thinking and feeling person behind it, the bodies turned into cruel dungeons. Each found itself facing the other again, as so often before, not knowing what to say, because for everything that longing might have still wanted to say or repeat, a far too steep overarching gesture was needed, as if leaning across an abyss, for which there was no solid foundation.

And it was not long before the bodily motions, too, inadvertently slowed down and froze. Outside the windows, the rain was still filling the air with its pulsing curtain of drops and the lulling, hypnotic sounds through whose monotony the sky-high desolation flowed downward. It seemed to Agathe that her body had been alone for centuries; and time flowed as if it were flowing with the water from the sky. The light in the room now resembled a hollowed-out silver cube. Blue smoke from cigarettes carelessly left burning twined around her and Ulrich like sweet-scented scarves. She no longer knew whether she was tender and vulnerable to the core of her being or impatient and sore at her brother, whose perseverance she admired. She sought his eyes and found them glaring like two moons afloat in this precarious atmosphere. And at that moment something happened to her—it did not seem to come from her will but from outside—: the surging water beyond the windows suddenly became like the flesh of a sliced fruit and was pressing its swelling softness between herself and Ulrich. Perhaps she was ashamed or even hated herself a little for it, but an utterly sensual exuberance—and not at all merely what is called sensual abandon but also, indeed much rather, a voluntary and free disengagement of the senses from the world—began to take possession of her; she was just barely able to anticipate it and even hide it from Ulrich by suddenly leaping from the couch, telling him with the speediest of excuses that she had forgotten to take care of something, and leaving the room.

26

UP JACOB'S LADDER TO A STRANGER'S HOME

A s s o o n as that was done she decided to look up the strange man who had offered her his help, and immediately proceeded to carry out her resolution. She wanted to confess to him that she no longer knew what do with herself. She had no clear picture of him; a person one has seen through tears that dried in his company is not likely to appear the way he really is. So, on her way, she thought about him. She believed she was being clearheaded; but actually her thinking was still imbued with imagination. She hurried through the streets, bearing before her eyes the light from her brother's room. But it hadn't been real light at all, she thought; it was more as if all the things in the room had suddenly lost their composure, or some kind of sanity they must ordinarily possess. But if in fact she alone had lost her composure, or her sanity, then that too would not have been limited to herself, because something had been set free in the things, a liberation that was stirring with miracles. "One moment more, and it would have peeled us out of our clothes like a silver knife, without our having moved a finger!" she thought.

But gradually she felt herself calming to the sound of the harmless, gray water pattering on her hat and coat, and her thoughts became more measured. Perhaps the simple clothes she had hastily thrown on helped as well, for they directed her memory back to schoolgirl walks without an umbrella and to guiltless states of mind. She recalled an innocent summer she had spent with a friend and her parents on a small island in the north: there, between the hard splendors of sea and sky, they had discovered a nesting place of seabirds, a hollow filled with white, soft feathers. And now she knew it: The man she was drawn to reminded her of this nesting site. The idea pleased her. Back then she would hardly have permitted herself, given the rigorous sincerity that is part of youth's need for experience, to abandon herself, as she was now deliberately doing, with such illogical, indeed juvenile, willfulness, to an unearthly dread at the thought of that softness and whiteness. This dread was related to Professor Lindner; but the unearthliness was related to him also.

The almost certain intuition that everything that happened to her was magically connected with something hidden was familiar to her from all the agitated periods of her life; she sensed it as something close by, somewhere behind her, and was inclined to wait for the hour of the miracle, when she would have nothing to do but close her eyes and lean back. Ulrich saw nothing helpful in supernatural reveries; his attention seemed mostly occupied with transforming, with infinite slowness, all unearthly content into an earthly one. Agathe realized that this was the reason why she had now left him for the third time in twenty-four hours, fleeing in obscure expectation of something that would take her into its care and allow her to rest from the afflictions, or perhaps just from the impatience, of her passions. But then as soon as she had calmed down, she would be herself again and back at his side, seeing in what he was teaching her the very possibility of salvation; and now, too, this lasted for a while. But when the memory of what had "almost" happened at home—and yet not happened!— obtruded more vividly, she was again profoundly at a loss. First she wanted to convince herself that the infinite realm of the unimaginable would have come to their aid if they had held out for another instant; then she reproached herself for not waiting to see what Ulrich would do; but in the end she dreamed that the right thing to do would have been simply to give in to love and grant overtaxed nature respite on a rung of the dizzying Jacob's ladder they were climbing. But no sooner had she admitted this than she appeared to herself like one of those incompetent fairy-tale creatures who cannot contain themselves and in their womanly weakness prematurely break silence or some other oath, causing everything to collapse amid thunderclaps.

If her expectation now turned again to the man who was to help her find counsel, he not only possessed the great advantages bestowed on orderliness, certainty, kindly strictness, and self-possession by an ill-mannered, desperate display; but this stranger also had the special distinction of speaking about God with serene certainty, as if he were a daily guest in His house and in a position to intimate that there, everything that was mere passion and vanity was despised. So what might be awaiting her at Lindner's? While she was asking herself this question, she pressed her feet more firmly on the ground as she walked and drew the coldness of the rain-drenched air into her lungs to make her mind completely sober; and then it began to seem highly probable to her that Ulrich, even though he was judging Lindner onesidedly, nonetheless judged him more accurately than she did, since before her conversations with Ulrich, when her impression of Lindner was still fresh, her own thoughts about the good man had been quite mocking. She was amazed by her feet, which were taking her to him anyway, and she even took a horse-drawn bus to get there faster.

Shaken about among people who were like rough, wet pieces of laundry, she found it hard to keep her web of reveries intact, for she wanted to bring it to Lindner. But she managed to protect it from tearing and withstood the ride with a determined face. She even belittled it, reducing its size, as it were. Her entire relation to God, if this name should even be applied to such adventurousness, was limited to a kind of twilight that opened up when her life became too oppressive and repulsive or, and this was new, too beautiful. Into that space she would then run, searching. That was all she could honestly say about it. And nothing had ever come of it. This she told herself between bounces and jolts. And then she noticed that she was now really curious to find out how her unknown acquaintance would extricate himself from this business that was being entrusted to him as God's deputy, so to speak—a vocation for which, surely, some degree of omniscience must have been granted him by the great Inaccessible One. For she in the meantime, squeezed between all kinds of people, had firmly resolved under no condition to deliver a full confession to him right away. But when she got out, she discovered within herself, remarkably enough, the deeply hidden conviction that this time it would be different from before and that she was determined to bring the Unfathomable out of the twilight and into the light, and to do so on her own if needs be. Perhaps she would have quickly extinguished this hyperbolic word if it had entered her consciousness at all; but what was there in place of a word was merely a surprised feeling that whirled her blood upward as if it were fire.

The man toward whom such passionate feelings and fantasies were en route was meanwhile sitting in the company of his son, Peter, at his midday meal, which he still ate, following a good rule of former times, at the actual hour of noon. There was no luxury in his surroundings, or, as it is better to say in German, no *Überfluss*; for the native word reveals the sense that the adopted foreign word—*Luxus*—obscures. Both words have the meaning of the superfluous and dispensable that idle wealth might accumulate; but *Überfluss* additionally means an overflowing, and thus signifies a padding of existence that slightly swells beyond its frame, or that surplus ease and liberality of European life of which only the very poor are deprived. Lindner distinguished between these two concepts of luxury, and just as luxury in the first sense was absent from his home, it was present in the second. One already received this peculiar impression, though one could not tell where it came from, when the front door opened and revealed the moderately large foyer. If one looked around, none of the furnishings created to serve mankind with a useful invention were lacking: an umbrella rack, soldered from sheet metal and painted with enamel, took care of one's umbrella. A coarsely woven runner rug removed from shoes the dirt that had not already been left on the doormat. Two clothes brushes were tucked into a pouch on the wall, and a rack for hanging outer garments was also provided. An electric bulb lit the room; there was even a mirror; and all these implements were maintained with the utmost care and promptly replaced when they suffered damage. But the bulb had the lowest wattage, by which one can just barely make things out; the clothes rack had only three hooks; the mirror encompassed only four-fifths of an adult face; and the carpet was just thick enough and its quality just good enough to enable one to feel the floor through it and not sink into softness. It may very well be futile, by the way, to attempt to describe the spirit of a place through such details, but one needed only to enter that house to feel wafting toward one the peculiar presence of something alive and intangible that was not strict and not lax, not affluent and not poor, not flavored and not tasteless, but simply a positive result of two negations such as might best be described as "lack of waste." However, this by no means precluded a feeling for beauty, indeed even a sense of pleasure, from making themselves felt as one entered the inner rooms. Sumptuous prints hung framed on the walls, the window next to Lindner's desk was adorned with a colorful showpiece of glass representing a knight who, with a prim gesture, was liberating a maiden from a dragon, and in the choice of several painted vases that held beautiful paper flowers, in the acquisition of an ashtray by the nonsmoker, as well as in the many small details through which, as it were, a ray of sunlight falls into the grave circle of duty represented by the upkeep and care of a household, Lindner had gladly permitted an unbuttoned taste to prevail. And yet, the twelve-edged severity of the room's shape permeated everything just enough to remind one of the hardness of life, which should not be forgotten even in comfort; and even where a touch of feminine indiscipline stemming from earlier times—a cross-stitched doily, a pillow with roses, or the petticoat of a lampshade—interrupted this unity, the containing whole was strong enough to prevent the voluptuous element from overstepping its bounds.

Nevertheless, on this day, and not for the first time since the day before, Lindner had appeared at mealtime nearly fifteen minutes late. The table was set; the plates, stacked three high at each of the two seats, looked at him with the round glare of reproach; the little glass knife rests, from which knives, spoons, and forks stared like gun barrels from their mounts, and the rolled-up napkins in their rings, were arrayed like an army left in the lurch by its general. Lindner had hastily stuck the mail, which he usually opened before the meal, into his pocket and with a bad conscience hurried into the dining room, uncertain in his bewilderment what it was that befell him there—it might well have been something like mistrust, for at the same moment, from the other side and just as hastily as he, his son, Peter, stepped in as if he had merely been waiting for his father to arrive.

27

THE DO-GOODER AND THE GOOD-FOR-NOTHING. BUT ALSO AGATHE

PETER was a quite robust fellow, about seventeen years old, in whom Lindner's precipitous height had been pervaded and reduced by a broader physique; he came up only as far as his father's shoulders, but his head, which was shaped like a large squarish-round billiard ball, sat on a neck of sturdy flesh whose circumference would have sufficed for one of Papa's thighs. Peter had lingered on a soccer field instead of in school and had on his way home unfortunately accosted a girl, from whom his manly beauty had wrung a half promise to meet with him again: delayed by this development, he had secretly slunk into the house and to the door of the dining room, uncertain till the last moment how he was going to excuse himself; but when to his surprise he heard no one in the room, he had rushed in, and, just on the point of putting on the bored expression of long waiting, was now very embarrassed when he collided with his father. His red face flushed with still redder spots, and he immediately let loose a great flood of words, casting sidelong glances at his father when he thought he wasn't noticing, but then letting his gaze leap fearlessly into the older Lindner's eyes when he felt them directed at himself. This was calculated, time-tested behavior; its purpose was to create the impression of a young man who was candid and unrestrained to the point of folly, and who might be capable of anything except keeping something hidden. But when that was not sufficient, Peter did not shy away from letting slip, apparently inadvertently, words disrespectful of his father or in some other way offensive to him, which then worked like lightning rods to attract a flash of displeasure and thereby divert his father's attention from more dangerous paths. For Peter feared his father the way hell fears heaven, with the dignity of roasting flesh on which the spirit gazes from above. He loved soccer, but even there he preferred watching from the sidelines with an expert mien and making weighty judgments to exerting himself on the field. He intended to become a pilot and perform heroic feats someday; however, he did not conceive of this as a goal toward which one must work but thought of it as a personal disposition, an innate attribute of people who will one day be able to fly. Nor did it make a difference to him that his aversion to work was in contradiction to the teachings of school: this son of a recognized pedagogue had not the slightest interest in being respected by his teachers; it was enough for him to be the physically strongest in the class, and if one of his classmates struck him as being too smart, he was prepared to adjust the imbalance with a punch to the nose or stomach. As everyone knows, one can lead a respected existence this way, but his method had one disadvantage: he could not apply it at home against his father, indeed it was imperative that his father find out about it as little as possible. For faced with this spiritual authority that had raised him and gently held him in its clutches, Peter's vehemence broke down into wailing attempts at rebellion, which Lindner senior called the pitiful shrieks of the desires. Exposed since childhood to the best principles, Peter had a hard time denying their truth to himself, and was able to satisfy his honor and virtue only with the cunning of an Indian brave by avoiding open verbal combat. He did, of course, employ many words in order to adapt to his opponent, but he never descended to the need to tell the truth, which in his opinion was unmanly and a waste of breath.

So this time too his protestations and grimaces bubbled forth at once, but they elicited no reaction from the master. Professor Lindner had hastily made the sign of the cross over the soup and was eating gravely, silently, and in a hurry. Once in a while, briefly and without focus, his glance would come to rest on the part in his son's hair. That part had on this day been drawn through the dense, reddish-brown hair with comb, water, and a good deal of pomade like a narrow-gauge railroad track through a reluctantly swerving forest thicket. When Peter felt his father's gaze resting there, he lowered his head to cover with his chin the red, screamingly beautiful tie with which his educator was not yet acquainted. For at any moment the gaze might gently widen at such a discovery and the mouth follow it with words about "submission to the slogans of coxcombs and buffoons" or "social preening and servile vanity" that offended Peter. But this time nothing happened, and it was only a while later, when the plates were being changed, that Lindner said kindly and vaguely—it was not even certain whether he was referring to the tie or whether his admonition was prompted by an unconsciously registered impression: "People who still need to struggle a lot with their vanity should avoid anything conspicuous in their outward appearance . . . !"

Peter took advantage of his father's unexpected lapse of character to produce a story about an "Unsatisfactory" he claimed to have earned by an act of chivalry, because, tested after another student, he had deliberately made himself look unprepared in order not to outshine his classmate by meeting incredible demands that were simply beyond the reach of weaker students.

Professor Lindner merely shook his head at this.

But when the middle course had been taken away and dessert was brought to the table, he began, pensively and circumspectly: "Look, it's precisely in the years of the greatest appetite that one can win the most momentous victories over oneself, not by starving oneself, which is unhealthy, but by occasionally renouncing a favorite dish after one has eaten enough."

Peter was silent and showed no understanding of this, but his head once again was blushing bright red up to his ears.

"It would be a mistake," his father continued, "if I were to punish you for this poor grade, because the childish lies you have added to it are evidence of such a lack of the very notion of moral honor that one must first make the soil tillable on which punishment can take effect. So I'm not asking anything of you except that you recognize this yourself, and I'm sure that then you will punish yourself."

That was the moment when Peter vigorously alluded to his weak health and also to the overwork that could have caused his recent failures in school and that made it impossible for him to steel his character by renouncing dessert.

"The French philosopher Comte," Professor Lindner replied calmly, "was accustomed after dining, often without any particular inducement, to chew on a crust of dry bread in place of dessert, just to remember those who do not even have dry bread. It is a fine trait that reminds us that every exercise of abstinence and simplicity has profound social significance!"

Peter had long had an extremely unfavorable view of philosophy, but now his father reminded him unpleasantly of the literary arts as well, for he continued: "The author Tolstoy also says that abstemiousness is the first step toward freedom. Man has many slavish desires, and in order for the struggle against all of them to be successful, one must begin with the most elemental ones: gluttony, idleness, and lust." Professor Lindner was accustomed to pronouncing any of these three terms, which occurred frequently in his admonitions, as impersonally as the others; and long before Peter was able to develop a concrete notion of what was meant by "lust," he had already been introduced to the struggle against it, along with the struggle against gluttony and idleness, without giving any more thought to the matter than his father, who did not have to give it any thought because he was certain that this was where basic instruction in self-determination begins. And so it happened that on a day when Peter did not yet know sensual pleasure in its most desired form but was already slinking around its skirts, he was surprised for the first time by a sudden feeling of angry revulsion against the loveless way in which his father habitually connected sensual pleasure with idleness and the craving for food. As he could not risk saying it directly, he had to lie, and cried: "I'm a simple person and can't compare myself with writers and philosophers!"—and though he was agitated, the words he chose were not ill-considered.

His educator did not respond.

"I'm hungry!" Peter added, still more passionately.

Lindner responded with a pained, disdainful smile.

"I'll die if I don't get enough to eat!" Peter cried, almost bawling.

"A person's first response to all intrusions and offenses from without occurs through the vocal organs!" his father instructed him.

And the "pitiful shrieks of the desires," as Lindner called them, died away. Peter did not want to cry on this particularly manly day, but the need to develop verbal agility in self-defense weighed terribly on him. He could think of nothing further to say, and at that moment he even hated lies, because one had to speak in order to use them. In his eyes, bloodlust and wails of lament alternated. At this point Professor Lindner said kindly: "You need to impose serious discipline on yourself in practicing silence, so that it's not the thoughtless and uneducated person in you that speaks but the one who is prudent and well brought up and whose words communicate peace and firmness!" And then, with a friendly face, he lapsed into reflection. "I have no better advice, if one wants to make others good," he disclosed to his son the conclusion he had come to, "than to be good oneself; Matthias Claudius also says: 'I cannot conceive of any other way than to be oneself the way one wants children to be!'" And with these words, Professor Lindner amiably and resolutely pushed the dessert away from himself—even though it was his favorite, rice pudding with sugar and chocolate—without tasting it, and by means of this loving obduracy forced his teeth-gnashing son to do the same.

At that moment the housekeeper entered the room and announced Agathe. August Lindner sat up in consternation. "So she did come!" a horribly distinct mute voice said to him. He was prepared to feel indignant, but he was also prepared to feel a fraternal indulgence guided by the natural empath's delicate moral sense of touch, and these two antagonists, each with a great retinue of principles, performed a wild chase through his entire body before he managed to give the simple order to show the lady into the living room. "You wait for me here!" he said to Peter severely and left the room with long strides. But Peter had noticed something unusual in his father, he just didn't know what; in any case, whatever it was inspired him with such recklessness and courage that after Lindner's departure and a brief hesitation he scooped into his mouth a spoonful of chocolate that was standing ready to be sprinkled, then a spoonful of sugar, and finally a big spoonful of rice, chocolate, and sugar, and repeated this several times before smoothing out the bowls for all eventualities.

And Agathe sat awhile alone in the strange house waiting for Professor Lindner, for he was pacing back and forth in another room, collecting his thoughts before confronting the beautiful and dangerous woman.

She looked around and suddenly felt anxious, as if she had lost her way climbing among the branches of a dreamed tree and had to fear not being able to find her way back safely from its world of twisted wood and myriad leaves. A profusion of details bewildered her, and in the austere taste that had found expression in them a forbidding severity was very peculiarly entwined with an opposite for which, in her unsettled state, she could not find a ready word. The forbidding quality may have been reminiscent of the frozen stiffness of chalk drawings, but the room also looked as if it smelled, in a grandmotherly, cosseted way, of medicaments and ointments; and there was a hovering presence within it of old-fashioned, unmanly spirits preoccupied with human suffering in a disagreeably ostentatious way. Agathe sniffed. And though the air contained nothing more than her imaginings, she gradually found herself being led further and further back, and now remembered the slightly anxious "smell of heaven," that odor of incense, stale and emptied of its spice, that clung to the habits her teachers wore when she was a girl being brought up together with little friends in a pious institute, and where she was far from languishing in piety. For edifying though this odor is for people who form the right association with it, in the hearts of worldly and resistant adolescent girls its effect consisted in a vivid memory of feelings of protest, not unlike those that imagination and first experiences associate with a man's moustache or with his energetic cheeks, redolent of pungent essences and a hint of talc. God knows, that scent, too, does not keep its promises! And while Agathe sat waiting on one of Lindner's renunciatory upholstered chairs, the empty smell of the world and the empty smell of heaven joined together and enclosed her inescapably like two hollow hemispheres, and a premonition came over her that she was about to repeat a lesson she had lived through without paying sufficient attention.

She now knew where she was. Reluctantly willing, she tried to adapt to these surroundings and remember the teachings from which she had perhaps allowed herself to be diverted too early. But her heart reared up at this compliance like a horse that is not amenable to any coaxing, and began to run wild with terror, as happens when there are feelings that want to warn the understanding but find no words. Nevertheless, after a while she tried it once again; and to support the effort, she thought of her father, who had been a liberal man and in his self-presentation had always exhibited a somewhat shallow Enlightenment style, but had nonetheless mustered a decision to consign his daughter to a convent school for her education. She felt inclined to regard this as a kind of atoning sacrifice and as an attempt, compelled by a secret insecurity, for once to do the opposite of what one takes to be one's firm conviction: and because she felt a kinship with every inconsistency, the position she had put herself into appeared to her for a moment like a mysteriously unconscious daughterly act of repetition. But this second, voluntarily indulged shudder of piety did not last either; apparently, during the time when her soul was placed under the all-too-solicitous care of the clergy, she had lost the ability once and for all to anchor her lively intuitions in a creed. For all she had to do was inspect her immediate surroundings again, and with the cruel instinct of youth for the distance that separates the infinity of a teaching from the finiteness of the teacher, which of course easily leads one to deduce the master from the servant, the sight of this home in which she sat like a figure in a framed picture, this prison in which she had willingly and, full of expectation, ensconced herself, suddenly and irresistibly provoked her to laughter.

Yet unconsciously she dug her nails into the wood of the chair, for she was ashamed of her indecision. What she most wanted to do was to fling everything that oppressed her, now and as quickly and suddenly as possible, into the face of this presumptuous consoler, if he would just finally deign to show himself: That underhanded business with the will—completely unforgivable if considered without defiance. Hagauer's letters, distorting her image as horribly as a bad mirror, yet still accurate enough so that a resemblance could not be denied. Then too, perhaps, that she had wanted to destroy that man, though without really, actually killing him; and that she had indeed once married him, but also not really, but blindly, blinded by self-contempt. Her life was filled with unusual half measures; but ultimately, the intuition or presage that hovered between herself and Ulrich, unifying everything, would have to be included in her confession, and this was a betrayal she could never commit, under any circumstances! She felt as surly as a child who is constantly expected to perform a task that is too difficult. Why was the light she sometimes saw instantly extinguished, every time, like a lantern swaying through a vast darkness, its glow swallowed up at one moment and set free at the next?! She was robbed of all resolution, and on top of that she remembered Ulrich's saying once that whoever seeks this light must cross an abyss that has no bottom and no bridge. Did he himself then, deep down, not believe in the possibility of what they were seeking together? That was what she was thinking, and though she did not really dare to doubt, she felt deeply shaken. So no one could help her except the abyss itself! This abyss was God: Oh, what did she know! With aversion and contempt, she surveyed the little bridges that were supposed to lead across: the humbleness of the room, the pictures hung piously on the walls, all those things simulating a confidential relationship with Him. She was as close to humbling herself as she was to running way in horror. Probably what she most wanted to do was run away: but when she remembered that she was always running away, she thought of Ulrich again and seemed to herself a "terrible coward." Hadn't the silence at home already been something like a windless calm before a storm? And then she had been propelled over here by the pressure of what was approaching. That was how she saw it now, not without a hint of a smile; and then it was not surprising that something else Ulrich had said should occur to her, for he had said at some time: "A person never finds himself to be a complete coward; because if something frightens him, he'll run away just far enough to consider himself a hero again!" And so there she sat!

28

A MIGHTY COLLOQUY

AT THIS moment Lindner entered the room, having made up his mind to say just as much as his visitor would; but as soon as they found themselves face-to-face, it all happened differently. Agathe immediately went on the attack with words that to her surprise turned out to be far more ordinary than seemed consonant with the events that had led up to them. "You probably remember my asking you to explain some things to me," she began. "I am here now. I still have a clear recollection of what you said against my getting a divorce. Maybe I've understood it even better since!" They were sitting at a large round table, separated by the entire length of its diameter. By comparison with her last moments by herself, Agathe, at the first moment of this meeting, felt deeply compromised, but then she regained her footing; she had laid out the word "divorce" like a bait, although her curiosity to learn Lindner's opinion was also sincere.

And Lindner actually answered at almost the same instant: "I know quite well why you are asking me for this explanation. All your life you have probably heard people whispering in your ear that believing in a suprahuman reality, and obeying commandments that have their origin in this belief, belongs to the Middle Ages. You have learned that such fairy tales have been disposed of by science. But are you certain that this is really the case?"

Agathe noticed to her surprise that at every third word or so, his lips beneath the sparse beard stiffened and bulged like two assailants. She gave no answer. "Have you thought about it?" Lindner sternly continued. "Do you know the vast number of problems this involves?

I see: You don't know! And yet you dismiss this with a grandiose wave of your hand, and you probably don't even know that you are merely acting under the control of extraneous forces!"

He had plunged into danger. It was not clear what whisperers he was thinking of. He felt himself carried away. His speech was a long tunnel drilled through a mountain in order to pounce on an idea, "lies of freethinking men," that was displaying itself on the other side, shining in boastful self-glory. He meant neither Ulrich nor Hagauer, but he meant both of them, he meant all of them. "And even if you had thought about it," he exclaimed in a boldly rising voice, "and were convinced of these falsehoods: that the body is nothing but a system of dead corpuscles, the soul an interplay of glands, society a ragbag of mechanical economic laws; and even if that were true, which is far from the case—I would still deny that such thinking knows the truth of life! Because that which calls itself science is not in the least qualified to elucidate by its superficial procedures what lives in a human being as an inner, spiritual certainty. The truth of life is a beginningless knowledge, and the facts of true life are not conveyed by proof: he who lives and suffers has them within himself as the mysterious power of higher claims and as the living exegesis of himself!"

Lindner stood up. His eyes flashed like two pulpit orators from the eminence provided by his long legs. Looking down at Agathe, he felt powerful. "Why does he talk so much right away?" she thought. "And what does he have against Ulrich? He hardly knows him, yet he's obviously speaking against him!?"

Then her feminine experience in the arousal of feelings told her more quickly and certainly than reflection could have that Lindner was only speaking this way because he was ridiculously jealous. She looked up at him with an enchanting smile. The way he stood before her, tall, lissome, and armed, he appeared to her like a belligerent giant grasshopper from a past geological age. "Good heavens," she thought, "now I'll say something again that will make him mad and he'll chase after me again. Where am I? What is this game I'm playing?" It confused her that Lindner made her laugh while particular phrases of his were not at all easy for her to forget—"beginningless knowledge," for instance, or "living exegesis"—such alien words in these times, but secretly familiar to her, as if she had always used them herself, though she could not remember having so much as heard these expressions before. She thought: "It's eerie, but he's already planted some of his words into my heart like children!"

Lindner noticed that he had made an impression on her, and this satisfaction appeased him slightly. He saw before him a young woman in whose face excitement and feigned indifference, even insolence, seemed to take turns in an untrustworthy fashion; but as he believed himself to be a connoisseur of the female soul, he did not allow himself to be deterred by this, knowing that the temptation to pride and vanity is extraordinarily great for beautiful women. He was generally unable to contemplate a beautiful face without an admixture of pity. According to his conviction, people distinguished in this way were almost always martyrs of their glossy exterior, which seduced them to conceit and its skulking train of coldheartedness and super-ficiality. Still, it can also happen that a soul dwells behind a beautiful countenance, and how often then has insecurity not hidden behind arrogance, and despair beneath frivolity! Often these are even par-ticularly noble people who merely lack the support of a true and unshakable conviction. And now Lindner was, little by little, once again completely overcome by the thought that it is the successful man's duty to put himself in the frame of mind of a person disadvan-taged by neglect; and as he thought this, he became aware that the form of Agathe's face and body possessed that lovely calm that is the very seal of all that is great and noble; and in fact her knee in the draped folds of its covering appeared to him like that of a Niobe.*
He was astonished that this particular simile, which to his knowledge could not be fitting or applicable at all, should urge itself upon him, but apparently the nobility of his moral pain had of its own accord

*In Greek mythology, Niobe was excessively proud of her beauty and that of her fourteen children. The gods punished her by destroying her children, after which she turned into a stone monument of never-ending sorrow.

associated itself with the dubious idea of many children, for he felt no less attracted than alarmed. He now noticed her bosom, which was breathing in small, rapid waves. He was aroused, and if his knowledge of the world had not come to his aid again, he might have even felt at a loss: but at this extremely awkward moment it whispered to him that this bosom must enshrine something unspoken, a secret that, given everything that he knew, might well have something to do with the divorce from his colleague Hagauer. This saved him from embarrassing foolishness by instantly offering him the alternative of wishing for the revelation of the secret instead of the uncovering of the breast. He wished this with all his strength, and the link between sin and the chivalric slaying of the dragon of sin hovered before him in glowing colors, much as they glowed in the stained-glass picture in his study.

Agathe interrupted this rumination with a question she addressed to him in a moderate, even restrained tone after she had regained her composure. "You claimed that I am acting under the influence of insinuations, that I am externally controlled. What did you mean by that?"

Disconcerted, Lindner raised his eyes, which had been resting on her heart, to meet her gaze. Something happened that had never happened to him before: he could no longer remember what he had last said. He had seen in this young woman a victim of the spirit that was confounding the age, and his victorious joy had occluded the memory of his own words.

Agathe repeated her question with a small alteration: "I confided to you that I want a divorce from Professor Hagauer, and you replied that I am acting under external compulsion. It might be useful to me to learn what you mean by that. I repeat, none of the customary reasons quite applies; even my aversion has not been insurmountable by the standards of the world. I have just become convinced that aversion to ordinary life should not be surmounted, but must instead be increased beyond all measure!"

"By whom?"

"Just that is the question you're supposed to help me solve." Again she looked at him with a gentle smile that was, so to speak, a horribly low-cut décolleté exposing an inner bosom covered with nothing but black silk lace.

Involuntarily Lindner protected his eyes from the sight with a movement of his hand feigning an adjustment of his glasses. The truth was that courage played the same timid role in his worldview as it did in the feelings he harbored for Agathe. He was one of those people who have recognized that the victory of humility is facilitated if humility first knocks out arrogance with a fist, and his learned nature made him fear no arrogance more bitterly than that of independent science, which reproaches faith with being unscientific. Had someone told him that the saints with their empty, beseeching raised hands were obsolete and that to update them for the modern age they would have to be depicted with sabers, pistols, or even newer instruments in their fists, that might have aroused his indignation, but he did not want to see the weapons of knowledge withheld from faith. That was almost entirely an error, but he was not alone in committing it; and this was why he had assailed Agathe with words that would have merited a place of honor in his publications—and probably occupied that distinction in fact—but were out of place directed at the woman who was confiding in him. Seeing this emissary of worlds hostile to him sitting modestly and thoughtfully before him, delivered into his hands by a kind or demonic fate, he felt this himself and did not know how to answer her. "Oh!" he said, in as generalizing and dismissive a way as possible, and accidentally hit close to the mark: "I meant the prevailing spirit of our time that makes young people afraid of looking stupid or even unscientific if they don't go along with all the modern superstitions. I have no idea what slogans there may be in your mind: Living it up! Life affirmation! Personal development! Freedom of thought, freedom in the arts! Everything, in short, except the commandments of simple and eternal morality."

The happy intensification "stupid, or even unscientific" pleased him by its subtlety and had aroused his fighting spirit again. "You are no doubt surprised," he continued, "that in conversing with you I attach such importance to science, without knowing whether you have given it a lot of your attention or just a little—"

"None!" Agathe interrupted him. "I am unfortunately ignorant of science!"*

She emphasized this remark with her voice and seemed to find pleasure in it, perhaps with a kind of false impiety.

"But this is your milieu!" Lindner corrected her emphatically. "And whether it's freedom in manners or scientific freedom, both are an expression of the same development: thought, will, and feeling detached from morality!"

Agathe again felt these words as sober shadows that were, however, cast by something darker that was in their proximity. She was not inclined to conceal her disappointment, but revealed it with a laugh: "Recently you advised me not to think of myself, but here you are talking about me incessantly."

He repeated: "You are afraid of seeming old-fashioned to yourself!"

Agathe's eyes flashed angrily. "I'm at a loss. So much of what you say has nothing to do with me!"

"And I say to you: 'Ye were bought with a price, become not bond servants of men!'" The manner of his delivery, so oddly contrasting with his physical appearance, like a heavy flower on a weak stem, amused Agathe. She asked urgently, almost coarsely: "So what should I do? I am hoping for a definite answer from you."

Lindner swallowed and his face darkened with earnestness. "Do that which is your duty!"

"I don't know what my duty is!"

"Then you should look for duties!"

"But I don't know what duties are!"

Lindner smiled grimly. "There we have it! The freedom of the personality!" he cried. "A vain mirage! You can see it in yourself: A person who is free is unhappy! A person who is free is a phantom!" he added, raising his voice further out of embarrassment as he spoke. But then he lowered it again and concluded with conviction: "You must return to your husband! Duty is what humanity in proper self-

*The German word *Wissenschaft*, here unavoidably translated as "science," refers also more generally to the pursuit of knowledge, learning, and scholarship.

knowledge has erected against its own weakness. Duty is one and the same truth that all great personalities knew in their hearts or pointed to in visionary foreknowledge. Duty is the work of centuries of experience and the fruit of the inspired vision of the blessed. But duty is also what even the simplest person knows with certainty deep within himself, if only he lives his life with sincerity!"

"That was a hymn with quivering candles," Agathe noted appreciatively.

To his annoyance, Lindner, too, felt that he had sung out of tune. He should have said something else but did not trust himself to recognize what the deviation from the genuine voice of his heart consisted in. He merely allowed himself the thought that this young creature must be deeply disappointed by her husband, since she was raging against herself so impudently and bitterly, and that despite all the censure she provoked, she was worthy of a stronger man; however, he had the impression that a far more dangerous thought was intent on following this one. But meanwhile Agathe slowly and very decisively shook her head; and with the instinctive assurance with which an excited person is seduced by another into doing something that brings a precarious balance to the point of collapse, she continued: "But we're talking about my divorce! And why are you saying nothing more about God today? Why don't you simply say to me: 'God commands that you stay with Professor Hagauer!'? Because frankly I can't imagine that He would want to command such a thing!"

Lindner shrugged his high shoulders indignantly; in fact, their swift rising movement made it seem as if he himself were ascending. "I never talked to you about this. That was just something you tried to do!" he gruffly repudiated her. "And as for the rest, don't believe for a moment that God concerns himself with our petty emotional squabbles! That is what His law is for, which we must follow! Or doesn't that seem heroic enough for you, since all anyone wants these days is the 'personal' touch? Well, in that case I'll challenge your standards with a higher heroism, that of *heroic submission*!"

Every word he had said implied considerably more, he believed, than a layman ought to permit himself, even if it were only in his thoughts;

Agathe, on the other hand, faced with such rude derision, could only smile steadily if she did not want to be forced to stand up and break off the visit; and of course she did this with such adroit assurance that Lindner felt himself vexed into ever greater confusion. He noticed how, more and more, an alarming influx of ideas was feeding an intoxicating ardor that robbed him of his powers of reflection and resounded with the will to break the obstinate mind and perhaps save the soul he saw before him. "Our duty is painful!" he exclaimed. "Our duty may be repulsive and disgusting! Don't assume that I have the intention of being your husband's advocate or that I am naturally predisposed to take his side. But you must obey the law, because that is the only thing that guarantees us lasting peace and protects us from ourselves."

Now Agathe laughed at him openly; she had guessed at the weapon that the effects stemming from her divorce had placed in her hand, and she turned the knife in the wound. "I understand little of all this," she said. "But may I honestly confess to you an impression I have? When you are angry, you become a little salacious."

"Oh, stop that!" Lindner rebuked her. He recoiled and had only the single wish not to admit such a thing at any price. He raised his voice in defense and implored the sinful phantom sitting before him: "The spirit must not submit to the flesh and its charms and horrors! Not even in the form of revulsion! And I say to you: Even though mastery of your carnal reluctance, which the school of marriage has evidently exacted of you, may be painful, you are not allowed to run away from it. For there lives in man a desire for liberation, and we can no more be slaves to the repugnance of our flesh than to its pleasures! This is obviously what you wanted to hear, otherwise you would not have come to me!" he concluded, no less grandiosely than spitefully. He stood towering in front of Agathe, the threads of his beard moving around his lips. Never before had he spoken such words to a woman, except to his deceased wife, and there his feelings had been different. For now they were mingled with lust, as if he were swinging a whip in his fist to chastise the entire globe, and at the same time he felt anxious as he found himself soaring at the height of his penitentiary sermon, like a hat swept away by a tornado.

"You just talked strangely again," Agathe noted dispassionately, intending to shut off his insolence with a few dry words; but then she imagined the enormous fall he would face and preferred to humble herself gently by checking her impulse, and continued with a voice that seemed suddenly to have been darkened by remorse: "I only came because I wanted you to guide me."

Lindner, helpless in his zeal, continued swinging his rhetorical whip; he sensed that Agathe was deliberately leading him astray, but he could not find his way back and entrusted himself to the future. "To be chained to a man for a lifetime without feeling any physical attraction is certainly a harsh punishment," he exclaimed. "But hasn't one brought this on oneself, especially if one's partner is unworthy, by not paying enough attention to the signs of the inner life?! Many women allow themselves to be beguiled by external circumstances, and who knows if one is not being punished in order to be shaken up?" Suddenly his voice cracked. Agathe had been accompanying his words with assenting nods; but the notion of Hagauer as a beguiling seducer was too much for her, and the amusement in her eyes betrayed it. Extremely bewildered, Lindner blared in falsetto: "For he who spares the rod hates his child, but he who loves him chastises him!!"

By now his victim's resistance had completely transformed the philosopher of life dwelling in his high watchtower into a poet of chastisement and its arousing secondary effects. He was intoxicated by a feeling he had not experienced before, born of an intimate connection between the moral censure with which he was goading his visitor and the excitation of all his manhood, an emotion that one might symbolically characterize, as he himself now accepted, as lustful.

But the "arrogant conqueress," who was supposed to be ultimately driven to despair by the empty vanity of her worldly beauty, responded matter-of-factly to his threats of the rod by quietly asking: "By whom am I being punished? Are you thinking of God?"

And that could not be said aloud! Lindner suddenly lost his courage. Beads of sweat stood among the hairs on his head. It was impossible to utter the name of God in such a context. His gaze, thrust out like a two-pronged fork, slowly withdrew from Agathe. Agathe felt it. "So he can't do it either!" she thought. She felt a mad desire to keep on tugging at this man until she heard from his mouth what he did not want to disclose to her. But it was enough for now; the conversation had reached its outermost limit. Agathe understood that it had only been a passionate subterfuge, transparent in its very fervor, to avoid having to say the essential thing. Besides, Lindner, too, now knew that everything he had propounded, indeed everything that had excited and upset him, even his own exaggerations, only came from his fear of all exaggeration, of which the most profligate kind, in his view, was the attempt to encroach, with the meddling instruments of sensation and feeling, upon that which must remain shrouded in sublime language, and that this hyperbolic young woman was obviously driving him in that direction. He now called it, silently in his own mind, "a violation of the decency of faith." For during these moments, the blood flowed back down from Lindner's head and resumed its ordinary course; he awoke like a person who finds himself standing naked far from his front door, and remembered that he must not send Agathe away without consolation and instruction. Taking a deep breath, he stood back from her, stroked his beard, and said reproachfully: "You have an unquiet and illusion-prone mind."

"And you have a peculiar idea of gallantry!" Agathe coolly replied, for she had no wish to go on any longer.

Lindner found it necessary to say something more to recover his dignity: "You should learn in the school of reality to rein in your subjectivity with unsparing rigor, for a person who cannot do this will soon be dragged to the ground by fantasies and illusions...!" He paused, for the strange woman was still eliciting unwelcome emphases from his voice. "Woe to him who departs from morality, it is from reality he is departing!" he quietly added.

Agathe shrugged. "I will attend the school of reality! I hope to see you at our place the next time!" she suggested.

"To that I must respond: Never!" Lindner protested forcefully and now perfectly down-to-earth. "Your brother and I have divergent views on life that make it preferable for us not to engage socially," he added as an excuse.

"In that case I will come to you," Agathe calmly replied.

"No!" Lindner repeated, but curiously enough, he blocked her path in an almost menacing fashion, for she had got up to leave. "That must not happen! You must not put me in the ambiguous position toward my colleague Hagauer of receiving visits from you without his knowledge!"

"Are you always as impassioned as you are today?" Agathe asked sarcastically, thereby forcing him to make way for her. She now, at the end, felt vapid, yet also fortified. The fear Lindner had betrayed had moved her toward actions that were foreign to her true condition; but while her brother's demands often discouraged her, this man gave her back her freedom to act at will from an inner impulse, and it comforted her to confuse him.

"Did I perhaps compromise myself a little?" Lindner asked himself after she had gone. He stiffened his shoulders and marched back and forth in the room several times. Finally he resolved to allow continued contact with her and summed up his considerable unease with the soldierly words: "One must be prepared to meet every discomfiture with valor!"

When Agathe got up to leave, Peter had quickly slipped away from the keyhole, where with considerable astonishment he had been eavesdropping on what his father was up to with the "big goose."

29

BEGINNING OF A SERIES OF WONDROUS EXPERIENCES

SOON AFTER this visit, there was a recurrence of the "Impossible," which was already hovering almost physically around Ulrich and Agathe, and it truly happened without anything happening at all.

They were changing to go out for the evening. There was no one in the house to help Agathe except Ulrich; they were late in starting and had therefore been in the greatest hurry for a quarter of an hour, when a short pause occurred. Almost all the ornaments of war a woman puts on for such occasions were distributed, piece by piece, on the armrests and surfaces of the room, and Agathe was bending over her foot, with all the attentiveness that pulling on a thin silk stocking demands. Ulrich was standing at her back. He saw her head, her neck, her shoulder, and this nearly naked back; her body was leaning a little to the side over the raised knee, and the tension of the process rounded three slender folds that sped merrily through the clear skin on her neck like three arrows: the lovely corporeality of this picture, sprung from the momentarily spreading stillness, seemed to have lost its frame and passed so suddenly and directly into Ulrich's body as to set him into motion, so that, not quite as unconsciously as a flag being unfurled by the wind but not with conscious deliberation either, he crept closer on tiptoe, and, taking the bent-over figure by surprise, with gentle ferocity bit into one of those three arrows, simultaneously wrapping an arm around his sister. Then Ulrich's teeth just as carefully released his overpowered captive; his right hand had gripped her knee, and while with his left arm he pressed her body to his, he pulled her aloft with him on upward-leaping sinews. Agathe cried out in fright.

So far, everything had happened in as playful and joking a manner as much that had happened before, and even though it was tinged with the colors of love, it was only with the essentially shy intention of hiding love's more dangerous uncommon nature beneath the garb of such lighthearted familiarity. But thanks to one of those accidents that are beyond anyone's control, when Agathe got over her fright and felt herself not so much flying through the air as rather resting in it, suddenly released from all gravity and in its stead steered by the gentle force of the gradually decelerating motion, she seemed to herself marvelously comforted, indeed transported beyond all earthly unrest; with a movement that changed her body's equilibrium and that she would never have been able to repeat, she now shed even the last silken thread of constraint, turned in falling to her brother, continuing, as it were, to rise as she fell, and lay, sinking down, as a cloud of happiness in his arms. Ulrich carried her, pressing her body gently to himself, through the darkening room to the window and set her on her feet beside him in the mellow light of the evening, which streamed over her face like tears. Despite the strength all this required, and despite the force Ulrich had imposed on his sister, what they were doing seemed to them curiously remote from strength and force; one could, again, compare it with the wondrous ardor of a picture that to the hand that takes hold of it from outside is nothing more than a silly painted surface. Thus they had nothing in mind beyond the physical process that completely pervaded their consciousness, and yet alongside its nature as a harmless, initially even rather coarse, joke that set every muscle in motion, it also possessed a second nature that with great tenderness paralyzed their limbs and at the same time enchanted them with an indescribable sensitivity. Questioningly, they wrapped their arms around each other's shoulders. The fraternal build of their bodies conveyed itself to them, as if they were rising up from a single root. They looked into each other's eyes with a curiosity as if they were seeing such things for the first time. And although they would not have been able to articulate what had actually happened, because their participation in it had been too compelling, they believed they knew that just a moment ago they had unexpectedly found themselves for an instant in the midst of that shared condition at whose border they had for so long been hesitating, which they had described to each other so often and yet had only gazed into from outside.

Of course if they considered it soberly, and surreptitiously they both did, it amounted to little more than a charming accident and should have dissolved into nothing at the next moment or at least with the return of some activity; and yet this did not happen. On the contrary, they left the window, turned on the light, returned to their preparations, but gave them up after a short time; and without their needing to confer with each other, Ulrich went to the telephone and informed the hosts of the party that they were not coming. He was already wearing his evening suit, but Agathe's dress was still hanging unfastened from her shoulders, and she was only now attempting to impart some civilized order to her hair. The mechanical resonance of his voice in the telephone and the connection to the world that had been established had not sobered Ulrich in the least; he sat down across from his sister, who paused in what she was doing, and when their eyes met, nothing was more certain than that the decision had been made and all prohibitions would now be a matter of indifference to them. Nevertheless, things turned out differently. Their mutual understanding announced itself to them with every breath; it was an agreement, endured in defiance, to release themselves at last from the discontent of longing, and it was an agreement endured with such aching sweetness that the images anticipating the fulfillment of that longing nearly tore themselves loose from them to unite them already in imagination, as a storm whips up a veil of foam ahead of the waves: but a still greater power bade them be calm and they were incapable of touching each other again. They wanted to begin, but the gestures of the flesh had become impossible to them, and they felt an ineffable warning that had nothing to do with the commandments of morality. It seemed that from the world of the more perfect if still shadowy union of which they had already had a foretaste as in a metaphor, a higher imperative had compelled them, and a higher intimation, curiosity, or premonition had breathed upon them.

The siblings now remained perplexed and thoughtful, and after they had calmed their feelings they hesitantly began to speak.

Ulrich said, aimlessly, the way one speaks into the air: "You are the moon—"

Agathe understood it.

Ulrich said: "You flew to the moon and the moon gave you back to me—"

Agathe said nothing: Moon conversations are so wholeheartedly used up.

Ulrich said: "It's a metaphor. 'We were beside ourselves,' 'We exchanged bodies without touching' are metaphors too. But what is a metaphor? A little reality with a great deal of exaggeration. And yet I could have sworn, impossible though it truly is, that the exaggeration was very small and the reality had already become quite big."

He said no more. He thought: "What reality am I talking about? Is there a second one?"

If one here leaves the conversation between brother and sister in order to follow the possibilities of a comparison that had at least some part in shaping it, it might well be said that this reality was truly most closely related to the fantastically altered reality of moonlit nights. For the moonlit world also cannot be fathomed if one sees in it only an occasion for a bit of romantic reverie that is better suppressed by daylight; but rather, if one wants to observe rightly, one must open oneself to the utterly unbelievable fact that all feelings really do change as if under a charm as soon as the piece of earth one happens to occupy plunges from the empty commotion of the day into the sentient corporeality of night. Not only do external relations melt away and re-form in the whispering nuptials of light and shadow, but inner relations, too, converge in a new way. The spoken word loses its selfwill in the listening presence of a neighbor. All affirmations express but a single streaming experience. Night clasps all contradictions in her shimmering maternal arms, and at her breast no word is either false or true, but each is the incomparable birth of spirit out of darkness that man experiences with each new thought. Thus every event on a moonlit night is imbued with the nature of the unrepeatable. It is of the nature of intensification, and is of the nature of selflessness and surrender. Every imparting is a parting without grudge, every giving a receiving, every receiving a conception pregnant with the vibrancy of night. To be like this is the only access to the knowledge of what is occurring. For the self holds nothing back on these nights, no condensed residue of self-possession, scarcely a memory; the intensified self shines out into a boundless selflessness. And these nights are filled with the senseless feeling that something is about to happen such as the world has never seen before, indeed such as the impoverished reason of day cannot even imagine. And it is not the mouth that pours forth rhapsodies, but the body, from the head down to the feet, is stretched taut above the darkness of the earth and beneath the light of heaven in an exultant gladness that vibrates between two stars. And the whispering with one's companions is full of a nameless sensuality that is not the sensuality of a person but of earthly life itself, of all that penetrates perception and sensation, the suddenly revealed tenderness of the world that ceaselessly touches all our senses and is touched by them.

To be sure, Ulrich had never been aware of harboring a predilection for exulting in moonlight reveries; but as one commonly gulps life down without feeling, sometimes much later one feels a taste of it, now but a ghostly shadow on one's tongue: and in this way he suddenly felt everything he had missed in the way of such raptures, all the nights he had spent heedless and lonely before he met his sister, as liquid silver poured over endless shrubbery, as flecks of moonlight in the grass, as pendant apple boughs, singing frost, and gilded black waters. Those were all details that did not cohere and that had never been together but that now commingled like the fragrance of a multitude of herbs arising from an intoxicating drink. And when he said this to Agathe, she felt it too.

Then Ulrich summed up everything that he had said with the assertion: "What made us turn toward each other from the first moment could really be called a life of moonlit nights!" And Agathe breathed a deep sigh. That could mean any number of things, but probably it meant: Why don't you know a magic spell against our being separated at the last moment? She sighed so naturally and confidingly that she did not even notice it.

And this in turn started a movement that inclined them toward each other and kept them apart. Every strong excitement that two people have experienced together to the end leaves behind in them the naked intimacy of exhaustion. Even a quarrel will do that; how much more a tenderness that hollows out the marrow of the spine as if to fashion it into a flute! Thus Ulrich, touched, would have almost put his arms around Agathe when he heard her wordless lament, and was as enchanted as a lover on the morning after the first tempests. His hand was already touching her shoulder, which was still bare, and at this touch she started, smiling; but in her eyes there reappeared immediately the signs of involuntary dissuasion. Strange images now arose in his mind: Agathe behind bars. Or fearfully waving her hand to him from a growing distance, torn away by the separative force of unknown men holding her in their grip. Then again he himself was not just the one impotently left behind, but also the one enacting the separation. Perhaps these were perennial images of the doubts of love, merely used up in the average life; then again, perhaps not. He would have liked to talk with her about it, but Agathe was now looking away from him to the open window and hesitantly stood up. The fever of love was in their bodies, but their bodies did not dare a repetition, and beyond the window, whose curtains were almost fully open, was what had seduced their imagination, without which the flesh is merely brutal or fainthearted. When Agathe took the first steps in that direction, Ulrich, guessing her intention, turned off the light in order to free their gaze into the night. The moon had come up behind the tops of the spruce trees, whose greenly glimmering black stood out in melancholy contrast to the blue-gold heights and the pallidly glittering distance. Reluctantly, Agathe surveyed that deep little piece of the world.

"So it's no more than moonlight romance after all?" she asked.

Ulrich looked at her without answering. Her blond hair had turned fiery in the semidarkness against the whitish night, her lips were parted by shadows, her beauty was painful and irresistible. But probably he stood similarly before her gaze, with blue eye sockets in his white face, for she continued: "Do you know what you look like now? 'Pierrot Lunaire.' This calls for prudence." She wanted to injure him a little in her excitement, which was almost making her weep. After all, it was behind the pale mask of Pierrot in his lunar loneliness that, ages ago, all useless young people appeared to themselves as creatures of dolorous whimsy, powdered-chalk white except for blood-drop red lips, and abandoned by a Columbine whom they had never possessed; this certainly did make the love for moonlit nights look rather ridiculous. But Ulrich, to his sister's initially growing sorrow, readily agreed. "That's true of 'Laugh, clown, laugh!' as well," he bitterly affirmed. "That song has sent shudders of inmost assent down the backs of a thousand philistines." But then he added softly, almost whispering: "This whole sphere of emotion is questionable! And yet I would give all the memories of my life for the way you look right now!" Agathe's hand had found Ulrich's. Ulrich continued softly and passionately: "What our age understands by an exalted state of feeling is a surfeit of emotion, and moonlight raptures have been debased to orgies of sentimentality. Our time does not even suspect that this elation must be either an incomprehensible mental disturbance or the fragment of another life!"

These words—precisely because they were perhaps an exaggeration—had the faith and with it the wings of adventure. "Good night!" Agathe said unexpectedly, and took them with her. She had released herself and pulled the curtains shut so hastily that the picture of the two of them standing in the moonlight vanished as if at one blow; and before Ulrich turned on the light, Agathe succeeded in finding her way out of the room.

Ulrich gave her more time: "Tonight you will sleep as impatiently as before the start of a great excursion!" he called after her.

"I do want that!" was what he heard as the door closed.

30

MOONBEAMS BY DAYLIGHT

WHEN THEY saw each other again in the morning, it was at first from a distance like coming upon an uncommon painting in an ordinary house, or even like sighting a significant sculpture among the haphazard displays of nature: unexpectedly, from the liquid lowlands of existence, an island of meaning, an elevation and condensing of spirit, comes to light in sensuous manifestation. But when they approached each other, they were embarrassed, and all that was to be felt of the previous night in their glances was the tiredness that was now shading them with tender warmth.

Who knows, by the way, whether love would be so admired if it wasn't tiring! When they became aware of the aching aftermath of the previous night's excitement, it made them happy again, the way lovers are proud of having nearly died of pleasure. Still, the joy they found in each other was not only such a feeling but also an arousal of the eye: The colors and shapes that presented themselves were diffuse and bottomless and yet starkly prominent, like a bouquet of flowers drifting on dark water. They were more clearly delineated than usual, but in a way that made it impossible to say whether this was due to the distinctness of the appearance or to its underlying emotion. This impression was as much part of the compact sphere of perception and attention as it belonged to the ambiguous domain of feeling; and that was precisely what caused it to hover between inside and outside, as a held breath hovers between inhalation and exhalation, and made it hard to discern, in peculiar contrast to its intensity, whether it belonged to the physical world or merely owed its existence to the heightening of inner participation. Nor did either of them wish to make this distinction, for a kind of shame of reason held them back; and for a long time afterward it still forced them to keep a distance from each other, even though their sensitivity was lasting and could well give rise to the belief that the course of the boundaries between them, as well as between them and the world, might have suddenly undergone some slight change.

The weather had turned summery again, and they spent a lot of time outdoors. Flowers and shrubs were blooming in the garden. When Ulrich looked at a flower—which was not exactly an old habit of this once impatient man—he now sometimes found no end to beholding what he saw and, for that matter, no beginning either. If by chance he knew the flower's name, it was salvation from the sea of infinity. Then the little golden stars on a bare, supple wand signified "forsythia," and those premature leaves and umbels were "lilacs." But if he did not know the name, he would call the gardener over, for then this old man would pronounce an unknown name, and everything would be all right again, and the ancient magic by which possession of the right word vouchsafes protection from the untamed wildness of things bestowed its calming power as it had ten thousand years ago. But something else could happen too: Ulrich would find himself deserted and without support facing some little branch or blossom and not even Agathe was nearby, with whom he could have shared his ignorance: then it suddenly seemed to him utterly impossible to understand the bright green of a young leaf, and the mysteriously limited profusion of forms in a little flower cup became an uninterrupted circle of infinite variation. In addition, it was hardly possible for a man like him, if he did not lie to himself, which on Agathe's account alone could not be allowed to happen, to believe in one of those bashful rendezvous with nature, whose murmurings and upturned eyes, sweet pieties and silent music-making are the prerogative of a special simplicity which imagines that no sooner has it laid its head in the grass, God is already tickling its neck, notwithstanding the fact that on weekdays it has no objection to nature being bought and sold at the fruit exchange. Ulrich despised this cut-rate mysticism at the cheapest price and praise, whose constant talk of being ravished by Grace is at bottom exceedingly lewd;* better to abandon himself to the impotence of trying to find words for an almost palpable color, or of describing one of those shapes that spoke for themselves in such a mindlessly haunting way. For in such a condition the word does not cut, and the fruit remains on the branch although one thinks it already in one's mouth: that is probably the first secret of daylight mysticism. And Ulrich tried to tell his sister about it, albeit with the ulterior motive that it should not, some day, disappear like an illusion.

But as a result, the passionate condition was supplanted by a very different state of serene, indeed at times almost desultory conversation that served to shield them from each other as if with a screen, even though they saw through it completely. They usually lay on two large deck chairs, which they were constantly dragging in pursuit of the sun; this early summer sun was shining for the millionth time on the magic it works every year; and Ulrich said many things that happened to pass through his mind and carefully rounded themselves, like the moon, which was now quite pale and a little dirty, or perhaps like a soap bubble: and so it happened, and quite soon, that he came to speak of the confounded and frequently cursed absurdity that all understanding presupposes a kind of superficiality, a penchant for the surface, which is moreover expressed by the idea of grasping entailed in the word "comprehend," and has to do with the fact that the primary experiences are not understood one by one but each in reference to the next and are thereby unavoidably connected more on the surface than in depth. He then continued: "So if I maintain that this grass in front of us is green, it sounds quite definite, but I have not said a great deal. Actually no more than if I told you that a man walking past us was a member of the Green family. And, good heavens, how many greens there are! I might as well content myself with the understanding that this green lawn is grass green, or even that

---

*The German phrase *zu billigstem Preis und Lob* involves an untranslatable pun. *Preis* and *Lob* both mean "praise" and are often used as a pair in liturgical language, but *Preis* also means "price."

it is green like a lawn on which it rained a little just a short while ago—"
He surveyed the plane of young, sunlit grass, blinking lethargically,
and said: "I imagine that is how you would probably describe it, since
you're adept at distinguishing dress materials by their color. I, on the
other hand, could possibly measure the color as well: I would guess
that it has a wavelength of approximately five hundred and forty mil-
lionths of a millimeter; and now this green does appear to have been
captured and nailed to a specific point! But already it's slipping away
from me, because look: something in this lawn's color has something
material about it, and that can't be described in terms of color at all,
because it's different from the same green in silk or in wool. And now
we're back to the profound realization that green grass is grass green!"

Agathe, summoned as a witness, found it very understandable that
nothing could be understood, and replied: "I suggest you look into a
mirror at night sometime: it's dark, it's black, you see almost nothing;
and yet this nothing is very clearly something other than the nothing
of the rest of the darkness. You sense the glass, the doubling of depth,
some remnant of the ability to shimmer, and yet you see nothing!"

Ulrich laughed at his sister's readiness to strip knowledge of all
its honor; he himself was far from thinking that concepts have no
value and was well aware of what they accomplish, even if he did not
exactly act as if he did. What he wanted to get at was the ungraspable
nature of isolated experiences, those experiences that for obvious
reasons one must cope with alone and in solitude, even when in the
presence of a companion. He repeated: "The self never apprehends
its impressions and productions in isolation, but always in a context—
in real or imagined, similar or dissimilar correspondence with other
things; and so all named things lean against each other in one or
another respect or regard, in series and alignments, as links in great
and not even remotely comprehensible totalities, each supported by
the next and pervaded by common tensions. But that is why," he
suddenly continued in a new direction, "if for some reason this system
of associations fails and none of the inner categories responds, we are
immediately left again to face an indescribable and inhuman, indeed
disavowed and formless, creation!" With that they were back at their

point of departure; but Agathe felt above it the dark creation, the abyss that was the world, the God who should help her!

Her brother said: "Understanding gives way to unslakable astonishment, and the slightest experience—this little pennant of grass or the gentle sounds when your lips over there pronounce a word—becomes incomparable, immensely solitary, unfathomable in its self-glory, and has a stunning, narcotic effect..."

He fell silent, irresolutely twirling a blade of grass in his hand, and listened with pleasure as Agathe, apparently as unentangled in thought as she was unconstrained by rigor, proceeded to restore physicality to their exchange. For now she replied: "If it were drier I would want to lie down in the grass! Let's travel! I would so much like to lie on a meadow, returned to nature as humbly as a discarded shoe!"

"But that also just means being released from all feelings," Ulrich objected. "And God alone knows what would become of us if they didn't show up in swarms, the loves and hates and sufferings and goodnesses that appear to be each person's exclusive property. We would probably be deprived of all capacity to think and act, because our soul is made for a life that repeats itself, and not for what steps completely outside the order of things..." He was dejected, believed he had ventured into a void, and searchingly looked into his sister's face with an uneasily furrowed brow.

But Agathe's face was even clearer than the air that surrounded it and toyed with her hair as she now responded with something she had memorized: "I know not where I am, nor do I seek myself, nor do I want to know of it, nor will I have tidings. I am as immersed in the wellspring of His love as if I were beneath the surface of the ocean and could not see or feel from any side any thing but water."

"What is that from?" Ulrich asked curiously, and only now discovered that she was holding a book in her hands. Without answering, Agathe opened the book and read aloud: "I rose above all my faculties up to the dark power. There I heard without sound, there I saw without light. Then my heart became bottomless, my soul loveless, my spirit formless, and my nature insubstantial." Now Ulrich recognized the volume and smiled, and only then did Agathe say:

"It's from your library." And closing the book, she concluded from memory: "Are you yourself, or are you not? I know nothing of this, I am ignorant of it, and I am ignorant of myself. I am in love, but I know not with whom; I am neither faithful nor unfaithful. What am I, then? I am ignorant even of my love; my heart is full of love and empty of love at the same time!"

Her good memory was not, as a rule, prone to shape its recollections into ideas but preserved them in their sensuous particularity, much the way one memorizes a poem; which is why there was always a participation of body and soul in her words no matter how unobtrusively she spoke. Ulrich recalled her performance before their father's burial, when she declaimed those wildly beautiful verses by Shakespeare to him. "How wild her nature is compared to mine!" he thought. "I haven't allowed myself to say much today." He reconsidered the explanation of "daylight mysticism" he had given her. All in all, it had amounted to no more than his conceding the possibility of transitory deviations from the familiar and established order of experience; and if one thought of it that way, her experiences merely followed a basic principle that was somewhat richer in feeling than that of ordinary experience and resembled little bourgeois children who have landed in a troupe of traveling actors. So he had not dared say any more, even though for days every bit of space between him and his sister had been full of unfinished events! And gradually he began to occupy himself with the question of whether there might not be more things that could be believed than he had admitted to himself.

After the lively culmination of their exchange, Agathe and he had reclined in their chairs, and the stillness of the garden closed over their fading words. Insofar as it has been said that Ulrich had begun to occupy himself with a question, the qualifying observation must now be added that many answers precede their questions as a man in a hurry precedes his open, fluttering coat. What preoccupied Ulrich was a startling idea that did not strictly speaking require belief but by its mere arising provoked astonishment and the impression that such an inspiration must never be allowed to be forgotten, which, considering such claims, was a little uncomfortable. Ulrich was used to thinking in a way that was not godless so much as God-free, which in the ways of science means leaving every possible turning to God to the emotions, because such an orientation is not capable of advancing rational insight but can only lure the mind to venture into the impenetrable. Nor did he doubt even now that this was the only right way, since the most palpable successes of the human spirit had only come about after the spirit decided to steer clear of God. But the idea that had come to beset him said: "What if this ungodliness were nothing other than the contemporary path to God? Every age has had its own pathway to the divine, commensurate with its most potent spiritual capacities; so would it not be our destiny, the destiny of an age of intelligent and enterprising experience, to disavow all dreams, legends, and ingenious conceptions for the sole reason that at the height of our study and exploration of the world we are turning to God again and will gain a relationship with Him through experience at its beginning?!"

This conclusion was completely unprovable, Ulrich knew that; indeed, to most people it would probably appear as perverse, and that did not trouble him. He himself really ought not to have thought it either: The scientific procedure—which he had just a short while ago described as legitimate—consists, aside from in logic, in immersing the concepts it has gained from the surface, from "experience," into the depths of phenomena and explaining the latter by the former; everything on earth is leveled and laid waste in order to gain mastery over it, and it seemed not unreasonable to object that this ought not to be extended to that which is not of this earth. But Ulrich now contested this objection: the desert is not an objection, it has always been a birthplace of celestial visions; and furthermore, prospects that have not yet been attained cannot be foreseen either! But it escaped him that perhaps he was in a second kind of opposition to himself, or had gone in a direction that veered away from his own. Saint Paul calls faith the confident expectation of things hoped for and the conviction of things unseen, a definition that, with its focus on grasping, has become the conviction of educated people, and Ulrich's opposition to it was among his most strongly held convictions. Faith as a diminutive form of knowledge was repugnant to his nature, it is always "against one's better knowledge"; conversely, it had been given to him to recognize in the presentiment of what lies beyond "the best of our knowledge" a special condition and a realm for adventurous minds to explore. That his opposition had now weakened would cause him much trouble later on, but for the moment he was not aware of it, as a swarm of ancillary considerations had come to engage and amuse him.

He singled out examples. Life was becoming increasingly uniform and impersonal. Something stereotypical, mechanical, statistical, and serial was insinuating itself into every entertainment, excitement, recreation, even into the passions. The will to life was becoming broad and shallow, like a river hesitating before it meets the sea. The will to art was already putting itself in doubt. It seemed as though the age was already beginning to devalue the individual person, but without being able to make up the loss through new collective achievements. That was its face. And this face, which was so hard to understand; which he had once loved and had tried to recast as the muddy crater of a deeply rumbling volcano, because he felt young like a thousand others; and from which, like those thousands, he had turned away, because he could not bear seeing it so horribly deformed; this face was becoming transfigured, becoming placid, slyly beautiful, and shining from within, by dint of a single idea! For what if it were God Himself who was devaluing the world? Would the world not thereby suddenly regain meaning and pleasure? And would He not have to be devaluing it if He were coming closer to it by even the smallest step? And would it not already be the one true adventure to sense just the annunciatory shadow of this?! These considerations had the unreasoning consistency of a series of adventures and felt so foreign in Ulrich's head that he thought he was dreaming. Now and then he cautiously looked over to his sister, as if fearful that she might perceive what he was up to, and several times he caught sight of her blond head like light on light against the sky, and saw the air that was toying with her hair also playing with the clouds.

For when that happened, she too was raising herself up slightly and looking around with wonder. She was trying to imagine what it would be like to be released from all of life's emotions. Even space, this always self-similar, contentless cube, was now different, she thought. If she kept her eyes closed for a while and then opened them again, so that the garden entered her view untouched, as if it had just been created, she perceived, with the disembodied clarity of a vision, that the line that connected her to her brother was distinguished among all others: The garden "stood" around this line, and without anything having changed in the trees, paths, and other parts of the real environment, of which she could easily assure herself, everything was oriented toward this connection as an axis and was thereby invisibly changed in a visible way. It might sound paradoxical, but she could just as well have said that the world was sweeter there, perhaps more sorrowful too: strangely, one seemed to be able to see this with one's eyes. And there was another conspicuous feature: All the surrounding shapes stood there eerily abandoned, but also ravishingly, and just as eerily, enlivened, in the semblance of a gentle death or a passionate swoon, as though they had just been bereft of something unnamable, which lent them an almost human sensuality and vulnerability. And as with the impression of space, something had happened to the sense of time; this flowing conveyor belt, this rolling staircase with its uncanny association with death, seemed at some moments to stand still and at others to be flowing along by itself, unrelated to anything else. In a single instant of external duration, time could disappear inside, without a trace of whether it had stopped for an hour or a minute.

Once, Ulrich surprised his sister during these experiments and probably had an inkling of them, for he said to her softly, smiling: "There is a prophecy that to the gods a millennium is no more than the blink of an eye." Then they both leaned back again and continued listening to the dream discourse of silence.

Agathe thought: "All this was his doing, he alone made it happen; and yet he doubts every time he smiles!" But the sun was steadily pouring its warmth on his parted lips, tenderly, like a sleeping potion;

Agathe felt it on her own lips and knew herself to be at one with him. She tried to put herself in his place and guess his thoughts, which was something they had come to regard as impermissible, because it was an intrusion and not the result of creative participation; but as a deviation it was that much more secret. "He doesn't want this to become just another love story," she thought; and added: "That suits my taste too." And then she thought: "He won't love another woman after me, because this is no longer a love story; it's in fact the last possible love story!" And she added: "I suppose we'll be something like the Last Mohicans of love!" At the moment, she was capable of this self-mocking tone, for if she was completely honest, the enchanted garden in which she found herself together with Ulrich was also, of course, more a wish than a reality. She did not really believe that the Thousand-Year Kingdom could have begun, despite the sound of terra firma in the name Ulrich had given it. She even felt quite deserted by her powers of desire, and wherever it was that her dreams came from, bitterly sobered. She remembered times, before she met Ulrich, when she had actually found it easier to imagine that a waking sleep like the one in which her soul was now being gently rocked would be able to escort her behind life to a wakefulness after death, close to God, where powers would come to fetch her, or just take her alongside life to a cessation of ideas and a passage to forests and meadows of imagination: it had never become clear what that was! So now she made an effort to recall those old visions. But all she could remember was a hammock suspended between two enormous fingers and rocked with infinite patience; then a calm state of being overtowered, as if by high trees between which she felt herself lifted up and removed from sight; and finally a Nothing, which in some incomprehensible way had a tangible content: —All these were probably the mixtures of intuition and fantasy in which her longing had found consolation. But was that really all they amounted to, mere hybrids or halves? For to her astonishment, Agathe was gradually beginning to notice something quite remarkable. "Truly," she thought, "it's just like the expression: It dawns on you! And the light keeps spreading the longer it lasts!" For what she had once imagined seemed to be present in almost everything that now stood around her in abiding calm, no matter how often she sent out a glance for confirmation. It had entered the world without a sound. To be sure, God—differently from the way a literalist believer might have experienced it—had absented Himself from her adventure, but to make up for that, this adventure was one in which she was no longer alone: those were the only two changes that distinguished the fulfillment from the premonition, and these changes were in favor of earthly naturalness.

31

STROLLS AMONG THE CROWD

IN THE time that followed, they withdrew from their acquaintances and astonished them by making a pretext of a journey and not allowing themselves to be reached in any way.

They mostly stayed secretly at home, and when they went out they avoided places where they might meet people of their social set; but they visited places of entertainment and small theaters where they believed themselves to be secure from such encounters; and generally, as soon as they left the house, they simply followed the currents of the metropolis, which are an image of people's needs and desires and with tide like precision amass crowds in one place and siphon them away from another, depending on the hour. They abandoned themselves to these movements without any particular purpose. It gave them pleasure to do what many were doing and to participate in a way of life that relieved them for a while of responsibility for their own. And never had the city in which they lived seemed to them at once so lovely and so strange. In their totality, the houses presented a grand picture, even if singly or in particular they were not beautiful at all. Noise streamed through the heat-thinned air like a river reaching up to the rooftops; in the strong light, muted by the depth of the streets, people looked more passionate and more mysterious than they probably deserved. All things sounded, looked, and smelled irreplaceable and unforgettable, as if to proclaim how it felt to be themselves in their instantaneousness; and the siblings gladly accepted this invitation to turn toward the world.

But it was not without reservation that they did so, for they could not help feeling the pervading dichotomy. Everything that was secret and undefined in their relationship, and that bound them together even though they could not speak openly about it, separated them from other people; but the same passion, which they felt constantly, because it had been thwarted less by prohibition than by a sublime promise, had also left them in a state that bore resemblance to the sultry intermittencies of a physical union. Desire, not finding an outlet, sank back into the body and filled it with a tenderness as indefinable as a last day of autumn or a first day of spring. And though they certainly did not feel for every person and for all the world as they did for each other, they still sensed the lovely shadow of "how it would be" falling on their hearts, and the heart could neither fully believe nor entirely escape the gentle illusion, no matter what it encountered.

This created the impression on the siblings, twins by choice, that by their anticipation and asceticism they had become sensitive to all the affections in the world that could not be dreamed to completion, but also to the limits reality and vigilance set to every feeling; and they saw very clearly the peculiarly two-sided nature of life, which dampens every higher aspiration with a lower one. It burdens every advance with a decline and every strength with a weakness; it gives no one a right that it does not take away from another, straightens out no tangle without causing new disorder, and even appears to evoke the sublime only in order to heap the honors it deserves on some trivial thing an hour later. Thus an all but indissoluble and perhaps profoundly necessary relation connects every sublime endeavor to the manifestation of its opposite and makes life for thinking or even just thoughtful people—beyond whatever differences and disagreements may separate them—rather difficult to bear, but it also drives them to seek an explanation for it.

This way in which the honorable side of life and its indignity adhere to each other has been judged in very different ways. Pious misanthropists have seen in it a consequence of earthly frailty; men of brawn, life's juiciest filet; denizens of the middle range feel as comfortable in this contradiction as they do between their right and left hands; and the circumspect simply say that the world was not created to correspond to human ideas. So it has been regarded as the imperfection of the world or of human expectations, has been accepted with childlike trust on one hand and melancholy resignation or defiant indifference on the other, and all in all, settling this question may be a matter of temperament rather than a soberly honorable task for reason. However, as certainly as the world was not created to correspond to human expectations, it is equally certain that human ideas were created to correspond to the world, for that is their purpose; and why it is precisely in the sphere of the right and the beautiful that this never comes to pass is a strangely open question. The siblings' aimless walks illustrated this like a picture book and gave rise to conversations that were accompanied by the loosely varying excitement of turning its pages.

None of these conversations treated its subject in a concrete and thoroughgoing way, each of them over their course turned upon the most various related themes; as a result, their overall context became more and more broad; their structure, determined by a succession of living occasions, broke down again and again, its borders flooded by an influx of new animated observations; and this continued for a long time, sometimes gaining, sometimes losing, before the result was unmistakably evident. The first hypothesis Ulrich adopted—whether by chance or not, with conviction or haphazardly—was that the limit imposed on feeling and also the advances and retreats, or at least the to and fro, of life—its intellectual unreliability, in short—perhaps fulfilled a not unuseful purpose, namely that of producing and sustaining a middling condition of life.

He did not want to demand of the world that it be a pleasure garden for genius. Only at its peaks, if not its excesses, is history the story of genius and its works; in the main it is the story of the average man. He is the material that the world works with and that continually emerges anew from it. Perhaps it was only a moment of fatigue that inspired this thought. Perhaps Ulrich was just building on the notion that it is the middling and average that is sturdiest and offers the best prospects for preserving the species; one had to assume that the first law of life is self-preservation, and that may very well be the case. But undoubtedly, a different outlook was adding its voice to this beginning. We may take it for granted that it is not the average man who creates the great upswings of human history; nonetheless, taking everything into account, genius and stupidity, heroism and indecision, history is precisely a history of millions of impulses and resistances, qualities, decisions, adjustments, passions, insights, and errors, which the average man receives from all sides and distributes in all directions. The same elements are mixed together both in him and in history; and this is the respect in which history is at all events a history of averages or, depending on how you might view it, the average of millions of stories, and if history as a result hovers forever around the undistinguished middle range, what could be more nonsensical than to take umbrage at the mediocrity of an average!

But another thought pushed itself into these deliberations: it was a memory of the calculation of averages as it is understood in probability theory. The rules of probability begin with cold, almost shameless nonchalance in the propensity of events to go one way at one time, a different way at another, or indeed to turn into the opposite of what they are. So one essential aspect in the formation and consolidation of an average is that the higher and special values are far fewer in number than the average ones, that in fact they hardly ever occur, and that this is true also of the disproportionally low ones. Both the high and the low remain, at best and at worst, marginal values, and this is the case not only according to the manual of calculation but also in experience wherever chance-like conditions prevail. This experience may have been obtained from hailstorm insurance and mortality surveys; but there is a clear correspondence between the low probability of marginal values and the fact that in history, too, one-sided arrangements and the unalloyed realization of exorbitant ambitions have rarely lasted. And if that seems but half the story from one point of view, from another we may consider how often, thanks to the same statistical law, the human race has been spared the enterprising mania of genius no less than the ravages of inflamed stupidity incited to action. Without deliberate intention,

Ulrich kept on extrapolating from the idea of probability to spiritual and historical events, and from the mechanical concept of the average to mediocrity in the moral sphere; and so he arrived at the two-sidedness of life with which he had begun. For the limits that are set on ideas and emotions, and the changes to which they are subject, their futility, the mysterious and treacherous connection between their meaning and the manifestation of its opposite—all this and the like of it is already given as an inherent consequence of the supposition that one outcome is as likely as another. But this supposition represents the fundamental idea from which probability theory draws its substance, and is that discipline's definition of chance; that it also characterizes the course of events in the world therefore permits the conclusion that life would not be much different from the way it is if everything were immediately left to chance.

Agathe asked if equating the course of the world with chance wasn't a capricious way of wrapping the truth in gloom, amounting to romantic pessimism.

"Anything but that!" Ulrich replied. "We began with the futility of all high-hearted expectations and thought there was a treacherous secret behind this. But if we now compare that futility with the rules of probability, we can explain this secret—which we could call, playing mockingly with its famous opposite, the "preestablished dishar-mony" of creation—very unpretentiously by the fact that nothing happens to contradict it! Evolution is left to itself, not saddled with a spiritual organizing principle; apparently it operates randomly; and while these premises all but exclude the True, they do at least consti-tute the foundation for the Probable! At the same time, out of this concept of probability, we can explain mediocrity as the statistical average that is the world's sole stabilizing factor and whose highly undesirable increase is palpable all around us. So there's nothing Romantic about this, and maybe not even anything gloomy; rather, whether we like it or not, I would say it's an adventurous possibility!"

Nevertheless, he did not want to say anything more about it, and he let the apparently ingenious venture rest without having got beyond the introduction.—He had the feeling of having touched upon something very large in an awkward and circuitous manner. The large subject was the profoundly ambiguous nature of the world, the fact that it seems to move forwards as well as backwards and is appalling as well as inspiring; and that it cannot affect a cultivated person otherwise, if only because history is precisely not the history of important figures but quite evidently that of the average man, whose confused and equivocal features have imprinted themselves on the world. That conclusion, on the other hand, so swiftly arrived at, had been encumbered with needless complexity in the attempt to give the well-known nature of the average man, by a comparison with the nature of probability, a background whose novelty had not yet been fully explored. But even in this comparison, the basic idea was no doubt seemingly simple. For the average is always also something probable, and the average man is the sediment of all probability. But when Ulrich compared what he had said with what could still be said about it, he almost gave up hope of continuing what he had begun with his juxtaposition of probability and history.

Agathe said with mischievous hesitation: "The concierge dreams of the lottery and hopes she will win! So presuming I had the honor of understanding you, the purpose of history would be to leave behind an ever more undistinguished breed of human being and justify its existence, for which I suppose there is no lack of evidence, or at least no lack of hints that this may be the case; and to accomplish this task, the simplest and soundest thing history could do would be to just leave everything to chance and let the laws of probability determine the distribution and combination of events?" Ulrich nodded. "It's an if-then. If human history actually had a purpose, and if this were its purpose, then history could not be better than it is, and would in this strange way attain a purpose of not having a purpose!"

Agathe laughed. "And that's why you're telling me that the low ceiling under which one lives has a 'not unuseful' purpose?"

"A profoundly necessary purpose, the promotion of the average!" Ulrich confirmed. "It is for this purpose that feeling and will are once and for all prevented from growing to the sky."

"Would that the opposite happened!" Agathe said. "Then my ear wouldn't be getting sore from paying such close attention before I know everything!"

It seemed to Agathe that a conversation like this about genius, the average man, and probability, which engaged the mind but left the feelings untouched, was a waste of time. Ulrich did not feel quite the same way, even though he was heartily dissatisfied with what he had said. Nothing about it was solid except for the proposition: If something were a game of chance, the result would evince the same distribution of hits and misses as life does. But the fact that the second part of such a conditional proposition is true does not permit the conclusion that the first part is true as well!

In order for the converse of this proposition to be believable, a more rigorous comparison would be needed, namely one that would first make it possible to project notions of probability onto historical and spiritual events and thus compare two such different mental horizons. This was something Ulrich no longer felt like doing; but the more conscious he was of that neglect, the more convinced he became that the problem he had touched upon was an important one. Not only has the growing influence of masses of people with lackadaisical habits of mind—which is leveling humanity more and more toward the midrange—given added significance to any question concerning the structure and development of the human average; but also the basic question of what is the nature of probability seems to tend more and more, for different reasons, including ones that are universal and of intellectual provenance, to assume the place occupied by the question of the nature of truth, even though originally it was merely a practical tool for solving particular problems.

All of this could have been expressed by saying that little by little the "probable human being" and the "probable life" were beginning to supplant the "true" human being and "true" life, which were nothing more than a vain illusion and pretense; rather like something Ulrich had suggested previously, when he said that the whole problem was nothing more than the result of a haphazard evolution. He himself evidently still felt somewhat in the dark trying to fathom the meaning of all such observations, yet precisely this weakness gave them the capacity to illuminate wide regions, like a Saint Elmo's fire, and he knew so many examples of contemporary life and thought to which they applied that he found himself vividly challenged to transform the felt sense he had of them into something more lucid. So there was no lack of a need for a continuation, and he now decided after all that he would not neglect to take it up on a more fitting occasion. He had to smile at his surprise when he realized that with this resolve he was well on his way, without wanting it, to introducing Agathe to something that long ago, in a skeptical mood, he had called "the world of 'the like of it happens.'" It was the world of unrest without meaning; he now called it the world of "probable humanity." With revived curiosity he observed the streams of people whom they had been following, by whose passions, habits, and alien pleasures they were being drawn away from themselves: it was the world of those passions and pleasures, and not that of a possibility not yet dreamed to its conclusion! And because it was that, it was also the world of limits, which set boundaries to even the most dissolute emotions, and it was the world of the middling condition of life. For the first time he was thinking, not just through his feelings but in the way in which something real is expected, that the difference that makes it impossible for emotion to come to rest and lasting fulfillment, in one case, or to find an evolving and worldly movement, in another, can perhaps be ascribed to two fundamentally different states or kinds of feeling.

Breaking off, he said: "Look at that!" and both of them became aware of what was meeting their eyes. It happened as they were crossing a well-known and, if one may say so, generally well-regarded public square. There stood the Neue Universität, an imitation of a baroque building overloaded with fussy little details; not far from it stood a "neo-Gothic" church, an expensive affair with two towers that looked like a successful carnival prank; and the background was formed by two expressionless institutions belonging to the university, a palatial bank, and a large, drably sparse building serving as courthouse and prison that was several decades older. Swift carriages and massive carts crisscrossed this view, and a single glance could encompass both the solidity of what had evolved over time and the preparations for future prosperity, exciting admiration for human agency no less than poisoning the mind with an imperceptible residue of vacuousness. And without actually changing the topic of conversation, Ulrich continued: "Imagine a band of robbers had seized control of world power, endowed with nothing but the crudest instincts and principles! After a while, works of the mind would grow from this savage soil! And again over a period of time, once the mind had become cultivated, it would stand in its own way! The harvest grows, and its substance diminishes; as if the fruits tasted of shadows once the branches are full!"—He did not ask why. He had simply chosen the image to express his sense that most of what calls itself culture exists between the condition of a band of robbers and a state of indolent maturity; for if that was the case, it might also excuse all the talk into which he had been diverted, even though a tender first breath of promise had inspired its beginning.

32

LOVE THY NEIGHBOR AS THYSELF

IT COULD be said of many things that they might have determined Ulrich's words or been obviously or tangentially associated with his thinking. For example, it was not long ago, on that unfortunate evening at Diotima's, that he had talked to his sister and even to others about the great disorder of the emotions to which we owe the disastrous tides of history in much the same way as we do the small upheavals of confused opinion, one of which happened to be taking place then and there. But as soon as he said something now that might have general significance, he had the feeling that such words were coming out of his mouth a few days too late. He lacked the desire to involve himself with anything that did not directly concern him; what interest there was would dissipate quickly. For his soul was exceedingly ready to abandon itself to the world through all the senses, however that world might turn out to be. His judgment played all but no part in this. It even meant almost nothing whether something was to his liking or not. For he was more affected by everything than he could understand. Ulrich was used to occupying himself with other people; but that had always happened in connection with feelings and views that are meant to apply in the large, and now it was happening on the scale of small, particular impressions, adhering to every detail for no discernible reason. It was almost a state that he himself, in conversation with Agathe not long ago, had brought under suspicion of being the desire for fellow feeling on the part of a nature that does not truly empathize with anything, rather than a capacity for genuine caring. That had happened on the day when, provoked by a not insignificant difference of opinion concerning an individual he did not know very well, Professor August Lindner, he had made a hurtful remark to the effect that one never participates in anything or anyone as one ideally should. And indeed, once the state he was in now had lasted a while and reached a full measure, it became unpleasant or seemed ridiculous to him, and then, with the same motiveless readiness he had felt for self-abandonment, he was prepared to take himself back.

But this time Agathe, in her own way, fared not very differently from him. Her conscience was oppressed when it was not uplifted; for she had swung into action too forcefully and now felt like a woman standing on a swing, exposed to judgment. At moments like this she feared the revenge of the world for the capriciousness with which she usually treated men who spoke of reality in earnest, like the husband she had provoked and the preserver of that husband's memory who was so eagerly concerned for her soul. In the thousandfold flurry of charming activities life is filled with by day and by night, not a single pursuit could have been found for her that she would have wanted to engage with wholeheartedly; and whatever she ventured to do of her own accord had to be safe above all from the reproach, deprecation, or even contempt of others. And yet what a strange peace there was precisely in that! Perhaps it is permissible to say, in variation of a proverb, that a bad conscience makes an almost softer pillow than a good one, provided the conscience is bad enough. The mind's ceaseless ancillary occupation of trying to eke out a good personal conscience from whatever wrong it is involved in then comes to a stop, and what remains is an independence without bounds or measure. A tender solitude, a sky-high pride occasionally poured their splendor over these outings into the world. At such moments, Agathe's inner experience could make the world seem bloated and rotund, like a tethered balloon circled by swallows, or degrade it to a background as small as a forest on the edge of the horizon. The violated civil obligations were only distantly alarming, like a far-off, rudely advancing sound; they were unimportant, if not unreal. An immense order that is ultimately nothing but an immense absurdity was what the world had become. And yet precisely for that reason every detail Agathe encountered had the tautness, the throbbing tension of the "once and never again," the almost exalted nature of a personal first discovery that is magically appointed and permits no repetition; and when she wanted to talk about it, it was with the understanding that not a single word could be said twice without changing its meaning. All of this endowed the irresponsibility of strolling through the crowd with a responsibility that was difficult to grasp.

The siblings' attitude toward the world at that time was therefore not an entirely impeccable expression of sympathy with others; in its own way, it contained affection and aversion side by side in a state of emotion that hovered in space like a rainbow, instead of these opposites setting up house as a hybrid blend, the way they do in the self-assured state of ordinary experience. And so it happened that one day their conversation took a turn that was indicative of their attitude toward each other and their surroundings, even though this exchange did not yet go beyond their familiar horizons.

Ulrich asked: "What does the commandment: 'Love thy neighbor as thyself!' actually mean?"

Agathe gave him a sidelong look.

"Apparently," Ulrich continued, "it means: Love even the person farthest away, the furthest from being your neighbor! But what does 'as thyself' mean? How does one love oneself? In my own case the answer would be: Not at all! In most other cases: More than anything! Blindly! Without question and without restraint!"

"You're too belligerent; a person who attacks himself will do the same to others!" Agathe replied, shaking her head. "And if you're not good enough for yourself, how could I be good enough for you?" She said this in a tone that lay between that of cheerfully borne pain and a polite turn in the conversation. But Ulrich failed to hear it and continued in a generalizing vein, gazing rigidly into the distance: "Maybe I should say instead: Usually everyone loves himself best and knows himself least! Love thy neighbor as thyself would then mean: Love him without knowing him and under all circumstances. And strangely enough, in loving one's neighbor, if such a joke is permitted, there would also be found, as there would be in every other love, the hereditary curse of eating from the tree of knowledge!"

Agathe looked up slowly. "I liked it when you once said about me that I was your self-love, which you had lost and found again. But now you are saying that you don't love yourself, and, by force of logic and example, that you love me only because you don't know me! Isn't it actually an insult that I'm your self-love?" The pain in her voice had now fully given way to amusement.

Her question provoked a counterquestion: Would it have been better if he loved her *even though* he knew her? Because that, too, is part of the commandment to love one's neighbor. This causes embarrassment for most people. They love one another without liking each other. "They find each other somehow unappealing or know that they will eventually, and then counteract that much too energetically!"

The cheerfulness of this exchange was contrived. Nevertheless it also served to scout out the boundaries of an idea, and of a feeling, whose pronouncement—irrespective of what had or had not transpired since then—had begun on that evening when Agathe, exhausted from her trip and arrival, retired to her new room and Ulrich, standing at her bedside, used the words "you are my lost self-love" during a conversation in which he confessed that he had lost both his love of self and his love of the world, and which had ended with their declaring themselves to be "Siamese twins." Since then, all their observations of ordinary and average life had served this purpose of exploration, even the banter they had just engaged in, though it had hurt them by its superficiality.

Abruptly, Ulrich's tone became morose: "We should have simply said that 'Love thy neighbor as thyself' is nothing other than the useful admonition: Don't do to others what you don't want them to do to you."

Agathe again shook her head, but there was warmth in her eyes. "It's a high-hearted, passionate, happy, magnanimous assignment!" she cried out reproachfully. "Examples of it are 'Love your enemies!'

'Repay their misdeeds with kindness!' 'Love without thought of reward!'" Suddenly she paused and looked at her brother dumbfounded. "But what is it that one loves in a person if one doesn't know him at all?" she asked innocently.

Ulrich gave himself time before answering. "Haven't you noticed today that it's actually disturbing when you encounter a person whom you personally like and find so beautiful you would like to say something fitting about him?"

Agathe nodded. "So our feeling," she conceded, "isn't about the real world and the real person."

"Which leaves us with the question: What is it that our feeling is responding to—what part of the world, or what transformation and transfiguration of the real person and the real world?" Ulrich quietly completed her thought.

Now it was Agathe who at first gave no answer; but her gaze was excited and lit up by imagination. Finally, she responded shyly with a counterproposal: "Maybe from behind the ordinary truth the great truth will appear?"

Ulrich hesitantly resisted this, shaking his head; but shimmering through Agathe's inquiring assertion was something undeniably evident. The air and the pleasure of those days were so buoyant and tender that one could not resist the impression that man and the world must perforce show themselves to be more real than real. There was a small suprasensory thrill of adventure in this transparency, comparable to the flowing transparency of a brook that allows one to see to the bottom, yet, even as one's wavering glance arrives there, makes the gaily colored mysterious stones resemble the skin of a fish, whose smoothness now all the more thoroughly hides what the eye thought to discern. By merely relaxing her gaze a little, Agathe, surrounded by sunshine, was able to feel that she had entered a supernatural realm; it was then quite easy for her to believe, for a very brief span, that she had come in contact with a higher truth and reality, or at least glimpsed an aspect of existence where a little door behind the earth secretly leads from the earthly garden to that which is not of this world. But when she returned her gaze to its usual range and let the full glare of life stream in, she would see whatever happened to be there: perhaps a little flag gaily and not at all mysteriously swung by the hand of a child; a police van with prisoners, its black-green paint flashing in the light; a man with a colorful cap sweeping away manure among carts and carriages; a division of recruits whose shouldered rifles were pointing their barrels at the sky. And all this was bathed in something that had a kinship with love; and all the people, too, seemed more ready to open themselves to this feeling than usual: But to believe that the kingdom of love was now really here, Ulrich finally said, was surely as difficult as it would be to imagine that at this moment dogs could not bite and no one could do anything evil!

It may be worth noting that there are many attempts at explaining the sense of a festively human high tide, as of a great wedding, and that some of those theories account for the experience of natural piety and love at such moments by supposing that behind the everyday earthly-round, bad-good, but at any rate definitely existing man or woman some far-off true human being can be expected to come to light. The siblings examined these well-intended attempts one by one and did not believe any of them. Not the Sunday wisdom according to which nature on her feast days brings to the fore all that is good and beautiful in her creatures. Not the more psychological explanation that while man, even in this tender transparency, does not turn out to be a different sort of creature, he nevertheless displays the lovable qualities for which he would like to be known: sweating out through his pores, like honey, as it were, all his self-love and inward-gazing indulgence. Nor the variant according to which human beings display their goodwill, which certainly never prevents them from doing bad things but on such days emerges from the ill-will that usually controls them, miraculously unharmed, like Jonah from the belly of the whale. And the briefest and most exhilarating explanation, which Agathe shyly touched on once more, that it is the immortal portion of our inheritance that occasionally shimmers through the mortal part, was certainly not believable to either of them either. Incidentally, all these solemn inspirations had one thing in common: every one of them sought the salvation of man in a state that does not come into its own under ordinary, inessential conditions; and just as the presentiment of salvation is clearly an upward-directed process, there is a second, no less plentiful group of self-deceptions where the same process clearly moves in a downward direction: These are all the familiar confessions and testimonies, not a few of them fondly preserved in historical record, according to which man is supposed to have forfeited the innocence of his natural state, his own natural innocence, through spiritual pride and other plagues of civilization.

Accordingly, there were two kinds of "true human being" that proposed themselves to spiritual perception with perfect punctuality on the same occasion; except that—insofar as one of them was supposed to be a celestial superman, the other an unalloyed creature of the earth—they were on opposite sides of the actual human being, und Ulrich's dry comment was: "All they have in common is that the real human, even at elevated moments, does not feel himself to be the true human, except plus or minus something that makes him appear enchantingly unreal to himself!"

And so the siblings had arrived from one limit case of interpretation to the other, and there remained only one last possibility of explaining this love, which was so gentle, settling on all things without distinction, like dew on an early morning. It was Agathe, finally, who gave voice to this possibility, with a graceful sigh of vexation. "So the sun shines, and one is gripped by an unconscious urge like a schoolgirl and a schoolboy."

Ulrich enlarged on it: "The social instincts expand in the sun like mercury in the thermometer, at the expense of the egotistic instincts, which ordinarily balance them out!"

Now brother and sister were tired of feeling; it happened from time to time that while talking of nothing but their feelings they neglected feeling itself. Also, because the profusion of feeling, when it found no outlet, was actually painful, they sometimes requited it with a little ingratitude. But after they had both spoken in this manner, Agathe looked at her brother sidelong once again and hastened to revoke what she had said: "And yet! It's certainly not like truant schoolchildren who want to hug the whole world and have no idea why!"

And the moment she exclaimed those words, they both felt again that they were not subjected to a mere fantasy but to something unknowable and unpredictable. Hovering within the overflowing emotion, there was truth; beneath the semblance, there was reality; peering out from the world were the shadowy outlines of a world being transformed. To be sure, it was a peculiarly coreless, only half-tangible reality they were divining, a half-truth as familiar as it was familiarly uncompletable that was wooing credibility: not a reality for the world's daily use nor indeed a truth for all the world, just a secret one for lovers. But obviously it was not mere caprice or illusion either; and its most secret insinuation whispered: Surrender yourself to me without reserve, and you will know the whole truth! But there were no clearly spoken words that said this: for the language of love is a cryptic language and in its highest perfection as mute as an embrace.

Smiling, Agathe knitted her brows and peered into the crowd; Ulrich followed suit, and together they gazed into the stream of people that flowed beside them and streamed toward them. Did they feel the forgetfulness of self and the power, the happiness, the goodness, the deep and high constraint that prevail within a brotherhood of human beings, even if it is only the accidental brotherhood of a busy street, so that one cannot believe there could be anything wrong or divisive in it? Their own existence, sharply bounded and set down heavily into that glory, stood out in wondrous contrast to it, as did the existence of every other person walking darkly through this cloudburst and loosed flood of tenderness whose radiance shone reflected in their eyes. At this moment, when a single vivid impression reprised and completely answered all questions concerning the "kingdom of love" and the meaning of the love of one's neighbor and the doubts surrounding that notion, Ulrich leaned over to his sister to see her face and asked her: "Do you think you can love someone in more than a vague sort of way when neither moral conviction nor sensual desire is involved?"

It was the first time since they had started going on these outings that he asked her this question so directly.

At first Agathe gave no answer.

Ulrich asked: "And what would happen if we were to stop someone here and say to him: 'Stay with us, brother!' or: 'Halt your steps, oh hastening soul! We want to love you as ourselves!'?"

"He would look at us flabbergasted," Agathe replied. "And then move on twice as fast."

"Or get mad and call for a policeman," Ulrich added. "Because he would think he was either dealing with good-natured lunatics, or with people who were pulling his leg."

"But if we went up to him straightaway yelling, 'You criminal, worthless scum'?" Agathe suggested tentatively.

"It could be that in that case he would not consider us crazy, and not think we were joking either, but take us for people with dissenting views, as they are called; apostles of some political faction who have a mistaken idea about him. Because obviously the societies for the blind who hate their neighbors don't have many fewer members than the one that espouses neighborly love."

Agathe nodded in agreement; then she shook her head and gazed into the air. The air was still the same as before. She looked down, and some humble detail, a basement window, a stray leaf of cabbage, seemed to be gently aflame, as if ignited by the light in the sky. Finally, she looked around for something that would appeal to her of its own accord, a face or an object in a shopwindow, and found it. And yet this real pleasure was a blind spot in the radiance of the day; Ulrich had already commented on this, but now she was even more aware of the contrast. It interfered in the general love of humanity and the world, instead of increasing it with its small contribution. And so Agathe replied: "It's all very unreal! Today I don't know whether I love real people and real things, or whether I really love anything!"

"Is that supposed to be the answer to my question," Ulrich asked, changing the question slightly as he restated it, "whether any love, even a great love, can be anything more than the shadow of a love if there is no sensual fulfillment? A desire that doesn't give the senses something to do already harbors a mute sadness!"

"I am full of love and empty of love, and both of these together,"

Agathe lamented, smiling and pointing to everything and everyone with a small, despondent gesture. —It was the lament of the heart into which God has penetrated as deeply as a thorn that no fingertips can grasp. In the confessions of the mystics, who yearn for Him with all their human soul and corporality, this strange despair again and again disrupts the moments of the most imminent transfiguration, and the siblings now remembered together the hour in the garden when Agathe had read such examples to her brother from a book. Then Ulrich said: "There is something of this mysticism in neighborly love; everyone feels and obeys it without understanding it. And perhaps every great love contains something mystical, maybe even every great passion. Maybe in all those moments that have a deeply opening effect on us, even in a temperate life, our participation in people and things is of a mystical kind, and different from real participation!"

"And what is mystical participation, if not just the opposite of a real one?"

Ulrich didn't stop to consider his answer, but he did hesitate. Finally, he said with great resoluteness: "Look, one is at the same time full of love and empty of love. One loves everything and nothing in particular. One is unable to detach oneself from the most trivial little thing, and at the same time the totality has no importance at all. This is a complete contradiction; both can't be real at the same time. And yet it is real; it would be pointless to deny it! So if I can't ask you to conceive of mystical participation as some kind of religious sorcery, there remains only the assumption that there are two ways of experiencing reality that more or less force themselves upon us!"

Sometimes at a propitious moment, and in close association, there arise the answers to such questions that, sporadically and haltingly, have troubled the mind with shifting unrest. Sometimes this abridgement is deceptive; but it is always a preview. One such moment was that of Ulrich's idea that there are two kinds of reality in the world, or rather that there are two kinds of worldly reality. Once that statement had been made, and before the siblings had persuaded themselves of its plausibility, there was no question in their life that had not been affected by this answer. The many unusual and boundlessly intertwined experiences and conjectures of the recent past, and the premonitory intimations of these at an earlier time, may not have found an explanation, but a refreshed confidence now pervaded them all. Thus a flame contracts darkly and holds its breath before flaring higher.

33
CONVERSATIONS ABOUT LOVE

MAN, THE speaking animal par excellence, is the only one that requires conversation even for his reproduction. And it is not only because he is talking in any case that he speaks while engaged in that activity, but apparently for him the delights of loving and those of talking are linked; and this in so profoundly mysterious a fashion that it almost calls to mind those ancients according to whose philosophy God, man, and things arose from the "Logos," by which they variously understood the Holy Spirit, reason, and speech. Well, not even psychoanalysis and sociology have taught us anything substantial about this, even though these two youngest sciences might very well compete with Catholicism in having had something to say about all things human. So one must make one's own rhyme and reason of the fact that in love, conversations play an almost greater role than anything else. Love is the most talkative of all feelings and consists to a large part entirely of loquacity. If the person is young, these all-encompassing conversations are symptoms of growth; in an adult, they form one's peacock's fan, which displays itself all the more vividly the later one starts, even if all it consists of are quills. The reason for this may be that contemplative thought is awakened by the emotions of love and forms lasting ties with them; but of course this would only displace the question, for even though the word "contemplation" is used almost as often as the word "love," its meaning is by no means clearer.

By the way, even though Ulrich and Agatha could not get their fill of talking to one another, we cannot on those grounds accuse the bonds between them of being bonds of love. That the subject of their talk was always and in some manner concerned with love is undeniable. But what is true of all emotions applies to the emotion of love as well: its ardor expands ever more largely in words the further removed it still is from action; and what induced the siblings after their initial obscure and intense experiences with each other to abandon themselves to conversations, and what seemed to them at times like an enchantment, was first and foremost their not knowing how they *could* act. But their consequent fear of their own feelings, and the curiosity with which they explored them, peering into them from their periphery, sometimes caused the conversations to veer into shallow waters that belied the depth from which they issued.

34

DIFFICULTIES WHERE THEY ARE NOT LOOKED FOR

WHAT ABOUT the example, as famous as it is gladly lived, of love between the proverbial "two people of the opposite sex"? It is a special case of the commandment: Thou shalt love thy neighbor without knowing what kind of person he is; and a test of the relationship that exists between love and reality.

People make of each other the dolls with which they have already played in dreams of love.

And what the other person believes and thinks and actually is plays no part in this?

As long as one loves him or her, and because of one's love, everything is enchanting; but this does not work in reverse. Never has a woman loved a man for his opinions and ideas, or a man, a woman for hers. These merely play an important supporting role. Incidentally, love fares much as anger does in this respect: If one understands without prejudice what the other person means, not only is anger disarmed, but usually, quite unexpectedly, love as well.

But isn't it true that especially in the beginning, delight in the concordance of one's opinions plays a major role?

When the man hears the woman's voice, he hears himself being repeated by a marvelous sunken orchestra, and women are the most unconscious ventriloquists; they hear themselves giving the cleverest answers without a word passing their own lips. Each time, it is like a small annunciation: one person steps out of the clouds to stand by another's side, and everything the first utters seems to the second a heavenly crown, custom-fitted to the size of her or his head! Later, of course, one feels like a drunk who has slept off his stupor.

But what of the works of love? Love's fidelity, its sacrifices, its attentions, are they not its most beautiful proof? But works, like all mute things, are ambiguous. If one looks back on one's life as a colorful chain of events and actions, it resembles a play of which one remembers not a single word of dialogue and all of whose scenes rather tediously have the same climaxes!

So one does not love in accordance with merit and reward, in the alternating chant of immortal spirits mortally in love?

That one is not loved as one deserves is the sorrow of all old maids of both sexes.

It was Agathe who gave this response. The eerily beautiful gratuitousness of love and the mild euphoria of injustice rose up from past love affairs and even reconciled her to the lack of dignity and seriousness she sometimes accused herself of on account of her game with Lindner, which she was always ashamed of when she was in Ulrich's presence. But Ulrich had started the conversation, and in the course of it had become interested in sounding her out about her memories, for her way of viewing these delights was similar to his.

She looked at him, laughing. "Haven't you ever adored someone and despised yourself for it?"

"I can honestly say I have not; but I won't reject the thought with indignation," Ulrich said. "It could have happened."

"Haven't you ever loved a person despite being eerily convinced," Agathe continued excitedly, "that this person, whether he has a beard or breasts, a person you're sure you know very well, and of whom you think highly, and who talks incessantly about you and himself, is actually just paying love a visit? You could leave out his way of thinking and his merits, you could change his fate, you could even furnish him with a different beard and different legs; you could almost leave *him* out, and you would still love him!—That is to say, insofar as you love him at all!" she added to temper her intensity.

Her voice had a deep sound, with an unsteady brightness in its depths, as if from a fire. Now she sat down guiltily, because in her unintentional eagerness she had sprung up from her chair.

Ulrich, too, felt slightly guilty because of this conversation, and smiled. He had not with any of his words intended to speak of love as one of the fashionably divided feelings that are termed "ambivalent" by the latest trend, which implies, more or less, that the soul, in the manner of tricksters, always winks with its left eye while pledging an oath with its right hand. Rather, he had taken pleasure in the fact that in order for love to arise and endure, no essential prerequisites are needed. That is, one loves someone despite everything, or, one could just as well say, for no reason; and that means either that the entire thing is a figment or else that the figment is itself an entire whole, just as the world is an entirety in which no sparrow falls from the roof without the All-Feeling-One being aware of it.

"So it doesn't depend on anything at all!" Agathe exclaimed by way of conclusion. "Not on what a person is, not on what he means, not on what he wants, and not on what he does."

It was clear to them that they were speaking of the soul's certainty, or, as it might be better to avoid such a grand word, the uncertainty which they felt (using the term now with modest imprecision and in the aggregate sense) in their souls. And that they were talking about love, reminding each other of love's mutability and its shape-shifting arts, happened only because it is one of the most intense and distinctive feelings, and yet such a suspect feeling before the stern bar of evaluative feeling that it causes judgment itself to falter. But of this the siblings had already received an inkling when they had barely begun to stroll in the sunshine of neighborly love; and remembering his assertion that even in this state of dazed beneficence one does not know whether one really loves people, and whether one loves people as they really are, or whether, and by means of what qualities, one is being duped by a fantasy and a mutation, Ulrich showed himself earnestly intent on holding the problematic relationship between feeling and knowing firmly in place with a knot, at least for now and in the spirit of the casual conversation that had just died away.

"These two contradictions are always present within it; they form a four-horse team," he said. "One loves a person because one knows him; and because one doesn't know him. And one knows him because one loves him; and knows not him, because one loves him. And sometimes this reaches such a pitch that it all suddenly becomes very obvious. Those are the notorious moments when Venus sees through Apollo and Apollo sees through Venus, and both behold a lifeless mannequin and are highly surprised that previously they had seen something else in its place. If love is stronger than astonishment at that moment, a struggle arises between them, and sometimes love—albeit exhausted, despairing, and irremediably wounded—emerges victorious. But if love is not as strong, it becomes a struggle between people who feel they have been deceived; it comes to insults, coarse intrusions of reality, endless degradation, all to make up for having been the trusting fool—." He had experienced these hailstorms of love often enough to be able to describe them quite comfortably.

But now Agathe put an end to this. "If you don't mind, I would like to point out that these marital and extramarital affairs of honor are for the most part highly overrated!" she objected, and looked around again for a more comfortable position.

"Love is overrated altogether!" Ulrich declared, laughing. "The madman who in his derangement draws a knife and stabs an innocent person who happens to be standing in the place of his hallucination—: in love, he's normal!"

35
LOVING IS NOT SIMPLE

A COMFORTABLE position and leisurely sunshine that caresses without being intrusive facilitated these conversations. They usually took place between two deck chairs that were not so much moved into the protection and shade of the house as into the shaded light that came from the garden and found its freedom tempered by walls that still glowed in the colors of morning. One should of course not assume that the chairs stood there because the siblings—stimulated by their relationship's sterility, which was, in the ordinary sense, already established and in a higher sense perhaps still impending—might have had the intention of exchanging opinions concerning the deceptive nature of love in Hindu-Schopenhauerian fashion, and to fend off with the tools of dissection the seductive delirium love proffers in order to perpetuate life; rather, the choice of this half-shadowed, indulgent, reclusively inquiring mode had a simpler explanation. The subject under discussion was so constituted that in the infinite experience by which the idea of love becomes clear and distinct, the most various associative pathways presented themselves, leading from one question to the next. Thus the two questions of how one loves the neighbor whom one does not know, and how one loves oneself, whom one knows even less, led their curiosity to the question, encompassing both, of how one loves at all; or, put differently, what love "actually" is. At first glance this may seem a bit too knowing and also all too sensible a question for a couple in love. But it gains in mental confusion as soon as one extends it to millions of lovers and their variety.

These millions differ not only as individuals (which is their pride), but also in their action, object, and relationship. Sometimes one cannot speak of lovers at all, and yet of love; sometimes of lovers but not of love, in which case things proceed in a rather more ordinary way. And the word comprises as many contradictions as Sunday in a small country town where the farm boys go to Mass at ten in the morning, visit the brothel in a side street at eleven, and enter the tavern on the main square at twelve to eat and drink. Does it make sense to explore such a word from all sides? But in using it one acts unconsciously as if underlying all the differences there were one common ground! One can love a walking stick and one can love honor; the difference between the two is as great as that between one and one thousand, and no one would think of naming them in the same breath if one wasn't accustomed to doing just that every day. One can cite other examples of what is one and one thousand yet one and the same, such as loving the bottle, tobacco, and even worse poisons. Spinach and outdoor activities. Sports or the mind. Truth. One's wife, one's child, one's dog. To this list, the siblings added further examples: God, Beauty, Fatherland, and money. Nature, a friend, one's profession, and life. Freedom. Success, power, justice, or simply virtue. One loves all of that. In short, there are as many things associated with love as there are endeavors and figures of speech. But what are the differences between all these loves and what do they have in common?

It might be useful to consider the word "forks." There are table forks, pitchforks, tree forks, gun forks, road forks, and other forks; and all these have a formative property of "forkness" in common. This is the decisive experience, the essence of all that is forked, the gestalt of the fork in the most dissimilar things that are called by that name. If we start from these things, it turns out that they all belong to the same category; but if we start from the initial impression of forkedness, it appears to be filled out and amplified by impressions received from the various particular forks. The common feature, then, is a shape or gestalt, and the differentiation lies first in the diverse forms it can assume, but then also in the objects that have such a form, their material, their purpose, and so forth. But while any fork may be immediately likened to any other, and is a sensory given, even if only in a chalk line or in the imagination, this is not the case with the various configurations of love; and the entire usefulness of the example is limited to the question whether here too, corresponding to the forkness of forks, there is a principal experience, a loveness, a lovehood, a lovelikeness, in every case. But love is not an object of sensory cognition that could be grasped with a glance, or even with a feeling, but a moral event in the way that premeditated murder, justice, or contempt is; and this means among other things that a variously ramifying, multiply supported chain of comparisons is possible between different examples of it, the most distant of which may be quite dissimilar, indeed distinct from each other to the point of being opposite, and yet be connected by a resonance that is passed from one link to another. In treating of love, therefore, one may arrive at hatred; and yet the cause is not the much-invoked "ambivalence," the divided nature of feeling, but precisely the wholeness and plenitude of life.

Nevertheless, such a word could also have preceded the segue that was beginning to develop. For forks and other such innocent aids aside, sophisticated conversation nowadays knows how to treat of the essence and nature of love without faltering and nevertheless express itself as grippingly as if this core inhered in all the appearances of love as forkness does in the pitchfork or salad fork. One tends to say then—and the habit of common usage might have tempted Ulrich and Agathe to do so as well—that the main thing in all matters of love is libido, or else eros. These two words do not have the same history, nevertheless, and especially in view of our time, their histories can be compared. For when psychoanalysis (because an age that refuses to have any truck with intellectual depth is intrigued to learn that it has a depth psychology) began to become the philosophy of the day and disturbed the adventureless life of the bourgeoisie, everything and everyone was declared to be the libido, so that in the end it is as impossible to say what this key and skeleton key to the psyche is *not* as it is to say what it is. And precisely the same is true of eros; except that those who with the greatest conviction reduce all physical and emotional bonds to eros, have experienced their eros in this way from the beginning. It would be futile to translate "libido" as "drive" or "desire," specifically sexual or presexual desire, and "eros," conversely, as spiritual or even suprasensory "tenderness"; one would then have to add a special historical treatment on the subject, a prospect so tedious it makes ignorance a pleasure. But this is what determined in advance that the conversation conducted between two deck chairs did not take the direction indicated but instead found appeal and refreshment in the primitive and insufficient process of simply registering as many examples as possible of what is called love in order to sort them in rows as if in a game, and indeed to allow themselves the utmost naivete and not to dismiss even the silliest examples.

And so, comfortably chatting, they classified the examples that occurred to them, and the way in which they occurred, according to the feeling, its object, and the action through which it expressed itself. But there was also an advantage in first taking stock of the behavior, and in considering whether it merited the name of love in a real or a metaphorical sense, and to what extent. In this way many kinds of material were brought together from various directions.

But spontaneously, the first thing they talked about was feeling; for apparently the whole nature of love is to feel. All the more surprising is the answer that feeling is the least part of love: to pure inexperience, it would be like sugar and toothache; not quite as sweet and not quite as painful, and as restless as cattle plagued by horseflies. This comparison may not seem a masterpiece to someone who is himself plagued by love; and yet the usual description is not much different: a sweet torment of joy and anxiety, pain and longing, an intangible ache of desire. It seems that since time immemorial nothing more precise could be said of this condition. But lack of emotional distinctness is not characteristic of love alone. Being happy or sad is also not something one experiences as irrevocably and straightforwardly as one distinguishes smooth from rough, nor can other feelings be recognized purely by feeling, let alone by touch. This turn in their investigation prompted a remark, which they might have elaborated with suitable examples, regarding the unequal disposition and formation of feelings. That was the term Ulrich gave it in advance; and he could just as well have said "disposition," "elaboration," and "crystallization."

He began by positing a natural experience: Every feeling involves a convincing certainty of itself that is apparently part of its nucleus. It must also be assumed, on equally general grounds, that the differences among feelings originate no less with this nucleus. He gave several examples. Love of a friend has a different origin and different traits from love of a girl, of a woman in full bloom, or of a woman who lives in saintly seclusion; and feelings that diverge even further, such as—to remain with the subject of love—love, veneration, lechery, sexual dependence, or the various kinds of love and kinds of antipathy, are already different at their source. If one allows both these assumptions, then all feelings, from beginning to end, would have to be as solid and transparent as crystals. And yet no feeling is unmistakably what it appears to be; and neither self-observation nor the actions prompted by the feeling provide any certainty about it. Now, this difference between the self-assurance and the uncertainty of feelings is certainly not negligible. But if one observes the birth of a feeling in the context of its physiological as well as its social causes, that difference becomes quite natural. These causes awaken in broad outlines, so to speak, merely the species of a feeling without determining it more specifically; for corresponding to every drive and every situation that triggers it, there is a whole bundle of feelings that can answer for them. That which is there at the beginning can be called the nucleus of the feeling still in a state between being and nonbeing; but if one wanted to describe this nucleus, irrespective of its nature, nothing more accurate could be said about it than that it is a something which, in the course of its development, and dependent on a great many things that are or are not added to it, will develop into the feeling it was supposed to become. Thus every feeling has, in addition to its original disposition, a destiny as well; and because what it later develops into is increasingly dependent on accruing conditions, there is no feeling that could unmistakably be itself from the beginning; indeed there is perhaps not even one that would purely and indisputably be a feeling. Put another way, it follows from this interplay of disposition and elaboration that in the domain of feelings it is not their pure occurrence and unequivocal fulfillment that predominate, but their progressive approximation and approximate fulfillment. And something similar is also true of everything that requires feeling in order to be understood.

This was the conclusion of the observation introduced by Ulrich, which contained approximately these formulations in this sequence. Hardly less curt and hyperbolic than the assertion that feeling is the least part of love, it could also be said that because love is a feeling, it cannot be recognized by feeling. Incidentally, this shed some light on the question of why he had called love a moral event. Those three nouns, however—disposition, elaboration, and crystallization—had been the main knots that held together the ordered understanding of the phenomenon of feeling, at least according to a certain fundamental view to which Ulrich, too, was not unhappy to turn when he had need of such an explanation. But because working this out properly would have demanded a more extensive and more methodical treatment than he was willing to take on, he broke off what he had begun at this point.

The continuation extended in two directions. In accord with the theme of the conversation, the object and the action of love should have been next in turn, in order to determine what it was in them that gave rise to their highly dissimilar manifestations, and finally to discover what love "really" is. That was why they had talked about the role actions played in defining a feeling at its very beginning, a determining influence which that feeling's subsequent destiny should be all the more capable of reprising. But Agathe asked another question: it might have been possible—and she had reasons, if not for distrust, then at least for fear of such distrust arising—that the explanation her brother had chosen really applied only to a weak feeling or even to an experience that wanted to have nothing to do with strong ones.

Ulrich responded: "Not in the least! It is precisely in its greatest strength that feeling is not at its most secure. In the greatest fear, one is paralyzed or screams instead of fleeing or defending oneself. In the greatest happiness there is often a peculiar pain. Too much zeal "loses the way," as the proverb says. And in general it can be maintained that at its most exalted, feeling loses its color and fades away as if blinded. It may be that the entire world of feelings that are known to us is suited to a middling life and ceases at the highest degrees, just as it does not begin at the lowest."

Tangentially related to this was the experience that often occurs when one observes one's feelings, especially if one "holds them up to scrutiny." They become indistinct and are hard to tell apart. But what they lose in clarity of strength they ought to gain, at least to some extent, through the clarity of attention, and they don't do even that. —That was Ulrich's reply, and it was not by chance that he associated the extinction of emotion under scrutiny and its dying away in the highest degrees of excitation. For both are states in which action is suspended or disrupted; and because the connection between feeling and action is so close that some people consider them a unit, the way the two examples complemented each other was not without meaning.

But what he avoided saying was precisely what they both knew from their own experience, that at its highest stage the feeling of love can involve a state of mental obliteration and physical disarray. This led him to turn the conversation somewhat arbitrarily away from the significance action has for feeling, apparently with the intention of coming back to the classification of love with regard to its objects. At first glance, this somewhat capricious possibility did seem better suited to the purpose of bringing order to love's multiplicity of meanings. If it is in effect a blasphemy, to begin with a concrete example, to use the same word for the love of God and the love of fishing, this is doubtless due to the differences between the beloved objects. Similarly, the significance of the object can be measured by other examples. When we love something, therefore, the factor that introduces the enormous differences in the relationship between love and its object is not be found in the love but in the something. Thus there are objects that make love rich and healthy; and others that make it poor and sickly, as if that were due entirely to them. There are objects that must reciprocate love if it is to unfold all its power and unique character; and there are others of which it would be meaningless from the outset to make any similar demand. This separates categorically a relationship with living beings from one with inanimate things; but even when inanimate, the object is the true partner of love, and its qualities influence those of love.

Now the more incompatible this partner is, the more skewed, not to say distorted by passion, love itself becomes. "Compare the healthy love of young people for each other," Ulrich admonished, "with the ridiculously exaggerated love of the lonely person for his dog, cat, or canary. Look at the passion between a man and a woman fading away, or becoming a nuisance like an ignored and importunate beggar, when it is no longer or not fully reciprocated. Don't forget, either, that in unequal relations like those between parents and children or master and servant, between a man and the object of his ambition or his vice, the balance between love and its reciprocation could not be more precarious and ultimately perishable. Wherever the natural regulating exchange between the state of love and its object is imperfect, love degenerates like unhealthy tissue!"

There was something special about this idea that attracted him. It could be elaborated in several ways and with many examples. While he was still thinking about it, something he had not foreseen but that crossed his intended path like a pleasant fragrance coming from faraway fields inadvertently directed his reflection to what in the art of painting is called still life, or according to an opposite but equally useful approach in another language, *nature morte*. "In a way it's ridiculous for a person to prize a well-painted lobster," Ulrich continued without transition, "grapes that gleam like a polished mirror, a hare hanging by its hind legs, and the inevitable pheasant, because human appetite is ridiculous, and painted appetite even more so." And they both had the feeling that this association reached back more deeply than was immediately apparent and was part of the continuation of what they had omitted to say about themselves.

For in actual still lifes—objects, animals, plants, landscapes, and human bodies magically cast, as if by a spell, into the circle of art— something other than what is depicted shows itself, namely the mysterious demonic power of painted life. There are famous paintings of this kind, so they both knew what they were talking about; but it is better, Ulrich said, not to speak of particular pictures but of a kind of picture, and one that moreover does not produce followers, but arises without rules at the summons of a creative impulse. Agathe asked by what signs one would recognize such a painting. Ulrich was visibly unwilling to indicate any definitive trait, but then said slowly, smiling, and without hesitation: "The exciting, indefinite, infinite echo!"

And Agathe understood him. Somehow you feel that you're on the beach. Small insects are humming. The air brings hundreds of meadow scents. Thought and feeling stroll busily side by side. But stretched out before your eyes is the unresponding wasteland of the sea, and what has importance on the shore loses itself in the monotonous motion of the infinite view. She was thinking how all true still lifes can arouse this happy, insatiable sadness. The longer one looks at them, the clearer it becomes that the things depicted in them seem to be standing on the colorful shore of life, their eyes filled with immensity and their tongues paralyzed.

Ulrich now replied with another paraphrase. "All still lifes really paint the world of the sixth day of creation, when God and the world were alone together, without man!" And in answer to a questioning smile from his sister he said: "So what they arouse in the way of human emotion would probably be jealousy, a mysterious curiosity, and sorrow!"

That was almost an "aperçu," and not even the worst of its kind: he noted it with displeasure, for he was not fond of these insights turned to precision as if on a lathe and hastily gilded. But neither did he do anything to improve what he had said, nor did his sister ask him to do so. For the obstacle that kept them both from adequately expressing themselves about the uncanny art of the still life, or *nature morte*, was its mysterious resemblance to their own life.

This resemblance had always played a great role for both of them. Without there being any need to recount in detail something that reached back to their shared childhood memories and that had reawakened at their reunion and ever since imbued all their experiences and most of their conversation with an indefinable strangeness, it cannot be left unmentioned that the narcotic breath of the still life was always to be felt in it. Spontaneously, therefore, and without adopting anything specific that might have guided them, they turned their curiosity toward everything that might be related to the nature of the still life; and the result was something more or less like the following exchange of words, which tautened and mobilized their conversation once again like a vortex:

Having to beg for something before an imperturbable countenance that grants no response drives a person into a frenzy of despair, attack, or humiliation. It is just as harrowing, but unspeakably beautiful, to kneel before an unmoving countenance in which life was extinguished a few hours ago, leaving behind a glow like a sunset.

This second example is even an emotional commonplace, if ever anything could be labeled as such! The world speaks of the benediction and dignity of death; the poetic motif of the beloved on his bier has existed for hundreds if not thousands of years; there is a whole genre of related, especially lyric, death poems. There is probably something adolescent about this. Who imagines that death bestows upon him the noblest of beloveds to keep as his own? He who lacks the courage or the possibility of having a living one!

A short line leads from this poetic puerility to the frissons of the séance and necromantic ritual; a second one leads to the abominations of actual necrophilia; perhaps a third to the pathological opposites of exhibitionism and violent coercion.

These comparisons may be disconcerting, and in part quite unappetizing. But if one does not allow oneself to be deterred and considers them from a medical-physiological point of view, so to speak, one finds that they all have one thing in common: an impossibility, an impotence, a lack of natural courage or of the courage for a natural life.

And if in this endeavor one does not fear risky comparisons, one learns something in addition: that silence, unconsciousness, and all manner of incomprehension in the partner are associated with the effect of driving the mind to eccentric extremes.

What is repeated in this way, above all, is the previously mentioned fact that an incompatible partner skews the balance of love; all that needs to be added is that not infrequently it is an already skewed emotional disposition that prompts such a choice in the first place. And inversely, it would be the responsive, living, acting partner who determines the emotions and keeps them in order, and without whom they devolve into mystification.

But what about the still life—isn't its strange charm also a mystification? In fact, almost an ethereal necrophilia?

And yet, a similar mystification takes place in the gaze of happy lovers as an expression of their highest feelings. They look into each other's eyes, cannot tear themselves loose, and languish in an infinite emotion that expands like rubber!

That was more or less how the exchange had begun, but here its thread got caught, as it were, and remained that way for quite a while before they were able to continue. They had looked at each other, and that had caused them to lapse into silence.

But if an observation is called for that explains this and even justifies such conversations at all and expresses their import: perhaps one could say what Ulrich at that moment understandably left unspoken: that it is by no means as simple to love as nature would have us believe when she entrusts every bungler among her creatures with the necessary tools.

36

BREATHS OF A SUMMER DAY

THE SUN, meanwhile, had risen higher; they had left the chairs like stranded boats in the shallow shade near the house and were lying on a lawn in the garden beneath the full depth of the summer day. They had been doing this for quite a while, and though their circumstances had shifted, they had almost no consciousness of any change. Not even the pause in their conversation brought this about; their speech had been suspended without any sense of a rupture.

A soundless stream of lusterless blossoms, coming from a group of trees that were past their flower, was drifting like snow through the sunshine; and the breath that bore it was so gentle that not a leaf stirred. It cast no shadow on the green of the lawn, but the green seemed to darken from within like an eye. The trees and bushes that stood on the sides or formed a backdrop, tenderly and lavishly decked out in their own green by the young summer, gave the impression of awed spectators who, startled and spellbound in their gay attire, were participating in this funeral procession and celebration of nature. Spring and fall, the speech and silence of nature, and the twin enchantments of life and death were commingled in this picture; hearts seemed to stop, removed from their breasts to join the silent procession through the air. "Then my heart was taken out of my breast," a mystic had said: Agathe remembered it.

She knew, too, that she herself had read this saying to Ulrich from one of his books. Here in the garden, not far from the place where they were now, was where it had happened. More details emerged. Other sayings that she had recalled to his memory occurred to her: "Is it you, or is it not you? I know not where I am; nor do I wish to know!" "I have risen above all my faculties up to the dark power! I am in love, and know not with whom! My heart is full of love and at the same time empty of love!" Thus, once again, there echoed within her the lament of the mystics in whose heart God has penetrated as deeply as a thorn that no fingertips can grasp. She had read many such blissful laments to Ulrich at the time. Perhaps her rendering now was not exact: memory deals rather imperiously with what it wants to hear; but she understood what was meant, and formed a resolve. As at this moment of flowery procession, the garden had once before looked mysteriously abandoned and animated; and that had been at the very hour after the mystical confessions Ulrich kept in his library had fallen into her hands. Time stood still, a thousand years weighed as lightly as the opening and closing of an eye; she had arrived at the Millennium; perhaps God was even making himself felt. And while she was feeling these things one *after* the other, even though time was supposed to no longer exist; and while her brother, so that she would not suffer anxiety in this dream, was *next* to her, even though space seemed no longer to exist either: the world, notwithstanding these contradictions, seemed in all its parts pervaded by transfiguration.

What she had experienced since then could not but appear to her as talkatively tempered compared to what had come before; and yet, what an expansion and affirmation that first revelation had bestowed on her subsequent days, even if the all but corporeal warmth of its immediacy had been lost! Under these circumstances, Agathe resolved this time to approach with deliberation the rapture that had previously befallen her in this garden in an almost dreamlike way. She did not know why she associated it with the name of the Millennium. It was a word bright with feeling and almost palpable, like a thing, yet it remained opaque to the understanding. That was why she could imagine that the Thousand-Year Kingdom could begin at any moment. It is also called the Kingdom of Love: this Agathe knew also; but only now did it occur to her that both these names have been handed down since biblical times and signify the kingdom of God on earth, whose imminent arrival is meant in a completely real sense.

Ulrich, moreover, occasionally used these words as ingenuously as his sister, without on that account believing in Scripture; and so it was not at all surprising to her that she seemed to know automatically how one should behave in the Millennium. "You must keep perfectly still," an inspiration told her. "You must leave no room for any kind of desire, not even the desire to ask. Divest yourself of your cleverness in handling your affairs. Deprive the mind of all tools, and prevent it from being used as a tool; both knowledge and will must be discarded; renounce reality and the desire to turn toward it. Contain yourself until head, heart, and limbs are nothing but silence. But if in this way you arrive at the highest selflessness, then at last outside and inside will touch, as if a wedge that had split the world in two had sprung out...!"

This may not have been exactly a sober plan of action. But it seemed to her that, with a firm intention, it must be attainable; and she pulled herself together as if she were trying to feign death. But it soon proved as impossible to completely silence all thoughts and all reports from the senses and the will as it had been in childhood not to commit any sins between confession and communion; and after some effort she completely gave up the attempt. In the process, she discovered that she was only superficially adhering to her purpose, and that her attention had long since slipped away. At the moment, it was occupied with a quite far-flung question, a little monster of dereliction: she was asking herself in the most foolish way, and was very intent on the foolishness of it: "Have I really ever been violent, mean, hateful, and unhappy?" A man without a name came to mind; who lacked a name because she bore it and had carried it away with her. When she thought of him, her name felt like a scar; but she no longer felt hatred for Hagauer, and now she repeated her question with the slightly melancholy stubbornness with which one gazes after a wave that has flowed on. What had happened to the desire to do him almost mortal harm? She had nearly lost it in her distraction and appeared to believe it must be possible to find it somewhere nearby. Moreover, Lindner might well be a stand-in for this desire for hostility; she asked herself this too and thought of him fleetingly. Perhaps now it seemed astonishing to her how much had already happened to her, young people being as a rule more prone to be surprised at how much they have already had to feel than older people, who have become as used to the inconstancy of passions and circumstances as they are to changes in the weather. But nothing could have meant more to Agathe than this: At that very moment, mysteriously detached from the great reversal in her life, from the flight of its passions and conditions, from the wondrous stream of emotion (in which youth ordinarily believes itself returned to the glory of primordial nature), there stood out again the stone-clear sky of motionless reverie from which she had just awakened.

So her thoughts, while still under the spell of the festive procession of flowers and of death, were no longer moving with it in its mute, solemn way; rather, Agathe was "thinking to and fro," as one could describe it in contrast to the state of mind in which life lasts "a thousand years" without a wingbeat. This difference between two states of mind was very clear; and she recognized with some amazement how often just this difference, or something closely related to it, had already been touched on in her conversations with Ulrich. Involuntarily she turned to her brother, and without losing sight of the spectacle surrounding them she took a deep breath and asked: "Doesn't it seem to you too that at a moment like this, and in comparison with it, everything else seems irrelevant?"

These few words dispersed the cloudy weight of silence and memory. For Ulrich as well had been watching the foamlike drift of blossoms floating past on their aimless journey; and because his thoughts and memories were tuned to the same note as those of his sister, no further introduction was needed to enable him to answer her unspoken thoughts. He slowly stretched his limbs and replied: "I've been wanting to tell you something for a long time—already in the state in which we were talking about the meaning of still lifes, and through all these days really—even if it doesn't perfectly hit the mark: There are, to set out the contrast sharply, two possible ways of living passionately, and two kinds of passionate people. One way is to start howling with rage or misery or enthusiasm at each provocation like a child, getting rid of one's feeling in a single brief, trivial whirl of intensity. In this case, and it's the usual one, emotion ends up being the everyday negotiator of everyday life; and the more violent it is and the more easily excited, the more it resembles the restlessness in a tiger's cage at feeding time, when the meat is carried past the bars, and the satiated fatigue soon afterward. Isn't that how it is? The other way of living passionately is to restrain oneself and not accede even in the slightest degree to the action toward which every emotion tends and is driven. And in this case life becomes a rather uncanny dream in which feeling rises to the tops of the trees, to the tallest spires, to the zenith of the sky! It's more than likely that this is what we were thinking of when we were pretending to talk about paintings and nothing but paintings."

Agathe propped herself up, curious. "Didn't you once say," she asked, "that there are two fundamentally different possibilities of living, and that they're almost like two different musical keys or tonalities of feeling? One of them was supposed to be the key of 'worldly' emotion, which never comes to rest or fulfillment; the other, I don't know if you gave it a name, but it must have been a 'mystical' feeling that resonates constantly but never arrives at 'complete reality'?" Although she spoke hesitantly, she had been overhasty and finished with some embarrassment.

Ulrich nevertheless recognized quite well what he seemed to have said; and he visibly found it difficult to swallow, as though he had something too hot in his mouth, and tried to smile. He said: "If that is what I meant, I'll have to express myself all the more modestly now! I'll just follow a well-known example and call the two kinds of passionate existence the appetitive and then, for its opposite, the nonappetitive, however unattractive that may or may not sound. Because in every human being there is a hunger, and it behaves like a ravenous beast; and there is no hunger but something that ripens tenderly, free of greed and satiety, like a grape in the autumn sun. In fact, in every feeling there is the one as well as the other."

"In other words a vegetal, perhaps even vegetarian, disposition, beside the animal one?" There was a hint of amusement and teasing in Agathe's question.

"Almost!" Ulrich replied. "Maybe the animalistic and the vegetative, understood as basic opposites in the sphere of desires, would be a trove for a philosopher! But would that make me want to be one? All I'm presuming to claim is what I've said, and particularly what I said last, that the two kinds of passionate existence have a model, perhaps even their origin, in every emotion, because every emotion contains those two aspects distinctly," he continued. But curiously, he went on to speak only about what he called the appetitive aspect. Its drive is toward action, toward movement, toward enjoyment; by its operation, emotion transforms itself into a work, or into an idea or conviction, or into a disappointment. Those are all different ways in which emotion discharges its tension, but they can also be means for it to recharge and gain strength. For emotion changes in being expended; it wears down, disperses, and ultimately expires even as it succeeds; or it encapsulates itself in its product, transforming its vital energy into stored energy, which later yields a return of vital energy, occasionally with compound interest. "And doesn't that explain one thing, namely that the robust activity of our worldly emotion, with its irrelevance, which you were so pleasantly sighing about, doesn't make a great difference to us, even if it is a profound difference?"

"You may be only too right!" Agathe agreed. "My God, this entire work of the emotions, its worldly wealth, the wanting, the rejoicing, the to-do, the infidelity, all for no reason other than that emotion drives us to it! Including everything one experiences and forgets: It's certainly beautiful like a tree full of apples of every color, but it's also meaningless and monotonous, like everything that grows to the same plump roundness each year and then falls off the branch!"

Ulrich nodded at his sister's answer with its breath of impetuousness and renunciation. "The world owes all its works of beauty, all progress, but also all unrest, and ultimately its meaningless cycling, to the appetitive side of the emotions!" he confirmed. "Do you know, by the way, that this term, 'appetitive,' is commonly used to refer to the share that our innate drives have in every emotion? Therefore," he added, "what we have said is that it's the drives to which the world owes its beauty and progress."

"Its crazed agitation too," Agathe added.

"Usually that is exactly what one says; so it seems useful to me not to disregard the other side! Because it's at the very least unexpected that man should owe precisely his progress to something that actually belongs to the animal stage!"—He smiled as he said this. He too had now propped himself up on his elbow and turned completely toward his sister, as if he wanted to elucidate something for her: but he went on hesitantly like one who wants first to be instructed himself by the words he is searching for. "Without question," he said, "the actively prehensile feelings of man—and you were right to speak of an animal disposition—have at their core the same few instincts the animal already has. This is quite clear in the major emotions: in hunger, anger, joy, self-will, and love, the soul's veil barely covers the most naked wanting—!"

It appeared that he intended to continue in the same vein; but though the conversation—which had arisen from a dream of nature, the peculiarly uneventful procession of blossoms still drifting through the space of awareness—did not for a moment leave any doubt as to the siblings' crucial question, but rather, from the first to the last word, stood under the influence of that emblem, was dominated by the enigmatic conception of "a happening without anything happening," and was taking place in a mood of gentle affliction: even though this was how it was, in the end the conversation had led to the opposite of such an ideal and its emotional tenor when Ulrich found himself constrained to emphasize the constructive activity of strong drives along with the disruption they caused. Such a clear vindication of the drives, and implicitly of the instinctual nature of man, and of active humanity altogether—for that too was implied—might of course have been part of a "Western, Occidental, Faustian sense of life," as it is called in the language of books in contrast to any sensibility that, according to the same self-fertilizing language, is supposed to be "Oriental" or "Asian." He remembered these pretentious vogue words. But it was not his or his sister's intention, nor would it have been consistent with their habits, to give a specious meaning to an experience that moved them deeply by employing such fly-by-night, poorly rooted notions; rather, everything they talked about was meant as true and real, though its source might be as remote and improbable as a walk in the clouds. That was why Ulrich had taken pleasure in subtending the fine haze of feeling with an explanation on the model of the natural sciences—even if that did seem to abet the "Faustian" idea—simply because the spirit of fidelity to nature promised to exclude everything that is excessively fanciful. At least he had sketched out an approach to such an explanation. It was of course all the stranger that he had done so only for what he called the appetitive aspect of emotion, while completely ignoring the question of how he might apply an analogous idea to the nonappetitive aspect, even though originally he had certainly not given it any less importance. It was not without reason that it happened this way. Whether the psychological and biological dissection of this aspect of feeling seemed more difficult to him, or whether he merely considered such analysis a cumbersome instrument altogether—both might have been the case—what influenced him primarily was something else, of which he had already given several indications since the moment when Agathe's deep sigh had betrayed the painful and elating contrast between the past, restless passions of life and the seemingly undying passion that was at home in the timeless stillness beneath the stream of blossoms. For—to repeat what he had already repeated in various ways—not only are two dispositions discernible in every individual emotion, through which, and in accord with their nature, that emotion can be developed to the point of passion; but there are also two kinds of people, or in every person periods of his or her destiny, that differ in that one or the other disposition predominates.

He saw a substantial distinction here. People of one kind, as already mentioned, reach vigorously for everything and take on every challenge; they dash over obstacles like a rushing stream or surge around them into a new course; their passions are strong and changeable, and the result is a strongly segmented career that leaves nothing behind but an echo of its tumultuous passage. This was the sort of person to whom the concept of the appetitive was meant to apply when Ulrich wanted to establish it as one principal notion of the passionate life;

for the other kind is in all essential respects the opposite of the first: such people are shy, pensive, vague; slow to decide, full of dreams and longing, and internalized in their passion. At times—in thoughts that were not part of their current conversation—Ulrich also called the second kind of person "contemplative," a word that is commonly used with a different meaning, and sometimes merely in the lukewarm sense of "reflective," but that for him had more than this ordinary significance, and indeed was equivalent to the previously mentioned un-Faustian, Oriental way. Maybe a key distinction in life was reflected in this contemplative mode, especially in conjunction with the appetitive as its opposite: That appealed to Ulrich more strongly than an axiom. But that all such highly composite and exacting conceptions of life could be reduced to a twofold layering already present in every emotion—this elementary possibility of explanation held deep satisfaction for him as well.

Of course it was clear to him that the two kinds of human being that were at issue could not signify anything other than a man "without qualities" in contrast to the one with all the qualities a man is capable of showing. The first could also be called a nihilist who dreams of God's dreams, as distinct from the activist, who, however, in his impatient mode of conduct, is also a kind of God-dreamer and anything but a realist who bestirs himself in the world with worldly clarity. "Why aren't we realists, then?" Ulrich asked himself. Neither of them was, neither he nor she; their ideas and their actions had long since left no doubt about that; but they were nihilists and activists, and sometimes one, sometimes the other, whichever happened to come up.

ACKNOWLEDGMENTS

I AM EXTREMELY thankful to Nicholas Berwin for conceiving this project and for reading and commenting on the translation at all stages of its development. His acute sensibility for nuances of meaning, both in English and in German, contributed to the refinement of many details.

I also want to express my gratitude to Edwin Frank for telling me about the "very interesting Musil proposal" that had come across his desk at New York Review Books, and asking me if I would like to do the translation, and for his astute and clarifying editorial scrutiny.

I am indebted to Walter Fanta of the Robert Musil Institut at the University of Klagenfurt for lending me the benefit of his scholarly expertise to help resolve several difficult problems of translation.

Thomas Frick read the manuscript in its first draft, chapter by chapter, with a writer's and editor's eye as it progressed. His always insightful comments and queries were wonderfully supportive and helpful.

I was fortunate in having a mathematician friend, Philipp Rothmaler (who is a logician to boot, like Ulrich), willing to hash out with me, in extended email exchanges and telephone sessions, several passages and formulations written in a scientific vein that were obscure to me.

I am grateful to Randy Cashmere for reading the book at a near-final stage and helping me to clear up needless obscurities by letting me know where a phrase or an image left him puzzled.

For full appreciation, Musil's language needs to be heard or at least silently intoned while being read off the page. My wife, Susan, listened to me read the book aloud as the translation developed; her critical discernment and sensitive appreciation were the first proof of each sentence's performative quality. For these gifts (and for her patience) I cannot thank her enough.

I gratefully acknowledge the financial support I received from the Literature Section of the Austrian Federal Chancellery.

And I owe very special thanks to Parabola, which was funded by the Nicholas Berwin Charitable Trust, for supporting this translation with a generous grant.

—J.A.

NOTES

44 *like a heap of stones spilled out from a mosaic*: This phrase, interpolated by Eithne Wilkins and Ernst Kaiser in their translation, elucidates the image to both Musil's and the reader's advantage.

52 *act of imagination and illusion*: This was Eithne Wilkins's and Ernst Kaiser's solution to the implications of the word *Einbildung* in this sentence. I don't think it can be improved on—or dispensed with.

108 *Sister Human*: The German *Schwester Mensch* is less peculiar and more evocative than it appears in English. It sounds Franciscan, or like something Adam might have said to Eve.

138 *The austere fervor that had lit up his face…*: I am adopting Eithne Wilkins's and Ernst Kaiser's lucid solution of a difficult problem posed by Musil's phrasing.

245 *something would have happened which, soon after, she was unable to name, as it was already gone*: One wants to rephrase this odd sentence to: "something would have happened which, soon after, she *would have been* unable to name, as it *would have been* already gone." But that is not what Musil wrote. The possibility that did not happen is as unknown to the reader as it is to Agathe—unknown even as a possibility—and that, I believe, is what Musil intended to express with this breach of grammatical convention."

249 *balletically disguised leap*: This is Burton Pike's ingenious solution to the challenge posed by Musil's phrase *tänzerisch bemäntelt*.

263 *will-o'-the-wisps of outings never taken*: The will-o'-the-wisps, suggested but not named in Musil's sentence, were invisible to me until I spotted them thanks to Burton Pike's rendition.

311 *Strolls Among the Crowd*: The chapter title in German, "Wandel unter Menschen," connotes a range of meanings that cannot be contained in a single English phrase. Musil's French translator Philippe Jaccotet rendered it as "Promenades dans la foule," which strikes me as a sensible solution.

318 *the world of 'the like of it happens'*: "The Like of It Happens" is the title of volume 2 of *The Man Without Qualities*. For an explanation of that concept and a description of the role it plays in Ulrich's thinking, see the introduction, page xiii.

OTHER NEW YORK REVIEW CLASSICS

For a complete list of titles, visit www.nyrb.com or write to:
Catalog Requests, NYRB, 435 Hudson Street, New York, NY 10014

* *Also available as an electronic book.*